An INNER Fire

JACKI DELECKI

This is work of fiction. Names, characters, places, and incidents either are the product of the author's imagination or are used fictitiously, and any resemblance to actual persons, living or dead, business establishments, events, or locales is entirely coincidental.

ISBN 978-0-9899391-02

Trademark disclaimer: The author acknowledges the trademark status and trademark owners of various products referenced in this work of fiction, which have been used without permission. The publication/use of these trademarks is not authorized, associated with or sponsored by the trademark owners.

Doe Bay Publishing, Seattle, Washington.
Cover Design and Interior format by The Killion Group
http://thekilliongroupinc.com

DEDICATION

To my Mom — the best story teller of all.
And to my Dad — the best listener.

ACKNOWLEDGEMENTS

Thank you to my "team" of experts who shared their incredible knowledge, enthusiasm, and unique abilities with me. I'm most grateful for their gifts of time and expertise. Any errors are my own mistakes or my imagination run amok: Helen Fitzpatrick, Executive Director of Administration, Seattle Fire Department; Captain Stephen Baer, Fire Investigator, Seattle Fire Department; Richard Panzer, DVM, Certified Veterinary Acupuncturist; Henny, Seattle Fire Department, rank—"Dog."

And to my "team" of editors who never stopped believing in me or my writing: My husband, children, Karuna, and Cynthia Garlough. Thank you for your continual love and support.

CHAPTER ONE

Grayce Walters' left hand twitched. Her universe spun on an altered axis. Her instincts swirled. Her intuition flared.

Earlier today, a cranky feline had gouged her, a sneaky dog had nipped her, and now, late for dinner with friends, the parking gods were messing with her. Something was coming. Something strange.

Her headlights probed the mist, dissolving in the murk of Puget Sound fog. Her intuition acted like an inner GPS, directing her to the far side of Seattle's Fisherman's Terminal. The beams shone on a yellow heap between stacks of crab traps. A dog lay on its side, barely visible in the shadow of a fishing shed.

Stepping out of her car, she inhaled the musky smell of salt water. A horn blared from the Ballard Bridge. Grayce jumped at the sudden sound. She grabbed a flashlight and moved into the mist toward the large canine.

She knelt on the damp cement next to the Golden Retriever. Relieved to observe the dog's shallow respirations, she released a slow breath *Baxter* was written in bold script on the dog's red leather collar.

She gently ran her hand along Baxter's inert body. Her cold fingers probed the crown of his head, locating an egg-sized lump on the back of his skull.

"Your head hurting, Baxter?"

The large retriever wagged his tail ever so slightly and then stilled.

Grayce scanned the cluster of corrugated fishing sheds. A deep foreboding flooded her senses. "Baxter, I need to get us away from here."

She searched the waterfront, looking for the perpetrator of Baxter's injury. The overhead lights on the docks cast an eerie halo on the boats bobbing in the black water.

Screeching hinges broke the silence. The sound raked her skin like dogs' nails skittering across the metal exam tables in vet school. Her nervous system ratcheted into high alert.

The sound of a door opening in the next row of sheds echoed in the night's silence. Then she heard footsteps on the cement, moving toward the water. The sound of the footsteps grew distant, swallowed in the darkness.

Under the dock lights she spotted him, a beefy man with a satchel slung over his shoulder. Wearing the slicker and boots of a commercial fisherman, he moved with an energized self-assurance toward the boats. Rage and elation radiated from him. Grayce was sucked into his dark violent energy. She fought the temptation to absorb his malevolence.

The footsteps stopped. He looked back in her direction. A raw chill penetrated Grayce's body. She bent forward to shield the dog and tightened her hold on the flashlight, ready to protect Baxter.

Moving in and out of the shadows on the wharf, the overhead beams caught the top of his head. His hair shone a fiery red. He walked into the fog.

Baxter whined, breaking the tense silence. She ran her hands along the damp dog searching for further injuries. "You're going to be alright, big guy."

Nerves stretched taut, she twisted to look for the man. She studied the entire area searching for him. Every sound boomed in her ears.

She fumbled in her jeans pocket for her phone, then hesitated. Grayce hit favorites for James, her best friend.

Damn! Voicemail.

Peeling off her coat, she covered the dog.

"Baxter!" A woman's voice, then a whistle.

The dog's ears shot up as he bolted upright. He gave a high-pitched yelp, shook several times, and loped in the direction of his owner's voice. Twenty feet away, a middle aged woman stood next to her Volvo station wagon with the hatch-back door open. Baxter jumped effortlessly into the car. The dog's large head was silhouetted in the rear window as they sped away.

She bent to pick up her rain jacket when a massive blast shook the wharf causing the cement to sway beneath her. The harsh sound reverberated in her ears as the tremor traveled through her legs.

She whirled around, trying to locate the source of the explosion. Shock waves continued to pulsate throughout her body.

She heard the fire before she saw it, a slow hiss followed by a roar. Twenty foot high flames shot out of a shed less than a few car lengths away. Heat blazed across her face, hot enough to singe her eyebrows and eyelashes.

Primitive fear imploded in her chest. She ran, ran as if the flames chased her.

The fire's heat penetrated her sweater to her skin. She sprinted, her feet and heart pounding.

When she reached the far side of the wharf, at the far side of the inferno, she dialed 911.

The wail of sirens filled the night's silence.

In the frenzy of noise and flashing lights, she spotted the red-haired man lurking in the shadows. He was crouched, half hidden by an industrial dumpster. As if he sensed her watching him, he turned and vanished into the darkness.

CHAPTER TWO

Grayce sat upright, uncomfortable on the cold metal chair in the fire investigator's waiting room. The chair creaked each time she shifted her weight.

Today was about facts and only facts.

Lieutenant Davis had been clear on the phone. "I'll take your statement. Nothing to worry about. Just routine."

Routine. There was nothing routine about last night's explosion, and plenty for Grayce to worry about. She came to the lieutenant's office because she didn't want last night's violence to disrupt her animal patients. She refused to allow that stress into her healing space.

"Ma'am? Lieutenant Davis will see you now, third door on the right."

With the help of three inches from her Jimmy Choos, a birthday present from her best friend, Grayce pulled herself up to a full five feet three.

Why was she worried? She was doing a public service, acting as a witness who had seen a suspect on the wharf, just before the blaze. Her certainty that this man had assaulted Baxter and started the shed fire wouldn't be mentioned.

She walked down a long white corridor. There was nothing creative about this workplace, although located above an eminent art gallery in Pioneer Square. The energy in the building was contained and functional, just like the lieutenant. From his efficient manner on the phone, she suspected that Lieutenant Davis would have no tolerance for her intuition. Though, who was she kidding, few people would. Her ability to read and heal energy states was hard to explain.

The historic building smelled of years of rain and mold. With each step on the uneven floor, her pantyhose began to slip and sag. She resisted the urge to pull on the damn things—they'd likely be puddled at her knees and feet by the time she got to the lieutenant's office. She hadn't worn tights since last year. She hated dressing up. She felt constricted, contained, and crabby.

A mass of black fur, nails clicking, bounded toward her. Shocked to see a dog running free in the fire station, she didn't notice a gap in the floorboards. Her heel wedged into a crack. The black lab tried to stop, but unable to get traction on the wood floor, slid straight into Grayce's legs. Grayce teetered then tumbled backward. She looked up into a pair of warm dark eyes. Doggie breath wafted across her face.

"Henny!" A loud voice reverberated in the narrow hallway.

"Oh, you're in trouble now." Grayce rubbed the dog's head, smiling into the soft eyes; then she tried to stand.

The dog placed one of her enormous paws on Grayce's shoulder and began to lick her face.

"My God, get off," a man shouted as he strode toward them. From her position on the floor, he looked to be at least seven feet tall. His white shirt pulled tautly across his broad chest and muscular arms, he was a man capable of carrying victims out of a burning building.

Grayce locked stares with the man who towered over her. His face was all angles and planes, like a model out of one of those edgy photo shoots in Nordstrom's catalogue. An electrifying shiver coursed through her. This man exuded the same controlled power as Samba, the Bengal tiger she had treated at the zoo.

"Henny!"

Both Henny and Grayce stiffened.

He pulled the dog by her collar. "I'm sorry. She never disobeys."

"I seem to have that effect on dogs." Grayce smiled and straightened her skirt that had hiked up to mid-thigh. She couldn't help noticing how his eyes trailed over her legs.

"I apologize, ma'am. I'm Lieutenant Ewan Davis, the Fire Investigator you spoke with on the phone. And now you've met Henny, usually a well-behaved part of our crew and our accelerant dog."

He grasped Grayce's hand to help her up. His giant hand enveloped hers, sending an elemental surge through to her toes. His heat radiated in her palm while she brushed off her skirt.

"It wasn't Henny. She's great. It was my darn heels."

Lieutenant Davis's gaze dropped to her shoes, then moved back up her legs.

Grayce felt fully exposed as if he saw her as a woman, not a witness. It wasn't just her Jimmy Choos knocking her off balance.

"Are you okay?" He stepped closer to her as if he meant to touch her, his professional demeanor transformed to concern.

Her heart skipped a beat. It was in no way related to the lieutenant's closeness. Her anxiety about the interview was causing her heart to palpitate. "Just proves why veterinarians shouldn't wear high heels to work."

Henny sat on alert next to Grayce.

"Get on your bed." The lieutenant pointed his finger down the hall.

The dog ignored the command.

"I'm not her handler but she usually obeys me," he shrugged his broad shoulders.

Henny nudged Grayce's leg.

Grayce put one hand on the dog's head and the other on the lieutenant's muscled arm. "She just wants to help."

"What?"

"She's just trying to make me feel welcome. She senses I'm nervous. I've never been a witness before."

"Knocking you down is a strange way to help."

Henny's tail thumped on the wood floor.

Grayce laughed.

Lieutenant Davis' hard angles softened with a slow grin. She usually wasn't distracted by outward appearances, but this man was more than the sum of his attractive parts with his black, closely-cropped hair, broad shoulders, and bright eyes. His energy was vital, forceful, not what she had expected.

"Guess you must like your job. You're the only person I've met who would laugh after being knocked down."

Grayce hoped the heat moving up her neck into her face wasn't noticeable.

While they moved down the corridor to the lieutenant's office, she kept a lookout for sneaky cracks in the floor and exuberant dogs.

"Please come in, Dr. Walters." He gestured to a nondescript white space.

The office was empty except for his metal desk, two chairs and a cabinet. Boxes were stacked against white walls.

She sat on another cold metal chair, pulling her skirt to cover her knees. Henny curled up in a ball next to her feet. Grayce scanned the sparse office. One lonely picture hung on the blank walls, an official photograph of the lieutenant dressed in full regalia, holding a plaque. An older man with the same penetrating blue eyes and same angled cheekbones as the lieutenant stood beaming next to him.

Lieutenant Davis settled behind his desk. "This won't take too long."

He hit the digital voice recorder on his desk and spoke in a quiet professional tone. "This is Lieutenant Ewan Davis. Today is the ninth of October, 2013. The time is 9:28 am. I'm interviewing Dr. Grayce Walters concerning the fire incident on Fisherman's Wharf on the night of October Eighth. Can you please state and spell your name, Dr. Walters for the record?"

Grayce did so, then crossed her legs, trying to maintain a nonchalant posture.

"All right then. Let's start at the beginning. Why were you in the commercial fishing area at night?" he asked.

The muscles in her neck tightened with the memory of the night. She cleared her throat. "I couldn't find parking by Chinooks so I drove to the back of the restaurant."

He gave an almost imperceptible nod. "Tell me exactly what happened."

She uncrossed her legs, sat up straighter, and tried to remember what she had planned to say. She already knew Lieutenant Davis would reject the idea of unseen talents or intuition. "As I reached to turn off my headlights, I spotted an injured dog. I'm a vet. I went to help. And while I was examining the dog, a man appeared, from a shed, off to my right."

A cold dread crept into her body with the mention of the man.

"Was there something suspicious about this man that you didn't ask him for help with the dog?"

An icy chill skittered up and down her arms with the memory of the man's elation over his violent destruction. How could she possibly tell the analytical lieutenant that she could feel the man's fury pulsating across the wharf? Her sensitivity to animal and human energy wouldn't fit into any of the investigator's rational categories.

"I was still evaluating the injured dog when the man came out of the shed. At that point I had things under control." She sat back and crossed her legs, trying to ignore the prickly shivers running up her spine.

"Do you know what shed he came out of?"

"I didn't see him, I heard him." She wanted to tell the lieutenant she didn't need to see the man; she could feel the dark energy surrounding him. "I heard the door open and then heard him walking toward the water. I didn't see him until he paused under the overhead light."

The lieutenant rubbed his hand back and forth on his chin. "So there's a possibility the fisherman didn't come out of a shed?"

What could she say? She had experienced the man's rage. She knew the man had hit Baxter on the head, had burned down the shed. She knew he was no fisherman. And she knew Lieutenant Davis would never believe her.

"I heard a door open and close. Then he appeared. I assumed he came from a nearby shed."

"Fair enough. Can you describe the man?"

She took a slow deep breath. "He was stocky... carried a duffel bag on his shoulder... had bright red hair." Her voice quivered on each word like a violin's string suspended over each note.

His hair had been dyed. Her heart leapt into her throat making it hard to pull air into her constricting chest.

"Is something wrong? What did you just remember?" His eyes focused on her, revealing tiny creases at the corners. Someplace in the back of her mind, she realized she liked the little imperfections.

Henny sat up and placed her head in Grayce's lap.

Grayce rubbed the solid head of the lab, avoiding eye contact. "His hair color wasn't natural." Her heart thumped against her chest like she had just sprinted across a finish line. "It was an unusual color. It had to be dyed." Breathless, her words came out in a whisper, "his hair was the color of fire."

Lieutenant Davis leaned forward. The concern she read in his eyes steadied her. He was first-rate, like Henny at her side, steady, loyal and ready to do the job.

"Go on, please." He gentled his tone, just like she did when soothing a frightened animal.

"He walked toward the boats and disappeared."

"You don't remember anything else about the man?"

"Nothing"

The brightness in the lieutenant's eyes turned frosty as did his tone. "Are you sure you don't remember anything else?"

She looked down at her lap unable to maintain contact with the lieutenant's intense inspection. "Nothing else."

He tapped a slow beat with his index finger on the metal desk. Grayce stared at the huge finger with the neatly trimmed nail and the deep pink nail bed.

"What did you do with the injured dog?"

Grayce looked up to find the lieutenant maintaining his scrutiny.

"One minute he was down, and then, with the sound of the explosion, he was up and loping toward his owner. I knew he was an adventurer."

"An adventurer?"

She heard the skepticism in his question. "Golden Retrievers like to roam."

"Did you see the owner?"

"No, I just heard her call for Baxter."

"Let's go over what you did see."

He reviewed every detail. What was the sound of the door opening? What kind of clothes was the man wearing? Did she smell anything before the explosion? There was no further mention of the man's hair color.

A half hour later, he completed her recorded statement and the interview was finished. She had achieved what she had set out to do as a responsible citizen. She had given the lieutenant the description of the arsonist without sharing any of her insight.

"Thank you, Dr. Walters. Your information may be helpful."

She was thankful to be done with the interview. She hoped never to think, dream, or come close to the red haired man again. The gigantic lieutenant with his aura of command looked totally capable of handling the dangerous man. "I hope my description will help you find him."

"Is this the best phone number to reach you?"

Grayce stared at the sheet of paper he handed her. She swallowed the rising panic and ignored the bone-deep awareness that the red-haired man wasn't finished.

"I may need to contact you," he said.

"I've told you everything."

"You never know what may come up with an investigation."

She forced her lips to curve into a smile of sorts. "Of course. You have both my office and cell number."

When she stood, Henny stood too.

For a man his size, the lieutenant was quick. He was next to her by the time she had picked up her purse.

She craned her neck to look up at him. His eyes were focused on her. They locked gazes briefly. Grayce looked away, trying to lessen the forceful connection between them, the heat racing through her body. She bent down to pet Henny. "It was great to meet you, girl."

Henny had been a bright spot in the morning, supporting Grayce with her gentle, loving spirit. Throughout the interview, Grayce had agonized over how much she should reveal about her intuitive grasp of the man's violent nature. She had almost confided in the lieutenant. She had almost believed he might be able to accept her gifts.

Almost. Almost wasn't good enough. Almost wasn't enough to trust. Almost would open up an abyss of her secrets.

CHAPTER THREE

Davis stared down the hallway after Dr. Walters left. He hated surprises. Getting back late to the office, he hadn't been able to do a rudimentary background check before the interview.

The delectable Dr. Walters was more than disorienting. Her big green eyes, short skirt, and the way she laughed, lying on the ground with Henny licking her face, was a shock to his system. And he wasn't sure he liked the jolt.

He sat down and opened his computer to do the witness profile he hadn't been able to do before the interview. The woman was brilliant, Phi Beta Kappa from the University of Michigan, Honors from Vet School at Cornell. There were endless pages on her research, papers, and presentations. Now, she practiced animal acupuncture. What the hell was that?

She was a good witness, factual not emotional. Her lack of reaction left him suspicious. Most witnesses needed to describe the experience of encountering criminals. Not the intrepid Dr. Walters. She seemed frightened as she described the man with red hair. But unlike most witnesses, she disclosed none of her fears.He appreciated the irony of the situation. She had given the perfect interview logical, precise and it made him suspect her. Dr. Walters hadn't offered any personal insights. He was familiar with the tactic; he used it all the time. When his neatly constructed world had careened out of control two years ago after his father's slow, agonizing death, Davis learned the only way to survive was not to reveal anything.

There was something inexplicable about Dr. Walters, something he couldn't grasp. She bore watching. God, who was he kidding? Her tight little body and her legs bore watching.

Skipping the elevator, Grayce took the stairs two at a time to her second floor office. She reminded herself, she had a normal life, a life filled with lightness and healing animals. A life not inhabited by red-haired men who beat dogs, set fires, and cause explosions.

Hollie's voice echoed down the wide hall from the partially open door. Bold black letters stood out against the white background. "Grayce Walters, D.V.M., Veterinary Acupuncturist." Maybe *normal* wasn't precisely the right word. Grayce entered the freshly painted, mint-green waiting room.

Hollie, with a phone perched at her ear, mouthed, "Mornin', Boss."

Grayce listened to her receptionist's husky voice, counseling a client. Hollie was the biggest surprise of this new endeavor. A technophile Goth, Hollie had attached herself to Grayce at Teen Feed, a program for homeless youths. Despite finding herself drawn to the thin, tattooed woman, Grayce still marveled that she had hired a street kid with a nose ring who was addicted to video games.

Grayce entered her office/exam room, peeling off her soaked North Face coat. She stretched the jacket over her chair since she still hadn't installed coat-hooks on the door.

She inspected the large space with its vaulted ceilings and generous windows overlooking the Montlake Cut, a waterway connecting Lake Washington to Puget Sound.

She was glad she hadn't allowed the lieutenant to interview her here. It was hard enough keeping the healing space balanced.

She had a regular life, a home, a cat, and an assistant. The last few days had been an aberration. She repeated the mantra, wondering how long it would be before she actually believed it.

Hollie had left today's schedule on the desk. Eight clients—her acupuncture practice was growing.

"Mrs. Leary and Beowulf are here." Hollie stood at the door. Today Hollie wore a pleated black skirt and a black T-shirt. Her tattoos were well concealed but the nose and brow piercing and the dyed jet-black hair stabbed by chopsticks couldn't be hidden. Her skirt barely grazed her thighs, but her black patent leather boots bridged the gap, reaching the hem of her skirt. Grayce enjoyed Hollie's original take on work attire.

From Hollie's sagging shoulders, Grayce knew immediately that Beowulf was faring no better today. The old gray tabby, the center of Mrs. Leary's life, had been diagnosed with leukemia months ago and had been holding on to allow Mrs. Leary time to adjust. Grayce was grateful she could relieve Beowulf's pain. Relieving Mrs. Leary's pain wasn't as easy.

Hollie returned with the gray tabby in her arms. Mrs. Leary followed, leaning heavily on her cane.

Grayce rose from her chair and moved to greet them. She spoke softly to Beowulf, petting his large head, opening her heart to his vibrations. Beowulf gazed back, the luster in his eyes diminished. His time was close.

"Mrs. Leary, why don't you hold Beowulf on your lap for his treatment?"

Although withered and wrinkled, Mrs. Leary always moved with a graceful efficiency. Today her shoulders slumped and she took small, measured steps to the treatment chair, overstuffed with chintz pillows. The giant chair dwarfed the delicate woman. Hollie tenderly placed the large cat on Mrs. Leary's lap.

"Would you like a cup of tea?" Hollie pressed her hand against the delicate woman's shoulder.

"I just couldn't drink anything. Thank you for asking."

Grayce knelt next to the cat. She focused her energy into gentle oscillating waves. "You're a handsome fellow, my friend. You've given so much joy to Mrs. Leary."

Grayce purred at the cat, speaking in a lyrical voice, "Mrs. Leary knows you're tired, and she doesn't want you to suffer."

Tears formed in Mrs. Leary's eyes. The woman's translucent hand rested on Beowulf's front paw, like mother to child, friend to friend.

Grayce steadied her breathing. She absorbed the woman's pain, feeling her sorrow. Grayce visualized ribbons of blue and yellow light surrounding Beowulf and Mrs. Leary, binding them together in the light of a white hot summer day.

Beowulf didn't budge when she placed the acupuncture needle into the crown of his head. Entry of the thin filliform needle pinched like the bite of a mosquito but Beowulf was oblivious to Grayce's ministrations.

She placed the next needle at the lumbar sacral junction, the Bai Hui, the center of energy. She raised her own vibrations to support Beowulf's deficient Bai Hui. Mrs. Leary's hand remained on the cat's paw, anchoring him in this world.

Grayce placed additional needles down Beowulf's spine. With needles in his head and back, the tabby drifted into a calm state. She slowed her vibrations while she rotated the needles then raised her heat into each one directing it in small increments until Beowulf slept peacefully.

There wouldn't be many more sessions.

After Mrs. Leary and Beowulf left her office, Grayce retreated to the large office window, trying to absorb the sun's warmth into her soul. The emptiness of grief sat on her shoulders pressing down on her, exhausting her. With her eyes closed, she took slow cleansing breaths through her mouth.

She had dedicated her life to healing animals. With all her clinical skills and knowledge and her intuitive healing abilities, she still couldn't prevent the end.

Her mentor had always attributed her great capacity for caring, her ability to heal, to her experience of losing her sister. He had taught her not to block her feelings of anguish but to honor them.

She continued to breathe slowly, visualized her sister's laugh and light filled the room.

CHAPTER FOUR

Davis and his jet-black standard poodle Mitzi climbed out of the Fire Department's Suburban and were surrounded by fishermen with knitted hats, flannel shirts and yellow rubber overalls, right out of "The Deadliest Catch." These guys could out-macho firefighters any day.

The fireground was still too hot to begin his investigation. Since he couldn't start digging, he had come to Fisherman's Terminal expecting to ask questions. Instead he had his hands full fending off the questions being fired at him.

"Is the fire department solving crimes with poodles these days?"

Laughter followed.

Always the tallest in a crowd, Davis was surprised to find himself looking up to a few of these Viking descendants. "This is my dog, guys."

He ignored the rolled eyes and knowing looks.

A burly man clad only in a T-shirt and overalls to protect against the forty degree chill, bent to pet the poodle. "What's the dog's name?"

"Mitzi."

"Did the dude say *Mitzi*?"

"Yeah. He said, *Mitzi*. More loud guffaws.

First rule of investigation was to build rapport. Davis spoke in a clear challenging voice. "Mitzi belonged to my ex-girlfriend."

Enjoying the attention, Mitzi mingled with the men, winning them over with her soulful dark eyes.

A huge man with a bulbous red nose, knelt down and scratched behind Mitzi's ears. The poodle leaned into his legs.

One of the giants queried in a deep bass voice, "So what caused the shed to burn?"

Questions were shouted from all sides.

"Any suspects? How you gonna find the guy? Got any witnesses?"

Rule Number2: Never, never give a press conference.

Davis cleared his throat. "Well, gentlemen, that's exactly why I'm here. Why would anyone want to burn down a shed? And just one shed? Any theories?"

"You're saying it was arson."

Davis scanned the group. Not a red-top among them. "Someone sure went to a lot of effort to burn just a shed."

"You think so, Sherlock?"

There was always one in a crowd. It was the same guy who'd made the crack about the poodle.

A brawny youth, his knit cap down low over his eyes, stood behind the wise-ass. Davis moved to get a better view, but the kid shifted position.

Davis raised his hands in the air. "Can someone tell me what's kept in the sheds? The Port office tells me that you store supplies in there. Would that include flammables?"

"Traps, rope. Nothing to catch fire." The men nodded. "Must be a grudge."

Davis searched for the face to match the ornery voice. The fisherman had a bushy red beard; unfortunately, the hair poking out of his baseball cap was brown. Davis asked, "Why would you think it's a grudge?"

A guy who looked like a bouncer who'd taken too many hits to his face growled.

"Cuz he's not from around here. He's a Russian."

"That don't mean nothing." The joker spoke again, the obvious leader of the group.

"Why was he unloading crab cases from the Jupiter in the middle of the night?" All eyes turned toward the bouncer but no one answered.

"Hey, help me out here. Don't you all catch crab?"

"No, we catch salmon. You can't store crab here."

"Where's it stored?"

"King Crab is put in cold storage either on Pier 91 or in the south end."

"So why was he unloading here?" Davis asked.

"That's what you've gotta find out," the bouncer countered.

Someone shouted. "Good luck with that." This was followed with another group guffaw.

"So how do I find this man? Does he have a name?" Davis asked.

Another guy who was petting Mitzi shook his head. "The Jupiter went out this morning. Won't be back for weeks."

"How convenient." Davis muttered under his breath. "Thanks, guys. I'll be around if you think of anything. Here's my card." No one budged, just like his days as an investment banker after the market tanked when no one wanted to talk about investments.

Suddenly Davis heard a loud insistent bark and then a man's angry voice. "Get off me."

Davis scanned the crowd for Mitzi. She had pinned the young man who had been hiding. She kept her paws on his chest and tried to lick his face.

A few guys laughed.

"Hey, Mike, afraid of a poodle?"

"What the hell?" Davis' surprise at his dog's behavior drew another loud hoot of laughter. "Mitzi, get down."

"Can't handle your women, Mr. Investigator?"

The men howled.

Mitzi sat down next to the youth. The dog gave a look of total innocence.

Davis moved towards Mitzi. "I apologize. I don't know what came over her."

A man put his gargantuan arm on Davis' shoulder, blocking any movement. "Just like my wife. Never does what she's supposed to."

The men chuckled and began to walk away. Mike, the kid with the low cap, merged with the crowd before Davis could get to him. The kid was probably afraid. It might not have anything to do with the fire, but he planned to ask Mike a few questions.

Davis bent to Mitzi. “Why did you jump on that kid? Is he in trouble?” Mitzi pushed against his hand. Davis watched the men move toward the boats docked at the pier.

“Okay, girl, I see what boat he got on. We’ll be back tomorrow to have a little private talk with Mike. Let’s get over to the Port Offices and see what they can tell us about the Jupiter and crab fishing.”

CHAPTER FIVE

Grayce ran but her legs wouldn't move. A faceless pursuer hounded her in a strange garden. She couldn't escape. His hard breathing grew closer and closer, sucking her into a black twirling mist.

She dropped to her knees and crawled behind a massive slab of steel. Crouched behind the twisted shadows, she waited. Her tracker's hatred surrounded her, devouring her into nothingness.

Grayce awoke with a start. Gloom pressed on her chest, making every breath a struggle. Gasping, she forced air down into her lungs. Cold sweat trickled down her back.

Sinister menace permeated her soul. She'd had the same dreams of catastrophe in her childhood after her sister Cassie had been killed, the same dreams of darkness, and the same sensation that she could never escape.

Trying to calm her ragged breathing, she climbed out of bed. She inhaled deeply into the mountain position and focused on purging her mind and body of the fear.

Exhausted, she crawled back into bed and dreamed of her sister and her family's devoted yellow lab, Gus. She and Cassie were being pulled up the hill by Gus at Gasworks Park. At the top, they dropped to the ground and rolled down the hill. Gus chased them trying to lick their faces. The presence of Cassie and Gus in her dream brought lightness and sunshine.

The dream shifted, and her feelings of safety vanished. Lieutenant Davis, his face contorted in pain, shouted at her to get back, away from the edge. He hovered on the brink of a disaster, of falling into emptiness. She had to save him. The backs of her knees tingled and her stomach trembled as she started to fall into the black void.

Grayce awakened herself and jumped out of bed. She had to shake out the night terrors, shake out the sensation that her world was spinning out of control.

Usually, she could control her dreams. In her work as an energy healer, she absorbed her client's emotions, fears, and illnesses. She processed and released their disturbed energy in her dreams, restoring her balance, replenishing herself. Since the wharf fire, her dream world had become disrupted. She had to regain her equilibrium or she wouldn't be able to work. Or heal.

CHAPTER SIX

Assistant Chief Stewart Maclean came down the hallway before Davis had time to make it into his office.

"You've got a witness to the fire?" Maclean asked.

"And a good morning to you, Officer Maclean."

"I told you to keep me informed."

"There's nothing to report," Davis said.

Maclean leaned on the door jamb. "Well, what did the witness see?"

"She saw a man carrying a duffel bag. It may have been the torch or she may have seen one of many fishermen on the wharf."

"A woman?" Maclean asked.

He bristled at the idea of Maclean knowing anything about Dr. Walters. "She didn't see anything, just a guy walking into the fog."

"Send me her statement. Anything else I need to know?"

"This fire just doesn't look like the work of any of our regulars. It's too good."

"Really?" Maclean stared at Davis, waiting for more.

"The calculated explosion to burn one shed makes me think the guy knew what he was doing. The question is, why an isolated shed?"

Maclean's beady eyes seemed to get smaller. "Go on."

"I'm planning to go through the list of our fired or should I say retired firefighters to see if anyone fits the bill. Do you want me to send you the list?"

"No. I know the loser's list."

"Peterson and Benson were really good firefighters." He felt a need to defend the men, even if their personal lives were a mess.

Emerging from the next room, Niles Olsen joined Davis and Maclean. "What about Peterson?" At six foot eight inches, the department's chaplain had to lean down to participate in the conversation.

"Davis thinks that one of our bottom feeders like Peterson might be behind the wharf fire," Maclean said.

"I said that the wharf fire has the markings of a pro and I need to rule out our ex-firefighters. I hope it isn't one of our own," Davis said.

"Peterson isn't a fire starter. And with counseling, he may have learned techniques to control his anger." Niles never gave up on any person in the department.

Maclean's lips twisted into a look of contempt and his voice got rougher. "He got busted twice for domestic violence before I kicked his ass out of the department. No counselor's going to change his behavior."

Davis gave Niles a small nod out of Maclean's view. Maclean didn't believe in any "new-age counseling bullshit."

Niles straightened his massive frame. "I don't think you should give up on a man because he's made a mistake. We've all done things we regret."

"Niles, you're burdened by regrets?" Maclean never missed the opportunity to probe and jab with his razor-sharp tongue.

The Norwegian's fair skin turned a bright red. "My mistakes aren't relevant to this conversation." Niles was no pushover. "My belief in a merciful God helps my regrets."

Maclean snorted. "Probably why you're the chaplain and not me."

Davis wanted to jump in and protect Niles, the finest in the department. But his friend didn't need his help in handling Maclean. "Forget Peterson. What about Redmayne or Conerton?"

He hated raising questions about the men, labeling them as possible criminals but Niles and Maclean knew more about the fired men's personal lives than he did.

Maclean rolled his eyes upward. "Redmayne? That stoner is lighting joints not fires. Sounds like another desperate theory."

"Niles, what do you think about Conerton?" Davis asked.

"The guy who wouldn't stop looking at porn while on duty?" Maclean asked.

"Yeah," Davis said.

"He's an idiot," Maclean fired back.

Niles face stayed bright red. But he refused to be further baited by Maclean.

Davis refused to back down until he had the information he needed. There was still one man left to discuss. "Benson has the skills. And I'm sure his drinking and need for money hasn't diminished."

"Are you kidding me? Benson couldn't stand upright long enough to pull off this stunt," Maclean said.

Despite the irony of Maclean calling someone else a drunk, Davis ignored the provocation. Maclean was well known throughout the department as a heavy hitter.

"This is the best you can come up with?" Maclean stepped closer. "FYI, Benson moved to Las Vegas after he was *retired.* Isn't that right, Niles?"

"It's true. In his exit interview, Benson said he planned to move to Las Vegas," Niles said. "I don't think you can consider Rob for your wharf fire."

"Davis, maybe you should consider returning to your previous career as an investment banker." Maclean chuckled and turned to leave.

Davis gritted his teeth, trying to suppress the need to pin Maclean against the wall. After his father's death, he left investment banking, the world of making the rich, richer, and sought a career in service. He was committed to his new work and to the people in the department who risked their lives every day.

"Don't try to make this into something big and dramatic. Just finish the damn investigation."

One more of Maclean's comments and the slow burn in Davis' gut would ignite. "Has the Port contacted the Chief's office yet?"

Maclean didn't answer. He turned and walked away. "Send me the pictures from the scene."

Niles put his arm on Davis' shoulder. "Working with him is a challenge."

"That's diplomatic. I can think of a better word."

CHAPTER SEVEN

Davis pulled the department's Suburban over next to the fire site. He opened the front door, then turned back to speak to Mitzi. "Stay put. No visiting with 'The Deadliest Catch' crew today. I've got to do some digging."

Leaning over, he pointed for emphasis. "Don't even think about getting out of this car." He knew animal trainers recommended limiting commands to short phrases, but since Mitzi understood everything, he saw no need. He wondered whether Grayce Walters would agree with him.

He opened the trunk to get his gear. Donning navy-blue overalls, steel-tipped boots, and a yellow helmet, he approached the heap of ash, charred wood, and hunks of metal.

"Damn." He had Grayce Walters on the brain. He marched back to the car and grabbed his filter mask and gloves. Mitzi whined, ready to join in.

"Sorry, girl, regulations. You're not allowed on a crime scene."

He made his way across the parking lot. The steel tips of his boots beat a cadence on the cement. Stacks of crab traps littered the sidewalks. The wind and rain had helped clear the air of the acrid smell of melted plastic.

He felt guilty leaving Mitzi in the car, but he was ready to start digging. He stepped over the yellow tape. The adrenaline rush hit him, the same high he got before a mountain climb. He was a junkie, addicted to the puzzle of a major hole in the ground, with most of its clues destroyed.

He assumed that N-4 had burned quickly after the explosion since the shed was built of heavy lumber with a corrugated metal shell. That not a single warehouse had burned was either the mark of a very experienced arsonist or a miracle. Since he didn't believe in miracles, he leaned toward the notion of a pro. The close proximity of the other warehouses, the flotilla of boats and their fuel could've caused a disaster.

The remains of the shed were scattered across the massive space. Misshapen chunks of pale blue metal, walls of partially burned fir, heaps of black ash, and piles of partially-burnt plastic formed a sci-fi landscape—Mars under the Ballard Bridge.

He bent over a shard of metal, most likely part of the ceiling. He sensed a presence. Frantically sniffing and barking, Mitzi ran through the site. He had never seen her act this of out of control.

"How the hell did you get out of the car?"

Mitzi leaped at him from two feet away. Her hundred pounds hit him square in the chest. He staggered backward from the impact. His heel caught on a part of the metal ceiling, sending him crashing on his ass.

"What in the hell's wrong with you? It's doggy daycare for you."

Mitzi stood over him, her dark eyes focused on his face.

He started to stand. He felt a gush of air blow across the empty space. Before he could grab Mitzi or roll away, a section of the charred thirty foot wall fell, shattering by his feet. Remnants of a burned plank broke off, striking the dog on the back. Mitzi gave a high pitched cry. His dog was down. "My God, Mitzi."

She lay very still. He scrambled over the rubble to reach her. He ran his hands down her spine and back legs looking for injuries. She whined when he touched her back leg.

"It's okay, it doesn't feel broken, but we've got to check it out." His voice sounded calm but seemed to echo in his head against the pounding beat of his heart. "I'm going to pick you up and take you to Dr. Herrick."

He carried the poodle next to his chest, trying to buffer her from the wind and rain. "How did you get out of the car?"

She licked his face, her rough tongue brushed his cheek.

At the truck, he wrapped her gently in his coat and laid her on the front seat. He sped toward Ballard and Dr. Herrick.

He patted her reassuringly as he drove. Mitzi could've been killed. And then came the thought he didn't want to explore: if it hadn't been for Mitzi, he might've been killed.

CHAPTER EIGHT

Grayce's morning passed quickly—a few minor behavior problems, adjustment to a new relationship, and hairballs.

Hollie appeared at her door. "Your new client's here." With her pierced eyebrow arched in contempt, Hollie emphasized *new* like it was infected.

Grayce nodded, trying to decipher Hollie's odd behavior. Always loving with the animals, Hollie kept a safe, cool distance from two-legged clients. Hollie didn't look cool.

Grayce scanned her schedule. "Mr. Davis with Mitzi, a standard poodle."

Hollie returned with the new client. Grayce stared. She blinked twice. Mr. Davis was Lieutenant Davis. Bewildered to see the fire investigator in her office after last night's nightmare, she blurted, "Has there been another fire?"

"No, I'm a patient. I mean my dog's a patient."

Grayce rechecked her patient list. "Mitzi?"

His face flushed when she used Mitzi's name. Had she gotten the name wrong? She seldom did. The black poodle's ears perked at the mention of her name.

"Yes, *Mitzi*." His face remained red as he led his dog into the room. Grayce focused on the haughty poodle, limping protectively next to her owner. There was something about the spunky dog she couldn't grasp.

Grayce couldn't envision the lieutenant comfortable in the overstuffed chintz treatment chair. She gestured to the chair across from her desk. "Please be seated. How can I help you…and Mitzi?"

"Mitzi was injured at the fireground," he said.

Grayce bent on one knee, not touching the stressed dog. "Mitzi, what an amazing protector."

She never knew where the words came from when she spoke to animals, but she knew they came from a deep part of her. She offered the words while observing the effect of her voice. Mitzi outwardly appeared calm but her eyes remained alert, watchful.

Grayce gently touched Mitzi's head, needing to comfort, connect with the injured dog. Showers of blue sparks danced in her peripheral vision like those from an overloaded circuit. The charge flowing from the dog to her hand topped any ampere scale. Lightheaded from the power surge, Grayce forced herself upright and stepped toward the old pine table that served as her desk.

Looking across the table, she saw Davis' concern.

"I'm fine, just got up too quickly." She knew he didn't buy it, but she couldn't think of anything else to say.

Grayce took a slow breath and focused on the sheet attached to the record. She had to concentrate to read the blurred words. "I see that Dr. Herrick referred you."

"He thought you could help with Mitzi's pain. And since I met you, I knew Mitzi would be comfortable."

She focused on the referral sheet. "A wood plank fell on her back legs two days ago?"

Davis leaned forward in his chair. "Mitzi was hit by a plank that missed me by inches." He stared at the poodle. "She knocked me down. Pieces of a charred wall crashed right at my feet. She saved me."

In the stillness of the office, foreboding floated around Grayce. She envisioned Davis on the ground with the wall crashing right before him. In his office, she had been shaken but she had thought it was caused by reliving the red-haired man's rage. Now, Mitzi had saved him from a near catastrophe. There was something about this accident that didn't feel like an accident.

"Mitzi's been acting crazy. She wasn't supposed to be on the crime scene. She jumped out of the window as if she knew I was in danger."

Grayce squirmed. She felt as if ants were walking up and down her spine. "Really? What else has she been doing?"

Davis shifted in his chair and hesitated as if not wanting to speak in front of the dog. "She howls when I leave the condo. The neighbors have complained. She chewed a hole in the wall as if she were trying to escape." His voice grew louder, clipped with each explanation.

"Is this new for her?"

"Since I started the investigation at Fisherman's Terminal, she's been a pain in the.... I can't leave her alone. I still can't believe she got injured. I left the car windows open, but I never thought she could fit through it." He rubbed his forehead with his broad fingers as if soothing away a headache. "Dr. Herrick thought you could help her. He couldn't praise your skills enough."

Grayce focused on Mitzi's pain and anxiety. She kept her voice low, trying to settle the fear pulsating in and around her and the apprehension traveling up and down her spine. "Acupuncture will help Mitzi."

"Great." Davis gave her the same lopsided grin as in his office softening all the harsh planes and angles of his face.

Grayce gave an inner sigh of relief with Davis' easy acceptance of acupuncture. She stood slowly, walked around the desk, and knelt beside the poodle. The dog thumped her tail when Grayce kneeled.

Davis watched. "Should I be doing anything?"

"No, you're fine."

Grayce took a deep cleansing breath and closed her eyes. She visualized waves breaking on the beach bringing the brilliant blue water onto the white sand, the fragments of broken shells tumbling into the wake, joining the rolling waves, melding into the powerful ocean. Calm, she readied herself to heal the traumatized dog.

She ran her hand along Mitzi's back, not actually touching the dog but feeling for changes in temperature. When she got closer to Bui Hui, the center of energy, she felt a burst of heat. The intensity of energy around the dog's lower spine confirmed her diagnosis: Mitzi was highly stressed and in pain.

Grayce placed the first needle into the top of the poodle's head. The dog's thick curly fur masked any reaction she had to the needle's insertion. Grayce visualized the waves surrounding Mitzi, taking her pain and fear out into the bigger universe.

She then placed the second needle at the base of Mitzi's spine. She needed to balance the intense energy flowing from the Bai Hui center. Rubbing the dog's springy coat, she whispered, "You're a brave dog. You kept him safe. I'll help you now."

Mitzi lay down after Grayce inserted the second needle and slept soundly. Grayce continued to place the needles, raising her own vibrations to absorb the dog's fear. She

felt heat dissipating through the needles.

Grayce wasn't aware of Davis during the treatment, not until she heard his voice, almost in a whisper.

"Unbelievable. It's the most remarkable thing I have ever seen." Grayce glanced his way. Davis' bright eyes gleamed. "Dr. Herrick was right. You're amazing with animals."

She couldn't look away. There was more to Davis than an eyeful of beauty. His feelings ran deep. She tore her gaze away and went back to moving several of the needles around Mitzi's injury.

"I think I should see Mitzi again next week." She ran her hand along Mitzi's chest. "She's strong and has a brave heart." Her words, spoken from a deep place, didn't only describe Mitzi.

Grayce stood and took the used needles to the disposal container, giving her more time to reflect on this confusing treatment. She had lessened Mitzi's anxiety and pain but she hadn't been able to remove the dog's deep fear. Deep fear wasn't part of the dog's nature. Mitzi sensed that her owner was in danger and was on alert to protect him. Grayce always trusted an animal's instincts.

She moved behind her desk and said her usual parting words to clients. "You can call me if you have any questions." Somehow saying the words to Mitzi and Davis had a totally different meaning, a commitment not recognized until she had spoken it out loud.

Davis leaned over the desk. “Thank you. You… I….” There was a long pause. He looked confused, struggling with uncertainty. He cleared his throat. “I’m sure you helped Mitzi.”

A knock on the door jarred them both. Grayce startled, exhaled the breath she hadn’t realized she had been holding. She stepped away from her desk and walked to the door, relieved by Hollie’s timely interruption.

“It’s Dr. Herrick on the phone. He has an important question for you. Should I tell him you’ll call him back?”

“No, I’ll take his call. Lieutenant Davis and Mitzi were just leaving.”

Davis followed the receptionist to the outer office. He hadn’t felt this uncertain since middle school and he certainly disliked the feeling.

This office jarred his every expectation of a professional visit with a renowned clinician. Dr. Walters was a highly respected veterinarian and a brilliant scientist. No one had a receptionist in thigh boots. No one had flowery chairs. No one served tea and cookies, and no one made him want to stay, to belong.

The receptionist brought him back into the moment. “Dr. Walters may be out of town for part of next week. I’ll call you once I know her schedule.”

Despite her appearance, the receptionist had won over Mitzi. Gentle and cooing in a sweet voice, she bent over the dog. Mitzi gazed back, showing none of her usual indifference.

Mitzi appeared recovered, with no indication of the limp she’d had earlier. The high-strung dog had actually slept during the insertion of the needles and then woke up energized.

He smiled at the receptionist. “Dr. Walters is really good, isn’t she? I mean, amazing with animals.”

The receptionist stared back at him. “Dr. Walters is a gem. She’s giving to everyone.” She leaned closer, her eyes direct. “And rather naive.”

“Excuse me?”

"Dr. Walters trusts everyone." The receptionist's red curled lip made it clear that she harbored no such illusions. She raised the eyebrow with the silver ball. "Didn't you just interview her?"

"Dr. Herrick referred me." He knew his voice was loud, but he refused to explain himself to an eighteen-year-old who looked like she painted graffiti on abandoned buildings in her spare time. He walked out of the office considering several comebacks. Outside the warehouse, the rain beat obstinately, matching his mood.

A moist nose pressed against his hand. "What?"

The poodle turned and looked back at the building.

"I know… you liked her."

He hadn't explained to Grayce how protective Mitzi became when women were around. Or the way she had growled when he arrived with Toni from Ladder 7. Mitzi had ruined his plans for romantic evenings more than once.

"Yeah, me too." He leaned over to stroke the dog's head.

It was more than liking; it was a connection, a force. When Grayce had looked into his eyes, he had a sensation of transparency, as if she peered deep into his soul. He'd had the same unfamiliar sensation when she'd gazed at his dad's picture in his office. She understood his loss; somehow she knew he had suffered when he could do nothing to stop the agonizing progression of his dad's bone cancer.

Oblivious to the rain, he crossed Fremont Avenue. What had the receptionist said? *"Grayce was always taking care of everyone."*

She had rushed to the rescue of an injured dog. It wasn't hard to imagine Grayce Walters consoling anyone in pain. Obviously, the receptionist was one of her charity cases. But who took care of Grayce Walters?

During this visit, like in his office, she had appeared worried. Was her fear more pronounced today or was he more attentive? He had the same gut reaction then. Grayce Walters was hiding something. He didn't suspect for a minute she was involved with the wharf fire. There was nothing criminal about the sensitive woman.

For the first time in his career, he doubted his ability to be objective about a witness.

Grayce sat at her desk. Flashes of heat followed by goose bumps galloped through her body. She rubbed her hands up and down her arms in an attempt to warm herself. A simple explanation for today's sensations was that she was coming down with the flu, but she knew better. She had absorbed Mitzi's fear for her owner. She had always been able to sense the energy states of all kinds of creatures but she had never experienced the transfer of an emotion from an animal for their human owner.

She had felt peril surrounding the lieutenant in his office. Mitzi, his defender, was still fearful and had been injured protecting him. How was she, an animal healer, supposed to help a dog protect her owner? Especially an owner whose job was to apprehend criminals?

CHAPTER NINE

Davis pulled his jacket collar up to stop the rain from dripping down his neck. He avoided the fire department's spot and walked across Jackson Street to his own hideout joint. He needed a caffeine fix before heading to Fisherman's Terminal and some time alone to sort out his impressions of the investigation. In his office, he kept getting distracted by the mental image of a small woman with luminous green eyes and a short skirt.

The funky coffee shop was crowded with tuned out Seattleites pouring over their computers. With the days dark and dreary, the coffee shops filled with people needing caffeine and a connection—that is if you considered sitting by someone while staring at a computer screen a connection. He spotted Niles scrunched in a worn chair in the corner.

"Niles, you hiding out?" Davis asked.

Niles head jerked up. The sleepy-eyed look that gave him the appearance of a gentle giant was gone. Instead a pair of steely gray eyes stared at Davis. "No."

"I haven't seen you around the department." Davis pointed to the adjacent chair. "Do you mind company?"

Niles looked down but not fast enough for Davis to miss the wariness in the chaplain's eyes. "No, join me."

"I needed to get out of my office." Davis sat down on another worn chair. "Take a break from my investigation." And take a break from his adolescent mooning over Grayce Walters.

"Any leads?"

"None. But I'm still convinced a pro set this fire. In your exit interviews, anyone come to mind that'd be willing to turn for money?"

Niles chuckled, sending ripples through his generous belly. He was the only department member who didn't pride himself in looking like a professional jock. "I'm counseling these guys about their career and personal mistakes. Do you think they'd share any criminal plans with the chaplain?"

"It would've been so easy if someone confessed," Davis said.

"Even if someone did confess, it would be privileged information. I'm the chaplain after all, but no one has given me any indications they'd set any fires, or were planning to turn to a life of crime.

"I'm not giving up on my theory."

"That's what I like about you, Davis. You're determined."

"Maclean would call me a stubborn son of a bitch. What am I talking about? Maclean has called me stubborn son of a bitch." Davis laughed.

Niles nodded but didn't laugh.

"Sorry for the shop talk. What kept you away from the department?" Davis asked.

"I've been busy with family matters."

"I've never heard you talk about your family." Niles was over sixty and single. The scuttlebutt in the department was that Niles was either divorced or had never recovered from a bitter relationship.

"I didn't have a family until last week."

Davis tried to read the inscrutable expression on Niles' face to see if this was a joke. Niles never clowned around with the guys. He distanced himself from the male crew's crude jokes.

"How can you have a family and not know it?"

Niles' face turned crimson. "I have a son."

"A son?" Davis shifted in his chair. Niles never spoke about himself. He had a way of deflecting anything personal.

Niles slapped his thigh. "Davis, it's going to be hard to forget the expression on your face."

"You had a baby? I mean your girlfriend had a baby?"

Niles' broad smile melded into his dimples. "That's good, Davis. No, I have an adult son. After my football injury and the end of my prospects of playing pro-ball, I went a little crazy partying, drugs. You know what I'm saying… and there was an exchange student." Niles shook his head. "She went home and never told me."

Davis relaxed, leaning back in the leather chair. "How did you find out?"

"My son, Nicholas, contacted me after his mother died."

Davis noted the warmth in "my son".

"Nicholas grew up believing his father had died. On her death bed, his mother told Nicholas the truth. Neither of us knew about the other."

Niles paused and stared at a distant point somewhere in the room. "Nicholas is married and has a six month old son." Niles' voice turned incredulous. "I learned I was a father and a grandfather on the same day."

Davis shut his mouth with a snap when he realized it hung open.

"At first, I just couldn't believe it. Then I could think of nothing else but getting them out of Russia."

"Russia?"

"Galina had relatives here. It's why she came to study in Seattle." Niles took a large gulp of his coffee. "I hardly gave her another thought after my senior year. What she must have suffered. I'm going to make it up to Nicholas and his family."

Niles had always been totally devoted to the department. He treated every member as family and now he had his own. Davis wanted to slap him on the back. "This is great news."

"It's going to look a bit irresponsible to have discovered at this late age that I'm a father. Can you put the best spin on the news when it spreads in the department? The crew respects you."

Davis felt Niles' intense regard and the emotion underlying his words. He flashed back to two years ago when his dad lay dying and he spilled his guts to Niles. The chaplain had been there in those long hours.

Davis smiled. "Sure Niles, whatever you need."

Niles stood up and shook his hand. "I knew I could count on you."

"Let me know if there's anything else I can do."

Leaning into the wind, Davis and Mitzi made their way along the dock. With the big gusts, the dock actually shook. Seattle's fishing fleet bobbed in the dark grey waters all around them.

Unlike yesterday, no one approached them when they arrived at the wharf. With the gusts blowing at forty miles per hour, the fishermen didn't appear to be in a convivial mood. Protected by yellow slickers, they worked under tarps, repairing their nets.

He followed Mitzi onto the fishing vessel. "Hey, anyone around?" Davis doubted anyone could hear him over the wind. He spotted a man in a flannel shirt and rubber overalls coming on deck from mid-ship. Davis extended his hand. "I'm Lieutenant Davis from the fire department. I'm investigating the shed fire."

The older man crossed his arms over his chest. "I recognize you."

Davis didn't need investigative skills to know how this was going to play. "I didn't get to meet anyone yesterday."

The older man glanced up at the rushing storm clouds overhead.

"I'm looking for Mike. He was on the wharf yesterday when I was talking with the men."

"What do you want with him?"

"Is he around?"

Mitzi pushed against the calloused man's hand. The fisherman rubbed the dog's head but refused to look at Davis.

"Mike's not here today. Some problem with his car."

"When do you expect him back?"

"Is he in some kind of trouble?" The man jutted his chin, his shoulders stiffened.

"I just want to ask him a few questions."

"Mike didn't start that fire."

Davis shook his head. "I'm not thinking he did."

"He's a good kid."

"I'm sure he is."

The big guy stepped closer to Davis. "Mike didn't start your damn fire. Go harass someone else."

Davis' hard wiring for domination surged through his circuits, but he restrained himself from going nose-to-nose with the captain. These fishermen thought they knew something about intimidation. He said, "Just want to tie up a few loose ends."

The man stood with his legs apart, braced against the rocking of the boat. "He's family. Everyone on this boat is family. So if you've got a problem, I wanna know."

Davis shrugged. "Look, this is no big deal. If you tell me how to contact him, I'll get out of your way."

Mitzi continued to sit next to the captain with her head leaning on his leg.

"He just moved down here from Alaska. He's been crashing on the boat."

Davis pulled out his card. "Tell Mike to call me. If he doesn't, I'll be back. Pleasure meeting you, too." Davis heard a grunt when he turned to leave. "Come on Mitzi, we've got lots to do."

CHAPTER TEN

Grayce quickened her pace through the Friday night party crowd in Belltown. Dinner with her dad had been the perfect antidote for her worry but spending the latter half of the night with her best friend, James, would make her forget her insane week. She was back in balance, no premonitions about violent men and no nightmares about Lieutenant Davis.

James was seated at a front table at the outside bar separated by a small fence from the sidewalk. He was absorbed in watching the people who paraded in front of him. His eyes glimmered when he spotted her. Standing, he kissed her on both cheeks.

"Darling, you look fabulous." He gestured with his manicured fingers. "We're both going to find gorgeous men tonight."

Grayce grinned at James' standard Friday night promise. "You always do. I'm not sure I'll be as lucky."

"Do you mind sitting outside? I do love watching the boys stroll by."

She pulled her coat around herself. "As long as I can sit under the heater…this little black dress isn't that warm."

He pulled her coat apart. "You wore this delectable creation by Helene for dinner with your dad?"

"I wore it for my two favorite men."

"How is the old man? Still wanting you to go to med school?"

"James, play nice. I've incredible news. You're going to go crazy."

"You met a man?"

"What? Why do you say that?"

He leaned forward, preparing his response.

She raised her hand. "No, don't answer."

James always had plans for Grayce's romantic life. He had been her friend since ninth grade chemistry class in high school. They were lab partners and both had secrets to hide. James liked wearing his mother's dresses and Grayce had unusual gifts. She never revealed the extent of her awareness, but James understood why she hid her sensitivity just as he hid his proclivities. Now as adults, Grayce maintained her self-protection while James abandoned his.

Grayce tapped her finger on her lips as if pondering her words. "Seems my reputation has spread to Hollywood." She watched James face, waiting for the change in his usual cool aplomb. Her good friend had two passions: movie stars and fashion. "I got an interesting phone call this morning." She paused building the moment. "From a movie star…someone you might have heard of."

"A movie star?" James, master of the sardonic tone, shouted. "What movie star?"

"Elizabeth Marley."

"Elizabeth Marley!" His voice pitched high, almost squealing with excitement. "Tell me everything and don't leave out one word."

"Her vet recommended acupuncture for her dog's fatigue."

"My God, you're going to Hollywood to meet a star."

"I'm going to Hollywood to treat her dog." Grayce moved her chair directly under the patio lamp.

James sat by her side, angling for a better view of the people walking down First Avenue. He enjoyed men of all shapes, sizes, and orientation.

Just then, the waitress, who wore a revealing V-necked tee and tight skirt, came by for orders.

"Come on, Jamesie, Grey Goose Martinis to celebrate? It's been an intense week." Tonight was about laughing and enjoying the company of the men who knew her best.

"You've twisted my… "

"James…Let's agree not to discuss body parts tonight." Grayce spent a great deal of time reacting to James' outrageous comments. They both enjoyed the game.

"Spoilsport." James moued masterfully. "Now tell me what was Elizabeth Marley like? Bitchy? I guess not, since you're treating her dog."

"Definitely a chain smoker, her voice is gravelly. I liked her sense of humor. And, she loves her dog."

"She must be so depressed, her husband is already living with his costar."

"Really? She said there were changes in her household. She probably assumed I would know the Hollywood gossip."

"Well, her husband has definitely run off with his costar and hasn't attempted to hide the affair. The press is going wild, painting her as the older wife, kicked to the dumpster for a hot younger woman."

"I didn't know it was that bad. I guess I haven't been spending enough time in the check-out line at the grocery store."

"You can't go to Hollywood in your usual Northwest style or, should I say, Northwest lack of style. I need to come over and help you pack."

"Would you? I hate making those decisions." Of course James knew all of her fashion deficiencies. "I don't have that many choices for a warm climate."

"If this becomes a regular gig, we're going to shop on Rodeo Drive. Don't you have those strappy Balenciaga sandals your mother gave you?" James could hardly breathe, plotting her Hollywood look. Her mother and James were onto her secret infatuation with designer heels. She never admitted to any correlation between her height and her closeted love of high heels.

"Remember when we found that little red dress at Macy's for the Prom. I thought my mother was going to pass out."

"The look on your mother's face when you came down the steps was hysterical. You were hot. That was the night I lost you to Mike Mallus. I still remember how his jaw dropped when we walked into the dance. Poor Lucy Vaughn—he never looked back."

"It was at that moment I think my mother finally decided you were a bad influence on me."

"God, I hope so."

They both laughed. She loved when James really laughed. Not the one he affected for drama but the laugh that softened the tense lines around his eyes and mouth.

"I still wish I could've seen your mother's face when you told her we were just friends. It took her a while to get used to the idea."

"She wasn't upset that you were gay but she regretted that I didn't have a boyfriend." Having a boyfriend was a sign to her mother that Grayce was beginning to recover from her sister's death.

"God, look at this guy coming down the street, and walking a poodle... my kind of man."

Grayce recognized Lieutenant Davis, heading straight toward them. Her heart rate accelerated. His face was calm, but his eyes never stopped watching the crowd. Moving away from the light, she leaned back in her chair.

James spoke in a sotto tone. "Oh God, all that dark hair."

"Mitzi, stop." Davis' sharp command didn't slow Mitzi from pulling on her lead toward Grayce.

James eyed the lieutenant and said in a voice loud enough to be heard at the next two tables. "What a great specimen."

Mitzi planted her two front paws on the wood beam separating the bar from the sidewalk and yelped.

Grayce leaned forward. No hiding now.

"Mitzi, get down." Davis' voice dropped low, almost to a growl, unconsciously acting as the alpha of the pack.

The dog sat.

Grayce willed her hammering heart to slow. Of all nights, why tonight? Tonight was about being with the men who cherished her, men who didn't give her nightmares and premonitions, men who didn't make her heart race into tachycardia.

"Grayce... Dr. Walters. What a surprise." Mitzi continued to yip straining to reach her.

"Hello." She pushed her drink to the side to pet the poodle. "How are you, Mitzi?"

"Darling, introduce me to this dreamy fellow."

Davis gave no indication that James had said anything out of the ordinary. "James Dewitt, this is Lieutenant Ewan Davis and Mitzi."

Davis bent and shook James' hand. "Nice to meet you."

Mitzi pulled on her lead, trying to reach Grayce.

"Ewan can you join Grayce and me for a drink? We're celebrating."

Grayce nudged James with her foot. "I'm sure he has other commitments."

"Really Ewan? Are you too busy to celebrate?"

Davis stared at her. "I would love to join you. What are you celebrating?"

James stood and pulled a chair from an empty table behind them. He placed Davis' chair between his and Grayce's.

Davis squeezed between the tables, trying to fit into the tight gap. His heat pressed against her back. His thighs brushed her when he pulled his chair closer to the table.

She caught a whiff of his scent—clean, fresh, a hint of spearmint. Her highly tuned intuitive system was bombarded, flooded by sensations, aware of Davis, all six foot four of him, struggling to sit comfortably in the small chair. This awareness wasn't about his dangerous job, or the rage of an arsonist—it was about a compelling, attractive male pressing against her.

"Call me Davis, everyone does."

"Really? Not Ewan?" James questioned unable to let anything pass.

"Davis seems easier for everyone."

"Doesn't your mother call you *Ewan*?"

"My mother passed away. My Aunt Aideen who raised me is the only person who calls me Ewan. So Davis it is."

"Well, Davis. We're drinking Grey Goose Martinis in honor of Grayce going to Hollywood. Can I get you one? Or is there something else you'd prefer?"

"Grey Goose works. Thanks."

Davis turned, focusing on Grayce. "You're leaving Seattle? I thought you'd just opened your practice?"

"I've been asked to treat a dog in California. I'll be gone for two days."

"Oh." There it was again, that crooked smile that reminded her of Dallas, the Doberman. Her patient was all sleek muscle and fierce growl, but had the same lopsided grin when he wasn't acting territorial.

"Excuse me." James waved his hand at their waitress, delivering drinks at the next table. The voluptuous blond stopped and stared at Davis, her eyes round with appreciation. "What can I get you?"

She leaned over the ledge placing a cocktail napkin in front of Davis, exposing her generous décolletage. She wiggled, giving her breasts a life of their own.

"Another round for the table." Davis' eyes stayed on the woman's face. She smiled at Davis and sauntered away.

James turned in his chair to look at Davis. "Do women always behave that way around you?"

Davis looked directly at Grayce. "Not all women."

Grayce couldn't look away. Her stomach twisted and rolled in rebellion, like the time she had gorged on an entire bag of vinegar and sea salt chips after trying to save a dog who had been hit by a car.

Contrary to the impression she formed during her interview at the fire department's headquarters and then at her office, she had liked Davis, the man who cared deeply about his poodle. By the way her stomach was twirling, it seemed she also liked raw male energy.

"So Davis, besides attracting women like bees to honey, tell me about yourself. How did you meet Grayce?" James leaned around Davis and placed his hand on Grayce's. "Darling, you've been holding out on me? Another man has replaced me in your affections?"

She hated when James acted overprotective. "James, behave yourself." She tried to glare at him. James winked.

Davis looked back and forth at them. "I brought Mitzi to Grayce's office for acupuncture." He didn't mention Grayce's role as a witness.

"Mitzi looks healthy, or has Grayce already cured her?"

"James, if you don't stop, I'm cutting you off. Davis is a firefighter. Mitzi was injured on his work site."

James perused Davis' broad shoulders and the way his thighs bulged in his blue jeans. "God, I might just need to start a fire in my condo."

Davis laughed out loud. Unlike other humans, whose stomach and shoulders shook, Davis' whole body rolled as a solid mass. "I'm definitely the wrong person to confide in about starting a fire. I'm a fire investigator."

James pursed his lips. "Oops."

Davis turned to Grayce. "When do you leave for California?"

"I'm going Monday afternoon and returning on Wednesday. Was Hollie able to give you an appointment?"

"Mitzi and I see you on Thursday." Mitzi's ears perked up when her name was mentioned. She placed her head on Grayce's lap and looked up into her eyes.

Grayce patted the dog's head. "Yes, I'll be taking care of you."

"I can't believe how Mitzi has taken to you. She really isn't that friendly," Davis said.

"Really?" James lost his flirty tone. "Everyone is attracted to Grayce. Especially strays." He angled his head, to inspect Davis. "Not that I meant Mitzi is a stray. Anyone looking at her knows she's a thoroughbred."

James wasn't referring to Mitzi but Grayce hoped Davis didn't realize it. Whenever she started dating, James got testy.

Davis straightened in his chair and faced James. "I'm sure we agree that Grayce has an amazing gift."

James crossed his arms and tapped his finger against his lower lip. "Oh, I'm aware of all of Grayce's gifts and her ability to attract lost souls."

"How is your investigation going?" She interrupted, hoping to derail the sudden turn in the conversation.

"It's moving slowly, the usual. But the good news is Mitzi hasn't needed to save me again."

The vision of Davis on the ground flashed through her mind. She felt light- headed, almost dizzy. Grayce pushed her Martini away. "Is Mitzi still going with you to the fire site?"

Mitzi pressed her cold nose under Grayce's hand. Grayce sensed a sudden tension from the dog.

"Yes, but she isn't allowed to get out of the car, right, Mitzi?"

The poodle pushed her nose against Grayce's hand again. Dogs' emotions were usually pure and easy to read but Mitzi's abrupt agitation was confusing.

Grayce focused her attention on the vigilant dog and fought the shadowy gloom creeping around them. She was absorbing Mitzi's fear. Panic slithered its way under her skin. She took a deep breath and tried to shake the apprehension. Mitzi needed her, needed reassurance. "What is it, girl?"

Mitzi looked up into Grayce's eyes and howled an eerie, disturbing sound. Grayce's vision narrowed into a black tunnel filled with murky energy. Blue sparks fluttered in the periphery.

The raucous bar scene quieted, and all heads turned toward Mitzi.

"Mitzi, what in hell is wrong with you?"

Grayce could hear Davis' voice but it sounded strangely muffled and distant.

"My God, Grayce, what is it?" The magnitude of James' volume broke the spell.

She didn't want James flying into one of his dramatic diva moments. "Sorry, I think the wine with my dad and now the Grey Goose has done me in."

Davis moved closer. "Are you sure that's all it is? Mitzi started to howl, and you got a strange look, like you were in pain."

Davis didn't miss a thing. What could she tell him? His dog was transmitting fear signals and she seemed to be the Bluetooth: the only network available to receive them.

"I'm fine. I really am, but no more martinis for this girl." She hugged herself, trying to stop the cold shivers running up and down her body as if she had jumped into the icy waters of Lake Washington.

"Grayce isn't the heaviest drinker. I remember a time in college…" James said.

"I'm fine but I think I'd like a cup of tea before I drive home."

Davis signaled their waitress. He ordered a tea for Grayce, a coffee for himself and when he gave James a questioning look, James said, "Oh, I think I'll have something stronger. I'm a pedestrian. A Vodka tonic, please extra lime."

Mitzi leaned against Grayce, crowding her and making her edgy. Soothing Mitzi, she ran her hand along the dog's chest, feeling the poodle's warmth and her pulsing heartbeat. "Mitzi and I are a bit fey today, a woman's prerogative."

No one laughed at her attempted humor. A pall had descended on her bright evening.

James answered a call on his cell. "Darling, do you mind if I meet Edward? He sounds verklempt."

She blew on the steaming mug. "No, no, go. I need to get going too."

She was glad not to have to run interference between the two men, but she wasn't sure she wanted to be alone with Davis.

"Do you want me to walk you to your car?" James' sideway stare indicated he was offering to help her ditch Davis.

"I'll make sure Grayce gets to her car." Davis said.

"Go ahead, James. I'm going to finish my tea before heading out."

James stood and ran his hands through his dark hair totally aware of the striking picture he presented. He bent over to peck Grayce on the cheek. "So we're on for Sunday? If we need to, we can head downtown to pick up a few things. How about eleven?"

"Let's be realistic, two?" She asked.

"Oh, so bitchy! Okay, so I like to sleep in, especially when I have someone to sleep in with."

Davis couldn't miss the leer James gave him. Leaning toward James, Davis countered, "I'm an early riser."

James laughed out loud, loving the sexual innuendo. Davis was holding his own with James, not easy for many straight men.

Grayce nodded to James. "I'll see you on Sunday. Give my best to Edward."

"*Au revoir, mon cherie*."

James sauntered down First Avenue.

"An interesting guy."

"James has been my good friend since high school. He isn't usually so dramatic. He was playing to a new audience."

"I wasn't sure at first if I should be jealous." Their eyes met again.

Her heart rate accelerated and then ran a trill as if she were going into atrial fibrillation. Davis' deleterious effect on her calm and steady heart rate defied medical reasoning and made her wonder about the benefits of yoga. "I really need to go. It's been a long week."

Davis searched her face. Whatever he saw caused his eyes to soften. "Are you sure you're okay? Do you want me to drive you home?"

She had no answer that Davis would like or understand.

CHAPTER ELEVEN

Blending in with all the other couples, Grayce and Davis walked with Mitzi toward her car. Dodging the crowds, their shoulders and hands brushed, except they weren't like any other couple. They were witness and investigator, client and veterinarian.

"Where are you parked?"

"I'm up on Second, where my Dad and I had dinner."

"You're a Seattle girl?"

"Born and raised. What about you?"

"The same."

She couldn't shake the sense of dread that sat in her stomach like a lump of greasy fries from Dick's. She had convinced herself that Mitzi's fear in her office had been a result of her injury. After tonight's bar scene, she knew she had been wrong.

"Where did you go to college?"

"University of Michigan." She found Davis studying her. "Family tradition. How about you? Husky?"

"No, I did the East Coast thing. Brown."

They continued to walk, side by side. Davis kept the conversation going. He appeared relaxed but she knew different. His energy was tight, controlled.

"I looked at Brown's medical school."

"But you went to vet school?"

She sighed. "Yes, to my mother's dismay. There it is, the red Subaru." She dug in her oversized bag for her keys. "Thank you for walking me to my car."

Davis hovered close, surrounding her with his jumpy energy. The man and his dog were definitely in the same state of agitation and she couldn't find her usual sense of calm with either of them.

She ran her hand along the dog's head. "Thank you too, Mitzi. You are a great girl."

"I was thinking the same thing."

Grayce looked up. The heat in Davis' stare surprised her. His face was flushed, the heightened color along his cheekbones made his eyes brighter. She didn't know where to look. Her heart fluttered, sending a rush of heat through her body.

He stepped closer. She backed up against the car. "Grayce?" The pitch in his voice vibrated deeper.

The air held an electric charge. She could hear the cars moving down Second Avenue. A homeless woman huddled in a corner. A street vagrant drifted toward them, a desperate frenzy in his reddened eyes. Pinpricks raced down her skin. She fought the lull of Davis' mesmerizing voice and eyes.

Mitzi growled.

Davis pulled on the lead. "Mitzi, it's okay."

The man continued, his amble slow, moving closer and closer. Violence radiated from him.

With her ears and tail pointed, the dog stood in attack mode.

"Spare change… for coffee?" Not the usual mumbling of the homeless but an imposing voice with a foreign cadence and accent.

The hairs on her neck and arms bristled. She widened her stance and rolled to the balls of her feet.

Mitzi strained on her leash.

Davis placed himself between Grayce and the advancing man.

"Move on." Davis snarled.

Ignoring Davis' threat, the man continued, now within arm's reach.

Her senses keen, she could smell a clean pine scent.

The man charged with a primitive ferocity, a knife in his raised hand. Bright lights flashed on the metal. He swung the knife in an arc at Davis' chest. Neither Davis nor Grayce had time to react.

Mitzi leapt through the air, emitting a hellish sound, hitting the attacker in the stomach and pushing him backwards. The man's head struck the sidewalk. A terrible thud resounded, followed by the clanging of the metal knife hitting the sidewalk.

Mitzi, her teeth bared, stood over the unconscious man. She kept up an insistent growl, her body poised for another attack, her white teeth gleaming.

Davis scanned the area before he bent over the man. "Grayce, get in your car. Call 911, and then get the hell out of here."

Ready to protest, Grayce swallowed the words and nodded in agreement. Her breathing was as choppy as her heart rate. Her body was primed for action, ready to do more than call 911. She wasn't going home and she definitely wasn't leaving Davis and Mitzi.

She fumbled with the keys. Her hand shook when she unlocked the door. She took a slow deep breath after being safely seated in her car. She relocked the car doors and then dug through her purse, searching for her cell phone.

Her medical composure took over as she answered the dispatcher's questions. Hyper-alert from the burst of adrenaline, she answered quickly, precisely. "Yes, Second Avenue and Bell… No, I'm not in danger. I'm in my car."

The dispatcher continued his questioning.

"Yes, unprovoked."

She focused. "My friend's dog jumped on him….Yes, hit his head… unconscious."

She watched Davis feel for the man's carotid pulse. The sirens started before she had answered all the questions.

"Yes, two police cruisers are arriving."

In another flash of violence, two cruisers careened onto the sidewalk forming an angle, boxing the crime scene. Bright lights glared on the two men and dog, surrounding them in a ghostly halo. Davis, leaning over the bleeding man, Mitzi in a fierce attack position, both surrounded by an otherworldly light. Two hefty police officers jumped out of their cars, their guns drawn. Davis raised his hands in the air.

Sirens blared in the distance. With their weapons pointed down, the police officers approached Davis. Her blood pulsated, expanding, into the keyed up muscles, readying her for the newest threat.

A two-ton fire truck sped toward them on Second Avenue. The bleating of an aid car could be heard in the distance.

Davis didn't move, but Grayce could see him conversing with the officers. Davis gave a shrug of his shoulders then produced his ID for the beefy, no-neck officer. With their guns holstered, the police spectacle slowed and the medical response began.

The ladder truck stopped, right in the middle of Second Avenue. A firefighter jumped out of the truck, medical kit in hand. By Davis' wide grin, it was obvious he knew the man.

Grayce's view of the assailant was blocked. She was about to leave her car when two firefighters joined the group.

Davis shook hands with the firefighters while the medics worked over the assailant. Mitzi and one police officer stood guard over the attacker, who appeared to have regained consciousness.

The evening had become a reunion of the fire department. Davis turned and walked toward her. His eyes were darkened with an emotion she couldn't read. He was under a great strain and it seemed to be directed at her.

Her heart did a weird run of flutters, then trills, a cacophony of irregular beats. She opened her door, unable to look away from his intense stare. He stood in front of the open car door. His massive form blocking the view.

"I told you to leave." His words were loud and clipped.

"I really would like to get out."

He didn't move.

"I'm used to emergencies." She looked up into his chiseled face and climbed out of the car. She slammed the door to make her point.

"This isn't about an injured dog." He swallowed hard. The muscles in his throat stretched rigid. "There is nothing for you to do."

A charge of righteous anger raced to all her meridians. They stood toe-to-toe. Too close, but he wasn't budging and neither was she. She stared at the black stubble on his jaw and the white texture of his skin.

"I want to make sure Mitzi and you are okay. He wanted to hurt you… I could feel…." She paused, aware of the assailant's deep drive to kill.

"He's a junkie; who knows what twisted thoughts he was having? It wasn't personal. Here comes Officer Lewis. Get in your car. Go. I'll take care of him."

She understood his need to take control. He didn't comprehend that she had the same drive. Women just didn't pound their chests, stomp, and command anyone within close range. "I'm not leaving. I can answer questions."

"I don't want you to put yourself through this. I'll call you tomorrow and give you all the details."

"I'm not leaving." She hadn't meant to shout, but she refused to be bullied.

He pulled her close to his body and kissed her, not the hard demanding kiss she expected but quick, soft and yet shockingly intense. He ran his finger across her lips. "Your eyes give you away, Grayce. I see your worry. Mitzi and I are fine. Please, let me handle this."

She wanted to respond, but he was already turning away.

"Lewis, she can't tell you anything I can't."

Davis walked away, looking confident that he could get both Lewis and her to do as he ordered. Ewan Davis, warrior chief, would've been perfect in medieval Scotland.

The police officer planted his feet and pulled out his notebook. "All I need is contact information if anything comes up."

"I'm happy to help in any way."

"I'm sure you are." The bulky man grinned. "Davis is in overdrive right now. This always happens. It's the rush, pushing him to be the boss, to be the man."

Grayce was embarrassed. The police officer had witnessed the battle between her and Davis. She wanted to tell Davis exactly what she thought of his domineering ways, but she'd wait until they were alone.

CHAPTER TWELVE

Grayce arrived home in a daze, her intuitive system shut down, her sensitivity overloaded. She went to the refrigerator, and reached for a can. Unlike many people who might reach for alcohol to soothe their distress, she reached for a Diet Coke. She tried to keep her addiction to one can a day. But there were days when resolve went right out the door. And tonight, after watching Davis almost get stabbed, was one of them.

She tapped her iPad, searching for her favorite Celtic singer and in seconds Enya's soothing voice played in the background. Grayce settled on the couch, Diet Coke in hand. She longed for potato chips but she refused to stock them for these moments of weakness. Napoleon snuggled against her feet. With the sound of the buzz of her phone, the gigantic Maine Coon jumped to the floor.

She didn't bother to look at the phone before answering.

"Grayce, are you alright? Officer Lewis assured me he didn't question you. I'm sorry you had to see the violence," Davis said.

Something in Davis' voice restrained her from bringing up his controlling behavior. "I'm okay. It's been such a bizarre evening. Are you alright? That man wanted to hurt you."

"I know. I'll probably have nightmares tonight when I think about it." He chuckled.

What could she expect—a combatant confessing unmanly fears? No, he was buttoned up and in control. She couldn't help but wonder if he ever let go of the invincible role.

"Grayce, you're very quiet. Are you upset about my high-handed methods? I wish I could see your eyes right now, are they still shooting fire?"

She laughed. It felt great to release all of her tension.

"You know I might be willing to be dominated in certain situations."

She couldn't keep up with his quick silver mood. Now he was flirting with her. She didn't know how to respond.

"Grayce? Don't fall off your chair." Again, the husky chuckle, "I don't want to be responsible for another disaster."

"Davis, you're not responsible for tonight's events. You don't need to shield me, I'm a grown up."

"I've noticed." His voice got low, silky.

"Don't you ever take anything seriously? Something felt wrong about the whole episode. I can't pin it down, but there was something strange about that man."

She wanted to confide in him about her foreboding and Mitzi's fear, but it was too soon. He wasn't ready or willing to discuss what had happened.

"Grayce, I'm taking the whole experience seriously, but I don't want you to worry. Remember, I'm the investigator; I even attended the Police Academy."

"Okay, I'll let you figure it out." She was confused and that irritated her. "Thank you for your concern."

"Listen Grayce, I value your insight, but you don't need to be concerned about a meth addict and his paranoid fantasies. It's late. Can I call you tomorrow? We'll talk more?"

"It's okay Davis. I'm fine."

"I'd just like to call you, okay, not to check on you, just to call you. I started to ask you if I could see you again before this all went down." She could hear another voice in the background.

"I've got to go, but are we settled? I'll call you tomorrow?"

"Sure. Good night."

Grayce hung up the phone. One moment she was laughing with Davis, feeling quite comfortable. The next, irritated by his overbearing command and his stubborn refusal to listen. Tonight's events, like Davis himself, had too many twists to navigate. Grayce sighed and headed for her tub.

She stepped into the lavender-scented bathwater and focused on the assailant. Davis had said the guy was a druggie but something was off with his behavior. Slipping into the deep water, she cleansed her mind of the whirls of sensations and images and reconstructed his distorted face.

She placed a hot wash cloth on her neck to relax her tight muscles. He wasn't a typical drug addict, clearly different than the ones she encountered as a volunteer at Teen Feed. She just knew in her gut that he wasn't a meth addict. The whole picture was wrong. Her eyes began to close. He was too focused, too vigilant. He was a man with a deadly purpose.

Davis stuffed his phone back into his pocket and headed toward Lewis. What was it about this woman? He never lost his cool. Under duress, he was calm, even nonchalant.

Lewis and Mitzi waited. Mitzi moved to stand next to Davis.

"Well, did she forgive you or are you on the couch tonight?" Lewis asked.

"You know how women are; she wanted to process my feelings," Davis said.

Both men laughed.

"I can't believe you got her to forgive you so quickly. My wife makes me suffer a lot longer than that."

Lewis thought they were a couple. He knew he hadn't behaved like himself, but felt he had acted reasonably professional. "It isn't like that at all. She's my dog's acupuncturist."

"Your poodle's acupuncturist?" That brought another round of laughter.

"Hey, Stone, does your dog have an acupuncturist?" Lewis yelled to his partner who smiled but didn't look up from his paperwork spread on the top of the patrol car.

"A what?"

"Never mind, I'll tell you later." And that made Lewis laugh again.

Davis knew Lewis enjoyed jerking him around. He had acted like an ass, taking over the crime scene and hovering over Grayce, but the woman elicited his most protective feelings. She was sensitive. Lewis was right. He had rushed to stand guard over her. There was something ethereal about her that made him want to keep her safe, away from the gritty way of the world.

He shook Lewis's hand. "Thanks for the help. Let me know what you run down on this guy."

"Yeah, I'll let you know, but I'm assuming he'll be headed to Harborview for a psych/drug eval. Probably a schizophrenic who's off his meds."

"Yeah, that was my impression, paranoid," Davis said.

Davis patted Mitzi. "Let's go home girl. What a night." He bent down and stroked her. "Mitzi, you're becoming a Lassie."

Mitzi had saved him twice. Who could've guessed that a pampered poodle could be a heroine? He had surprised himself when he felt so strongly about keeping the well- coiffed dog, and not the cheating girlfriend. He had liberated Mitzi from jeweled collars and endless grooming appointments.

Davis and his rescuer made it down Second Avenue to his condo in no time. Tonight, he knew he could've subdued the man without Mitzi's help, but she had saved him from forcing Grayce to watch him take the guy down.

He had believed he was helping Mitzi by adopting her, but he was proving to be the one who needed to be rescued. The words of Grayce's friend James replayed in his mind. "Grayce is always collecting lost souls." Did James see him as another of Grayce's lost souls? Was he? James had been drunk.

CHAPTER THIRTEEN

Leg work was the third rule of investigation.

Davis leaned against Mike's beat-up Corolla. He wanted to ask the kid a few questions without the captain of the boat looking over his shoulder, trying to protect his fledgling. Davis pulled up the collar of his department jacket. Any true Seattle native would reckon tonight's rain as no more than a drizzle.

Mike was afraid that made him a suspect. The captain had called Mike a good kid, which translated as Mike has a troubled past. The kid had no rap sheet, which meant that he had been too young to start one.

Mike strolled down the dock toward the parking lot. He looked up and slowed his pace.

Davis hoped the kid wouldn't run. Wearing his regulation shoes, he just didn't feel up for a chase. "Hey, Mike." He also hoped he wouldn't need to get physical with the kid, who was built like a linebacker and outweighed him by 50 pounds.

Mitzi bolted toward the kid and jumped paws first, trying to lick his face.

"Mitzi, get down." Davis moved to grab her, his plan to intimidate the kid foiled by his dog's affectionate greeting.

The big kid bent down to pet the poodle. Mitzi sprang, going for his face. Mike laughed at Mitzi's antics, his tough guy façade fading.

"You got a buddy, Mike."

Mike continued to rub Mitzi. "Wish I could have one of these."

Davis heard in those few words everything Mike had never gotten in his short life.

"You want to get some food?" Dinner hadn't been part of his plan.

Mike looked over his shoulder. "Not around here."

"How about Pioneer Square? J&M has great burgers."

Mike shrugged.

"Here or the J&M. Your choice."

The kid shrugged again. "Okay."

"Meet you in twenty. And if you don't show, we'll be back." He would've sounded threatening if Mitzi weren't still licking the kid's hand. Mitzi was telling Davis to go easy with Mike. Davis believed in his instincts, but he'd be a fool not to trust Mitzi's.

Davis watched Mike down his second burger. The kid could eat. Davis hung out with mountain climbers and firefighters, but this kid devoured burgers like he might never eat again. Mitzi leaned against Mike's leg.

They sat at the J&M café, a seedy bar in Pioneer Square. The J&M had probably served the same burgers to the men headed to Alaska for the Gold Rush. And like the prospectors, Davis and Mike sat on the same beat-up, uncomfortable woods chairs.

"Are you from Alaska?' Davis asked.

"Nah, Aberdeen."

"You got family up there?"

"My mom's."

"That's where you learned to fish?"

"Yeah."

"Your mom still in Aberdeen?"

"Nah, she died. Her family took me in." Mike stuffed three fries into his mouth.

Davis had a pretty good idea about the answer to his next question. "How about your dad?"

Mike swallowed the gob of fries. "What about my dad?"

The answer he expected. "Is your dad in the fishing business?"

"Nah, my old man's a logger."

He had hoped that he was wrong about how Mike's life

went down.

"Is the captain part of the family?"

"Mom's brother."

"Seems like a good guy... trying to help you out."

"Uncle Burt's all right."

"What kind of work did you do in Alaska?"

"Fishing, processing."

"Tough work."

"I don't mind hard work."

"Yeah, that's what your uncle said." Davis sat back in his chair, maintaining his relaxed posture. "Did you see the guy loading the crab boxes?"

Mike shifted in his chair and blinked rapidly, several times. "I didn't see anything."

Davis leaned forward. "Are you sure?"

Mitzi pushed her head under Mike's hand. He looked down at his plate then around the room. Avoiding eye contact, he stared back at the food on his plate. "Yeah, I'm sure."

Davis leaned back in his chair and crossed his arms. He had his answer.

"Tell me more about catching crabs. I know there's Dungeness around here."

A flicker of relief flashed across Mike's face before he added more ketchup to the fries. The kid thought he had dodged the bullet.

"What about King Crab? Is it all from Alaska?" He needed to learn a lot more about crabbing if he was going to solve this case.

"Alaska and Russia."

"Interesting. Tell me about Russian crab."

"Russian Red King Crab, caught in the Sea of Okhotsk, ships out of Vladivostok."

Davis nodded. He didn't have a clue about the Sea of Okhotsk. "You know a lot about Russian crab?"

Mike sat up straighter in his chair. "You pick up things."

"How does the crab get shipped from Russia?"

"The frozen crab is packed inside poly liners, and then into cardboard cases."

"Big cases?"

"Not that big, somewhere between twenty to sixty pounds."

Not big for burly Mike. "So no crab comes to the terminal. It goes to Pier 91 or down to the South End, right?"

Mike took the final bite of his burger and nodded.

"So what's the big deal about a guy stealing some crab and taking a cut for himself?"

He had a pretty good idea of what was in the box and it wasn't crab. The kid didn't answer. "The guy didn't have crab in those cases, did he?"

"Have no idea." Mike's eyes went left and he blinked nonstop while he lied.

The kid could be videotaped for training investigators. He was that easy to read.

Mike gulped his Coke.

No doubt that the kid knew and was afraid.

"Have you done business with the Russians?" Davis asked.

"Business?" The high pitch of Mike's question was hilarious. His anxiety made him sound like he was twelve and back in the throes of puberty, his voice cracking.

Davis cleared his throat to stop himself from laughing. "I meant fishing business."

"Nah." Mike sat back in his chair.

"I've heard the Russians can be intimidating."

Mike snorted.

"You and your uncle don't look like you scare off easily."

"You learn not to mess with them. You don't wanna end up in the brine tank."

"Brine tank?"

"Where they freeze the crab, before it gets shipped out."

"The Russians give their competitors a swim in the brine tank, huh?"

"Yeah."

"Sounds like a tough way to go. You ever see anyone go into the tank?"

"I gotta get back to the boat. You need anything else?"

No need to scare the kid off. "That's it. Stay around. I might need to talk with you again."

Davis watched Mike walk out of the bar. The kid definitely knew the contents of the crab cases or had a pretty could idea.

He needed to talk to someone who knew about the criminal fishing business. Was it the FBI or the Coast Guard?

CHAPTER FOURTEEN

Grayce took the office steps two at a time. Drug addicts, Hollywood stars and the attractive Ewan Davis had converged on her usually calm life. Sheesh! At least James was going to be highly entertained. And before her trip to California to meet a movie star, she needed to talk with Hollie about drug addiction.

"Mornin' Boss."

Today, Hollie wore a white concoction layered with lace that skirted the neckline and sleeves revealing her multiple tattoos. A black dragon's sinewy path ran the entire length of her right arm and peaked through the lace. Hollie's dress was reminiscent of the Laura Ashley dresses Grayce's mother made her wear when she was an adolescent— feminine, with no hint of sexuality.

Grayce following Hollie into the office, stared at the finishing touch to Hollie's ensemble—black combat boots, laced to the ankle. The young woman buried her soft, sensitive underpinnings beneath a tough armor, like a giant tortoise.

"Am I seeing the new client this morning?"

"Yes, Rowan's at nine. The owner was quite anxious for an appointment before you left."

"How did this client hear about us?"

"Another referral from Dr. Herrick, your biggest fan."

"Dr. Herrick understands the benefits of acupuncture."

Hollie's nose flared, jiggling the small piercing on her right nostril. "Sure…it's the acupuncture."

"Phil Herrick? Please, he's a colleague."

"The man practically drools when he sees you." Hollie rolled her huge doleful eyes in a pitiful manner.

Grayce laughed. "You look more like a Bassett Hound than poor Phil. How about telling me about Rowan."

"Just an old guy with arthritic hips. Otherwise, pretty healthy. Did I mention that he's a one hundred and eighty-five pound Rottweiler?"

"Okay. I'll try to get some calls in before Rowan arrives. Any word on how Beowulf did over the weekend?"

"No, but I'm thinking that's good news, isn't it?" Hollie's deep voice got softer.

Grayce wanted to touch Hollie and reassure her, but Hollie wouldn't appreciate the concern. Hollie never acknowledged or admitted any feelings of vulnerability. "Mrs. Leary would've called us if she needed anything. So no news is good. How is the schedule for the rest of the week? Were you able to get everyone in?"

"You'll have a long Thursday when you get back, but I got everyone in."

Grayce still marveled at the transformation in her receptionist. Hollie had come to Teen Feed for weeks, always dressed the same—stringy hair, leather wrist bands, and a T-shirt with the guild characters from her World of Warfare game. Grayce never questioned her ability to identify the suffering of others. As long as she could remember, she had had the ability to divine the hearts of all creatures.

"Do we still have the jasmine tea?"

"I got more pearls yesterday."

Hollie, new to the world of tea drinking, tried to surprise Grayce with new types of tea. "I would love some jasmine before I see Rowan the giant. I also need to talk with you at some point this morning."

CHAPTER FIFTEEN

Standing at the fire scene, Davis kicked a pile of charred wood. This fire just didn't add up. He didn't have a good theory on how it had reached a high enough temperature to ignite the forty-foot-high lumber. He nudged a large piece of fir with the steel tip of his boot. He was missing something but fatigue blocked any brilliant insights.

Absorbed in sorting through the rubble, he didn't see Assistant Chief Maclean barreling toward him until he heard, "Davis." By Maclean's curt tone, his stride, and the angle of his head, Davis knew the other man was in a mood. Already peeved by his intrusion, Davis didn't feel up for a verbal skirmish.

"Glad to see you working." The assistant chief pressed his lips into a sneer that made him look more like someone who'd had a stroke than the angry bastard he was.

"Glad to see you too." He tried to swallow the sarcasm.

Maclean's beady eyes focused on Davis. "I heard your damn dog got injured on the site? Why in hell would you bring a dog on the site?"

It was just like Maclean to have discovered his only breech of procedure in two years and come out to harass him about it. He tried to tell himself it wasn't personal. Maclean couldn't handle change—the words firefighter had never passed the man's disapproving lips. Maclean still believed only a fire*man*, a Caucasian male, should work for the department.

"I didn't bring my dog to the site. She jumped out of the car." The excuse sounded lame.

"Your dog could've disturbed or destroyed evidence."

"I know. The wall fell right after she got on the site."

He was glad he had told no one how close the collapsing wall had come to crushing him. Things happened on the fireground.

"So did your dog find an accelerant?"

"My dog isn't trained to smell for accelerants. She's a French poodle." He could see Maclean eyeing him. He knew exactly where the assistant chief's thoughts were going. It was hard enough to live up to his Scottish background. "She's my ex-girlfriend's dog."

Maclean stepped over the yellow tape, avoiding getting ashes on his shoes. Davis found it hard to believe his boss had ever gotten "wicked dirty" from the tar, the creosotes, and other by-products of the fire that clung to your clothes and skin at a fire scene.

"Are you planning on using Henny?"

Once he finished his digging, Davis planned to bring in Henny, whose nose was trained to detect possible accelerants. But to annoy Maclean, he refused to give him a straight answer. "I haven't finished my digging. I'm going to need a crane."

"Do you know how fricking expensive cranes are? You've got to fill out the paper work. And good luck with that."

Maclean could see by the giant fallen lumber, a crane was necessary to excavate the scene. Davis took a slow, deep breath and swallowed the words he was dying to unleash.

"What about the pictures? Have you taken them yet?"

Maclean had a bigger bug up his ass than usual. Why was he here on a Saturday? He never got personally involved.

"I took some photos early this morning."

"Have you uploaded them yet?"

He thought about the pleasure he would get from telling Maclean to go to hell. "I'm going back to the station after I finish the digging. Why so much interest in this fire? Don't tell me the mayor and the press are going to show up tomorrow?"

"The press hasn't started yet, but the Port wants answers now. There's a lot of interest in the wharf since they started filming that TV show down here. The Port doesn't want any bad press and neither does the chief."

Maclean hadn't just come to harass him about Mitzi. He came to tighten the screws on Davis, to demand that he finish the investigation, tidy and quick.

"Are you up for this one? Or should I assign a real fire*man*?" Delivering his sunny message, Maclean walked away. He spoke over his shoulder in his familiar patronizing voice. "And none of the usual attitude, no independent bullshit. Keep me in the loop."

Davis could feel the blood pulsating at his temples, right above his clenched jaw. Independent... bullshit! It wasn't an attitude. Fire investigators were separate. They solved crimes.

Something about this fire made him uneasy. Maclean hassling him added fuel to the fire, literally. He would've laughed at the pun if he wasn't so frustrated.

Before he left, he needed to finish his inspection of the area surrounding the fire scene. Ordinarily, he would've scouted out the perimeter well before this, but the crashing wall and Mitzi's injury had interfered. Davis headed to his Suburban to get Mitzi, glad that Maclean hadn't seen the dog in the department's rig.

"Come on Mitzi, let's go for a walk." The dog stretched her length on the back seat and then jumped out of the door.

He and Mitzi walked the entire wharf. They inspected other sheds that extended toward the Ballard Bridge, then turned and walked along the waterfront. The air hung with a salt water tang. They walked past rows of moored fishing boats.

A few clouds scuttled across the sky. The night walk was helping to clear his head of his crazy, disorderly thoughts. To solve a fire, you needed to fit the pieces together in a logical methodical process. But with this fire, everything was out of order, out of sync.

Underneath a monument to the Chinese who'd migrated to the Pacific Northwest in the early 19th century, Mitzi found the only clump of grass left in the area to relieve herself on. As a responsible citizen, he had his dog bag on hand for clean up, but he needed a garbage can in which to toss the full bag.

Scanning the area, he spotted two large dumpsters across the parking lot behind a metal fence. The gate to the fence hung open. He and Mitzi headed toward the dumpster, bag in hand.

The sign "For restaurant use only" induced a little guilt, but he reasoned one little baggie wasn't going to hurt.

Lifting the large lid of the dumpster, he was hit with the smell of rotting fish. He peered into the dumpster for possible clues. Nothing. It figured. It would've been just too easy to discover evidence sitting there, waiting to be taken to the landfill.

He lowered the lid. Mitzi had disappeared behind the dumpster. "Mitzi, come." He used his command voice, but no response. Irritation prickled his skin. "I'm not up for this tonight."

He heard a faint sound from behind the dumpster. He hoped it was Mitzi and not a Norwegian Rat the size of a small cat.

"Mitzi, come out. I don't want to go looking for you. And I sure as hell don't want to tangle with a rat."

Davis could barely squeeze into the recess between the side of the dumpsters and the fence. Debris blocked his progress. He heard the rustle of papers and a scratching noise. A shudder coursed through his body. Shining his flashlight beam in front of him, he spotted his dog. "Mitzi, get out of there."

She looked up briefly and then resumed her efforts to grab onto an empty container. At least it wasn't something rotten or alive. On closer inspection, he could make out an empty canister of brake fluid. Brake fluid mixed with chlorine could make a big bang, just the type to set the forty-foot wall of solid fir ablaze.

"Good dog. Let's see if we can find anything else of interest around here." Together they combed the area around the dumpster and office building. They walked up to Nickerson Street and scanned the grass along the curb, retracing the route the torch might have used for his exit. No chlorine bottles had been left lying on the side of the road. An empty container of brake fluid might be a dead end. But in this business, nothing could add up to something big.

CHAPTER SIXTEEN

Grayce took the steaming mug of tea from Hollie. Intricate patterns of blue and red tattoos wrapped around her assistant's arm. "What time is Lieutenant Davis and Mitzi's appointment this week?"

Hollie pulled the comfy treatment chair from against the wall and sat down across from Grayce. "He and Mitzi are scheduled for Thursday at 4:30."

"Mitzi will need another treatment. She attacked a homeless man in Belltown."

"What the f…? Mitzi's not aggressive."

"Mitzi jumped on the man to stop him from stabbing Lieutenant Davis."

The idea that someone tried to kill Davis was doing weird things to her nervous system. She felt jittery, jumpy—like she had chugged a super-sized Diet Coke.

Hollie's lips, the color of an eggplant, twisted into a smirk. "Mitzi, a street-fighting Poodle. I can just see the gangsters hangin' with Poodles."

Grayce laughed at the outrageous image.

"Did Davis know the dude?"

"No."

"What was he after? Money? Drugs?"

"Neither, according to Davis. He is convinced that the guy was either mentally ill or high on something and didn't know what he was doing."

Now came the difficult part. She had never probed Hollie's past. In their quasi-job interview, Grayce asked if drugs would interfere in Hollie's ability to work. Hollie had declared "she was clean" and Grayce believed her. In the two months of her employment, Grayce had never had reason to doubt her.

Grayce chose each word carefully. She could feel the red moving into her face to the tops of her ears. "I'm not sure the guy was an addict...my only experience with drug addiction was volunteering at Teen Feed."

Hollie's purple lips emitted a brash laugh. "And you thought I'd know about junkies?"

"I wanted to get your perspective."

Hollie arched her blackened eyebrow. "The dude must have been strung out to take on Davis."

"That's my point. Why would anyone take on a man of Davis' size? There are so many easier targets. This guy didn't act like an addict. He just didn't have the detachment I've seen in kids who were high."

Hollie cracked each knuckle painfully slow. The harsh sound punctuated each word. "Nothing matters to an addict 'cuz the junk owns 'em. They don't care about anyone. My dad only cared about cooking meth."

Grayce flinched at Hollie's detached recital. Teen Feed was filled with kids who were running from either their abusive families or their abusive foster care placement.

Hollie sat upright and crossed her leg exposing black combat boots. "What does Davis think?"

"Davis is convinced that the guy is a street druggie with paranoid delusions," Grayce answered.

"I'm with Davis, sounds like he was paranoid, probably snorting crank."

"Maybe you're right, but something felt wrong about the guy." She envisioned the man's steely determination. "This guy was focused... as if he was hired to hurt Davis." As the words left her mouth, she knew. The man was a hired assassin. She took a big gulp of the hot tea, scalding her tongue.

"Are you alright?"

"I'm fine." Except she didn't feel fine. Her stomach plummeted and sunk to her knees like the drop on the roller coaster.

"Where did it happen?" Hollie asked.

"Second and Bell."

"I could go down and check it out. See if anyone knows the guy."

"What?" Grayce jerked her hand and spilled tea on the scattered papers on her desk.

"I'll ask about the guy." Hollie had the instincts of a pit bull and the loyalty of a yellow lab. "What did he look like?"

"If anyone is going to ask questions, it's going to be me. Right now, I'm trying to figure things out." She blotted the wet papers with Kleenex. She didn't know exactly what she was trying to figure out.

Hollie flung herself forward in the chair. "The street is no place for you."

"I'm not going to Belltown. I'm trying to understand what happened." She didn't mention that she was trying to gain perspective on her deep belief that someone was hired to kill Davis.

"Let Davis take care of himself. He can definitely handle it."

"You're probably right."

Grayce's logical brain agreed with Hollie's take on the situation, but the twisted knot in her stomach vehemently reacted, sending spasms throughout her gut like a bad case of tourista.

CHAPTER SEVENTEEN

"Davis, do you have any time this week to do Mt. Si?"

Davis turned toward Pete, a triathlon competitor who spent a great deal of his day at the gym. "Isn't six a.m. a bit early for you, Pete?"

A grin crossed Pete's sun-weathered face. He strode toward Davis. "I needed to get in a workout. Gotta be in Tacoma all day."

Regulars already filled the Y-Gym. When Davis had first returned to Seattle during his father's illness, Y-Gym had provided a refuge. A stranger adrift in his own hometown, Davis felt anchored at the popular gym among serious athletes like himself.

Pete inspected Davis' regulation navy blue pants and shirt. "Man, you gave up your designer suits for that outfit? Those pants look like the ones I wore in parochial school. You shouldn't have listened to Rod."

A mutual buddy at the gym had provided the initial push for Davis toward fire investigation. "Hey, I want you to know these pants don't have to be dry cleaned."

"No time for Mt. Si?" Pete asked.

"Don't think I can swing it. I'll call you if this case magically solves itself."

Both men left the gym, oversized bags slung over their shoulders. Davis took a deep breath when he stepped into the gray rainy morning. His workout had helped get his focus back.

"Good luck with the investigation. Maybe we can hit the mountain next week."

"Yeah, I'll need it by then. Hope traffic isn't too bad."

"With this rain, it's going to be a bitch." Pete swung into his jeep.

Davis started the steep climb to his condo, making a mental list of all he had to do during the day. Top of his list was to talk to Dr. Grayce Walters. He was going to make one final call. He didn't seem to be able to get her or her guileless stares out of his mind. It wasn't as if he was desperate for a woman's attention, he just wanted to make sure she was okay.

He entered the black glass and steel building. At this early hour, the place was deserted. He wasn't in the mood to be friendly. He assured himself his short fuse had nothing to do with Grayce Walters. At this stage of an investigation, he usually had a working hypothesis. With the wharf fire, nothing was falling into place except wild speculation.

Why hadn't Grayce returned either of his phone calls? He couldn't stop visualizing her face, so vulnerable after the attack on Friday night. He replayed the danger. What if he hadn't walked her to her car? What if he hadn't been there to protect her from the paranoid druggie?

He was heading down a familiar path—the knight in shining armor. Women loved a man who wanted to rescue them.

But Grayce was different than most women. She'd tried to shield him after the assault. Strong but sensitive, she confused him.

He punched the elevator button harder than he needed to.

Despite Napoleon and his 18 pounds walking on her head at four a.m., Grayce had slept without nightmares. Energized after her meditation, she was ready for a run. She brought up Sufi music on her iPod, stretched her hamstrings and twisted her hair into a pony-tail.

The phone rang. There was only one person who called her this early. After her sister died, both she and her mother had trouble sleeping. When Grayce left for college, they had established a routine to talk in the morning if either had a rough night. They never changed the routine.

"Sweetie, I hope I didn't wake you."

"I've been up for a while, Mom. Are you ready for your trip?"

Her mother answered in her professional, no nonsense mode. "I'm leaving for the airport in a few minutes but wanted you to know how much your dad enjoyed dinner with you."

"It was great for me, too."

"Guess who your father ran into at the University Club?"

God, she hoped it wasn't Peyton Archley, a former college boyfriend. Her mother still clung to the hope that they might take up their romance again. "I've no idea."

"Dean Williamson. Your father had a nice chat with him about your interest in medical school."

The muscles in her jaw started to tighten. Her mother was fixated on Grayce attending medical school again. Never a good sign. "Mom, I went to vet school."

"He was quite impressed with your advanced degrees in the sciences and the awards you garnered at Michigan and Cornell. It sounds like your father couldn't restrain himself from bragging."

She wasn't sure whether to scream or laugh. She unclenched her jaw. Her belief that the higher species should be able to moderate their response to adverse stimuli wasn't working this morning. Knowing her mother was trying to take care of her, she felt like the lowest of worms. "Really?"

"Dean Williamson told your father to have you call him. He'd love to talk about your future in medicine."

Her mother still hoped that as a "real doctor" no one would discover Grayce's unconventional gifts. She attributed Grayce's "quirkiness with animals" to the effects of Cassie's death.

Grayce had been forced into therapy after that. She had made the mistake of revealing that she continued to feel Cassie's presence. The psychiatrist had told her parents that Grayce's "symptoms" were part of the grieving process, a refusal to accept her sister's death. And in time Grayce's visions would fade. He had been wrong.

Cassie still came to Grayce in her dreams—a bright energy that wrapped her in love. Many nights after Grayce had helped an injured or dying animal, Cassie would whisper words of comfort to her in her sleep.

"Honey, are you there?"

"I'm here, Mom." Grayce had learned not to share her visions or her gifts. What did it matter if there were no words, no scientific explanation for her reality?

"I think you shouldn't let this opportunity pass."

Grayce stretched her masseter muscle, the highly developed muscle in dogs for biting, opening her mouth wide then moving her jaw back and forth, searching for a response that would soothe her mom.

"Grayce? Do you want his number? I have it right here."

"Sure, Mom." What was the Gandhi quote about the path of least resistance? "Have a safe flight. I hope your meetings go well."

Would she find herself at the age of sixty, still feeling guilty that she couldn't make up for her mother's immense grief over Cassie? Grayce had achieved outstanding academic success, excelled in mastering acupuncture skills in China and had established her own practice. All these accomplishments and she still didn't feel that she had done enough to lessen her mother's suffering. She couldn't take away her mother's pain, but she couldn't give up trying.

Her mother still worried about her. Grayce still worried about her mother. Her mother wanted her to fit in. She wanted her mother to be happy. There were some days it all seemed impossible.

CHAPTER EIGHTEEN

Davis sat in front of his computer. He almost lost it on Saturday night when he couldn't upload the fire scene pictures. He had wanted to get home and instead he spent an hour looking for the cord to connect the camera to the computer. Finally, he transferred the pictures to his phone.

No one could find the cord this morning either. He emailed the pictures from his phone to the email server and then downloaded them to his work computer. He stood to close the door before calling Grayce.

Tom Vaughn walked by Davis' office. "Hey Davis, figure out what caused the wharf fire? Dirty rags that combusted?"

Tom had been the officer on-call the night of the wharf fire and had been one of the first responders.

Davis stood at the door. "Rags wouldn't be enough to start that fire, but brake fluid and chlorine would do the job."

Tom stood with his feet apart, looking up at Davis. "Arson?"

Tom was the smallest man of the department's brass, but everyone's favorite. Tom loved to joke, lighten the seriousness of their work.

"Who owns it?" Tom asked.

"Can't find the owner. I've got a PO Box out of Alaska and a disconnected cell phone."

Davis didn't explain that the guy fished on the Jupiter, the same boat carrying the crab cases. "The fire had to be lit by a pro with the skill to burn a solid wood shed without burning up the rest of the sheds or the wooden wharf."

"Got someone in mind?"

"Not yet." Davis had talked with the men on the list of retired firefighters. Nothing panned out. Every one of them had an alibi for the night of the fire. Benson was the only one he couldn't find. For twenty thousand dollars—the going payment for arson—Benson could fly in from Las Vegas.

Tom moved down the hall and spoke over his shoulder. "Good luck. I wanna hear how it goes down."

Davis shut the door before anyone else could talk to him. He couldn't believe he was this nervous—as if he were a teenager, calling a date for the prom.

After Mitzi's appointment on Thursday, he didn't need to see Grayce Walters again. The receptionist put him straight through to Grayce without any dire threats this time.

"Is everything all right? Is Mitzi okay?" Grayce asked.

"Yes, we're both fine. I was hoping you might have a break in your schedule. I'm headed your way this morning and thought we could get a cup of coffee."

"I can't. I'm leaving for the airport in two hours and have lots of fires to put out before I go…sorry, forgive the pun." She gave a nervous laugh.

It boosted his confidence. He didn't want to be the only one feeling unsure.

"Are you alright about Friday? You didn't answer the phone yesterday."

"I had to get ready for California. I went shopping with James all day."

He recognized a puny excuse when he heard one. Grayce didn't seem the type to shop all day. He really didn't know her. And, obviously, she didn't want to know him.

"Mitzi didn't suffer any injuries from Friday?"

"Mitzi's fine." He recognized a brush off when he heard it. He had given plenty in his lifetime. But he had never been on the receiving end before.

"Have you heard anything about the man who attacked you?"

"No, I was going to call Lewis and see whether they kept him, but I've been too busy."

"You don't know if he's in the hospital?"

"I'm assuming he got admitted for evaluation and will be back on the street once his meds start working or sent to drug rehab for his meth addiction."

"They'll just let him go?" He could hear her sharp intake of breath.

"They won't release him until they're sure his delusions are manageable."

Grayce wasn't going to admit that she was afraid of the guy. "They won't let him back on the street until he's safe." He was going to say *until they know he won't try to stab someone else,* but he didn't want to remind Grayce about Friday night.

"I'm bringing Henny to the fire site today."

"How is she?

"She hasn't knocked anyone else down."

"I'm glad to hear it."

He relaxed, hearing her light laugh. "If you ever would like to watch her and Steve work, I could set it up. But maybe you don't want to spend your time off meeting dogs? I didn't mean like bad dates… I meant... you know what I mean."

She giggled like a young girl. The tension in his body uncoiled.

"I guess…well…you know I've been on a few dates that might qualify."

"When you get back from LA, I can make it happen. It is pretty amazing to watch Henny work."

"I love watching the trusting relationship between handlers and dogs. Oops, here's Hollie. My client must be here."

"Have a great time in Hollywood meeting movie stars. I'm so impressed."

"Don't be or you'll start to sound like James."

They both laughed.

"Really need to go. Thanks for calling."

"See you Thursday, Dr. Walters."

He hung up. He liked the way he had ended the conversation. Impersonal. Who was he kidding? His palms were sweating from holding the phone. He didn't feel anything impersonal about Grayce Walters. He was intensely drawn to her. A glimpse of a chaotic household, filled with children and stray animals flashed through his mind. He took a deep breath and blew it out in one burst. He had never in his life connected a woman with the idea of children. Definitely off his game. Children were an abstract idea, a someday, just like marriage.

Davis refocused on his computer. He checked whether the fire scene pictures had finished downloading. Download icon still showed 47 percent. He clicked the 'cancel' button with his mouse and nothing happened. Damn, the computer had crashed. Nothing was flowing in this investigation.

His only suspect was nowhere to be found. Benson's cell was disconnected. The last address he had given the personnel department was a motel on Aurora Avenue. Davis had checked with the motel. Benson hadn't stayed there in months, not since he had been fired from the department. He was married or had been married, but Davis had had no luck locating his wife.

And he still hadn't been able to have an off-the-record chat with his friend, Zac, from the FBI. He hoped his friend would have time for coffee since Grayce didn't. The Federal Bureau of Indolence—FBI agents were never busy.

CHAPTER NINETEEN

The first thing Grayce noticed when she entered Elizabeth Marley's Malibu Beach house was how cold it was. Like a mausoleum. Icy pinpricks beat a fast tempo up and down her body. Neither the bright sunlight nor the sound of the crashing waves coming through the open French doors could mask the deep gloom.

With her signature blonde hair flowing, the movie star looked exactly like she did on TV. In cutoffs, a white T-shirt and flip flops, she was the epitome of a California girl, not a Hollywood star. Elizabeth's weariness, etched in the lines of her wan face, showed through her weak smile. A rotund grey schnauzer barked incessantly at her feet.

"Welcome to California. I hope your flight wasn't too difficult."

"Thank you. The flight was easy."

Grayce bent to acknowledge Frank who kept barking and circling Elizabeth. "And you must be Frank." The dog didn't approach her, but he had stopped barking. Grayce didn't try to touch Frank whose pointed dark ears and stubby tail signaled he was on alert.

"I knew he would act all energetic once you got here." Elizabeth Marley attempted another smile, but failed. The woman was in pain. It was raw and close to the surface and penetrated right into Grayce's being.

"Frank is trying to protect you."

"Where do you want to treat him? Do you need a table?"

"Wherever you and Frank are most comfortable. I don't need a table."

"I guess that would be the couch. We spend a great deal of time there. Come this way."

Grayce followed Elizabeth and the dog into a living room lined with expansive windows. The room was designed for the viewer to experience the grandeur of the ocean, but Grayce couldn't enjoy the beauty. She couldn't shake the pall that hung in the air. Stark loneliness pervaded the space. "Why don't we sit on the couch and you can hold Frank on your lap."

"Can you treat me too?" Elizabeth asked in a joking manner, but there was a hungry edge to the question.

"I'm not good at treating anyone without a tail."

Elizabeth sat on the pale yellow overstuffed couch. Everything in the space spoke of a calculated style of relaxation and warmth, much like the movie star's finely honed image as comfortable and unassuming.

"Come Frank." The small dog jumped into the arms of his owner.

"Tell me more about Frank. How long have you had him?"

Another pained swallow. "Four years." Elizabeth hung on the four years, the length of her marriage.

"Any health problems?"

"No, he's never been ill."

Grayce moved to the couch and sat within easy reach of Frank. The dog watched her take the needles from her pocket, his nose twitching in the air. She presented the needles, still wrapped in their paper package, in front of his moving nose.

"What do you think, Frank?" She used her most soothing voice, a tone that engendered trust. She waited for Frank to become curious. The schnauzer left Elizabeth's lap and moved closer to the hand with the needles.

"He has a great nose," Elizabeth said.

Grayce patted the dog's head. "You are a wonderful dog. What an incredible companion."

Grayce moved her hand along Frank's body, allowing him to adjust to her touch. He had tucked himself between his owner and Grayce, still protecting, doing his job. Canine devotion always made her heart lighter. If only Elizabeth Marley's husband had possessed one ounce of Franks' loyalty.

"What a faithful critter you are," Grayce whispered to Frank.

"He hasn't left my side," Elizabeth said.

Grayce slowed her breathing, making it synchronous with the sound of the braking waves. She ran her hand an inch above the dog's back, concentrating on the depleted energy, assessing the acupuncture points along the dog's spine—definitely deficient lung points, the organs associated with grief. She continued to touch, connecting from her quiet spot to Frank's sadness. He was siphoning his owner's grief, absorbing it into his body. He offered his soul to Elizabeth, healing through his constant devotion.

Grayce visualized harnessing the ocean's power to fill Frank and renew his lung points. She placed the first needle into the crown of his head. As she expected, he showed no reaction. She then placed a needle at Bai Hui point, the bottom of the spine. She needed to balance Frank's top-to-bottom energy, the yin-yang, encouraging his stagnant Chi to flow, like the high tide crashing outside his front door.

Grayce heightened her vibrations for Frank's deficient Lung Chi. She rotated the needles while Frank slept. His black lips curved upward as if smiling. He usually was a happy dog. She had seen this condition many times as devoted pets depleted their chi trying to comfort their owners. Grayce looked up and saw tears in Elizabeth's eyes.

"I'm amazed you could do this. I've had acupuncture. Honestly, I didn't think Frank would let you. I didn't know what to do for him." A sob punctuated her recitation.

More than a husband's abandonment, a deeper desolation plagued this woman. Her primitive anguish seeped through Grayce's defenses, stirring up an unexpected wave of grief.

Sorrow pressed on Grayce making it hard to draw air, the same heavy feeling of dread after Cassie's death; like a boulder that would never budge, a despair that would never end. Why this woman, why her pain?

Grayce repressed the churning emotions and returned to the treatment. Frank needed the lung points to stay longer. She rotated the needles allowing the heat to dissipate. The schnauzer continued to rest between the two women.

"How long will Frank stay relaxed?"

"Once I take out the needles, he'll wake up. He won't want to miss any of the action."

Elizabeth gave a genuine radiant smile, the one that made her one of Hollywood's most admired actresses. When Grayce had contemplated the trip, she expected this woman to be a narcissistic Hollywood cliché. She couldn't have been more wrong.

Grayce removed the needles. Frank remained asleep, a whisper of a snore vibrating through his soft, relaxed body.

"I'll plan to come down next week to treat him again."

"What's wrong with him?"

"Frank's an empath. He's responding to your stress."

"You have an amazing gift," Elizabeth spoke in a low, gravelly voice.

Their eyes met—such a strange bond. She was revisiting the loss of her sister through a famous movie star's loss. It didn't make the pain any less or any better.

She removed the last needle. "The acupuncture will lighten the tension and give him back his spunk."

The schnauzer awoke slowly, looking toward his owner. He licked her hand. Elizabeth Marley rubbed his head. "I love you, boy."

Frank slowly thumped his tail, making both women smile.

Grayce brushed her hand along the dog's head. "Frank is going to be fine. His big heart can carry the load."

The dog stood and stretched.

As was her practice, she acknowledged the hard work Frank was performing. "You're a loyal companion."

When they stood, Grayce realized she was taller than the star—an unusual experience since she was usually the shortest person in the room.

The slight woman looked up into Grayce's eyes. "Your light is strong. Don't be afraid to use it."

Hearing the words, the words that Cassie used, was like a kick to her solar plexus. No air moved in or out of her body. She waited for her lungs to start working, her heart to return to beating.

"Thank you for coming to treat Frank." The actress reached for Grayce's hands and squeezed them tight. Elizabeth's soft hands worked like a balm, spreading warmth, soothing Grayce, as if Cassie was there holding her hand.

Leaving the beach house, Grayce gulped the moist air, taking her first deep breath since Elizabeth had spoken Cassie's message.

She squinted in the bright light and pondered the unplanned instant, the serendipitous moment which can alter one's life. This California trip to treat a dog was an illusion. Cassie was here, forcing Grayce to peel away another layer of the profound loss she allowed no one to glimpse.

Grayce inhaled, tasting the hint of salt in the air. Elizabeth Marley had recognized Grayce's hidden pain because of her own acute state, as if fellow grievers shared a secret handshake.

When she had entered Elizabeth's house, Grace felt the same hopelessness, the same dark void that she had felt after Cassie's funeral. Her sister was killed at the age of seventeen in a car accident. Less than two years apart, she and Cassie shared every confidence. Cassie was the only person who had understood Grayce's sensitivity to people and animals. Grayce never had to explain how she was different. Cassie understood and accepted. Grayce struggled to forgive herself, for despite her intuitive gifts, she had been unable to prevent her sister's death. She had worked hard to develop her skills to save animals in part because of guilt.

She stepped into the chauffeured car and tried to remember the happy moments. She thought of Cassie's quip that Grayce's light was so bright that she glowed in the dark.

Grayce understood that if Cassie had lived, she would've wanted to shelter Grayce from a world that wouldn't understand or accept Grayce's uniqueness. Cassie was still trying to protect her baby sister with premonitions and dreams.

She gazed out the window at the endless ocean. Today was a giant nudge from her sister to move on and forgive herself.

"Back to Shutters, ma'am? Excuse me, ma'am." The driver broke her reverie.

"Oh, sorry."

"Back to Shutters?"

"Yes, thank you."

Grayce thought about another person who had learned to keep his emotions hidden. She wondered how Davis would react if she divulged her worries about his safety and how she came to her concerns. His warrior response to the assault was proof of his unwillingness to admit to something as fragile as feelings.

CHAPTER TWENTY

"Dr. Walters, Mitzi and Mr. Davis are here." Hollie entered Grayce's office ahead of Davis and Mitzi.

What was with the *Dr. Walters*? Hollie was definitely in her watch dog mode when Davis was in the office.

Grayce stood up from her desk. She tried to ignore the familiar surge of vital, male energy that accompanied Davis when he entered the room. Davis' second chakra, the life force center, was strong and potent.

Mitzi made a dash toward Grayce. Leaping forward, the poodle placed her paws on Grayce's shoulders and licked her face. Up on her hind legs, Mitzi was almost as tall as Grayce. Surprised by the poodle's enthusiasm, all she could do was laugh at the greeting.

"Mitzi, get down." Davis' deep baritone resonated in the spacious room. He moved forward trying to grab Mitzi by her lead.

Grayce couldn't stop laughing. Her eyes met Davis'. Their connection hit her with a turbulent force, like getting smacked by a tidal wave. Her heart started the same gallop, the same palpitations, the same thumping against her chest. She had never responded to anyone like she did to Davis. His second chakra disrupted her balanced chakras, throwing them into chaos.

He shook his head. "I'm sorry. She is obviously glad to see you."

"I'm glad to see her, too."

All three of them stood in the middle of the room. She was aware of Davis' accelerated breathing, a perfect match to her short, staccato breaths. He smelled fresh, clean, of the outdoors. His large, rough hand was curled around Mitzi's leash.

"You can let Mitzi off the lead." She bent to pet Mitzi, needing time to settle herself. "Please sit down."

Mitzi licked Grayce's hand before rejoining Davis at the chair.

She walked to her desk. "Obviously, Mitzi's feeling better? No limp?"

"Obviously."

Grayce glanced up. Davis leaned nonchalantly back in his chair. Although he positioned himself in a relaxed pose, with one leg crossed over the other, tension radiated from him. His shoulders and jaw were set in hard, stiff angles. His whole body was ready, ready for action, ready to jump out of the chair. Grayce could feel his stare as she made her notes.

She focused on Mitzi, ignoring Davis' scrutiny and waited for him to give her an opening to discuss Mitzi's tension. "She's settled down?"

"She seems calmer. There haven't been any more episodes of her howling, or chewing things up." His tone was jagged, impatient.

"It does sound like she's calmer." She didn't look up but proceeded to rearrange the sheets of paper on her desk. The interview was bordering on the absurd. It would be a lot easier if she could blurt out "your dog is anxious because someone wants you dead."

"She's back to her old self. Except, I don't know, it's as if she's always on alert."

She wanted to high five or shout out "finally," but instead she leaned forward across her desk. "Dogs can pick up on their owner's mood. You're in the middle of a dangerous investigation. Mitzi is picking up your anxiety. "

Looking at Davis was a mistake. The space between his eyebrows had disappeared into a harsh furrow. His mouth was clamped together. No hint of a crooked smile. "Anxious? I'm not anxious."

She was usually so facile communicating with people and their pets but not with these two. Connecting Mitzi's symptoms with her owner had been a tactical error.

"I'm not trying to imply you're anxious, but, if an owner is surrounded by danger like you are, dogs can pick up on the tension. They do read people's emotions."

He now sat upright. His light playful eyes were dark and directed at her. It didn't take an intuitive to know that he was a bit aggravated, maybe more than a bit. Not the way to begin an important discussion with a forceful male, by making him defensive and suggesting something girly like he might be nervous.

"I don't think Mitzi needs any treatment for her injury but she…"

"You're going to put yourself right out of business if you heal your patients so quickly."

Now, she was starting to get aggravated. The man was stubborn. He wasn't listening to her.

"As I was starting to say… I think Mitzi is still…" She had almost slipped and used the word anxious. "I think she is still hyper-vigilant. I would like to treat her today to help her relax."

Grayce looked at Mitzi, who sat erect next to Davis. She refused to dissect or analyze her gifts. This man was in danger and his dog knew it.

Grayce needed to retreat to her inner quiet space to do the treatment. After the treatment, she would try again to warn Davis. Taking a deep breath, she stood and went to the cabinet to get the needles. She focused on Mitzi and what the dog needed to feel safe and protected— if only she could do the same for her owner.

"Okay, Mitzi?" Centering, she sat down next to the dog to begin.

Mitzi's chi was low from her constant vigilance, the cost of protecting Davis. Grayce needed to balance and replenish Mitzi.

She closed her eyes and visualized Mitzi running in a field of tall grass, the sun shining on the poodle. The air was fresh, clean and the light was hot, bright and surrounded Mitzi. Grayce placed the needles, directing her energy as the heat of the sun.

She envisioned Mitzi rolling in abandonment on her back in the grass, her legs pumping, pointed to the sun, to the center of all life force.

Prepared this time for the rush of fear being released from the stressed dog, she didn't resist the negative force. Grayce breathed in and out in a slow, steady, deep rhythm and allowed the dark currents to flow around her.

Like in her dream, a black mist whirled about her, but unlike in her dream, she was present and in control. The mist remained at her feet, unable to suck her into the void, into the fear.

She continued to rotate the needles, envisioning Mitzi in the field, in a cocoon of heat, light, and safety.

Completing the treatment, Grayce removed the needles from the sleeping poodle. When she stood, she realized how exhausted she had become from the treatment. She walked to the cabinet to dispose of the needles.

She kept her back to Davis, grappling with the evil that hovered around him, like circling vultures waiting to attack.

His voice was gentle, clearly concerned. "Grayce, are you alright?"

Lost in sorting out Mitzi's treatment and a way to approach Davis, she hadn't realized how long she had been standing at the cabinet. She inhaled and turned, attempting to appear composed. "I'm fine. It's been a long day."

"You look done in. Can I take you out for a drink, dinner?"

An opportunity to speak to him—this is what she wanted. She couldn't allow him to proceed blindly in his investigations.

"Right now, I could eat a horse." He patted his stomach. "I guess I shouldn't talk about eating animals in this office."

"Most of my clients are carnivores."

They both laughed.

"So, what do you say? Mitzi's been stuck in the truck all day. I'll walk her and come back."

"Okay." She was worn out from trying to support his dog. She didn't know if she had enough energy to take on the owner.

"I'll be back in fifteen minutes. We'll walk to one of the places around here."

She watched the odd couple leave her office. Davis' massive frame dwarfed the gigantic poodle. With her head and nose pointed upright, Mitzi promenaded next to Davis. Her perfect carriage reflected centuries of careful breeding.

She wasn't fooled by the elegance. Poodles had been bred to be hunters. Mitzi's alert, close proximity to Davis clearly demonstrated her role as defender. Watching them leave, Grayce felt a need to shield them. She had to help Mitzi protect him.

It sounded so dramatic but she knew it to be true. Davis wouldn't accept it. He would want an explanation. He would want proof. She had none.

Communicating with animals was simpler.

CHAPTER TWENTY-ONE

He sat knee to knee with Grayce, squeezed in a corner of the hectic Thai restaurant. The smell of lemongrass mixed with the sweet smell of Grayce Walters made him ravenous. The intimacy of their small corner and the light touch of her knees softened his mood. He enjoyed touching her. Oblivious, Grayce stared at the menu.

"How was your trip?"

"Great."

"Was it another cure?"

She didn't look up from the menu. "I think I helped."

"I'm sure you did."

She nodded, still not looking at him. "Thank you."

He was getting better at reading her. She was upset. He didn't blame her. He had acted like an ass in her office. He had been looking forward to seeing her but she had ignored their connection, ignored the way the air seemed to constrict when they were together like an oxygen deprived fire ready to combust.

"You've really made a difference to Mitzi."

"About Mitzi…

An eager waiter appeared. "Would you like to begin with drinks?"

"Grayce, how about Grey Goose?"

"No, I don't think it's a martini night." She was pale with violet smudges under her eyes.

"Wine, then? Red or white?"

"Either. I don't care."

The waiter hovered. "Would you like to see the wine list, sir?"

"Sure."

Grayce sat studying the menu as if it were an instruction manual.

"Are you going to return to LA?"

"Next week."

"Sir, the wine list. Would you like to start with some appetizers?"

"I'm starving. What do you recommend?" He was hungry, but mostly for Grayce's attention.

"The spring rolls are our house specialty."

"Bring two orders."

He leaned across the table and tried to find a way to lighten her mood. "I warned you, I'm hungry, and I could devour…" He couldn't finish because erotic images danced before his eyes. His heart pumped fast. His face must be the color of a department rig. The erotic images wouldn't go away. He reached for his water glass.

"Have you decided on a wine?" God, he might have to kill the waiter.

"How about a Syrah? Grayce?"

"Sure." She gazed at the crowd behind him.

"I think you will be quite satisfied with your choice, sir."

Satisfied? Hardly. He couldn't even get Grayce to look at him.

She smoothed a nonexistent crease on the tablecloth. Her nails were clipped short with no bright polish like other women wore. "How is the investigation going?"

He had no desire to talk about work. He wanted…He didn't know what he wanted but he knew who he wanted. She had agreed to the dinner, but, as in her office, she was keeping him at a distance. "Grayce, what's wrong? Something's bothering you?"

She shifted in her chair, pulling her knees away, avoiding his touch. "I need to talk to you."

Her forehead was puckered into a fretful shape. He had never seen her anxious. She chewed on her lower lip. He knew what was coming. She was going to tell him she wasn't interested in a relationship. He wasn't either. But when she was close, with her knees pressed against his, he forgot all of his logical rationale against involvement.

"Have you heard what happened to the man who assaulted you?"

What? She was still upset by Friday night?

"Grayce, I'm sorry you had to come in contact with that creep."

Her wide eyes stared at him, but she wasn't really seeing him. She was lost in thought, probably reliving Friday night, remembering the crazy.

"Witnessing violence is disturbing," he said.

"It wasn't the violence. Well, it was the violence. But that man. Have you heard anything? What's happened to him?"

"The guy escaped, got away in Harborview's Emergency Room. Lewis was embarrassed to tell me."

She hugged her arms around herself. Her pale eyelids fluttered. "The man escaped," she whispered. "He's back on the streets."

"He won't bother you. He doesn't know who you are."

She looked up. For the first time since they arrived at the restaurant, she really looked at him. "You think I'm worried for myself?"

"I'm not sure what you're worried about. I'm trying to figure it out."

She gave a little shake of her head.

"What is it Grayce? Tell me." He wanted to touch her, soothe the crease in her forehead, kiss away the worry in her lower lip.

The waiter arrived with their wine.

Davis poured Grayce a glassful, hoping it would help restore her to the vibrant, laughing woman he first glimpsed on the floor in his office.

"You have nothing to fear from that guy."

She sat taller. "I'm not afraid of the guy. Well, I'm afraid, but not for myself."

"You're not?" He wasn't sure if she heard the disbelief in his question.

Restless, she shifted in her chair. She took a deep breath and held it too long, like a swimmer dreading the jump into freezing water. "I'm worried for you. I tried to tell you the night of the attack. The guy wanted to hurt you." She was back to fingering the tablecloth, not looking at him.

He reached over and took her hands between his—so small and cold. He rubbed his thumbs on her palms, pressing deep, wanting to take all her troubles. He never had anyone who worried about him. "Grayce, you're amazing. I'm really touched."

She pulled her hands away. "You don't understand. The guy is dangerous. I can sense it."

He wanted to take her hands back, to stay connected. "I know how sensitive you are. I've seen you with Mitzi."

"I don't mean sensitive in the way you mean." Her eyes flitted, inspecting the crowd. "Davis, listen to me," She spoke in a hushed voice. "I feel things other people don't."

"You're not telling me you're a psychic? Do-do-do-do, Do-do-do-do," he hummed the Twilight Zone music. "My aunt calls herself a witch—once she takes a few shots of Glenrothes whiskey. In fact, every time a cups comes up while she's reading the cards, she tosses back another."

Grayce closed her eyes. Her chest moved in her prim green sweater. She seemed focused on her breathing. She opened her eyes and reached for his hand. "This isn't about me or my gifts. The guy isn't crazy; he was on a mission, like a hired killer."

He didn't want to laugh, but a hired killer was too much. He lowered his head, but Grayce must have caught his smile. She pulled her hand out of his and leaned away.

"Grayce, what you saw was the meth pushing him to violence. He was in his own drug-induced world."

Her eyes were shining but with the dim candlelight, he couldn't be sure if there were tears. "He wanted to kill you."

"Of course, he wanted to kill me. He was crazed. It wasn't personal. Who knows what twisted thoughts drove him to attack me. Maybe he didn't like the shirt I had on or I reminded him of the father he's always hated. It's never logical."

She shook her head back and forth. Her ponytail had come undone, a lock of blonde hair dangled in front of her ear. He wanted to press the hair back, tuck it behind her perfectly formed ears, and feel the smooth silk. Gentle, sweet Grayce, worried for his safety. A strong, compassionate woman caring for him stirred something deep, unrecognizable. His lungs did a hitch, or maybe it was his heart.

"You look tired. Let's get out of these damn uncomfortable chairs. Let me walk you home."

"Davis, someone wants to harm you. You need to be on your guard."

Her warning stirred the hairs on his neck. The threat ran down his spine. Suddenly, a sense of dread lingered in their little corner. He must really be tired, too. He was beginning to pick up on Grayce's worries.

"Mitzi senses it too." Grayce leaned forward. "You've told me how Mitzi is tense, on alert."

"And you told me Mitzi was picking up on my tension from the investigation. You said dogs can pick up on their owner's feelings."

"It's true. Animals are conduits for their owner's emotions. It's different with Mitzi. I can't explain but she and I... "

"I see how attached Mitzi is to you. She doesn't even like women."

"There is more to it." Her face was as white as the tablecloth, the sparkle in her eyes dimmed.

"Grayce, you're exhausted. You had a big week, your trip to LA. You need to get some rest. I'm going to take you home."

"I am tired but something is wrong. When I'm with you and Mitzi, I experience overwhelming sensations. I know you're in danger."

He pulled both her hands back into his, he had to touch her. "Grayce, you're absolutely right. I'm in danger, but not from that thug."

Her whole body stiffened. "Someone else has threatened you?"

He squeezed her hands and gazed into her eyes, trying to communicate his need for her. "Yes, there is a person who is a threat to me."

She gasped. "Who?"

"Mitzi is probably tense when you see her because I'm tense. Not from the investigation but from trying to deny what is between us. Don't you know when we're together the room vibrates? All those sensations you're feeling are between us."

"What?"

He didn't usually have to convince women they were attracted to him. Grayce definitely needed some convincing, judging by the astonishment in her voice.

"All the strain is us trying to ignore what's happening."

"You think everything I'm feeling is...is an attraction between us?"

By the shock on her face, Grayce wasn't driven by desire for him.

"I'm very drawn to you, Grayce. Didn't you know?"

"No, I...no, I didn't know...I thought you...I don't know what I thought."

He moved his chair back. He shouldn't be declaring himself, pushing her tonight. She was exhausted and he didn't want to blow his chances. "Come on I'll walk you home."

She reached across the table, touching him gently as he had seen her do to Mitzi. "Davis, I'm..."

"Don't worry, my feelings aren't hurt." At least, not that he would admit. "I'm going to give you time to realize what a wonderful guy I am." He liked a challenge and convincing Grayce Walters was going to be a challenging pleasure.

Grayce nearly bolted from the cramped corner and the pressure of trying to explain herself to Davis. Once outside, she filled her lungs with the damp autumn air. She had tried to tell him. Instead, they now walked side-by-side, hips and hands brushing in the most tantalizing way.

"Grayce you're getting that worried look." He took her hand, enfolding it in his. The hard edges of his face were softened in the shadows of the street lights and the gray mist.

She had allowed him to misunderstand. He thought she was concerned about their relationship. He was right—she was attracted to him, but not because he exuded male pheromones that had women buzzing around him like yellow jackets at a barbeque. But because the big macho man wasn't the least bit embarrassed about worrying and caring for his French poodle. He was more than a gorgeous man.

He kept her hand tucked into his. Heat radiated up her arm. She listened to his slow breaths, the sound of leaves rustling when they walked, and the sound of water dripping off sodden branches. A water drop landed on her upper lip. She flicked her tongue to catch it.

She heard Davis' breath quicken. His eyes brightened and focused on her. "Grayce." His voice was urgent, breathless as if in pain.

He pulled at her hand, bringing her closer, closer until they were pressed together. He lowered his head and caressed her lips. His urgency vanished. He outlined her lips with the tip of his tongue, slowly exploring.

He kissed her eyelids, her forehead, her cheeks. He nibbled on her earlobe. Playing, enticing, tempting. His gentleness overwhelmed all her senses, so hypnotizing and exciting. The tingling in her frazzled nerves rushed to her fingertips and the back of her knees.

Her need to tell him about the danger and her abilities faded away. Davis returned to her lips. He lingered, rubbing his warm lips against hers. He tasted of wine and wonder. Her body softened around the heat from his body.

She put her arms around his neck, wanting to pull him closer, to feel him against her. She hadn't realized he held her hand. The pull of her hand stopped Davis.

He blew out a breath. His warm breath moved across her face. "I didn't mean to start." He rubbed his nose against hers. His voice was rough. "I can't resist you."

This night couldn't get more confusing, confounding and lovely.

"God, this is embarrassing. I know that sounds like a pick-up line."

She pulled on his hand. "It's okay, Davis."

But now that he had brought it up, she couldn't help but wonder how many other women had heard him say those exact words. She'd rather not think about all those other women.

"Grayce, don't look at me like that. I've never been here before."

Her pulse beat a little faster. "Everything is getting muddled."

She started to walk. Davis followed.

"Wait."

Where was her knowing when she needed it? She knew about out-of-body sensations, but nothing prepared her for the in-body sensations Davis provoked.

"I just wanted to talk and somehow everything got twisted into…" Her face flushed when she remembered her enthusiastic response to Davis.

"Grayce, I'm sorry. I really meant what I said in the restaurant. Let's just take it slow. No pressure."

"It's not that…. It's just."

How could she explain? She really liked Davis but her job was to warn him about the danger, not start dating him. She started walking again.

"Is there someone else?"

She stopped, hearing how vulnerable Davis sounded. She couldn't imagine this man feeling unsure about any woman. "No, there isn't anyone."

"So we're both free." His wide grin was contagious.

She couldn't resist. She smiled back. "But you're my client. I've never dated a client."

"I would hope not since your clients are four legged. Besides, I'm not your client, Mitzi is. And I know she won't mind at all."

"I'm a witness in your investigation. Isn't that a problem for you?"

"The wharf fire is a small job. And it isn't like you really saw anything. No conflict for me."

He made it sound so simple.

"On Saturday night, I'd like to take you to my favorite Italian restaurant. Are you up for it, Grayce?"

She hesitated.

"Come on, Graycie. You'll like it."

No one but her dad had ever called her "Graycie."

"Okay."

"It's in Pioneer Square. The department loves to get their fix of carbs there. You do eat carbs?"

"I eat everything. I lived in China."

"China? You didn't eat dog did you? On second thought, you'd better not answer that."

CHAPTER TWENTY-TWO

Grayce waited for Hollie to plop into the chair. "I've decided to speak with the homeless men in Belltown." Last night she had remembered that Davis' attacker had smelled like pine and musk. Meth addicts didn't smell like the men's department in Nordstrom.

"You're going to give a talk at the Mission?"

"What? No. I'm going to try to find out about the man who tried to stab Davis. Davis believes the man was a drug addict with paranoid delusions."

Davis would never accept her inner convictions about the man's malevolent intentions. His clear disbelief in anything existing beyond his logical world was reinforced last night by his jokes about his aunt's Tarot card readings. In the middle of the night, she had devised a plan to gather enough evidence to convince the hardheaded fire investigator that she was right.

Hollie snorted, flaring the silver crossbones in her nose, today's fashion accessory, which complimented the black Goth look. "You wanna prove Davis wrong?"

"No, I just want to give Davis something more to go on about the guy." She didn't mention her forebodings that the guy was a hired killer.

Hollie snorted again. "Like I said, you want to prove macho Davis is wrong?"

"I'd like to prove Davis wrong, but only because I think he's in danger."

"But, isn't the guy in jail?"

"No, the police took him to Harborview's ER and he escaped."

Hollie stared, her almond-shaped eyes growing round. "A guy tries to stab Davis, runs from Harborview, and you… you're gonna go looking for him?"

"I'm not looking for him." Grayce shuddered at the memory of him thrusting the knife towards Davis' chest. Her heart fluctuated in wild rhythm. "I'm going to ask about the man. I need information to prove he's not a drug addict."

Hollie raised one blackened eyebrow, the pierced silver skull lifting.

"I want to ask a few questions about the guy."

"No one will talk. They might pretend they're talking, but it'll all be bullshit. They'll say anything they think you'll believe."

"I was going to offer money."

"Are you nuts? You can't go down there and wave money around."

"It's one idea."

"I'll do it. I'll go down while you're in LA."

"You're not going down there."

"I know the streets. You don't."

"I'm not as wimpy as you think."

Hollie rolled her eyes. Grayce watched the silver skull nod.

"I don't want you involved."

"I'm involved."

Grayce resisted the urge to roll her eyes back at the young woman.

"What if we prove he's not a drug addict? Davis is one big dude; he can take care of his business."

Grayce stood up. "You're not going to do anything."

"I need to be there to cover your back." Hollie leapt out of her chair and stood in front of Grayce. "We can go together. I'll be your front woman." Hollie's animated face had lost the toughness she painted around her eyes and lips with the hard black lines. The excitement in her voice and eyes clashed with her death statement of cross bones and skulls.

"I don't know…."

"I know the streets. And I can tell who's lying. They won't try any shit…they won't give you a hard time if I'm with you."

"Well." Grayce was wavering. "Why not?"

"I'm going with you!" Hollie's low pitched voice went up an octave. "We should go at night. That's when it goes down. It better not rain. No one will talk."

Hollie slowly inspected Grayce. "You're gonna need to do something about how you look. No offense, but you'll stand out. You…look so…"

This from the woman who had multiple piercings, multiple tattoos, and wore thigh high boots year-round.

"I look like everyone else in this town."

"Yeah, everyone who's got money."

"You're right. Seattle's rain-gear is expensive." She could find something to wear in her parent's closet. "Promise me, you won't go down there while I'm in LA?"

Hollie raised one of her tattooed arms. "Scout's honor." Not the image Scout Masters of America were aiming for. "We could go this week, Thursday. We'll bring 'em cigarettes."

"That's brilliant. I guess I do need you." Grayce was joking but the radiant glow in the young woman's eyes stopped her. "Any giant Rottweilers today? Maybe we should be taking a Rottweiler with us to Belltown?" The vision of Mitzi accompanying them flashed across Grayce's brain.

"They'll think you're a drug dealer."

Both women laughed.

"You've got a lot of phone calls and one twelve pound dachshund who nips. The owner said she would be bringing Ganesh in a muzzle. She's hoping acupuncture will help his attitude."

Grayce stared at Hollie's painted black fingernails when she handed Grayce the dachshund's chart. Her nails matched her black lips. Last night, the idea of approaching the homeless in Belltown seemed rational. In the light of day, maybe not—rather like dating a man who had a hired assassin trying to kill him.

CHAPTER TWENTY-THREE

Grayce stood with Davis and Mitzi on the front porch of his Aunt Aideen's house.

"I can't believe you're nervous. Everyone loves you and so will my aunt." He squeezed her hand.

"I'm not nervous. I don't want her to get the wrong idea about us." Grayce held a bouquet of sunflowers, the last of the season, flowers that magically turned toward the sun each day.

"You have nothing to worry about. I told her we've only gone on one official date. But when she discovered you're Mitzi's acupuncturist, she wanted to meet you. You don't know my aunt. Once she gets an idea, there is no convincing her otherwise."

Aunt Aideen opened the door wearing a caftan of jewel tones in bright blues and purples and a necklace with oversized exotic purple stones. A large boned woman, she was almost as big as Davis and looked like she could bench press Grayce. Her big frame spilled over the door jam.

Davis hugged his aunt, wrapping his thick arms around her. "Welcome home Aunt Aideen. How was your trip? I hope India wasn't too hot."

Aunt Aideen had the same bright blue eyes as Davis, but her black hair was peppered with silver streaks.

Squeezed to Aunt Aideen's bosom, Grayce got a whiff of orange and hibiscus, warm and sunny.

"Come in, come in. Hello Mitzi, how are you?" Mitzi sat primly in front of Aunt Aideen. No jumping on this woman.

"I'm just finishing the dinner. Come into the kitchen." The kitchen was a large rectangle with Italian tiled floors and windows looking out on an expansive garden. Plants and herbs overcrowded a bay window and hung over the window sills.

"It smells heavenly." Grayce took a deep whiff of tomato and basil.

"I've decided to make my famous Scottish dinner." Aunt Aideen's lips were pressed together as if she were suppressing laughter.

Grayce had been warned to expect the possibility of a Scottish dinner.

Davis waggled his eyebrows. He had also warned her that Aunt Aideen was a lousy cook and they would go out to eat once they visited with his aunt.

Aunt Aideen stopped, tying her apron around her waist. "Grayce, I can't believe Ewan hasn't already warned you that I'm an abysmal cook."

"You know?" Davis's voice was incredulous. His mouth hung open, his eyes wide.

Davis' question made Aunt Aideen laugh. She bent over at the waist, holding her side. Mitzi, not wanting to miss out on the excitement, pawed Aunt Aideen's shoe.

Aunt Aideen rubbed the poodle's ears. "Mitzi, they think I've gone dotty. I've always known I was a terrible cook."

"But you made Scottish dinners." Davis drawled out the words as if the memory was torture.

"Well, not that many. They stuck in your memory…and probably other places too." Aunt Aideen chuckled at her witticism. "Grayce, you can watch me cook the cod's head."

"Cod's head?" Davis' lips paled with the question.

"Ewan, why don't you take Mitzi outside and give us ladies some time alone."

"But Aunt Aideen…"

"Go ahead, Laddie. I don't bite and Grayce looks like she can handle a few questions."

"Questions?" The notch between Davis' brows came together in a deep groove. "Aunt Aideen, you promised no questions, remember?"

"Run along, Ewan. Mitzi is ready to go outside. Aren't you lass?"

With the high pitch of Aunt Aideen's voice, Mitzi started to yelp.

Davis paused as if he was ready to say something, but instead shook his head.

"Why don't you come back in fifteen minutes? Everything is almost ready and I know how hungry you get."

Davis stood at the door, hesitating.

"Ewan, how will you be back here in fifteen minutes if you don't leave?"

"Let's go Mitzi. We're being kicked out," he said.

Aunt Aideen waited until Davis left and then turned to Grayce. "I thought I'd never get him to leave. Come along to the living room, Grayce, I've opened a bottle of champagne to celebrate."

"But what about the Cod's head?" Grayce had spent six months in China and had been exposed to the various eating practices of Asia. She had never acquired a taste for fish head or eyeballs, which the Chinese considered a delicacy.

"We're not having a Scottish dinner. The food is atrocious. Have you never wondered why there aren't any Scottish restaurants?"

The laughter bubbled up and burst out of Grayce.

"I've got a little Italian restaurant down the street. I call Marcello and he prepares what I want. We're having Marcello's fabulous lasagna. I didn't know if you ate meat so I ordered his vegetarian."

Aunt Aideen took out two flutes and poured Champagne into each. "Please sit down."

Grayce sat on a deep maroon couch in the enormous living room, filled with books, plants and art, a room of scattered, relaxed comfort. Her feet sank into the thick rug which had the same rich reds of the couch.

An end table was covered in pictures of children. Prominent in a heavy silver frame was a picture of Davis and his sisters with a black lab. Grayce picked up the picture. Davis, a young boy, looked back at her with the serious smile that she was getting to know well. Already tall, he stood with his arms around his sisters.

"Fine-looking children. They have the Davis family size, dark hair and blue eyes but it's their mother's inner beauty that made them wonderful human beings. My sister-in-law was warm and generous and everything my brother needed to help him get past our repressive Scottish upbringing."

Grayce held the picture of the children, feeling their tragic loss, their secure world obliterated. She was fifteen when Cassie died. She couldn't imagine how young children experienced the loss of their mother. "How old was Davis when his mom died?"

"Ten. It was hard on him. He was very close to his mother and old enough to understand what was happening."

Grayce stared at Davis' picture. Her chest tightened, deep pain pressing on her chest for the sweet little boy who had suffered. "It must have been terrible for all of them."

"My brother tried to do the best he could, but he was grieving too."

Grayce couldn't imagine Aunt Aideen's burden of helping the children and her brother adjust to the devastating loss.

"Davis inherited my brother's sense of responsibility and the tendency to be a bit controlling, especially when their feelings threaten them. I had years of practice loosening up my two older brothers, so it wasn't too hard to get the household to lighten up."

Grayce could only nod. The ache sat in her throat, not moving.

"I've had this joke going for years about my Scottish cooking. Ewan warned you, didn't he? I hate to give up my secret, but I'll swear Ewan to secrecy from his sisters."

Aunt Aideen took a big gulp of the champagne. "Just imagine arriving and finding a well-organized but cold household. I'm not criticizing my brother. But he went right back to work, shutting out all his feelings. I had planned to stay for a few months but ended up living with them for twelve years." She sighed, her eyes gazing at the picture of the children.

"You did an amazing job."

"They carry a few scars, but I tried my best to help them.'

She leaned toward Grayce. "You're a lot like Davis' mother. She had the same gentleness about her. You're good for him. I already see it. He seems younger, ready to laugh."

Grayce felt the heat moving into her cheeks. "We've just met…"

Both women heard the back door open and Mitzi's clicking toenails on the tiled floor.

"Where are the chefs? I'm starving," Davis yelled from the kitchen.

"Ewan, we're just having a little champagne."

Davis and Mitzi came into the living room. "I left for a few minutes and you two have already given up the cooking?"

"There is Auchentoshan on the sideboard, 'a good Scottish Whiskey; everything else is dish water'—as your dad liked to say." Aunt Aideen looked out the window lost in a happy memory.

"I'm happy to drink champagne, but I'm a bit hungry," Davis said.

Aunt Aideen jumped out of her chair. "Grayce bring your champagne. Ewan bring the bottle. Everything is ready."

Davis walked to the couch to help Grayce. "Did my aunt ask you a lot of questions?"

"She didn't ask any. She told me about your mom."

His hand was warm, although he had been out in the cold, wet evening. He saw the picture she held in her hand, but he didn't mention it.

Grayce didn't release his hand when he pulled her up. She held it tight, sending her own warmth.

Aunt Aideen stood in the doorway between the kitchen and dining room. "The cod's head is ready. We're having a feast. Sheep's head too. Please sit down."

Grayce tried to suppress the shudder that rippled through her body at the idea of eating a sheep's head. Aunt Aideen was kidding, wasn't she? Did the Scots only eat heads of animals?"

Aunt Aideen walked into the dining room with the fragrant lasagna. "How do you like the sheep's head that Marcello prepared?"

Davis laughed aloud, his mouth open wide, his body shaking. "Aunt Aideen, you did that to torture me. Didn't you? I have a mind to pick you up and put you over my knee."

Aunt Aideen started the same laugh, the same loud sound with her mouth spread wide. "Grayce, I used to threaten to put the children over my knee. Well, my lad, I suppose if you're strong enough to toss the caber then you're strong enough to toss me."

Davis insisted that he clear the dishes after dinner.

Grayce, Aunt Aideen and Mitzi remained seated in the dining room, lingering over their tea and blackberry pie.

"I know the children warned you about the Scottish cooking but what about my palm reading and Tarot card readings?" Aunt Aideen asked.

Still struggling with the idea of his aunt referring to Davis as a child, Grayce wasn't quick enough to hide her reaction to the question.

"Oh, I can see it in your eyes." Aunt Aideen gave another loud chortle, her endless joy exploding and expanding into the atmosphere.

Davis had warned Grayce about his aunt's beliefs. He'd been very clear about his feelings concerning intuition and psychic phenomenon. He couldn't believe anyone as intelligent as his aunt could believe in such crap.

Grayce had hoped to avoid the whole conversation about other worldly gifts.

"I should live up to my reputation and read your palm tonight, but I'm a bit fagged from the jet lag. Make sure when you meet Ewan's sisters, you tell them I'm going to read your palm and cards." There it was again, the loud chortle. Then she whispered conspiratorially, "Don't tell the girls this, but I don't need to read your palm to know how special you are. It'll be our little secret."

Aunt Aideen stood when Davis came back into the dining room. "I'm sure you both have lots to do tonight." The Davis' family eyes danced with mischief. Aunt Aideen thought she knew exactly how they were going to spend their evening. What was she thinking? This was only their second date.

Grayce picked up the last plates and headed to the kitchen.

Mitzi woke from her deep slumber and trotted behind Grayce into the kitchen. The dog rolled over and played dead for the crust of Grayce's pie.

"I always knew she was an amazing actress, but I had no idea she knew that trick," Grayce said.

"My grandkids taught it to her. Mitzi is an amazing dog. Best thing Daphne ever did."

Aunt Aideen's mention of Davis' old girlfriend and Mitzi's previous owner seemed to be a signal between Davis and his aunt.

Davis picked his Aunt Aideen up and squeezed her. In the Davis family, it seemed demonstrations of brute strength were part of their communication. "Okay, okay. You're right as always," was all she could hear Davis whisper to his aunt.

Aunt Aideen was giggling when Davis put her down. "That boy just doesn't know his strength."

Aunt Aideen hugged Grayce tight. "Welcome to the Davis family."

CHAPTER TWENTY-FOUR

Rule Number Four: Trust your gut.

Davis' gut was dancing, boogying and doing the cha-cha after his conversation with Zac at the Seattle Division FBI Headquarters on Third Avenue. A major heroin route went through Alaska. Afghanistan's one hundred billion dollar heroin business was exported to Russia, then dispersed throughout the world and Alaska was one of the conduits.

His hypothesis that heroin was packed in crab cases and delivered straight to Fisherman's Terminal didn't seem so improbable. All he needed was proof. There lay the challenge and the struggle of fire investigation. The proof was under fallen lumber, buried in ashes. He needed a crane to get under the fallen roof. He was willing to beg Maclean if it meant he would uncover evidence of drug smuggling.

Once he had definite proof that this was a drug smuggling case, he'd call the Feds. Then everyone would be involved—Coast Guard, DEA, ICE, FBI and he would lose total control of the case. At this point, all he had were disjointed clues. He liked to solve his own problems, especially when one of his problems might be a retired firefighter.

Steeling himself against his truculent boss' inevitable harassment, Davis knocked on the assistant chief's door. "Do you have a minute?" He took in the gold-framed pictures of Maclean's wife and two children, filling a third of the polished desk; honorable commendations covered the wall behind.

"Does it look like it?" Maclean gestured at the neat stacks of paper in front of him.

He ignored the antagonism in Maclean's question. He needed to play nice if he wanted to get the crane. "What's the status on my crane?"

"What crane?" Just like Maclean to pretend he didn't remember.

"I spoke with you at the fireground. I need a crane."

"You're kidding? No way. Do you have any idea how much a crane costs?"

"This fire was torched by a pro."

Maclean laughed harshly. "Someone paid for one shed to be burned?"

"They knew what they were doing. Brake fluid and chlorine."

Maclean stood from behind his desk. Even working alone, in his own office, the assistant chief always wore his uniform jacket, displaying his rank. "You found evidence of the brake fluid and chlorine?"

"I found the brake fluid bottle but haven't gotten any results yet from the lab."

"You need my job for a while. Then you wouldn't have time to spin fantasies about a shed and spend the department's money."

Maclean walked around his desk. Davis stepped forward. He wouldn't let Maclean try to intimidate him.

"I want to dig under the fallen roof."

Maclean scowled. "I'm not going to spend department money on a fire that will never be determined."

"Someone with skill and experience burned down that shed." He withheld the mention of drug trafficking, since he knew Maclean would love nothing more than to take this case from him and hand it over to the Feds.

Maclean locked his eyes on him. "Any idiot could've burned a wooden structure."

"Nah, the wood planks were thick, logs, in fact. It would take a hot explosion to start that fire. And someone knew how to do it, someone with experience. There can be only one type of person who has that kind of skill."

"Come on, any dumb shit can read how to do it on the internet."

"Nah, this was too good. I'm thinking it has to be one of us."

He waited, expecting an eruption from Maclean. When nothing showed on Maclean's face, he continued. "And you know who came to mind?"

"We've already gone over the list. There's no one worth considering."

"One stands out and I plan to find him."

"Who?"

"Benson."

"Benson?" Maclean scoffed.

"Benson was a damn good firefighter and I can't find him. Personnel doesn't have any information about him moving to Las Vegas. They gave me a local number that's disconnected and an address for a motel on Aurora Avenue."

Maclean leaned back against his desk and crossed his arms.

"You said he moved to Las Vegas. How did you know that?" Davis asked.

Maclean shrugged. "Hell, I don't know. Office gossip."

"Wasn't Benson married? I thought I'd call his wife."

Maclean straightened. "I don't need you spending your time trying to embarrass this department. The chief is still taking flack in the press about that disgruntled woman who didn't make the cut." Maclean's mouth twisted as he spat the word woman. "Just what he doesn't need right now is an ex-firefighter lighting fires on the terminal. Can you see the media circus? You weren't around when the Blackstock Lumber or the Mary Pang fires went down. Back off."

Davis recognized the stubborn set of Maclean's jaw. "How about my crane?"

"You never give up, Davis, do you?"

Maclean walked behind his desk and sat down. "Is the paper work in?"

"Yeah."

"Okay, you can have your damn crane, but give up on Benson. You got that?"

Davis walked down the hallway, trying to sort out the meeting. Maclean hadn't meant that he shouldn't pursue his investigation even if it included exposing Benson. Nah, Maclean was just trying to cover the chief's ass.

CHAPTER TWENTY-FIVE

Grayce made a wide U-turn and pulled the Subaru in front of her office. At yesterday's visit in Los Angeles, she had declined Elizabeth Marley's offer to foot the bill for a stay at Malibu's Villa Constanza Hotel "or in the guest room here… It would be no imposition." Poor Elizabeth—so starved for human interaction. But Grayce had been firm—she had to be on the 4pm flight to Seattle, she had plans—even though she couldn't tell Elizabeth what those plans were. So now, instead of relaxing in style in a five star hotel, or playing gin rummy with one of America's shiniest celebrities, she was in pursuit of clues to convince Davis he was in danger—a target for a hired killer.

She spotted her assistant, looking out of place in front of the slick development that had sprouted up next to her funky warehouse/office. Hollie was dressed in her World of Warfare guild T-shirt, wrist bands, torn blue jeans and jacket. Her hair hung around her face, shading her eyes.

"There's Hollie."

James jumped out of the car and opened the back door. With his forest green fedora, black wrap arounds and black suit, he looked like *The Green Hornet.* "Good Evening, I'm James, your escort for this evening of adventure and mayhem. Do you prefer the front or back position?" Grayce leaned across the front seat. "James, stop."

He tittered. "I didn't mean anything. It slipped out."

James hadn't even met Hollie and he had already started his salacious banter. If James had his way, Grayce was convinced he'd turn the night into a farce.

Hollie stood on the sidewalk, arms at her side, motionless.

"Come on guys. Let's go." Grayce tried for her enthusiastic voice.

Apparently she'd hit the right note of animated optimism, because Hollie brushed past James and climbed into the back seat. James swooped low in a grand bow. "And good evening to you, too."

Settled in the front seat, James twisted to talk with Hollie. "You really dressed the part. Where did you find those atrocious clothes?"

Grayce gripped the steering wheel, unable to think of anything to say to alleviate the awkward moment.

"Hollie, this is my good friend James Dewitt and I'm thinking of dropping him off at the next corner, if he doesn't mind his manners." She tried to sound teasing but heard brittleness in her voice.

"Grayce, I meant it as a compliment to Hollie. Honestly, I thought we were all trying to look…Okay, never mind. Let me apologize. I think you look fabulously homeless."

Grayce looked in her rearview mirror to gauge Hollie's reaction. The young woman's face was hidden in the shadows.

"I included James because I felt we would be less conspicuous, you know… not stand out…if there were more of us."

"I love it. James Dewitt, making two women look normal. Let's face it girls, you need a man on this mission."

The only response from the back seat was the sound of cracking knuckles. Not a good sign.

"Do I understand you ladies don't believe I can be called upon to do the manly thing? Just because I'm wearing my Louis Vuitton shoes doesn't mean I can't protect you. I refuse to wear tennis shoes. My God, who deemed tennis shoes a fashion statement?"

Of course, James would see this evening's attempt to get information about the person who tried to stab Davis as a fashion challenge.

"Hollie, he's kidding."

"Who's kidding? Hollie dear, you didn't get those piercings just for tonight?"

"James. Please." She used the same voice as her mother. The night was deteriorating.

"Okay, okay. Hollie, is Grayce always this grim?"

No answer from the back seat.

"Ladies, you know what your problem is? You both lack a sense of *joie de vivre*. You don't need me along for my karate training. You need me for entertainment. The idea of me standing in for Ewan Davis, the hulk, is amusing enough."

Grayce needed to get control of the evening, but James, in his usual style, was turning this into a social event, as if they were all headed to a club. She used her rearview mirror to talk with Hollie. "It's true. James has a black belt."

A snort of derision came from the back seat.

"Right now, my only black belt is Armani."

Grayce heard Hollie's snort change into a loud laugh.

"Underneath this perfectly coiffed stud is a fighting machine."

Hollie snickered. Her snorts became mixed with laughter.

James continued. "The woman is skeptical."

Another answering snort from the back seat.

"I'm endowed with great *kokoro*."

Grayce laughed aloud right along with Hollie. The tightness in her neck and shoulders began to loosen for the first time since she had decided on this attempt to help Davis.

"The ladies are contemplating my Kokoro…I like where your minds are going but you're wrong. In karate, *kokoro* is attitude, your dedication and perseverance. I did achieve a black belt in karate, but it was a long time ago. My father realized I wasn't going to excel in the manly sports, you know, football, baseball. He decided on martial arts. It appealed to his sense of humor to have me trained as a finely-honed, aggression machine, when he knew I'd prefer reading fashion magazines."

Grayce tried to stay focused on her driving. The traffic was backing up on Elliot Way.

"Also, I was slow in growing, slow in a lot of things, but I've made up for it."

Grayce checked her rearview mirror again. Hollie was leaning against the far side of the car staring out the window.

Grayce reached over and squeezed James' hand. "I'm not anticipating that you'll need your karate skill tonight. The plan is only to talk."

James coughed dramatically.

"I know, I know. You think tonight is going to be useless. That it's totally illogical that we're investigating on the behalf of an investigator." She didn't expect them to understand why she had to protect Davis.

"I didn't say anything."

"You didn't need to say anything. Your cough said it all. Thank you for coming, anyway." She felt incredible gratitude for the two people who hadn't questioned her plan and who willingly accompanied her.

James, always sensitive to her moods, filled in the silence. "Next time we go on a mission, I need more time to plan our clothes. I've almost given up on Grayce with North Face as her designer. But Hollie, with your dark eyes and hair, I could do so much. You're a knockout."

James was right. Hollie was a natural beauty. Grayce didn't pay much attention to people's outer appearance. To her, Hollie was a young woman who had suffered and was still in pain.

"Are we seeing some Italian in those almond eyes?"

"Part Navajo, at least that's what my father said when he was sober."

Seeking some relief from her tension, Grayce pushed the stereo button. Enya's voice vibrated in the background.

"Sounds like you'll fit right in, honey. Grayce and I didn't have perfect childhoods either."

From the backseat, Hollie muttered. "Yeah, life sucks."

Grayce searched for a supportive, positive comeback. But true to form, James got there first.

"Join the club, honey."

"Can you do the moves, like the Karate Kid?"

James had passed some sort of test with Hollie. Who could know what made people trust? James always said exactly what he thought. People never reacted indifferently to him. But surprisingly, children and animals loved him. He feigned disgust when around children, but "the little rug-rats" were always drawn to him.

"You're joking right? I can do better than Jackie Chan."

Modesty never inhibited James.

Stopping at a red light, Grayce turned toward her companions. "We've got to get serious. We need to go over our plan."

"Grayce, we know. We'll get serious right now." James pretended to slap his face, sat up straight and squared his shoulders. "Is this better?"

Ignoring James, she continued. "I'll decide if we talk with anyone."

"Boss, we've got to see who's around before we make plans."

"Okay, but I'll ask the questions. I want us to have a signal, a warning that it's time to leave. If I sense danger, I'll say that we need to meet Jesse and we'll get the heck out of here, okay?"

"I promise, on my Boy Scout honor." James raised his three fingers.

"Promise me you won't make your usual risqué comments."

"You're going to muzzle me? Honey, you only want me for my brute strength, not my quick wit?"

Hollie was laughing again.

Grayce felt like a mother preparing to take her kids to the Puyallup fair, trying to warn them about too much cotton candy and scary rides, all the things that made the fair dangerous and thrilling.

"Okay, okay. I will not speak unless spoken to…" This brought another snort from the back seat.

"Hollie, I need the same promise from you."

Hollie paused before her answer. "I'll try. But if anyone gives you any shit. I'll…."

"No." Grayce's response seemed to echo off the roof of the cramped car. She tried for a more conciliatory tone. "Hollie, you can be friendly while you pass out the cigarettes."

"You're giving out cigarettes? This evening is getting better. I'll smoke with them."

James was perennially trying to stop smoking. Grayce wasn't about to get sidetracked, arguing about smoking and its health hazards. "You know you really don't need to smoke tonight. You know how bad they are for you."

"I don't need to, but what if I want to?"

She cleared her throat, striving to regain control over the adolescents, "Okay, so we're all agreed. I'll take the lead and when I say it's done, we leave."

CHAPTER TWENTY-SIX

Grayce maneuvered her car into the small space in Belltown. "James, read the sign. Am I okay to park here?"

James leaned out the window. Street parking was always tight in Belltown, quite a change from the days when this was Denny Re-grade, home to Seattle's homeless. Now hip and sexy, Belltown flowed with the highly paid thirty-something crowd. Upscale restaurants and condos mixed with shelters, missions, and community services, a daily reminder of Seattle's other population.

"James, what does the sign say?"

"Parking for two hours. No problemo."

Trying to bring harmony back to the troops, Grayce offered words she knew no one believed, "Finding this spot is a good omen."

From the unhappy backseat. "Whatever." Hollie obviously wasn't pleased about her role of passing out cigarettes.

James opened his door. "Might I point out, parking a red Subaru at the corner isn't too undercover."

"Who said anything about undercover? I want to make sure we can get out of here," Grayce said.

"I was thinking along the lines of a slow getaway to El Gaucho for martinis. What has Grayce promised you, kid? I get Grey Goose for this evening's work."

Hollie climbed out of the backseat and gave James an exasperated look.

Grayce came around the car to the sidewalk. The evening had the feeling of warm spring. She inhaled deeply and waited for the wafts of damp grass, hyacinths and lilacs. Instead she got noxious car fumes, the kind you could taste on your teeth.

James stood with his hands on his hips, inspecting Grayce's attire. "My gawd, please tell me I'm in a bad dream. What's that black thing?"

"I found it in my parent's closet."

"Black trench coat with tennis shoes—Dear Lord, I hope you're not naked underneath."

Grayce ignored James' fashion-faux pas-stare-of-horror, and locked the car.

Hollie demanded, "Is fashion the only thing you think about?"

Great, the troops were back to arguing.

James raised his eyes to the sky. "Does the woman dare to ask me what I think about? Honey, in deference to Grayce's wishes and your obvious youth, my lips are sealed." With a grand motion, James locked his lips and threw away the key.

Hollie smirked almost into a smile. Leave it to James to get Hollie out of her funk.

"Honey, you know what they say, if you're talking about it, you ain't gettin' it."

"James…you promised."

"Okay, okay." James put his arm around Grayce's shoulder. They started, three abreast, down the sidewalk.

"Have I mentioned how much I hate tennis shoes?"

"James…" She pleaded for the fiftieth time.

"Grayce, you worry too much. Tonight is about dressing up and having a cig in the name of saving that hot fire investigator. By the way, Hollie dear, you didn't buy any of those menthol girly cigs, did you?"

Hollie reached into her blue jean jacket and flashed a pack of cigarettes. "Do Camels meet with your manly approval?"

James reached over and pinched Hollie's check. "Don't get sassy with me, girl."

"Boss, is this where Davis almost went down?"

"Pretty close, the end of this block." Grayce pointed to the empty corner. "Second and Bell."

James scrunched his lips together in a pout. "All dressed up and no homeless to talk with."

"Strange to see it deserted. When Davis and I were here, there were loads of people lolling around," Grayce said.

"Everyone is down on first. It's Thursday night, bar night, the night for roaming singles," James said.

Hollie shot a serious look at James. "We stand around and wait and try not to attract attention to ourselves."

"What fun is there in that?"

Grayce stopped walking, put her hands on her hips and stared at James.

"I'll behave. But you must see the humor in this evening." Met with silence, James sighed theatrically. "God, give me a cigarette."

Hollie dug into her jacket and pulled out the pack.

"So authentic." James took one and rolled it between his fingers. Next, he held it to his nose.

Hollie stood, poised with matches. "Man, you gonna smoke it?"

"It's been three months and I'm savoring the moment."

"You really don't need to smoke." Grayce couldn't stop the reprimand. She really hated being the only responsible adult on this field trip.

James placed the cigarette between his full lips. "Light it, baby."

Hollie struck the match and leaned toward James. He inhaled deeply and slowly, blew out smoke rings. The smoke lingered under the street light. "Do I look like James Dean?" He leaned against the street light. "How about Brando?"

Within minutes of James's theatrical antics, a man staggered toward them, his progress irregular. He swayed side to side.

Grayce felt his emptiness etch into her soul. She hated to watch human wretchedness and not be able to do anything to alleviate it.

"Got a fag?" He asked.

Complete silence followed except for a sound resembling gagging. Hollie's face was contorted in pain, the pain of trying not to crack up laughing.

James rolled his eyes as only a dramatic diva could, but restrained himself from speaking.

Hollie reached for the packet "Sure."

Deep pock marks lined the man's craggy face, his alcoholic heritage etched in his bulbous nose and red eyes.

Hollie lit the cigarette and handed it to him. His hand shook when he took it.

No one spoke. Grayce could smell cheap liquor and the stench of his dirty clothes.

Hollie's face showed no reaction except for her whisper, "Move on."

"Thanks." With his slurred appreciation, he shuffled down Second Avenue.

"Probably a relative," Hollie muttered under her breath.

James tweaked her nose. "Nah, your nose is smaller." He took a deep draw from his cigarette. "Tell me what you plan to tell Davis about tonight, Grayce?"

She didn't know.

"You're not planning to tell him?"

"I don't know if I can explain why I needed to do this."

Grayce and James exchanged looks, a look that spoke of a long term understanding and acceptance. Thank God for James' friendship. He never asked for explanations, never hinted that her request was crazy or strange. He was just trying to make the evening into a funny adventure.

She paid no attention to James' and Hollie's discussion of tattoos until she spotted two men approaching them. There was at least a six inch height discrepancy between them. Both were dressed in the same brown oversized down jackets. The tall man dragged his feet with his boots untied. He wore multiple socks of different colors, obvious donations from a shelter, like the identical coats.

Dressed in fatigues, the older man had the hood of his coat wrapped around his head even though the autumn evening was balmy. His generous pink lips curved and softened his worn, black face. "Got one to spare?" He looked directly at James.

Hollie answered, "Yeah, why not?" She pulled out two and handed them over with the matches.

"My buddy don't smoke. I'll keep 'em for later." The older man took the cigarettes and carefully placed them into zipped jacket pocket. The tall one's mouth hung open with a vacant stare.

Grayce stood close to the older man. His muted pain, the suffering in his eyes, enveloped her. He had been making do his whole life and had no expectation of anything different. Hope had been beaten out of him.

Hollie spoke first, “This used to be the place.”

“It’s early.” The older man didn’t seem the talkative type, but his eyes warmed when Grayce smiled at him. The street light gave a yellow hue to his eyes—aging or liver failure.

James grabbed her by the elbow and whispered, “We’re here to ask questions, not save lost souls.”

She nodded, but it didn’t stop her from absorbing the man’s pain. She touched his arm. “I was here a few weeks back and there were lots of men standing around on this corner.”

“You folks ain’t lookin' for drugs are ya?”

“Nah. We’re just sightseeing,” Hollie answered.

“This ain’t the corner.” The old man leaned toward Grayce. “Cops all over. They know Old Joe…they know I ain’t doin’ nothin’. Not Tom here neither.”

Grayce was confused. Did he think they wanted drugs? The younger man kept smiling. She didn’t think he was high, but what did she know?

Joe pointed to the young man. Tom’s grizzly Adam’s apple bobbed, drool pooled on his lower lip. He seemed to have difficulty synchronizing his swallowing. She wasn’t very knowledgeable about human disabilities, but Tom had some type of motor problem. It was also evident that Joe looked out for Tom.

“We’re not looking for drugs. We want to ask some questions.”

Hollie rolled her eyes at Grayce telling their purpose. James continued smoking.

Hollie moved in front of the man and took out a fresh pack of Camels. “There’s a pack of cigarettes if you can answer our questions.”

A glint emerged in Joe’s eyes. “I might be able to help.”

Grayce asked, “Where are all the men?”

“The police keep comin’ down here. People go to other places when the cops are around.”

"Really?" Grayce scanned the area. A man stood across the street in the shadows, waiting or watching. The light of his cigarette flickered in the dark.

Ole Joe watched her. "The police not here yet, too early."

Hollie asked, "Why are the cops hangin' around?"

Joe hesitated. Hollie raised both of her eyebrows in question and played with the pack of cigarettes.

"Keep askin' about a dude who tried to stab a guy."

"You know about the stabbing?" Grayce's heart knocked against her chest, forcing her breath to tighten.

Joe turned toward Grayce.

"You sure you're not a cop?" Joe's rheumy eyes moved up and down, taking in her tennis shoes, tattered black raincoat.

"Do I look like I'm with the police?"

Joe's moist lips curved. "Guess not."

"Please tell me what you know about the stabbing."

"A dude tried to stab someone important. I'm thinking an undercover cop. The police keep coming down, askin' the same questions."

Her heart knocking had turned to deep thuds resonating from her chest into her head. "What questions? Do you know the guy?"

Joe chuckled, his voice raspy. "Nah, don't know anyone important." He was enjoying playing with them.

Hollie stepped closer to Joe, her relaxed pose gone. If she were a dog, her ears and tail would've been pointed in the air, ready for the attack. "Do you know the guy who did the stabbing?"

"Nah, by the way the police are acting, he's someone," Joe drawled out the last word.

Hollie leaned on one hip, waiting. James blew smoke rings.

"The police keep askin' if Ole Joe has seen him."

Hollie switched the pack of Camels into her other hand, crumpling the paper. "Well, have you?"

"For a few weeks, he just hung here and now he's disappeared. But, like I told the police, there are lots of guys who show up for a while then split. No big deal, but the police think it's a big deal…you know they gotta protect all the people up there." Joe pointed to the condos towering over Second Avenue.

"So the guy wasn't a drug user?" Grayce cringed at how lame that sounded.

"He stood around and never spoke to anyone. I asked him for a cig. He gave me one, it was foreign and he talked like he wasn't from here."

Little pinpricks of expectation ran from her stomach to her fingers and toes. "Where do you think he was from?"

"Don't know, but he wasn't a Mexican. They all hang under the bridge." Joe pointed down to Western Avenue.

A disheveled youth in shirt sleeves with tattoos covering each arm strode toward their little group. Grayce felt her neck hairs stand on alert. Like Hollie with her street swagger, this kid had mastered the aggressive attitude of alpha of the pack. "Don't mess with me" was written all over his walk.

James dropped his cigarette and crushed it with *savoir faire.*

The kid's pupils were constricted and a sheen of perspiration was beaded on his forehead. His coiled energy rushed out in a single breath. "What do we have here?"

A large scar crossed his nose just like George, her battered tom-cat patient. No one answered.

Ole Joe and Tom drifted away.

His blood shot eyes focused on Hollie. "You holding?"

Not one to decline a challenge, Hollie moved closer to him. "No way."

He spoke into Hollie's face, "Haven't seen you before?"

Hollie didn't flinch. "So?"

Grayce cleared her throat and spoke in her most commanding voice. "Remember, we're meeting Jess. We should get going."

The kid's reddened eyes zeroed in on her. "Stick around. I feel like talking." Although said offhand, it was clear he wasn't offering a choice. "You liked talking to those two idiots."

When he leaned closer to her, she could feel his aggression and his lack of control. A blur of Vuitton passed at the periphery of her vision.

The kid lay on the sidewalk, holding his stomach and gasping.

After his kick, delivered to the kid's abdomen, James bent down and wiped off his shoe.

"Did you just kick my friend?" A new voice from behind grated on Grayce's already hyper-sensitive nerves and had her neck hair bristling. She focused her center, shifted her weight to the balls of her feet and waited.

She felt a rush of air pass close to her ear. The newest antagonist was bringing his hand down on her shoulder to push her out of the way, to get to James. Using his downward momentum, she swung her arm in an arc in one swift motion, striking his forearm.

His knees buckled from the pain she had delivered to his radial pressure point. She wrapped her arm around his head, rotated his body and dropped him to the cement.

"Oh my God, Boss, that was incredible!"

James pulled Grayce away from their attackers. "Get in the car. Go! Go! Go!"

The first guy pushed himself to his knees, breathing hard. "Get up, Jarred. Let's kick their asses."

Jarred made a feeble effort to roll over. Not because she had injured him badly, but because he knew she could take him down again.

James took Grayce's arm. "We're leaving. Come on Hollie."

They sprinted to the car. Hollie grumbled from behind, "Those chicken shits aren't going to chase us."

In seconds, they were in the safety of her car with the doors locked.

James spoke in his British voice, "I almost lost my Vuitton with that kick."

They all burst into laughter. The adrenaline was flowing, making them punchy.

Hollie was exuberant. "Awesome. I didn't know you knew karate, Boss. It was like a video game or a movie."

Grayce pulled the car out of the parking spot. She tried to calm down, but neither her heart nor her body was listening.

Hollie leaned forward from the back seat. "Next time I wanna be the one to take them down. Can you show me how?"

"There isn't going to be a next time. And aikido isn't something you just take up."

"Aikido. I don't know what it is. You were better than a video game."

Grayce basked a bit in the high praise since she had never used aikido in a real fight. "I used the reverse kubishme on him."

"I had no idea you were so cool."

James feigned a cough into his hand.

"Your karate kick was cool too, rad, man."

"I don't know, kid." James grabbed his groin in mock pain. "I should've stretched before coming. I need a martini to ease my pain."

James and Hollie laughed. Grayce wasn't so entertained. Her body was relaxing, but she grappled with the depressing, low vibrations of aggression. The thugs just wanted to cause trouble, nothing personal to them. Men who just needed to beat someone up to feel alive.

"Thanks for all your help tonight. I shouldn't have involved you," she said.

"We weren't in danger. I could've taken the guy down. Not quick and pretty like you two did, but I grew up handling mean sons of …." Hollie said.

Hollie, needing to learn to fight to protect herself, made Grayce feel discouraged. She was feeling the after effects of dealing with anger and hostility.

"I can see you're not in the mood for El Gaucho." James reached over and rubbed Grayce's neck. "Darlin, don't start berating yourself. We're all okay. We just got a little too close to street-living."

Grayce looked at James. He winked at her, not his affected pick-up wink, but a wink that bolstered her. "No need to don the shroud. We're okay. And we did learn that the police are still looking for the guy."

"And it sounds like he's foreign," Hollie added.

"But we didn't disprove Davis' theory of a drugged assailant," Grayce said.

They drove in silence over the Fremont Bridge.

"Hollie, should I drive you to your apartment?"

"Nah, drop me off at the office. I'll go check our phone calls before I head home."

She should've known that Hollie would maintain her privacy. All she knew was that Hollie shared an apartment with some other gamers.

"These night duties aren't in your job description. And, come in late tomorrow. I'll take the messages off later."

"I'm not tired. This was better than any night of World of Warfare."

Grayce wondered if she was the only one whose energy was depleted.

Grayce plunked down on her couch with a bag of Hawaiian chips. Since the night of Davis' near stabbing, she had begun stocking potato chips in her house.

With the sound of the crinkling paper, Napoleon appeared and wrapped his 25 pound body around her feet. He didn't eat potato chips but seemed to understand her need for comfort.

She knew junk food wasn't the answer, but she still succumbed to the comfort of chips and Diet Coke. She reached into the greasy ocean blue bag. She should be meditating on the calmness of the blue water. Instead, she savored the burst of sweet onion flavor and salt lingering on her tongue.

Diet Coke and chips echoed a time in her childhood when she felt secure. On Friday nights, she and Cassie were allowed special treats and TV. The sisters shared a refuge in a world of their own making, where nothing bad could happen.

If Cassie had lived, she wouldn't have allowed Grayce to eat alone. Grayce thought of her growing relationship with Elizabeth Marley, the unspoken understanding and acceptance between the two women. And she didn't feel the intensity of loneliness she usually felt at these times without her sister.

She wasn't sleeping more than four to six hours a night since the wharf fire, and when asleep, her dreams were mostly filled with visions of reflective eyes in the dark, staring at her intently. Sleep deprived, she was having trouble sorting out what was real. When awake, she got the prickly sensation of being watched, and followed, and she was afraid to turn her head, to look over her shoulder—even in her own living room.

She continued to munch chips out of the bag. If someone was following her, it was time to return to practicing aikido.

CHAPTER TWENTY-SEVEN

He never came to Capitol Hill, a place filled with tattooed kids and gays, except for his dirty dealings with the Russians. The wail of police sirens punctuated the noise of the crowded streets. They wouldn't kill him in a public place, around the corner from the police station, would they? They could and would, once he had served his purpose. He was expendable.

He paused to look through the darkened window of the bar, lit up by a three-foot neon cocktail glass. Inside, the first floor bar was dark and nearly empty, with just a few regulars drinking away their Sunday.

He glanced over his shoulder to make sure no one was in close enough range to see him climb the stairs and join the Russians. At the top of the iron stairs, he heard the low murmur of voices.

The large mezzanine featured leopard-skin couches, blood-red walls, and gold frame mirrors. The upper floor was completely deserted, except for the mob boss, Ivan Zavragin, with his body guard, Kirill, and another minion he had had never met.

His palms were already sweating. He was tempted to wipe them on his church pants.

"Come, sit." Zavragin pointed to the chair opposite him. The gold from Zavragin's tooth glowed in the dim light.

The boss was flanked by his stocky underling and Kirill, the bodyguard, at the end of the spotted couch.

He sat down, imagining the leather straps around his feet and wrists, immobilizing him for the torture.

Kirill's stare burned into him, marking him as a potential dead man. He stared straight back at the pock-marked heavy. Kirill's flat dark eyes were a soulless black void, those of a killer who had been to hell and taken the long way back.

Zavragin poured from the bottle that had been propped in the ice bucket at his side. "Genuine Russian vodka. Nothing better."

There was always a ritual when he met with the Russians. He would drink and smile. It was all part of the game they played. Bowls of nuts and olives sat on the table that separated him from Zavragin and Kirill.

He never got used to the thugs who were always present. The new thug, half his size, stood behind Zavragin, his tattoo of four turnip-shaped church spires symbolic of his four prison terms boldly displayed across his arm. He recognized the intimidation, but it wasn't necessary. They had him by the balls. He threw back the shot, matching Ivan and waited.

"How is the investigation going?"

This was no social tête-à-tête. "I've got it under control."

Zavragin watched him, his dark eyes hooded, his face hidden in the shadows. "Really?"

He had given the wrong answer. Fear traveled at warp speed through his body, settling into his gut.

"Under control?" Zavragin's tone had gotten smoother, unlike the harsh Vodka that burned your throat and guts.

"Did you know Lieutenant Davis has been down at the wharf asking about crab shipments?"

He didn't know. How could he know? He knew Davis would be a problem. His usual machinations wouldn't deter a man like Davis.

"By your silence, I'm assuming you didn't."

"Let him poke. There's nothing to find."

"Easy reassurance from the man who said he had the situation totally under control."

"It's under control." He hoped it was under control. He only needed two more weeks and it would be finished.

Kirill sat up straighter. Ivan laughed, contorting his face into a grimace, frozen like an Egyptian death mask. "I want to be back on the wharf. Now! It's been almost a month."

These criminals acted like it was his fault that their drug smuggling business had to relocate. He had done what they asked. "I warned you. The investigation could go on for several months. If you didn't want the heat, why burn the shed?"

Kirill unlocked his crossed legs and leaned over the table; he clenched and unclenched his fist over the nut bowl.

He imagined Kirill's lethal hands around his throat, tightening, closing off his airway. He tried to appear relaxed. He had learned over the last months not to show any fear to these sadists. He refused to give them the pleasure of watching him squirm. "The other fires I managed for you weren't under public scrutiny. Why such a conspicuous building this time?"

"So curious today? You weren't so particular about our work when you wanted to bargain." Zavragin leaned forward. "The shed fire was a message to the greedy bastard who decided to help himself to a few crab cases. No one cuts me out and lives."

Did Zavragin suspect his escape plan? His lungs were trapped in his rib cage. The air didn't move in or out.

"But there was no body in the shed."

"I didn't want to make your job too hard." Zavragin smiled but it didn't move beyond his lips. "Fishing accidents happen especially around the dangerous brine tank."

Zavragin didn't want the police involved. The police would take over the investigation if a body had been found on the wharf. An icy chill settled over him. He was a dead man once Zavragin learned of his double dealing.

"I can trust you to take care of things in the fire department. Just one more little difficulty…"

"Just one?" Fear twisted his guts into tight ropes.

"Davis' girlfriend, the vet, she's been asking around Belltown about the stabbing. My guy is long gone. She learned nothing, but I don't want problems."

Grayce Walters, Davis' witness was in Belltown?

"Don't hurt her. You'll only make things worse." Zavragin gave another of his contrived laughs.

He would never kill for them.

Zavragin stood. Kirill followed. "Nice seeing you."

Kirill descended the steps ahead of his boss. The ex-inmate followed Zavragin down, covering his back.

Did they think he'd shoot Zavragin in the back? If he was going to kill anyone on this earth, it would be the evil mobster, but he'd like to see the fear and pain on Zavragin's face, the same pain and fear Zavragin had caused so many to suffer.

The waiter appeared a few minutes later.

He was in no rush to go home. "Glen Livet—neat. Make it a double."

Why hadn't Benson told him about seeing Grayce Walters on the wharf? Nothing had changed. Benson required supervision, just like when he was a firefighter. He had needed Benson to light the fire, and now he needed him to follow Grayce Walters. He hoped Benson could keep it together until this atrocious charade was finished.

He took a deep swallow of the unpeated, smooth Scotch, waiting for the woody heat to smooth his ragged, torn edges. In fourteen days, he would be a wanted man. Zavragin would get to him before the police.

CHAPTER TWENTY-EIGHT

Grayce stepped into the elevator and pressed number thirty-four, the top floor of Davis' condo building. His distraught message from last night played over and over in her mind—"I'm at the Emergency hospital. Mitzi's in trouble."

Davis was at the elevator when the door opened. He was dressed in a wrinkled blue shirt; several buttons were undone, revealing black chest hair. A five o'clock shadow darkened his chin; a shadow of vulnerability darkened his eyes.

"Thanks for coming."

She took his callused hands in hers. "How are you doing?"

He gripped her hands tight. "Better, I think. Exhausted, and at the same time, wound up."

He looked so lost. His second chakra was diminished. "It must've been awful."

He swallowed hard. "I've been angling to get you to my place. I should've known you'd come for Mitzi." His forced smile never left his lips. His face and eyes were as flat as his energy.

"How is she?"

"I can't tell. She just sleeps. Dr. Herrick said she might be like this for another day or two."

"I spoke with Phil on the way over. Mitzi's labs are all normal." She was glad Davis didn't know how close Mitzi had come to kidney failure. "I can't believe she ate chocolate."

"She didn't eat it. Someone poisoned her with chocolate." The violence in his voice lashed across her skin, making her breathless.

"Poisoned?" She could barely get the word out. It seemed like all the oxygen had been sucked out of the condo.

"Who would poison Mitzi?" She had been so worried about the threats against Davis; she hadn't considered that they would try to hurt Mitzi.

"I've no idea, maybe a neighbor who got tired of her barking."

Mitzi had saved Davis' life twice. Whoever was after Davis was going to try a third time, and they were insuring their success.

Davis pointed to the living room. "Here's our patient."

The spacious room was dark except for a lone corner lamp and the lights from the city below. Mitzi was lying on an oversized bright pink circular bed in the middle of the room.

"Pink, Davis. I wouldn't have thought it was your color."

"Daphne, my ex-girlfriend's taste, not mine."

She tried to ignore the twinge of jealousy, the sudden and unfamiliar feeling of rivalry toward the woman. She heard a gentle thump and moved closer to Mitzi. The lack of an enthusiastic greeting from the spunky poodle told her more than Phil's entire medical description.

She knelt next to Mitzi's bed. "How are you, girl?"

The poodle looked up, her dark eyes dull and listless.

Grayce met Davis' stare. His eyes were more than tired—they were vacant. He was as fragile as Mitzi. She wanted to fix them, make it all better. "You're both gonna be back to your old selves in a few days."

She didn't need to perform an extensive exam to know Mitzi's diagnosis. The poodle's chi was low from the assault to her body. Her lung points most likely were inflamed. Going through the logical process of diagnosis helped her separate her emotional reaction to this newest threat against Davis and Mitzi. She needed to focus on healing the damage.

She didn't touch Mitzi but ran her hand an inch above her fur, searching for any change in temperature, any reactive acupuncture points. "You've been poked and prodded. Do you think you can tolerate a few more needles?"

There was the gentle thump again. “I think that’s a *yes*.” She smiled at Mitzi and then Davis. “The treatment will balance her energy and speed up her healing.”

“I’m sure you’ll help in any way you can,” he said.

She pulled the needles from her jeans pockets, then settled herself into a crossed-legged position next to Mitzi and spoke in a gentle voice, “I know you’ve been through a lot.”

She placed the needle into the top of Mitzi’s head to release the stagnant chi. Grayce was blasted with raw emotion. Cold stark fear arced between Mitzi and her.

Unprepared for the raging force, Grayce’s body reacted. Anxiety pressed her down, holding her too tight to move, too tight to breathe. Her heart sped up as did her breathing.

Mitzi’s eyes were on hers. The dog licked Grayce’s hand; her tongue was hot, too hot.

Exhaling deeply, Grayce closed her eyes and visualized Mitzi cavorting, jumping. She centered on the joy, raising her own vibrations with Mitzi’s exuberant movements. She then placed the needles making her way down Mitzi’s spine.

Grayce rotated the needles. Hot currents moved between them, an excess of blocked chi. She opened her mind and heart with the image of a strong Mitzi, vital and vigorous. A blaze of agony seared Grayce’s brain, as if she had been forced to stare into a blinding light. A snake filled her vision, slithering down into blackness, into emptiness.

Her heart pounded. Her breathing got choppy. This was the energy of the poisoner, an animal killer.

She needed to calibrate the spiking energy. She began to remove the needles. She left the lung point’s needles in place to intensify the treatment of the emotional center.

Mitzi’s muscles start to relax. Stretching her paws out in front, she slept.

Grayce breathed into her center and deepened her visualization, delving into the darkness. The snake twisted on a man’s arm.

Mitzi gave a god-awful howl and started to shake, jarring Grayce out of her meditative state.

"What the hell is going on?" Davis voice grated on her ears, irritating her already hyper-vigilant state. He stood over her and touched her shoulder. "Are you all right?"

With his other hand, he petted Mitzi. "You okay, Mitzi?"

Grayce didn't have any way to describe the treatment. Nothing like this had ever happened.

Dread pressed on her chest, making each breath a strain. Mitzi licked her hand. The now cool, wet tongue brought her back. When Grayce rubbed the soft, springy fur on Mitzi's chest, she could feel the dog's racing heartbeat.

"Nothing. Mitzi and I ...we're fine." Avoiding Davis' gaze, she busied herself removing the final needles. She had never had a patient get agitated in response to acupuncture. A few might get restless but never frenzied like Mitzi. Clearly, the acupuncture had released a whole flood of blocked energy.

Davis was bent over both of them, his voice filled with worry. "I didn't mean to scare you, but your breathing got loud and fast. And then Mitzi gave that howl, like in Belltown."

"We're fine. I was picking up on Mitzi's experience, feeling her stress."

Davis helped Grayce from the floor. They stood toe to toe. She could feel his warm breath on her face, the heat from his body, the clean fresh smell of him. She clung close, needing her senses to be revitalized by his integrity.

"Mitzi's going to recover quickly. But it's too bad, I don't treat humans, you look like you need acupuncture."

"A glass of wine will have to do. No Grey Goose tonight," he said.

"I could use a glass of wine." She had never meant that more than now. The image of the man's scarred arm was burnt into her mind.

"I've only got red."

"Red sounds perfect."

She followed him into the shiny metal kitchen, the exact opposite of her kitschy space. Davis' was new Seattle. Hers was definitely old Seattle, overflowing with plants and her cat Napoleon. His refrigerator was bare, unlike her fridge, covered with pictures of her patients. The cold silver shined back at them.

He opened the wine bottle. In his stark, impersonal kitchen, she felt his solitude. He didn't spend much time here.

He pulled the cork out of the bottle. "If it weren't for Jim Herrick, I don't know if Mitzi would've made it. He's an amazing vet."

"I'm sorry I wasn't available." She started to move toward him to touch him, connect. He turned and reached for the glasses on the shelf above.

He poured the wine, his back to her. "It's okay. You're here now."

Was he angry? He must regret his emotional message on her phone. Always in control, Davis wouldn't have wanted his feelings exposed, to be vulnerable. He rarely let his guard down, even with himself.

"I wish I could've been with you and Mitzi. I've been having trouble sleeping so I turned off my phone."

His body was taut, hovering over her. "You don't owe me any explanation. It's really okay."

She inched closer to him, wanting to ease his guilt, his burden. "It must've been hell. I know how much you care for Mitzi."

"It's over. Mitzi's fine. I'm fine. We're just tired." He pulled his lips back in imitation of a smile, but managed only to contort his face into grimace.

"Anyone would've been scared."

The heat in his look would have caused a lesser woman to run for cover. His jaw muscle pulsated in the hollow of his cheek from his clenched teeth.

"You know you're off the clock now. I'm fine, just tired and pissed. Someone tried to kill my dog."

She tried to remind herself his attack wasn't personal. "I'm not working now, just a friend, willing to listen."

He began to pace in his shiny kitchen, taking up more of the cold space. "Why do women always think talking about something makes it better? I'm going to get the guy who hurt Mitzi. End of story."

Grayce was offended. Not by his attack but because he had lumped her together with other women, other women like Daphne. After their time together, she believed they were becoming friends, more than friends. A flush came to her face. "It was just an offer to talk, Davis."

She sipped her wine. She wasn't going to apologize for trying to help him. It was time to go. She had helped Mitzi. Davis obviously didn't want her help tonight.

She put her glass on the grey granite. "I should be heading out. It's late."

He nodded. "Yeah, it's late. I'll walk you down."

"No, don't leave Mitzi. I'm fine." She walked to the living room to say good-bye, but the poodle slumbered deeply. What had his anger been about? She couldn't think about it right now.

She gathered her coat and purse. Davis watched her. She walked toward the door.

"Good night."

He touched her arm. "Grayce, I'm sorry. I didn't mean to be an ass. It's just been a hard few days."

She patted his hand. "You'll feel better when you get some sleep." She walked to the elevator.

She wasn't surprised that Davis didn't want to process his feelings, but the disconnect hurt. He was exhausted and needed sleep. After treating Mitzi, she was worn out, too. She stepped onto the elevator, ready to be home. Based on Davis' reaction tonight, he would never accept her intuition. Intuition got too close to feelings, emotions.

How could she explain to him, in any logical terms, the impending threat she perceived to him and Mitzi and now her vision of a man's scar?

She had to keep her focus on preparing herself, save her energy for the coming battles with his enemies. She didn't know why she was involved in protecting Davis and Mitzi. But the w*hy* wasn't important now—only the *how*.

CHAPTER TWENTY-NINE

Why the hell had his boss picked this bar? The boss sat across from him in the slick cushioned booth. Fuck, nobody needed to park under a chandelier to throw back a few cold ones. Benson missed the J&M with its wood tables and waitresses in tight ass jeans and its perfect location, close to the station but far enough away that you wouldn't get spotted having your morning belt. In his new line of business, the J&M was off limits.

"You want another?" Benson signaled the waiter.

The commander shook his head.

"Somethin' wrong?" Benson asked.

The commander never got pissed, but you knew when he was disappointed, just like his old man. Except unlike his old man, he never beat the shit out of you.

"What's with the red hair?"

Benson ran his fingers through his hair like the commercial. "It's a statement. I've always wanted to be a redhead." Benson laughed, but the commander didn't. "It's my signature: fiery red, get it?"

The commander tapped on the table, his massive finger beating a slow rhythm, like all the years at the station. "There's a bit of a complication with your signature."

"What complication?" No one, not even the commander, could reprimand him now. He was a free agent.

"You and your red hair were seen. A woman saw you."

"The woman takin' care of the dog?"

"You knew someone saw you?" The commander never raised his voice, but the way he asked felt like he had.

"I had to shut the fucker up, he kept barking." God, this was just like work. Nothing about what a good job he'd done. No respect for how perfect the shed burned, or how perfect he had planned. He purchased each item from a different location, paid cash for the five gallon container of chlorine from a pool supply store in affluent Bellevue, the gallon canister of brake fluid from the hood in White Center, the thin cotton rugs from Kmart.

"She didn't see me come out of the shed."

"But she heard you."

That's all the commander could say, that some stupid bitch had heard him? His plan to set the explosion in a corner, to ignite two walls simultaneously, had worked. The Martha Stewart rugs had served as a fucking great wick.

"So? There's no way she can connect me to the fire."

The commander sat up straight. He was one big son of a bitch.

"So she saw me. I'm some dude on the wharf. Davis can't prove nothin."

"Don't underestimate Davis. He's no fool."

"I thought Davis was going to be taken care of?"

"His poodle keeps getting in the way."

"No shit. Davis has a poodle?" The idea was too funny.

The commander threw back the rest of his Glen Livet.

He didn't need a pricey drink. His Corona went down real smooth. "What's the big deal if a woman saw me?"

"The people who invested 20K expect the job done right."

"The shed burned beautiful. Fuckin' good job." He had saturated the rug closest to the wall with brake fluid. He wanted the biggest explosions next to the forty feet of fir. And his timing had been perfect.

"They won't be happy if they find out there's a witness."

"Nothin' will come of the witness."

"I know that, but they don't."

"So, who cares?"

The commander slowly leaned forward as if he was thinking about grabbing him and hurting him. In the years at the station, he had never seen the commander do anything violent. The man was always in control.

"You don't get it. When they're unhappy, things happen."

"I did the fuckin' job. What they gonna do to me? Ask for their money back?" Shit, he'd already spent most of it. He had obligations, his bookie, his shiny red Corvette.

"If they want their money back, you'll be glad to give it to them."

"They'd have to kill me first."

The commander raised his eyebrows as if it was a possibility.

Those bastards wouldn't come after him, wouldn't kill him, would they?

"We've got to take care of our little complication. I've got her addresses for work and home."

"What do you mean?" His voice cracked. He was still thirsty. He reached for the comfort of the cold Corona.

"Just follow her. Make sure she doesn't contact Davis."

"Why should she?"

"She shouldn't, but I don't want any messes."

"Why don't I follow Davis?"

If he hadn't been watching the man's face closely, he wouldn't have seen the change, the way his face got redder, his eyelids closed for a second before he gave the hard look. "Davis will spot you, even with your signature. He'll recognize his old buddy."

Davis and all his work pals had deserted him after he was sacked. No one believed the sauce gave him an edge, didn't matter to anyone that he was one damn good firefighter.

"Just do what you're told."

"Hey, I'm no Columbo. How much to follow her?"

"Are you kidding? This isn't a job. Our asses are on the line."

"Okay, okay."

He could just let the witness know he was watching her, give her something to think about.

The commander started tapping his finger again. "Don't say or do anything. Just watch her."

"I could scare her."

The commander clenched his fist into a tight knot, the size of a sledge hammer. "If you scare her, what do you think she'll do?"

"Shut the fuck up and go away."

The commander took a deep breath and spoke as if he had trouble breathing. "She'll go straight to Davis. Do you understand? We want to make sure she doesn't go to Davis."

"So I just follow her?"

"And call me if she visits Davis' office or meets with him."

The commander handed him a sheet of paper.

"Grayce Walters, Veterinarian. That's hilarious. The woman who rescued the dog was a vet." He was starting to feel mellow. His third Corona must be kicking in. Watching a woman might not be bad at all.

The boss didn't answer, but shook the ice in his glass.

"Call me if Grayce Walters makes any contact with Davis. Use my personal cell phone. Don't contact me otherwise."

"I know, I know. We can't be seen together." The commander always treated him like he was a dimwit.

"One other thing."

"Sure."

"Lose the red hair."

The commander threw down a fifty and walked out. Hell, with fifty bucks, he could live with the bullshit. Even the chandelier was startin' to look good.

CHAPTER THIRTY

Grayce negotiated her Subaru over the Fremont Bridge, her tires slipping slightly on the wet grills in the middle of the span. She and Hollie were on their way to an aikido demonstration at Smiling Crane Aikido Studio and, a fine mist hung in the morning air.

"Why did you study aikido? It doesn't seem like your kind of thing," Hollie asked.

Without the heavy black eyeliner and her hair knotted on top of her head, Hollie looked fourteen.

"When I got interested in acupuncture, I wanted to learn everything about the East. Studying aikido helped me improve my acupuncture skills."

"Martial arts helped your acupuncture?"

"Aikido teaches you to focus, to direct your energy. By studying aikido, I mastered controlling and channeling my energy into intention, the very center of my healing practice.

"I've never taken any kind of martial arts. But I had to take a self-defense course at the shelter. It was a joke." Hollie cracked the joints on her left hand.

"Sounds like a good idea in theory."

"They had some Pollyanna telling us how to be safe on the streets—like she knew the streets. You know they're putting on this demonstration today just for us. They don't usually do private demonstrations. Of course, the fact that you studied with that famous master helped."

"Thanks, Hollie, for getting this together." She had asked Hollie to research aikido studios. She didn't know what her assistant had said but she had a feeling the people at the studio expected a master, not someone who hadn't studied or practiced aikido in years and wanted to brush up on her skills.

Twenty minutes later, Hollie and Grayce hung their wet jackets on bamboo hooks on the grass-colored wall in the Smiling Crane Studio. The vibrations in the space were peaceful, harmonious.

"The instructor is almost a third degree black belt. How cool is that? Just like James," Hollie said.

"One designer kick and James is your hero?" Grayce said.

"His kick was awesome and he has a black belt. I'm getting a feeling that aikido is for me."

"Remember, this is a scouting trip, to assess whether this is the studio for either of us."

"No problem, Boss. I get it. We're on a reconnaissance mission."

"Why do I always feel as if I'm in a video game when I'm with you?"

A tall woman dressed in a gi and the distinctive trousers called *hakama* that practitioners of aikido and kendo traditionally wore, entered the hallway. "Dr. Walters, welcome to Smiling Crane. I'm Elaine Mitchell."

"Thank you for meeting us early on a Saturday morning."

"It's not early for me."

The woman's highly coiled vigor radiated in the tiny space. The dim light shaded her face, accentuating her pointed angles. Her black hair was pulled so tightly, it seemed to pull her eyes back. She smiled but her dark pinpoint eyes didn't hide her distrust. The tightness around Elaine's eyes and mouth communicated that despite years of studying aikido, Elaine still had much to do to work through her demons.

"I understand you're a veterinarian and you've studied aikido. You're hoping to continue your study here?"

"Yes, it's been years since I've practiced."

"Everyone needs more study. And I'm sure aikido will continue to help you develop deep focus and compassion in your work with animals."

Hollie's chin thrust forward, her eyebrows gathered in one deep crease, and the piercings bobbed. Not a good sign. Her assistant never did well with new situations, especially those involving controlling personalities.

"Dr. Walters doesn't need to study aikido. She's already a master and she's an amazing, compassionate person."

Grayce wanted to laugh out loud. Not exactly the way to embrace aikido, the way of serenity and balance.

Elaine Mitchell's lips pulled back. "You're the receptionist who called?"

Elaine was in deep trouble now. Grayce envisioned fireworks shooting out of Hollie's darkening eyes. Hollie didn't consider herself a lowly receptionist, but Grayce's assistant. Hollie edged next to Grayce, widened her stance and crossed her arms on her chest. Grayce moved between the sparring women. "I'm really looking forward to today's demonstration. Hollie has been explaining the history of your studio to me, a wonderful, restful spot." Not exactly restful at this moment.

"One of my students has volunteered to help. If you'd like, I would love to demonstrate with you, Dr. Walters. I've heard you're very accomplished." Elaine's voice was deceptively soft and clashed with the challenge in her words and the rigid set of her shoulders and neck.

"Thank you, but Hollie and I would like to watch today." She used her calming voice, the one she used for agitated animals needing to establish their territory.

Elaine tilted her head, assessing Grayce. "You can decide whether you'd like to practice after my demonstration." Elaine pointed down the long hallway. "This way."

The women followed Elaine into the bare practice room. Two orange mats placed against the wall provided the only relief to the monotony of brown.

Elaine pointed to the two mats. "You can watch from there."

Grayce and Hollie sat on the mats. When they were seated, Hollie whispered, "Why didn't you tell her about your teacher?"

Elaine turned and stared at Hollie as if she had heard the comments. Elaine joined a young woman who waited in the center of the padded floor. "This is my student, Mary."

Mary, like her teacher, was dressed in a gi.

"I will answer your questions after the demonstration." Like her speech, Elaine's movements would be precise, no motion or emotion wasted.

The two women bowed to each other. Elaine nodded. Mary stepped back then charged with her hands raised above her head, ready to attack Elaine.

With a broad drop, Elaine deflected Mary's arms. Dancing on the balls of her feet, she circled, awaiting Mary's next move. Similar to a boxing ring, each woman circled, moving and feinting in constant motion.

Mary rushed her instructor, her hands upright, tight to her chest, a position for direct assault. Elaine stepped to the side, Mary flew right past Elaine.

Mary circled to Elaine's front and attempted another attack by running forward swinging her arm to the side as if to deliver a chop. Elaine flipped Mary onto her back with a flick of a wrist. An impressive demonstration, since Mary outweighed Elaine by at least 30 pounds.

"What do you think, Boss? I could take her, right?" Hollie whispered behind her hand.

Grayce had no confusion about which woman Hollie referred to.

Elaine walked toward them, her face less tense and almost serene. "What do you think, Dr. Walters?"

Grayce smiled. "You're very talented. Your movements were graceful, lithe, as if I was watching PNB dancers." She sensed how much the woman wanted her to be impressed.

"Would you like to try?" Elaine challenged. Grayce wasn't in the least tempted to demonstrate her skills in this venue. Her aikido skills would be needed to take down a real enemy.

"No thank you."

"I will." Hollie jumped up from the mat. She pushed the long sleeves of her World of Warfare T-shirt, revealing the blue and red snake on her arm, hostility vibrating off of her.

Elaine's small eyes got smaller. Grayce knew that Elaine would never harm Hollie, but wondered how her assistant would handle defeat.

"Come this way." Elaine pointed to the mat. "We'll begin by bowing to show our respect."

Hollie followed Elaine, acquiring her street swagger, with her shoulders and hips swaying to her own music of attitude. Hollie marched toward the center, her ponytail bouncing on top of her head. Her smirk was reflected in the mirror. The women bowed.

Tension radiated down Grayce's neck and back and into her gut. Hollie had experienced violence in her childhood and she didn't want her to suffer any further trauma. She took a deep breath and crossed her legs into a lotus position.

Elaine instructed Hollie to attack her in any way. Elaine's posture was upright on her toes but her body was loose, relaxed. Grayce read the moment Elaine focused. She also read the unfocused antagonism in the tightness across Hollie's raised shoulders and her fisted hands.

Hollie turned and walked toward Grayce. She winked. Grayce could only nod in response. She knew what was coming.

Hollie rushed Elaine with her head down like a charging bull. Hollie's obvious intention was to plough into the woman and knock her off balance.

Grayce watched Elaine's face. Nothing registered but the intensity of her focus. Hollie ran toward the woman, her ponytail whipping. Grayce saw a flash of fear move across Elaine's face. The instructor was mastering her own fears. Old fears Grayce surmised. Elaine was taking on other's anger. By diffusing their rage, she healed herself and others.

In seconds, Hollie was flipped to the ground. Her loud exhalation upon impact with the mat echoed in the cavernous space. Grayce's stomach and heart thumped with the sound and sight of Hollie on the ground.

Hollie stood quickly, her ponytail had relocated itself to a spot above her left ear and her oversized T-shirt twisted. Hollie's eyes were dark. She walked to the corner and put her ponytail back on the top of her head before she moved toward Elaine again.

Hollie circled Elaine, her back hunched, ready to do damage. Elaine's face and body remained relaxed.

Grayce couldn't guess Hollie's next move but she worried about what her street fighting repertoire might include. Hollie rushed Elaine for the second time, with her arm flexed and hand fisted. Elaine pushed Hollie back to the mat in one motion, as if batting at a pesky mosquito.

Each time Hollie hit the mat, Grayce's stomach did somersaults and dives, dropping to the back of her knees as if she got flipped and slammed.

Hollie jumped up and charged again with her arms in the same attack position as Mary had demonstrated. Elaine easily deflected Hollie's raised arm by grabbing it at the wrist and taking Hollie to the ground. The two women continued to circle. Hollie tried to change her timing and slow her charges, but Elaine continued to anticipate and redirect each motion.

Hollie's white T-shirt stuck to her back. It was obvious after watching this demonstration that Hollie had survived her childhood by fearless tenacity.

Hollie was flipped on her back again. The silence in the room was shattered with Hollie's shout and burst of laughter. "Uncle, Uncle."

Elaine smiled widely, the first genuine of the day. She extended her hand to Hollie. "You'll make a good aikido student. You have agility, strength and focus."

Hollie's need to decimate Elaine was ignored.

The two women came toward Grayce. Hollie had just found a way to heal herself, like Elaine.

The purpose of the visit was a reminder, a serendipitous instant of the universe. Grayce needed to trust, trust her intuition, and trust Cassie for back up. She would return to her practice of aikido, but not in this studio. Her practice would be solitary, in the silence of her house, her energy focused on stopping a scarred enemy who had attacked Davis and poisoned Mitzi.

They drove back to Fremont. Grayce listened to Hollie's enthusiastic description of Elaine's moves. "When I get good, I'm going to challenge James to a match. I would love to flip him."

"I'm not sure James will be willing to do matches. I don't think he does karate with people he likes."

"I can get him mad enough to want to take me on." The young woman wasn't exactly on the path to spiritual enlightenment yet.

"I wasn't planning on sharing today's excursion with James or Davis."

Grayce could feel Hollie's stare.

"Why don't you want them to know?"

"James would make too many jokes and Davis would ask too many questions."

"No problem. It will make it more of a surprise when I flip James."

"You definitely would surprise James." She could imagine James' response to Hollie trying to take him down. It actually might be pretty funny.

"Men don't like it when women are powerful. I think Elaine does aikido to feel powerful." Hollie said.

And just like back in the studio, Grayce's stomach dropped and dove. Hollie had recognized Elaine's anger. Grayce had learned from treating the abused how adept they were in reading the moods of those entrusted with their care. It was a key to their survival.

"That is quite insightful, Hollie. I do believe Elaine is working on whatever happened to her in her past."

Grayce waited to hear the familiar cracking of the knuckles.

"I'm going to get as good as she is. And Boss, you don't need to worry about doing aikido. I'll take care of you."

Did this mean Hollie would be giving up her video games for real life action?

"Thanks, Hollie. I appreciate it." She wasn't about to reveal to her assistant that danger was grinding closer each day and she believed someone was stalking her. If Hollie got a whiff of a threat, she would never leave Grayce alone. The young woman already acted like her personal body guard.

She couldn't shake the feeling that the man with the scar loomed somewhere, waiting. But she did not confide in Hollie. How could she tell anyone that she was preparing herself against a man with a scar from a vision she had received from a poodle?

CHAPTER THIRTY-ONE

He smiled, then Grayce did.

She once told Dr. Zao that his gentle smile resembled the Dalai Lama's. He chuckled, the light sound floating on the air, like the sweet music of the wind chime in her garden.

"Tea?"

"Yes, please."

He poured from a plain brown ceramic tea pot. The ritual was the same. Time paused when she visited her mentor. Her fears and worries dissipated like the steam from the tea pot. "How are you?" He was always polite.

He really didn't need to ask. He already knew. His kindness enveloped her like a soothing balm.

"I've been having a nightmare, the same nightmare. Someone is chasing me in a garden. It started with a new patient. During her treatments I have the most overpowering sensations—I go to a fearful place. When I treat her, waves of hostility overcome me. Her chi is low; her lung points sticky. I attempt to balance her kidney, liver and lung points. Instead of relaxing with treatment, she gets agitated." Even to her own ears, her words sounded rushed, harsh, too intense.

She was leaning forward as she spoke, but now she sat back and took a deep breath.

He sat still in his wooden chair. "Yes?"

"During her last treatment, when I closed my eyes to focus, I had a vision of a man with a long twisted scar on his arm." She took another deep breath. "I don't understand what is happening to me."

Another gentle smile.

"Mitzi has been injured twice. I first thought I was feeling her fear through my nightmares." Her voice trembled. "But I've never had visions before."

"You have a great connection with this dog." Dr. Zao smiled.

"It's different than any other patient. I can't treat Mitzi's fear. Instead, I'm taking it on, as if I'm always spinning with dark feelings when she's near me. I've tried to explain my worries to her owner. He misunderstood. He believes the strong feelings are the attraction between us."

She felt her face flush, the heat moving across her cheeks. Dr. Z, as she affectionately called her mentor, had known her since college when she first became interested in acupuncture. He was the only person who understood the extent of her gifts, and the connection with her sister.

She owed so much to Dr. Z. He had saved her in many ways. He helped her accept the "yin and yang of Grayce Walters" as he liked to tease her. She had begun to accept that a scientist could also have a strong bond with a deceased person and have gifts that science didn't accept. He never saw any discrepancy in her warring sides. He saw only her goodness. He appreciated the goodness in everyone. He nodded. Dr. Z never asked prodding questions. He let you wander until your mind became so tired you would eventually get to the heart of the matter and finally acknowledge the real problem.

"So her owner is a good man, yes?"

No pretending with Dr. Z. "Yes, I like him a lot." It was true. She had let her heart get involved. "He's a fire investigator. He holds deep pain. I can feel it. When I've tried to talk to him, he becomes angry, resistant."

Another nod from her wizened mentor. She didn't know Dr. Z's age, but she thought of him as young and old at the same time.

"Getting too close to his pain, yes?"

It was always like this with Dr. Z—just one comment opening a world of understanding.

"Yes."

"Do you know what causes so much pain and darkness in this man and his dog?"

"He grieves the loss of his mother as a child, and the recent loss of his father." She looked into Dr. Z's black eyes.

"It is hard, Grayce, yes? You want to solve other's problems."

"I've never encountered anyone I couldn't help." Davis and Mitzi were the exception. "Davis is in the middle of a fire investigation. I believe someone wants to harm him. Mitzi knows and is trying to tell me."

Compassion and concern flickered across his face. Dr. Z looked like he was sifting through all the words and delving deep into her heart.

He knew what her real fear was, why she was here today. To admit out loud that a poodle had given her a vision seemed delusional. She knew full well that science didn't support such phenomena.

"Someone tried to poison Mitzi by feeding her chocolate. It was during the treatment, after the poisoning, when I saw visions of a black snake but further in the treatment I realized it was a puckered scar on a man's arm." Grayce leaned back in her chair. "I can't make sense of what's happening."

He was silent. Dr. Z never rushed his thoughts or speech. The silence lengthened.

Grayce bristled. "Should I change my treatment?" She wanted a direct answer, an easy solution. She had never felt irritated with Dr. Z.

"Maybe your skills are changing, expanding."

"My skills aren't working. I'm having nightmares and now visions."

"Mitzi was close to death, open to a different consciousness, yes."

She could only nod her head.

"Is it possible some barriers were unlocked by Mitzi's altered state? Maybe new channels of understanding were released for you?" Dr. Z didn't expect her to answer; his questions were always rhetorical. "You are a great empath. You've always been able to feel other creatures' suffering and pain. Is it so hard for you to imagine you might be able to experience their thoughts?"

She sat upright. It wasn't possible. It was too absurd. She never believed in the charlatans who could communicate with an animal over the phone. She wasn't a quack.

Dr. Z shook his head. "So much fear for you?"

It always eased her burden when Dr. Z labeled her worries. The words spoken aloud lost their potency, like a nightmare remembered in the morning,

She was leaning forward again in her chair "But how is it possible?"

"What is the difference when you see pictures in your dreams and see Mitzi's pictures?"

She let the thought settle, trying to understand words that were more than words—a wisdom that defied logic.

"It sounds like you've opened your heart to this dog." Dr. Z pressed his hand to his chest. "And this man."

Her heart sped. Heat moved through her body, pooling in her face and chest. She barely acknowledged her feelings for Davis. She was beginning to realize the truth in Dr. Z's words.

"Dogs protect their owners, yes? Mitzi almost died and still wants to protect her owner. How could she do this?" He leaned toward her, closing the space between them. His black eyes focused on her, seeming to see beyond her, looking into her soul. "You've always told me that dogs' hearts are open and can identify people who care about them, who need comforting. Is it so outlandish that Mitzi knows you care about her and Davis?"

"She knows. But that doesn't mean I can read her thoughts. I care a great deal about many animals but I've never been able to share their thoughts." The heat moved to the top of her ears. Her voice got louder. "I saw Mitzi's thoughts. A man with a scar on his arm."

Dr. Z waited. He was really good at waiting.

"Did I really read Mitzi's thoughts?"

Again, Dr. Z didn't reply.

"Are you able to see other's thoughts?" She had barely uttered the words when the realization struck her. Dr. Z could see other's thoughts.

"I'm sorry, I didn't mean to pry." Her mind reeled.

He sat back in his chair, his posture open, accepting. "Does knowing of my abilities change yours?" He never raised his voice but somehow she always knew when he was using his quiet force to make her look more closely.

"No."

"We all have different gifts. It's our own journey to discover them." He smiled. "I will treat you, yes? It's been a long time. It will help your mind to slow down, calm your fear."

Grayce left the little house in Ravenna. She found herself sitting in her car, but didn't remember the one block walk to her car. Her entire being was still in another space, a space that sparkled with bright light, her heart chakra open, resonating with awareness.

Grayce didn't know how long she sat in her car but finally, she turned the key in the ignition. It was dangerous for her to drive when she was still woozy from acupuncture, but she had to get back to her office. Between her trips to LA and her investigation, she had a lot to catch up on. At least at this time of night, the office would be empty. She needed the silent time and space to digest Dr. Z's wisdom, his treatment.

A light of hopefulness radiated through her being. Dr. Z's treatment prepared her for what was waiting, for whatever shock might come next.

CHAPTER THIRTY-TWO

Grayce climbed the wooden stairs to her office. With each step the aging wood creaked, fracturing the nighttime silence. The smell of pine wax that Mr. Lopez used on the fir floors and banisters assaulted her nose.

Every cell in her body went on high alert, synapsing at high frequency, heightening her awareness of every sound, smell, and sight. Her acupuncture treatment hadn't calmed her nervous system as she first thought, but intensified her sensory input. Her neurons fired, as if she were on speed, on Dexedrine.

Reaching the top of the stairs, she was breathless, not from exertion of climbing but from her agitated state. She groped for the light switch. The school house fixtures barely lit the cavernous hallway. She walked down the passage to her office. Shadows danced on the walls.

The click of the rusty lock she'd inserted into the office door echoed in the quiet. She glanced over her shoulder down the hallway. Nothing.

In her office, Hollie's familiar chipped tea mug positioned on the right side of her desk and the smell of lavender, used to calm her patients, soothed her jagged nerves. She inhaled the comforting scent, imagining she walked in bright sunlight through the purple French fields. She moved to the filing cabinet and the accumulated stacks of invoices and bills.

Staring at the bulging file, she wished she had hired an accountant. The problem was her system of bartering, discounting special rates for seniors or anyone who fostered abandoned pets didn't fit on a spreadsheet.

With the heavy file in hand, she opened the door to her office. She heard a noise in the hall. Walking back to the heavy door, she peered down the hallway. "Mr. Lopez?"

No answer. Her nervous system was wacky from her treatment.

She needed to discuss her reaction to today's treatment with Dr. Z. Her overstimulated response was similar to Mitzi's. Instead of the deep sense of calm after acupuncture, like Mitzi, she was tense, edgy, hyper-vigilant.

She shut and locked her outer office door. The metal resisted. The old locks had to be replaced.

Weary after only an hour at her desk, Grayce stood, stretched and began to pack up the files. It was time to head home. The chamomile tea had relaxed her but also had made her sleepy, like the bear on the package.

She checked her cell phone one last time. Davis hadn't texted to cancel their third official date. After their disagreement, she wished he had cancelled. Getting involved with him wasn't a good idea. Who was she kidding? She was involved.

Fumbling with her keys in the hallway, she bent to lock the door. She could barely see the keyhole. The hall lights were out. A wave of fear surged through her body, settling in her feet, rooting her to the floor.

Just like on the wharf, danger seared down her spine. A draft of arctic cold rushed down the hallway. She straightened, pushing against the resistance of her tight lungs, frozen muscles and inert feet.

The fir floor creaked. Heavy footsteps moved toward her. Her heart bolted from her rib cage into her throat. The old floor creaked again.

She ran into the darkness toward the front stairwell.

Her harsh breathing reverberated in her head. Out of the darkness, massive hands clamped down on her arms, hot breath on her neck.

She twisted, trying to use her weight to break the grip. The grip tightened.

"Going somewhere?" His rough laugh grated against her ear, her skin. Shivers of revulsion rolled through her body. He lifted her off her feet.

The stench of alcohol, sweat and tobacco enveloped her. Repulsed, she fought the bile that rose up in her throat. Her feet hung in the darkness. Cold sweat dripped down her back. She had panicked but needed to get back in control.

With his hands pinning her arms to her body, he held her over the top of the stairs. "If you don't stop moving, I might drop you," he snickered.

She relaxed into his hands. She couldn't break his grip, but she could kick him, force him to release her. And then she would fall down the twenty wood steps.

"If you had just learned to stop sticking your high and mighty nose in places it didn't belong, I wouldn't have to hurt you."

Her feet dangled in the air. She waited, marshaling her energy. His hands squeezed tighter, his nails digging into her skin. She ignored the pain and waited for the moment.

"You need to forget the wharf. Get my meaning, bitch?"

He shook her hard, hard enough to make her teeth hurt. His fetid breath blew across her neck.

"Do you understand?"

She nodded.

"If you know what's good for you and your fuck buddy, Davis, you'll forget our little conversation. I'd hate for something to happen to the almighty fire investigator." He placed her on the edge of the steps. This was the moment.

The back of her knees and her stomach fluttered. Her heart sprinted, speeding out of control.

He pushed her forward. "This should help your memory."

He let go. She teetered, twisted in mid-air, lashed out with a kick. She felt and then heard the snap of his knee. The thrust of her movement pitched her faster into the black emptiness. Her shoulder hit first. Unable to stop, she tucked her head and rolled into a tight ball.

As if in one of her nightmares, she waited for the void to take her. Aware she was falling, she couldn't stop. The sound of her shoulder striking each step echoed in the silence. Eventually sweet darkness came.

She lay on her side, afraid to make a sound, but she didn't know why.

Then she remembered. She'd been attacked, knocked down the stairs.

Was he still there? Waiting?

She rolled to her side. Pain shot down her right arm. She had to move, had to get out of here.

She struggled to a sitting position. A wave of nausea hit. Dizzy. White dots paraded before her eyes. Leaning against the bottom step, the queasiness went away.

Everything hurt. Her head throbbed. Her neck was sore. Taking deep breaths, she palpated each rib. No sharp twinges, no rib fractures.

Her teeth chattered, and she realized she was cold. Way too cold. She clenched her jaw, tried to keep her teeth from chattering, but couldn't.

She shivered and shivered. Had to get warm.

Her thinking was muddled. She knew she was in shock. And she knew she had to get out of there. Had to go home, to reach safety.

She pushed herself to her knees, sharp pain shot through her arm again. Nausea threatened. She bent to pick up her purse. Another wave of nausea. She stood, motionless. If she sat down, she wouldn't be able to get back up.

The pain and her churning stomach receded enough for her to open the door. She wanted to go home. She waited for her intuition to alert her if he waited outside.

She didn't perceive any threat. He had delivered his message, loud and brutal. Exiting, she turned to lock the door. She wanted to laugh at the idea of locking the door but it would hurt too much.

A bath, a hot bath to wash away his touch. The thought of his breath on her neck sent waves of revulsion down her body.

Getting into her car was torture. Every part of her body screamed. She checked her rearview mirror for him. His words, threatening retribution if she told Davis, were embedded in her brain. The man was filled with rage, rage capable of murder.

If she called the police, they would contact Davis. Tomorrow she would think about who to call. Tomorrow she would treat herself with acupuncture. Tonight, she needed an Epsom salt bath and some serious western pain killers.

CHAPTER THIRTY-THREE

The ringing phone woke her from a deep sleep. Grayce rolled over. A stabbing pain shot down her arm. Remembering last night's assault, she wanted to put a pillow over her head and pretend it was all a nightmare, a nightmare that didn't end with intense pain and threats.

Her cell sounded like it was coming from the kitchen. She swung her legs over the side of the bed and her entire body rebelled. Everything hurt. The cold floor jolted her fully awake. Napoleon jumped from the bed—breakfast time. At least someone was functioning.

She stood, all her muscles tightened. The phone's insistent ring continued. Napoleon wrapped himself around her ankles, purring in anticipation of his kibble.

The journey from bedroom to kitchen, all five steps, hurt as if she were eighty years old and racked with rheumatoid arthritis. The bright sunlight burning her eyes intensified the throbbing in her head.

She searched for her phone in her polar fleece draped over the chair. The ringing stopped.

She leaned on the chair. The only person who would call at this hour was her mother. She squinted at the missed call; Davis called at 12:10pm. She had slept until noon—courtesy of over-the-counter sleep aids.

She couldn't bring herself to talk, feeling as if she had been hit by a Mack truck. If Davis showed any concern, she might let down her guard and tell him about the attack. She hadn't had time to think through what she should do about last night's threat. She needed to shore herself up with a Diet Coke and another hot bath, and a few acupuncture needles, and, most likely, a few more pain pills.

By the time she got herself together enough to talk with Davis, the day would be over and she still wouldn't know if they had a date for tonight.

Pushing away from the chair, wincing from the sudden jolt to her shoulder, she walked to the refrigerator, reaching for a Diet Coke. Daunted by the idea of having to stretch to reach for a glass, she drank out of the can. The cold liquid was soothing on her dry lips and throat, a side effect of the PM in the medication.

She walked the three steps back to the table. Sitting down, she reached for the pill bottle, inclined to sleep the afternoon away. She put down the bottle and dialed Davis.

"Grayce, how are you?"

"Great." She tried to sound chipper.

"You sound funny. Are you sure you're all right?"

"The week caught up with me." If he only knew who caught up with her.

"You're still planning on coming to tonight's department party?"

She heard the uncertainty in his voice.

"I wouldn't blame you if you didn't want to come. I was an ass."

Exhausted from last night's episode, she was too tired to discuss the finer points of whether Davis was an ass. She didn't blame him for not wanting to talk about his feelings the night Mitzi was poisoned. She understood about not wanting to talk when you've been through hell.

"I feel really badly about not wanting to talk about what happened to Mitzi. Can we sort it out?" Davis asked.

His sincere apology tempted her to divulge the assault. The memory of the threat stopped her. "Of course."

"Great." His voice was lighter. "We may have to be a little late for the party. I've got a meeting at five with a fisherman from the wharf."

Suddenly she was wide awake. "Really?"

"Yeah. The guy's being kind of strange. He doesn't want to meet at the wharf, but at some hole-in-the-wall bar in

Georgetown at five. I'll just have time to get home and shower before I pick you up."

"I thought you already met with the suspicious kid from Alaska."

"This guy rents the shed next to N-4. Hopefully he'll show."

"What do you mean?" Uneasiness pulsed in her stomach.

"I spent days tracking the representative of the company who rented the N-4 shed. The Port only had the company name with a PO Box in Alaska for the rental agreement. I finally talked to a guy who said he worked for the company and he agreed to a meeting. He never showed. You'd think he'd want an explanation about the fire and how the investigation was going."

"But what did he say about not showing up?"

"Can't find him. He's gone, disappeared." Disappeared? Her hands trembled. She didn't know if it was the side effects of the pain meds or the apprehension that sank in her stomach making her feel quivery. "You said that you couldn't talk to the men because they're out fishing?"

"But why would the company phone be disconnected?"

Prickles of hot then cold flashed across her skin, as if she had influenza with a high fever.

"This is the strangest case I've ever worked on. Every time I think I've got a lead, it evaporates as if someone is ahead of me, anticipating my next move."

The words of her assailant drummed in her ears and his threat of what he would do to Davis, the star investigator.

"I would love to skip the whole party, but the guys have spent tons of time organizing. We don't have to stay long."

She swallowed against the lump of fear that moved from her stomach into her throat. "I'm looking forward to it."

She could barely walk, hardly talk, but she would be social at a fire station party. She didn't know what else to do. She needed to be with Davis.

"I'll pick you up at 7:30 or so."

"Davis..." She had difficulty forming the words. They came out as a whisper, "Be careful."

"I'll try." His voice sounded strained when he said good-bye.

Grayce reached for the Tylenol. She needed pain relief and sleep before the party.

Davis hung up the phone. Grayce worried about him, had told him to be careful. No one ever worried about him. Since his mother died, he spent his life convincing everyone including himself that he was invincible.

He didn't know how to proceed with a woman like her. She was straight-forward, honest. No games, no secrets with Grayce Walters. She wasn't anything like the lying Daphne.

This was totally foreign territory. He had no idea how his apology would go tonight, but he was eager to try. All because one ethereal woman worried about him.

CHAPTER THIRTY-FOUR

A crew of beefy firefighters huddled around Grayce. Davis' colleagues exuded testosterone, intense male energy. She had covered herself in long sleeves, tights, and high boots to hide her bruises. From the frequent glances, she surmised that the men approved of the outfit or at least the short skirt.

The firefighters joked, pushed, and jabbed each other with insults. They mocked Davis' usual serious veneer. She smiled and nodded, allowing Davis to do the talking. The men hooted loudly, entertained by the idea that Davis was dating Mitzi's vet.

The men quickly dispersed once the buffet line opened, leaving Grayce and Davis alone.

"Are you hungry, Grayce?"

"I had a late lunch. What about you?"

Davis watched her as if she had an answer to a problem he needed to solve. "I can wait."

He was different tonight, more relaxed, openly affectionate, touching her at every opportunity, a brush across her back, a hand briefly on her shoulder. His gentleness was helping her forget the assailant's brutal hands.

Davis shifted his weight from side to side and looked directly into her eyes. "I want to apologize for the other night. I know you were trying to help."

Like in his childhood picture at his aunt's house, Davis' face was open, vulnerable. Mesmerized by the emotion in his voice and his unguarded look, she wanted to touch him, to run her finger along his rugged cheekbone, to soothe away his troubles.

"When Mitzi almost died…I felt like I let her down. She saved me, you know that."

She wanted to tell him that he hadn't failed Mitzi, but he wouldn't want easy words of reassurance.

"It felt like when my dad died. I couldn't save…"

"What do we have here?" An older officer, with multiple ribbons on the blue suit of the fire department, inspected her from her blond hair to her black leather boots. "Am I interrupting?" He feigned concern, but his tone wasn't the least bit regretful.

"Oh, hell," Davis said it loud enough for his superior to hear.

"Davis, introduce me to the lovely lady. I don't think I've had the pleasure." He stretched the word pleasure with sexual innuendo.

"Grayce, this is Assistant Chief MacLean. Maclean, this is Dr. Grayce Walters."

"My pleasure, ma'am, excuse me, I mean doctor."

The assistant chief's slip was intentional. The grooves around his thin lips and above his eyebrows were deep from years of scowling in dissatisfaction.

"What kind of doctor?" Like a child with a stick, Maclean needed to poke everything and everyone in his vicinity.

Davis moved closer to her. He and Mitzi made a great pair of a watch dogs.

"Grayce is a vet."

"Your name sounds familiar. Are you the one who saved the poodle?"

"No, a colleague took care of Mitzi."

"How did you hear about my dog?" Davis's voice was sharp. He angled his body toward Maclean, ready for a face off.

Maclean ignored Davis but stared at Grayce. "I make it my business to know everything."

Did he know she had been on the wharf? Was Davis not supposed to be dating a witness?

"Do you have any pets, Officer Maclean?" She asked.

Maclean gave Grayce an oily smile. He stepped closer, too close, invading her personal space. "With such attractive animal doctors, I might have to reconsider."

"Maclean." Davis loomed over his superior, his body tight, ready to defend.

Maclean's lips and face moved in an imitation of a laugh. "How archaic, Davis. I'm sure Dr. Walters has many admirers." Another smarmy smile.

She touched Davis' arm. "I'm starving and, by the looks of these firefighters, the food will go fast."

"You're right. Let's get in line. Excuse us, sir," Davis emphasized the sir.

"I wouldn't want to detain you."

Davis pulled Grayce to his side and moved them away from Maclean. "Are you all right? He's such a…"

"Does he know I'm a witness?"

"What does that matter?"

"He was so antagonistic. I thought you might be in trouble for bringing me to the party."

"He doesn't know. And there's no policy that prevents me from dating you. He treats everyone badly. He enjoys goading people, getting under their skin."

"It seemed more personal," She said.

"You're probably right. When I first arrived, he wanted us to be buddies over our shared Scottish heritage and I wasn't interested."

"He holds that against you?"

"And that I'm an investigator. We're known for our attitude, not kowtowing to the brass."

She shivered. Her own energy was depleted from last night and Maclean's primitive aggression drained what little she had left.

"Are you cold?"

"Just a bit."

Davis placed a warm hand on her back, guiding her. She scanned the room for the assistant chief. He stood engrossed in conversation with a large blond woman in a revealing black dress. She had her hand on his arm and the assistant chief was focused on the woman's exposed cleavage.

Grayce looked down the long table, filled with egg rolls, sushi, barbeque ribs, salads, a smorgasbord of Seattle's ethnicity. "Wow, a lot of food."

"The guys usually choose quantity over quality, but this looks decent."

Davis held her plate. She chose from the assortment of salads. He looked at her heaped plate. "Lucky you had a late lunch."

She laughed and looked up at Davis to share the joke. His eyes were warm, light.

"We've made our appearance. Let's get out of here." He bent over her, as if he were about to kiss her in the buffet line.

"Davis." Someone behind them murmured his name in a low sensual tone.

Davis straightened.

The same blond she had seen with Officer Maclean.

"Toni." Davis' relaxed teasing was gone, his shoulders hunched.

"How are you, Davis? I haven't seen you in a while."

"Great."

The woman had the stature and presence of a Wagnerian soprano. Everything about her was larger than life.

"Grayce, this is Toni Williams from Ladder Seven. Toni, this is Grayce Walters."

Grayce smiled, ignoring Toni's open perusal. She wasn't good at these female games, never knowing how to respond to the layered subtext.

"Are you a new firefighter?"

Davis' burst of laughter at the idea of Grayce as a firefighter didn't help her mood. She wished she had worn her Jimmy Choos so she didn't have to look so far up at Toni. "I'm a veterinarian."

"You take care of Mitzi?" Toni made it sound as if she groomed dogs.

The three proceeded down the buffet line.

"Toni is part of an elite group of firefighters. They do the rescues the regular guys can't do—high angle rescues, confined space. They're also trained as divers."

"Impressive." She could imagine the gargantuan woman pulling someone out of a burning building. Toni radiated the same physical confidence as Davis. Grayce tried to stand taller, all five feet of her.

Toni put her hand on Davis' arm. "Davis, did you hear about the rescue down on the Duwamish?"

Grayce waited for Davis to finish his conversation. Officer Maclean sidled up next to her.

"I seem to have forgotten silverware." He pressed against her, his shoulder rubbing against her back, reaching across her.

She moved away from him, moving closer to Davis. "May I get something for you?"

"Thank you. I've got it."

His long, manicured fingers stretched across the table to the stack of rolled silverware. A dark blemish was partially exposed below the cuff of his crisp white shirt—a purple striated scar.

Her heart skidded and stopped for a micro-second, leaving a hollow feeling, like a cave in her chest. Was this the scar from Mitzi's vision?

He leaned closer to her. "Have you seen the Sculpture Garden?" She could smell his expensive musky aftershave.

She needed a closer look at his scar. Was it the scar from her vision after Mitzi's poisoning? He was very knowledgeable about Mitzi's near-death experience. Her heartbeat did skips and leaps defying normal sinus rhythm.

"No, I haven't yet, but I would like to," her voice was rushed, breathless.

He stood too close, leering down at her. "You shouldn't go home until you've seen Richard Sarro's piece—right outside the doors, down the steps." His bleached white teeth exaggerated their size-large canines in his large mouth.

"It's called *Wake*—walls of steel, shaped like hulls of ships moving through the water. Impressive, massive." He turned to walk away. "Don't miss it."

"Thank you. I won't." Was he trying to get her outside to prove his sexual prowess or for something more dangerous? She was more familiar with the nearby dog park than the sculpture garden. Both had been built on an old railroad bed running along Puget Sound. Several of her clients were regulars at the dog park. They had the same aggressive and territorial behavior as the assistant chief.

"Let's find a table?" Davis' voice made her jump. He was half-turned toward Toni, listening to her story. He gestured with his head toward an expanse of window looking down on the gardens. "How about over by the windows?"

Grayce was confused. The scar on the assistant chief's arm was very similar to her vision. Most of the men and women at this party probably had scars, occupational hazards, even Brunhilde from Ladder Seven. Davis had most likely explored each and every one of her scars, judging by his obvious discomfort introducing Grayce.

"I'll get us drinks and be right over." Davis bent close. "Are you alright?"

"I'm fine." She wanted to add. *I'm fine, if thinking your boss might be a criminal because he has a scar on his arm that I've seen in a vision from your dog is fine. I'm fine if I don't have a concussion from being pushed down steps by a man who might have started the wharf fire. Sure I'm fine, darn fine.* She walked to an empty table by the windows, the heels on her boots clicking on the concrete floor of the cavernous space.

People were busy eating at nearby tables; no one paid attention to her. She put her plate down on an empty table. A door was open to a deck, overlooking the gardens. She turned to look for Davis. He was walking toward the bar.

She scanned the room for the assistant chief. He sat with his back to her, at a table filled with men in identical blue suits.

Last night's experience was affecting her, clouding her judgment about the assistant chief and his scar. She couldn't intuit if the man was a threat.

The room felt crowded and claustrophobic. She walked outside to the end of the deck, away from the door, out of view of the party goers. She drew fresh air into her lungs. Inhaling deeply, she ignored the throbbing of her bruised ribs. A train rumbled below the park.

"You must be new in the department?"

A man twice her size towered over her. Were there any average sized people in the fire department?

"I'm a guest." Shivers ran through her body, another side effect of her nighttime activities and pain medications.

"I'm Niles Olsen, the chaplain."

She had felt paranoid at the party and now she felt paranoid talking with the chaplain. He moved out of the shadows. His face was round with baby fat, although he was at least in his fifties. It was time to go home, if she was too afraid to talk with a chaplain.

"I'm Grayce Walters. I'm here with Ewan Davis."

"Grayce Walters, I've heard that name before. You're the witness to the wharf fire?"

Her scalp tingled. "I really didn't witness much."

He stepped closer, his large frame blocking the light from the party. "I thought you saw someone."

She had to crane her neck to look up at him. Shards of light broke his face into harsh slats. She didn't know if she was supposed to talk about evidence. It couldn't be a problem to tell the chaplain, could it?

"I did see a man but Davis thinks he was a fisherman." Discussing the man on the wharf stirred the memory of his rage, the same rage as last night's attacker. She remembered how hard he had gripped her, squeezed her. Trying to blot out the memory, she rubbed her arms, as if she could erase his fingerprints from her skin.

"Are you going to walk in the sculpture garden? I personally love Richard Sarro's piece *Wake*. I believe he meant it as a metaphor for death."

The little hairs on her neck stood up. She tried to keep her voice steady. "The piece seems to be very popular. I may need to see it."

He had stepped back into the shadows. She could no longer see his face. "Pleasure to meet you, Grayce, who didn't see our culprit." He wandered back into the party.

Why did both men want her to go into the garden and see the same sculpture?

The immense sculpture stood, beckoning from below. Lights, strategically placed on the sculptures, gave the space a surreal, other-worldliness.

She followed the small lights on the steps. Sarro had curved forty-foot walls of steel into soft waves, giving the colossal inert pieces a feeling of movement. She walked between the gigantic slabs with shadows as big as the monsters of childhood dreams. "Wake" wasn't a metaphor for death. It was a blatant demonstration of uncompromising male power.

She felt minuscule against the strength of men who shaped steel to their whims or planned attacks on women. She wasn't the size of a Valkyrie, but she was strong when it came to protecting the vulnerable, not that Davis would ever perceive himself as vulnerable.

The sound of footsteps on the gravel ricocheted off the steel barrier. It came from the path that wove through the park. She peered toward the pavilion. Bright lights from the deck reflected back in her eyes.

This was her reoccurring nightmare, except she wasn't asleep or safe in her bed. In the nightmare, an unknown adversary chased her between walls of steel. She always awoke in a panic, never knowing if she had escaped. Her hand pressed to her mouth, she tried to smother the rising fear.

The footsteps stopped. She was visible to anyone coming down the path. She stepped into the shadows and inched her way along the icy steel, away from searching eyes. The sound of feet grinding into the gravel came closer.

She held herself rigid, afraid to breathe, taking tiny steps toward the lights and the party. Each step in the gravel shouted her location. She paused at the end of the sculpture. To reach the stairs, she would have to step into the open. Her heart thundered in her eardrums.

"Grayce?" Davis walked down the stairs, looking into the darkness. "Grayce, is that you?"

"Davis." Her voice was barely audible over the throbbing in her head.

"I've been looking for you."

She walked toward him and the deck. She didn't turn around to see if anyone followed her, ready to grab her like last night. A shiver wracked her body.

"What's wrong?"

When she didn't answer, Davis pulled her into his arms.

"Why are you out here in the cold?"

"I wanted to see the sculpture. Did you know it's called *Wake*, a metaphor for death?" She was talking fast, trying to gather her wits, trying to control the feelings of shock that replayed from last night.

"Grayce, are you okay?"

She didn't want words, just his heat. She breathed in the scent of Davis and pressed her head against his chest.

A shadow moved in the right corner of her eye. On the path above them was Niles Olsen. She had panicked and hid from the chaplain. Her nervous system had imploded. Her defenses were fried, as if someone had failed to flip the safety switch.

"You're freezing. Let's get you inside," His voice was jagged, tender.

"I don't want to go back to the party. Can you take me home?"

"Are you upset about Toni? Is that why you came outside, why you want to go home?"

Why did he mention Toni? Was she another one of his ex-girlfriends? Did he know Toni was involved with the assistant chief?

She knew the adrenaline pumping through her made her giddy because she wanted to laugh out loud. She wished her problems were as mundane as an ex-girlfriend, instead of violent assailants and visions of scars.

Rubbing her face against Davis' chest, she talked into his shirt. "I just needed some air. Truly. Toni wasn't my reason for leaving."

"Toni and I…"

She felt his chest move with each breath. She kept her arms wrapped around him, wanting to hold on to solid Davis, hold onto his integrity and decency.

"Uh, we did consider dating but there just wasn't a connection… for me."

She didn't want to talk about Toni, but it seemed Davis did. She wanted to tell him about last night, about the fear crushing her. "She's seems perfect for you. She's your type."

"My type? What does that mean?"

"She's your size, strong, and she obviously likes danger."

Laughter burst out of him. His warm breath rustled through her hair. "Your size fits me perfectly." He pulled her against him. "You're the dangerous one with your softness." He kissed her eyelids, her cheeks, her jaw. He spread kisses along her neck, kisses that skidded and skimmed over her cold skin, heating her.

"I'm going to disgrace myself if we stand like this too long," He chuckled.

She loved the lightness in his laughter. His enjoyment made the darkness fade in the starlit night. She pressed her lips into his, wanting a taste of him.

He tightened his grip. His tongue invaded her mouth, searching, possessing. She kissed him back, moaning into his mouth. Davis' hands came down her back, squeezing, lifting her against him. She wasn't cold any longer.

"Get a room." The shout from a firefighter on the deck jolted her away from Davis.

"Hell… those adolescent bastards."

She must be in shock. She had been kissing Davis in front of the entire fire department's holiday party.

"Grayce, I didn't mean to embarrass you. I only meant to warm you."

"Well, I'm definitely not cold now."

"Let's get out of here."

They climbed the stairs. Davis put his arm around her, anchoring her next to him. The men disappeared from the deck. At least the boys showed some discretion.

She cringed. "I don't want to go back in there, not now."

"It's my fault."

"Davis, it was mutual."

"Don't look at me like that or I might have to start kissing you again. Right here in front of all the windows."

"Now that the entire fire department has seen us, why not?"

He laughed, his mouth wide open, the lines around his eyes crinkled, the strain gone from his face.

"Let's walk around the building and go through the entrance to get our coats. I don't trust the guys. They never miss the chance for a practical joke."

CHAPTER THIRTY-FIVE

"Can I make you tea? Coffee?" Grayce tried to sound nonchalant but her voice quivered with the question. Davis' six foot broad frame and male force overwhelmed her tiny kitchen. Little trills of anticipation hummed low in her stomach.

"I'll have whatever you're having." His manner was relaxed, but she felt the tension radiating off his body, igniting white sparks of awareness in her.

He inspected the photos covering the refrigerator. Napoleon was wrapped around his feet.

"These all your patients?" He seemed genuinely impressed.

"Yes."

"And who's the Chinese man?" He pointed to a picture of her and Dr. Zao in China.

"He's my acupuncture mentor."

"He doesn't look like a veterinarian."

"No, Dr. Zao only treats people."

Davis looked down at his feet. "Do you think Napoleon's comfortable with me now?"

Her cat wasn't the least bit nervous around Davis. He rubbed against Davis' leg, leaving marmalade-colored hairs all along the cuffs of his black pants.

"I would say he's ready." They weren't speaking only about Napoleon.

"He's gigantic. Is he a special breed?"

Davis bent down and rubbed Napoleon's head. The cat, not in the least bit shy, stretched on his back and allowed Davis to stroke his generous stomach.

"He's a Maine Coon cat, one of my first patients."

Davis peered up at her. "What was wrong with him?"

"Oh, he's never been sick."

Napoleon's purr revved up to small motor boat volume. Davis continued to rub the cat.

An odd half smile came to his lips. "I'm jealous."

"You're jealous?"

"How did he get to be your roommate?"

She laughed. He didn't laugh. He closed the space between them, his eyes hot and predatory. "I think he's one lucky guy," His voice was gravelly.

His intense stare caused her to lose her concentration. "Uh, I guess…" He stood so close she could smell the lime in his scent. Warmth spread through her, pooling in sensual heaps of heat.

"How did Napoleon come to live with you?"

"His elderly owner asked me to take Napoleon if he died. I couldn't say no."

"Saying no is hard for you, isn't it?"

"I guess." His nearness scattered her thoughts. "How could I say no? I liked Mr. Johnson a lot."

"That's my point."

She was having trouble following the conversation. "What point?"

"I know you don't like to hurt people. Don't worry about disappointing me tonight, if you've changed your mind."

His breath rushed fast and hot against her cheeks.

"If you want to wait, I'm okay but once I start kissing you, I'm not sure I can stop."

Her heart accelerated pulsating to every pressure point. She had never met a man like Davis. He didn't want her to feel pressured, to feel she couldn't say no. She could see the dark grains of stubble on his chin, his chest rising and falling with an uneven force.

"I haven't changed my mind."

He let out a shaking breath. "Now, I'm worried about disappointing you."

Her heart expanded, danced. Davis, the tough, invincible male, showing his vulnerability. "Davis, you could never disappoint me."

His calloused hands held her face and his lips explored her jaw, nibbling playfully. He teased her ear, whispering how sweet she was and how much he wanted her.

She outlined his full lower lip with her tongue, tugging on the sweet fullness. She felt the hitch of his breath against her chest. Wrapping her arms around his neck, she explored his mouth with her tongue, searching.

He pressed her against the refrigerator. The cold metal against her back with the heat of Davis moving against her front sent waves of pleasure. She wanted to feel his skin, to touch all of him.

"Can we move to the bedroom?" His voice strained against her ear, his breath burning.

She took his hand and led him the five steps to her bedroom. He pulled her back and kissed her deeply, his tongue thrusting in and out, showing her what he wanted from her. She sucked on his tongue, pulling it deep into her mouth, pulling them both into passion.

"We've got to get out of these clothes," his voice came out as growl.

His hand had descended down her back, his finger working its way between the pulsating crevices.

"Let me light a candle." She walked to her bedside stand. She could hear him kick off his shoes.

He peeled out of his dress shirt. Black hair covered his chest and narrowed to a V above his belt buckle. His wide torso glistened in the shadows.

"Come here, Grayce. Let me help you get out of that little skirt—it's been driving me crazy all night."

"Really?'

"Did you see the way the men were staring at you? I thought at one point I might have to put my coat on you."

She ran her hands along his chest, exploring the wiry hair. The taut muscles flexed under her hands. His heart beat fast, furious against her palm.

He eased her sweater over her head, released her bra and began to caress her breasts. He squeezed her breasts hard, causing pleasure to shoot down between her legs. He explored each nipple, circling, rubbing them between his fingers. "Perfect."

He bent and took her breast in his mouth. Sensations streaked to the back of her knees, making it hard to stand. She ran her fingers through his hair, followed the curve of his neck, and back, feeling his heat and moisture.

He suckled her other breast. She held his head on her breast, wanting to keep him there, wanting more, wanting everything.

He lifted her off her feet and lowered her to the bed. "Do you know how long I've wanted you like this?" He gazed at her body, leaving a trail of sensations with his fervent look. "You're so damn beautiful."

The passion in his eyes and the huskiness of his voice made her squirm on the bed. She reached her arms to him. "Can you warm me like you did at the party?"

"Oh, I plan to more than warm you." He took off his pants, reaching in his pocket for a condom. He knelt next to her and began to place wet kisses along her neck, taking his time to search for the sensitive hallow behind her ear.

"Let's see. Where did I leave off?" Stretching next to her, he took her breast into his mouth, twirling his tongue around her nipple, sending shock waves of sensation through her. "I think I was right here."

His touch became urgent. He pushed his finger into her wetness and moaned her name, his breath rushed and frantic. She pushed against his hand, arching her back. He put a second finger in her and slowly imitated the rhythm to come. He maintained the same slow languorous rhythm as he sucked on her breast. She couldn't stop moaning and writhing, bucking her hips off the bed.

"Please. Davis," she first pleaded then commanded.

"I can't wait either." He lowered himself on top of her, holding all of his own weight with his arms. Nestled between her thighs, he slowly entered her, filling her. She tightened her hands on his back, pulling him closer and kissing him hard. His breathing accelerated, rushing in and out past her ear with each thrust.

"Grayce, I want to make this good for you."

His strangled words excited her. She wrapped her legs around him, pulling them both into the vortex swirling around them. Her desperate need drove them to a frenzied pace.

She held on to Davis, closed her eyes and got lost in the pleasure.

"You're so damn perfect." With one last thrust, his body wracked with his climax.

He lay on her, his body shuddering. She soothed the moist skin on his back, tracing each vertebra. She inhaled the salty, sweaty smell of Davis.

"I don't want to move. I want to stay right here but I'm squishing you."

She wanted Davis' body on top of her, filling her, heating her. She wanted this shelter, this feeling of security that nothing could ever go wrong, tomorrow would never come.

Davis rolled over and pulled her close to him. They gazed into each other's eyes, shocked by their intense lovemaking. He kissed her hair, her eyes, and then gently kissed her lips. "Pretty quiet. Are you okay?"

She laughed. "I'm in awe."

"Me, too. My fantasy didn't come close to the reality of being with you in the flesh, and oh what flesh." His hand caressed her hip, her thigh. "This is one of my favorite places, so soft, tender and this little hollow. I want to spend the night sucking on this supple flesh, to feel you shiver against me when I touch you here." His tongue probed and licked the space behind her ear. Her heart thrummed like a hummingbird.

"We were kind of in a rush but I promise you, next time we'll go slower." She saw the heat in his look. How could he already stir her feelings?

She snuggled deeper and turned on her side, pressing against his warmth and safety.

Disoriented and sore, Grayce rolled over. She looked straight into Davis' eyes. He was dressed and standing over her.

"Good Morning. I'm sorry I've got to get to work."

"It's Sunday."

They had spent the whole night in each other's arms, talking, between fierce and sweet lovemaking.

"Of all the worst timing." His tone was bemused. He bent down to kiss her. "I'm thinking maybe the guy on the wharf could wait."

He pulled back her covers, grinning. His face softened in the morning light. "I don't want to forget what you look like."

He was beaming, like a mischievous little boy. "What the hell? Are those bruises from me?"

She reached to pull back the covers.

Davis tugged back. "Let me see." He touched her shoulder and rolled her gently to her side.

"This isn't from last night. What happened to you?"

This was the moment she had tried to prevent by turning off the lights and lighting candles. This was the moment when she should tell him. He probably was used to threats on his life, but she wasn't. The words and the rage of the man were branded into her brain.

"I tripped on my stairs when I was working late on Friday night." The rehearsed words came out easily. But her body shuddered with the memory of her dark descent down the steps.

"You could've been killed."

The thought of the man dangling her over the steps brought the same tingling behind her knees as before she fell. The knot in her stomach twisted.

He sat on the bed next to her. "I'm sorry. I didn't mean to scare you. But you must've been in pain." His eyes held concern.

She was tempted to blurt out the truth. Tell him everything, including her suspicions about his boss.

"Why didn't you tell me last night?" Patches of red streaked across his cheeks. "Were you in pain? You know we could've waited."

"I wasn't in pain last night. I was…" Her face started to heat too. "Honestly, I forgot."

He leaned forward, trailing his finger, followed by his kisses along the bruises on her shoulder. "Last night was amazing. You're amazing Grayce Walters."

"Ditto, Ewan Davis." She felt cherished this morning. Last night was more than sex for her and she hoped for Davis, too.

"I hate that I have to leave. I want..." His knuckle brushed on the underside of her breast. Her breast began to swell with his touch. His breathing got rough, loud. He stood and pulled the covers over her. "I mean it when I say I can't resist you."

His laugh was delicious to her ears.

"You're covered in bruises and I can't stop wanting you. I better not even start or I won't leave." His face flushed with color again.

She would never not want Ewan Davis.

"Why do you have to meet on Sunday?"

"The guy I met in Georgetown yesterday gave me a lead. He saw two men in leather coats go into Shed 4, late at night. They drove a black SUV and loaded it with crab crates. I wanted the guy to do a sworn statement but it made him so paranoid I let it drop for now. He really believes someone might come after him. It's strange."

"Why is it strange?"

"The guy's bigger than I am and one rough dude. He didn't strike me as someone who would be easily intimidated."

Even with the heat of Davis pressed against her thigh, she got cold, bone cold.

"I called the guy from the port and told him I wanted to look into a few sheds, with no one around. Nothing official, of course. If I had known about last night, well, if I had known..." He waggled his eyebrows. "I definitely wouldn't have planned this for early Sunday morning."

Her mouth was dry. "Will the assistant chief be there?"

"The brass don't work on Sunday."

Grayce touched Davis' hand. "There's something about that man I don't trust."

"He was baiting me. He was trying to get to me by hitting on you. He has no respect for women."

"It felt like more than harassment." She wanted to tell him about the scar and her suspicions, but it wasn't a simple conversation. Davis was in a rush and she needed time to explain. This morning or any morning wouldn't be the right time. And she didn't want to ruin last night's magic. She wanted to savor the delight of being loved by Davis.

"I need to get going." Davis pressed his warm lips to hers. "What are your plans for the day?"

"James and I have lunch together on most Sundays. I listen to his salacious description of his Saturday night at the clubs."

He brushed her hair away from her forehead. "Are you going to describe your salacious Saturday night?"

"I'll report it was like most of my Saturday nights, nothing out of the usual."

The relaxed lines around his mouth and eyes vanished. He straightened, pulling away from her.

"I'm joking. You know that, right?" She pulled on his hand bringing him closer.

"I've just been with…" His tone got low. "You're so different."

She rubbed the skin on his hand with her finger. "I'm not planning to share any details about last night. It was our night."

"This isn't about one night."

She pulled the sheet up around her neck.

Davis smiled. "I'll call you later. And you can tell James my intentions are honorable." He walked out of the bedroom humming.

CHAPTER THIRTY-SIX

Grayce grinned at James when he arrived at the restaurant. She couldn't stop smiling after her night with Davis.

James unwrapped his black cashmere scarf and scanned the café, making sure everyone noticed his entrance before he sat. "You look like hell. What happened?"

"I do? I don't feel bad."

James' thick lashes veiled his close inspection of her face, hair and lips. He bent around their little table to look at her body.

"Honestly, James. What is the matter with you? I'm wearing the same blue jeans."

"You did it!"

"What?"

"You did, don't deny it."

She giggled. She seemed to be doing a lot of smiling and giggling. A passionate night with Davis had turned her into a giddy teenager.

"After the party last night, his place or yours?"

"Mine."

"God, give me more details. What were you wearing? The little black dress from Helene?"

Shivers of pleasure skittered along her spine with the memory of Davis unzipping her skirt.

James gestured, raising his hands toward the ceiling. "Why didn't you call me? I'm so good at seduction dressing." No topic could make him happier. She could imagine James, during an earthquake, his condo shaking, pausing for the appropriate disaster fashion statement before rushing to safety.

"I wore a skirt, turtle neck and my Stuart Weitzman boots. And I didn't plan to seduce Davis."

"A turtleneck? That proves it."

"Proves what?"

"The man's in love."

Her stomach plummeted and rolled, the sensation of falling out of your seat, tumbling into space during the rollercoaster's loop-to-loop.

He leaned across the table and beckoned with his index finger. "Come on, give Jamesie some details."

She and James had shared years of intimate sex details. Well, James's had shared them. She wasn't going to discuss her night with Davis. It was too new, too private.

"There aren't many details to share. What can I say? We left the party early and Davis drove me home and came in."

James twirled his mustache as if he were a villain in a silent movie. "Came in? Yes, he did."

"James." He usually couldn't shock her with his coarse comments.

"Okay, okay, just a tiny tidbit. Something to whet my imagination about the gorgeous firefighter. Is Davis as hot as he seems?"

Her face burned from the memory of Davis' intense lovemaking.

"The color of your face, my God, its crimson. I've never seen you like this, such a glow; you either had a facial by Yugaslava or fantastic sex."

She pressed her hands to her cheeks.

"You're in love."

"Love after one night?" She thought of her intimate night with Davis—the laughter, the teasing, and the non-stop talking. Last night was more than sex, it was sweet sharing.

"Oh honey, after one long night, you know. I see it in your eyes. I might not be the intuitive, but I'm the expert about love if you consider how many times I've been in love. You're a goner. Admit it."

"Well, maybe a little bit."

James placed his hand on hers, his dark eyes glistened with tears. "Davis is a lucky guy."

"I'm not sure he'll think he's lucky, when I tell you what's been happening."

She described the man attacking her, dropping her down the stairs. For once in his life, James didn't joke. He listened during her description of the vision of Maclean's scar and the sculpture garden. His jokes would come later.

"What am I going to do? I hinted to Davis about Maclean and he thought I was offended by Maclean's sexist attitude."

"Darlin', you've gotta tell Davis."

Her entire body tightened, sending spasms of pain from her fall down her shoulder to her arm. "I can't."

"He'll understand."

"What makes you so sure?"

James ran his fingers through his hair, lifting the thick curls into a tousled GQ look. "How can he not believe you? You're the most sincere person I know."

"It has nothing to do with my sincerity. Davis was an investment banker and now he's an investigator. The man believes in facts."

"Men in love are more open, accepting. It's why I love falling in love every other week." He raked his hair one last time, achieving the perfect finished style.

The idea of Davis in love skidded along her nerve endings. Scintillating pricks of pleasure skipped along her skin.

It didn't matter. Davis wouldn't discount his logical world because of his attraction for her. He wouldn't accept that Mitzi communicated images to her. She had moments of not believing it herself.

"It won't work. He values logic. Nothing about my abilities can be understood with deductive reasoning."

Davis would never believe in her ability to protect him, the power that set her apart from others and made her steadfast. He would only see her five foot, 90 pound body.

"If I tell Davis, he'll rush in and they'll kill him. I can't believe I'm saying it out loud but it's true. I need to protect him in my own way. It sounds crazy, but that's how I feel."

It was time to use her abilities for something other than healing sick animals. She didn't have the physical prowess of Davis and Toni. Her strength came from an inner power.

James reached across the table and patted her hand. "Honey, if you believe it. I believe it."

Their friendship had a lot of fluff and silliness, but it was their way of finding humor in their painful pasts. James had suffered under his father's brutal hand. Grayce didn't have scars like James, just bruising on her heart from losing Cassie.

"What's going to happen when Davis finds out? What will you tell him?"

"Maybe I'll never have to tell him. Maybe it's all in my imagination."

"Like the guy knocking you down the stairs or burning down the shed—that's all in your imagination."

"I need to protect Davis. It's all I know."

"I think you should tell Davis."

She shook her head. "I plan to tell him once I'm sure the assistant chief isn't involved. Can you see what would happen if I tried to tell him I saw a scar on his boss's arm from a vision from his dog?"

"When you put it like that, it does sound a bit flakey."

"Flakey? I think it would be called clinically psychotic."

James snickered.

"Will you help me?"

"I'll have to start working out." James pretended no interest in fitness, but he was a gym rat. After the years of being under his father's power, he would never defer to another man's force.

"How can I find out about Maclean?"

"I'll Google him. I might find something, but I doubt it. He has a position to uphold for the fire department. Didn't you say that Hollie is a computer whiz? Why don't you have her do a search?"

"Great idea."

"And we can follow him."

"Follow him?"

"While Hollie's getting the lowdown, we'll just tail him for a few days; see if he's up to something."

"Tail him, how?"

"I'll drive. You'll have to wear sunglasses and maybe a scarf, like Grace Kelly in *To Catch a Thief.* How about a wig?"

"You're kidding, right?"

"No," James answered with dramatic flair, his head thrown back with insouciance, as if the movie cameras were rolling.

"Okay, no Grace Kelly how about Angela Lansbury, or Miss Jane Marple?"

"This isn't a movie. This is real life."

I'll call the fire department at the end of the day and find out when he leaves his office and we'll follow him from work."

"God, you're scary."

James gave a wide unrepentant smile. "Thank you. I'd like to think so."

"Is it legal to follow someone?"

"Legal? Someone knocks you down the stairs and they want to kill Davis?"

"This is too crazy."

"Do you have another plan to get evidence that Davis will believe?"

"I haven't thought it through."

"Besides, I don't think it's illegal. How do all those private detectives do it in divorce cases?"

"I guess you're right."

"Are you going to involve Hollie in the sleuthing?"

"No. I've learned my lesson after Belltown. These guys are serious."

"So you're willing to risk my life?"

"James don't joke. You're the only one I can trust."

CHAPTER THIRTY-SEVEN

Davis checked his watch for the third time. Patience wasn't his strong suit. Five more minutes and he might explode. He had the urge to punch something or someone, preferably the someone who had the balls to break into his office.

"Lieutenant Davis, come in. Sorry to keep you waiting. I've been on the phone with reporters. The fate of the Alki is the story of the day. Hundreds have been protesting against junking the old fireboat." Ms. Ferette showed her sharp little teeth in imitation of a smile. "I know how busy you investigators are."

Davis had only spoken to Julie Ferette by phone. Her tailored suit, pearl necklace, and painted nails, the uniform of a bureaucrat, meant he was in trouble. Ms. Ferette wouldn't be easy to convince to deviate from department policy and procedures.

"No problem."

"There must be something important to bring you downtown. How can I help you?" There was another flash of spiky teeth.

"I need you to agree that everything I tell you will be kept completely confidential."

Ms. Ferette's eyes, heavy with painted dark lines, widened. Her expression resembled the surprised look of a raccoon caught in the act of pilfering from your garbage can.

"If I can." She ran her red nails on her cheek.

"My office was broken into last night. My computer was hacked. Pictures and the files from my current investigation were stolen."

She stiffened in the straight back chair. “How is that possible? Key cards are assigned for office access. Every entry and exit is registered.”

“I need the name of the guy who entered my office.”

“No one has access, but department employees.”

“Exactly.” He leaned forward, purposely crowding her. “I want this kept quiet. No one is to know.”

“I need to notify the chief and then the police.”

“Give me a little time before you bring everyone in. Let me get to the guy before he can cover his tracks.”

Her little teeth gnawed on her lower lip.

He pitched his voice low, suggesting every bureaucrat’s worst fear. “It’ll save the department a public scandal and prevent a lot of questions about your security system if I bring the guy in quietly.”

“I’ll get my IT person on it.”

“Call this number. It’s my cell. Once you give me the name, you can do whatever you need to do.”

Ferette let out an exaggerated breath. “This is most irregular. I’ll need to…uh…”

“Just give me the guy’s name before you report him. I’ll be happy to report to the chief once I’ve nailed his sorry…. Thank you. I appreciate your help.”

Ferette stood. “Forms will need to be filled out.”

“I’m used to paperwork.”

Davis proceeded down the hill to Pioneer Square. Someone with access to the department’s server had rifled through his office and removed the shed files and pictures. The perp hadn’t known the FI’s procedure of uploading all fireground pictures onto a disc.

The file contents were routine, with one exception. It contained Grayce’s personal information. Had they stolen the file for the information about her? How could he warn her to be careful and report anything suspicious without frightening her?

He needed to report the break in to the chief and discuss when to bring in the feds for the possible drug smuggling. But when he spoke with the chief, he would lose control of the investigation. He wanted the bastard's name before he turned over the case. The bottom line—he wasn't going to trust Grayce's safety to the feds, to strangers.

Davis stopped in front of his building. How was he supposed to greet everyone, when they were all suspects? He felt the tick of his tightly clenched jaw.

Everyone in the department knew he would be able to track the key card owner. Either he was dealing with a skilled idiot or a mastermind.

CHAPTER THIRTY-EIGHT

Davis lifted Grayce's hand from his chest and kissed her palm. She draped an arm and a leg over him as if to shield him, sighed and slept on.

His plan had been to invite her for dinner and then warn her she might be in danger. He wasn't going to tell her about the break in. He didn't want to alarm her, just make her aware that the investigation had heated up. Things could get nasty. Instead, they had eaten a snack in bed after amazing sex.

He peeled himself out of her embrace. She mumbled something, then reached for him without waking. He had considered putting some distance between them until the investigation was finished. Who was he kidding? He couldn't stay away from her. And besides, he could protect her if she were close-by.

Mitzi slept at Grayce's feet and didn't stir when he left the room. Mitzi had made her loyalties clear. She hadn't left Grayce's side.

Davis sat on the couch with his laptop and studied each fire scene picture. Someone had found them threatening. The first time the pictures disappeared he had thought it was a technical glitch. When the pictures disappeared a second time, he started to get suspicious.

"Davis?"

Grayce stood in the doorway wearing his shirt. Mitzi stood behind her. A surge of possessiveness hit him in the gut. He wanted Grayce Walters to belong to him and only him.

"How long have I been asleep?" She stretched her arms over her head. He watched his shirt hike up to reveal her thighs, high enough to tantalize, high enough to cause heat to pool under his clothes, under his skin.

"Three hours."

"Wow, I was really out. I had no idea I was so tired."

"My fault. I didn't plan on a workout when I invited you for dinner."

A patch of red appeared on each cheek. A woman who blushed, a woman with no artifice. How had he gotten so lucky?

"Are you working?"

"I was." He stood. He wanted to go back to bed and do all the things they had done to each other and more. Desire drummed through him in a slow, steady beat. With her hair sleep-tousled around her shoulders, she looked like the cover of Maxim, like every hot-blooded male's fantasy.

He pulled her into his arms. She smelled of lemon and warm, sleepy woman.

"Are you hungry?"

"I am, but you keep working. I'll fix something."

"I'm hungry too." He leaned down, taking bites of her earlobe, nipping at her neck. "So tasty."

He started to remove her shirt when her stomach growled loudly.

"I guess I'm pretty hungry."

"I did promise you dinner." He pulled her by the hand to the kitchen. Her fingers linked with his felt right. The two of them felt right. It was strange to have the roles reversed. Women always brought up to the topic of commitment at this point. For the first time, he wanted to have the *c-word* discussion.

"More wine?" Their unfinished second bottle of wine sat on the counter.

"That would be great."

"There's still salmon. Can I reheat it?"

"I like it cold."

"Sit down. Let me serve you."

"I can help."

"I like taking care of you."

"Your dinner was great."

"I can do steaks and salmon. Sprinkle with a rub and grill. Quite the gourmet."

Grayce moved next to him and cut the bread. She fed him a crusty piece. He licked her fingers one by one. He was as winded as if he had climbed to Camp Muir. He rested his chin on her head, trying to regulate his breathing. Mitzi got up and nosed her way between them.

Grayce asked, "What do you want, girl?"

Mitzi held her nose in the air and sniffed.

"Davis, do you give Mitzi bread?"

Mitzi yelped.

"I feel bad if she's not eating when I'm eating."

Mitzi gazed up at Davis, her dark eyes beseeching.

"I swear she knows I feel guilty."

Grayce cut a small piece and gave it to Mitzi. "You're such an actress."

Mitzi licked Grayce's fingers. He and Mitzi both had the same need to taste Grayce.

"Do you want salad and salmon?"

"I'll have both."

"For such a small woman, you sure can pack away the food."

"I burned quite a few calories tonight."

The heat started to gather under his skin again. "Should we eat at the table for a change?" He liked making her blush. He carried the wine and glasses.

Grayce searched in the cupboard for the plates. "Davis, I didn't know you carried a gun."

"I don't usually."

"Why now?" Her voice sharpened.

"It's the reason I wanted you to come to dinner."

"To show me your gun?" Her voice and eyes were lit with mischief.

Now, he was blushing.

Mitzi moved to lie under Grayce's chair. Grayce bent over and patted Mitzi, giving him an eyeful of her round luscious breasts. Desire drove through his body like the leader on a NASCAR racetrack. This need to keep touching, to get closer, to know someone intimately was new.

He leaned down, their faces close. “I can’t resist you, Grayce Walters. They’re going to have to put that on my gravestone. *The man who couldn’t resist Grayce Walters*.”

She ran her tongue over his lips. “I taste Merlot. Let me see if I can taste the salmon.” She pushed her tongue into his mouth.

An erotic thrum traveled through him. “Grayce I want…I want... ”

“I want it too. The feeling’s mutual, Davis.”

Grayce sat back in her chair and flipped the thick curls over her shoulder, looking young and innocent. “But first, tell me why you’re carrying a gun.”

Some bastard had access to Grayce’s home and work addresses. Maybe he should tell her.

As if Mitzi understood his need to protect Grayce, she placed her head on Grayce’s lap. Grayce spoke to the poodle in a low soothing voice. Mitzi nuzzled deeper. He and Mitzi did think alike.

Mitzi could stay with Grayce and guard her when he couldn’t be with Grayce. The poodle had already proven herself as a ferocious watchdog.

“You’re looking very serious.” Grayce sat up in the chair, putting her feet on the ground, her playfulness gone. “What is it, Davis?”

“Some interesting things have turned up about the shed fire.”

“Tell me.”

“Well, it’s mostly speculation, but I believe I’m onto something big.”

“The sheds are being used for criminal activity. I don’t think the fire was started by a fire bug as it was made to look. The Russian mob may be involved.”

“In Seattle?”

“When I searched the sheds on Sunday, one of the Port employees told me about the strange activities in the N-4 shed.”

Grayce leaned forward.

"The port employee went into the shed to leave paperwork for the renter. He found crab cases sitting out, unrefrigerated. It had him baffled."

"I don't understand."

"These guys aren't in the fishing business. There was something worth a lot more than crab in the boxes. My guess is drugs. I've been doing a little research. One of the major heroin routes from Afghanistan is through Russia to Alaska."

"Oh my God, if that's true..." She shot out of her chair. She began to pace in front of him. Mitzi sat at attention, watching Grayce.

"I was right. You're in danger. The guy who stabbed you was hired by the Russians. Remember? He had a strange accent." Her speech was fast, rushed.

"What are you talking about?"

"You're in danger. I knew it. And you know it. That's why you've started carrying a gun."

How in the hell had she turned the conversation to him? "I'm not worried about my safety. My job is dangerous."

She stopped pacing and stood over him. "James, Hollie, and I went down to Belltown to ask questions about the guy who tried to stab you. We found out that he wasn't a street person, he had an accent and smoked foreign cigarettes. Don't you see? He's Russian and was hired to kill you."

His entire body clenched. Anger and fear beat through him. He shoved his chair back. "You went to Belltown? Looking for the crazy guy?"

Grayce backed away. "I knew you'd be upset. I tried to tell you. You wouldn't believe me."

"I am upset." The vein in his temple pulsed as if it was about to burst.

He took a deep breath. "I can't believe you would put yourself in danger after you saw what that guy was capable of."

"We weren't in danger. We only asked questions. I would've gotten more information, but some guy tried to harass us. James had to use his karate."

"What?" He was going to explode, like the shed after its big blast. "James had to fight someone off?"

Mitzi now stood in front of Grayce shielding her from his wrath.

"The guy wanted to pick a fight. James knocked him down."

"Listen to yourself. Why did James have to use karate if you weren't in danger?"

He had worried about frightening her. What a joke. She and her friends had gone out searching for suspects. Mitzi lay back down.

"This isn't a game. This isn't some damn TV show." He heard her quick intake of breath.

"You think I'm doing this for entertainment?"

He had never seen Grayce angry. Her green eyes darkened to the color of the granite in his kitchen. Her chest heaved in and out. Always calm and centered, his little animal healer's face was red, red hot. "How absolutely unfair. I was trying to help."

"By getting yourself stabbed?"

"I know how to defend myself."

"God damn it, Grayce. You're a veterinarian."

Mitzi's head came up in alert. Even his dog was on Grayce's side. He could see the tears of frustration pooling in her eyes. He reached for her. She turned and walked to the bedroom. Mitzi followed her. This was just like with his sisters. Women stuck together.

"You don't need my help. I forgot you're the invincible man."

He shouted, "Grayce, come back."

Her eyes widened. She stood straighter, spreading her feet apart. He recognized the stance for what it was. He had seen it enough with the punks who started fires. Grayce would argue with him before backing down.

"I'm sorry. I didn't mean to shout. Please, can we talk about this rationally, calmly?"

Their breathing was the only sound in the room.

His nerves whirred, giving him an edgy, out of control feeling. "This investigation might get dangerous. I want to make sure nothing happens to you."

She dropped her hold on the door. Mitzi lay back down at Grayce's feet.

"Why would you ever take such a risk?" He shook his head. "I just want you safe."

"You don't understand, Davis. I feel the same. I don't want anything to happen to you."

"You don't?"

She stepped away from the door and touched his arm. "Wasn't that what tonight was about?"

"Tonight has been perfect, but the idea of you going to Belltown." He felt himself getting agitated again.

"You didn't believe me. I knew the guy was more than a drug addict."

"You might've been right. But you still shouldn't go looking for trouble. Grayce, those guys kill without flinching."

"I understand. But the guy James kicked was like the kids at Teen Feed. He was mean, angry at the world but not dangerous."

He pulled her into his arms. "Promise me you'll stay out of it." Her body stiffened against him. "You need to tell me when you have any suspicions and I'll do the investigating."

"I tried to tell you and you didn't believe me. I told you the guy was hired to stab you and you laughed."

When she had told him about the assailant, he had thought she was distraught. He kissed her hair and held onto her tightly, wanting to keep her in his arms. "I stand corrected. I didn't listen to you, and I should've. But I'm still not convinced you're right."

She tried to pull out of his arms.

"Okay, okay. Listen to me. If drugs are involved, this investigation will get treacherous. I don't want you involved."

Grayce ran her hand along his chest as he had seen her do with Mitzi, trying to soothe him. And it seemed to be working. "I know you have great instincts. Let me pursue the criminals. Can we agree on that?"

Her hand had stopped and one finger jabbed at his chest. "You need to promise to listen to me."

He bent down and captured her finger and brought her palm to his lips, brushing, caressing the soft surface of Grayce. "I'd do anything for you. Don't you know?"

She twined her arms around his neck and pulled him down. "I know—it's the way I feel too."

"Before we get to the making up part, let's settle on something. I want Mitzi to stay with you. She's proving to be an incredible guard dog. I'll feel better knowing she's with you."

Mitzi sat up and nuzzled Grayce's hand. He swore Mitzi understood every word he said.

"That's unfair, Davis. You know I could never hurt Mitzi's feelings by saying I don't need her. I'll agree if you'll have Mitzi protect you too."

Mitzi barked and jumped on Davis.

"Two women protecting me. Let the Russians come after me."

"Don't say that Davis. Please, don't say that. Promise me you'll keep Mitzi with you when you're working."

"Honey, I can take care of myself." If the other FI's could see him, promising his 90 pound girlfriend to let his poodle protect him, they would laugh their asses off. He would never admit it to the guys, but he liked the feeling that Grayce was worried for his safety.

"Mitzi is always with me or in the car. That's not hard. But I want Mitzi to be with you when you're at home or I can't be there. Agreed?"

Grayce did a half nod.

"You haven't said the words," he said.

"I'll keep Mitzi with me. Does that make you happy?"

"It does make me happy. He pulled on her hand and backed toward the bedroom. Now, can I make you happy?"

Grayce bent down and whispered to Mitzi. "Your job is to keep him safe when I'm not with him. Understood? It's not over."

CHAPTER THIRTY-NINE

Grayce opened her desk drawer and reached for her hidden stash. The big gulp of warm Diet Coke helped quell her gnawing anxiety. She should be breaking the habit but today wasn't the day for self-improvement.

Last night she had jumped out of the proverbial frying pan right into Davis' arms. She tried to justify not divulging her secrets. She had made him promise to listen to her observations. It was a beginning. How could she explain visions from his dog? Visions she didn't understand.

He promised to cherish her. But he had reacted badly after her visit to Belltown. How would he respond to her cover up of the attack and following his boss? Once her suspicions were substantiated, she would tell Davis everything. He deserved her full honesty.

Hollie knocked, then leaned her head in the door. "Diet Coke, Boss? What's wrong?"

Busted by an eighteen year old, and she thought she had hidden her indulgences so well. The end of all of her secrets loomed.

"Rasputin is here, and he's one very unhappy cat."

"Give me a minute before you bring that charmer in."

Grayce flashed on the Russian connection—maybe this was a good omen.

"I can't believe we're doing this." Grayce stared at the long line of cars ahead of them.

"God, I hate I-5." James eased his red Beamer into the northbound merge lane. "The one time I'm legal in the carpool lane, and I'm stuck tailing Davis' boss. Grayce, you and Mitzi better be right about Maclean."

"James, it's a hunch, just a hunch." She didn't have any way of processing her other world information into a practical approach.

"Definitely beats Monday night football," he said.

"This is insane. We're following an assistant chief on a vision from a French poodle?" The sensible thing would be to disclose the threats, the visions, and her premonitions to Davis. She had been down this path after Cassie's death and she didn't want to repeat the painful experience.

"Would you be happier if it were from a pit bull? How about a Rottweiler? Any messages from Chihuahuas lately?"

This wasn't the first time her inner world collided with the workings of the outer world, but it was the first time Grayce needed to use her inner world abilities to protect a human and she wasn't sure how to proceed.

"Okay, this is crazy. You should be home with your hot new boyfriend. Is that what you want me to say?"

"Yesterday, following Maclean sounded pretty reasonable. Now, it feels too weird."

"Honey, stop. What do you want to listen to? Pretend we're on a road trip. Remember the time we went down the Oregon Coast." James began to run through the music selection on his I-phone.

"James, please watch the road. Let me pick the music."

"No way, I'd have to listen to some soothing flute music."

Grayce willed herself to relax and leaned into the leather seats. "What did Hollie tell you while I was seeing my last patient?"

"Maclean lives in Magnolia, with a wife, a son, and daughter. The picture she found was from years ago, looked like a 1950's "Leave it to Beaver" perfect family. Republican, hates gays."

"You got that all from a photo?" She asked.

"Everything but the Republican."

"Where was the picture of him from?"

"*Seattle Times*. He was receiving a citizenship award from the mayor."

"That isn't helping."

"Oh my God!" James shouted.

"What?"

"Praise the Lord. Traffic is moving."

James turned up Madonna's *Express Yourself* and began to gyrate. This felt like a usual car trip with James, except for the fact they were spying on one of Seattle's most model citizens. James trailed several cars behind Maclean's green Ford Explorer. Like most commuter evenings in Seattle the freeway looked like something out of B-movie with everyone trying to escape a city taken over by space invaders or Godzilla.

"Is he going to take a ferry?" James asked when they approached the Whidbey Island Ferry exit. "No ferry."

"What if he's heading to Vancouver? We're not going to follow him all the way to British Columbia. Let's agree to stop at some point," Grayce said.

James continued to move side to side, dancing. "The Outlet Mall. I knew this evening would turn out great. We'll stop at the mall. I've only been there once, but you can find some great deals." James tweaked her knee. "Come on, admit it, you love to shop."

"You know I hate to shop."

"Let's find you some sexy underwear for your next date. How about red for the firefighter?"

She felt the familiar flush on her cheeks. "I guess I could look around."

"When will you be seeing the hunk again?"

"I'm making dinner for him on Thursday. He made me dinner last night."

"Gorgeous and cooks. God, the guy's a keeper."

"He doesn't really cook, he grills."

"He wanted to lure you to his place to have his wicked way with you." James raised his eyebrows. "No matter what, we've got to get you some new lingerie."

The traffic thinned when they got past Everett.

"My God, he's actually going to the Outlet Mall."

She was in no mood to be amused. Spying on Maclean, spying on anyone felt wrong.

James followed Maclean down the curving exit. They were two cars behind. She slid down in her seat, trying to hide. There was a long line of cars, all waiting to get to the destination discount shops, Tulalip Casino, and a high-rise hotel.

"The Tulalips developed the American dream—gambling, entertainment and discount shopping. Did you hear me say the part about discount shopping?" James was almost drooling.

"The revenge of the modern red man on their invaders," she said.

"Grayce Walters, I'm shocked. You almost sounded cynical and completely politically incorrect. You sounded like me."

"I wasn't criticizing the Tulalip Tribe. They're known to be very generous, donating a lot of money to charities."

"He's turning into the casino parking lot." James said.

They followed Maclean to the parking lot of the gigantic brick casino.

"So let's take bets. What do you think he plays?" James asked.

"Roulette, Black Jack?" She asked.

"Looks like the assistant chief is a gambler," James said.

"I was having trouble believing he was a family man."

"He's getting out, taking off his officer's jacket. You stay in the car and I'll follow him," James said.

"What?"

"He knows you."

"I'm not letting you go in there alone. Something could happen," she said.

"Yeah, I can get a drink and lose some money. I think it's what usually happens at a casino." James turned off the car.

She put her hand on James' arm. "I'm going in. It's a big place. I can watch him without being seen. And if he sees me, I'll pretend I don't recognize him." Goosebumps of repulsion ran up and down her skin at the idea of being seen by Maclean.

James rolled his eyes, fluttering and flitting as only a drama queen can. "All right, Nancy Drew, let's go." He put his arm around her shoulders.

Entering the casino, she stepped into an alien world. The massive dark space flashed with shards of light, and vibrated with a repetitive sound and the low hum of voices. Music played in the background as if to the rhythm of the slots.

The place was mobbed on a Monday night. Lost in a world of immediate gratification, hordes of dazed women and men played the shiny machines. Grayce felt breathless, claustrophobic. The energy in the room was suffocating, desperate.

Maclean walked directly to the back of the deep building. His step was purposeful. He had been here before.

"Let's go see where he's headed," James said.

They walked slowly, stopping, pretending interest in the slot machines that lined the room. Traces of smoke lingered.

James sniffed the air. "I forgot you can smoke here. I like these sleuthing jobs."

She couldn't keep up the banter. The tension of pursuing Maclean and the sensory overload of the casino had drained her.

As though sensing they were trailing him, Maclean turned and looked back. She slipped behind James, as James turned toward the wall with a disinterested expression and began to whistle. How lame! He was going to make them for sure.

When Maclean didn't rush them or angrily demand what they were doing, James zeroed in on their quarry again. "He's going into the VIP room. Guess I'll be joining him."

"The what?"

"The room that separates the real men from the wannabes. It's just for the high-stakes gamblers."

"How are you going to get in there?"

"Through the entrance." James smiled down at her. "Go play the slots. If you sit right over there, you can keep an eye on me and Maclean."

"But what are you going to do?"

"I'm going to gamble, watch our man, see how much he bets. You know—the typical James Bond stuff."

She tried to think of an argument against his plan. She grabbed his arm. "James, don't talk to Maclean."

"The gamblers in the VIP room aren't in there to be social. Don't worry so much. Nothing's going to happen."

James prodded her, pointing her toward the slot machines that faced the exclusive lounge. "You can watch from there."

The monotonous noise of the slots and the artificial light disturbed her. The imbalance of energy in the gambling space and their pursuit of Maclean agitated her. "This feels wrong. I don't want you to gamble with Maclean."

"Give me a signal and I'll come out. Honestly, I'll just play for twenty minutes, half an hour. Come on, you wanted to know about this guy. We're here. Let's do it."

James, impeccably dressed in a tailored pea coat, a cashmere scarf knotted at his neck, belonged in the VIP lounge. Her North Face polar fleece and ponytail clearly said slots.

She didn't know if you had to buy tokens to play the slot machines. She sat at the machines which gave her a clear view of the VIP lounge. A gray-haired woman in white tennis shoes was settled in the same cluster of machines. Grayce peeled off her coat and sat down, avoiding eye contact with the older woman.

"Gonna try your luck with that one, Darlin'?" The older woman's hoarse voice cracked with a hacking cough.

"Going to try." Grayce inspected the machine. Did it come with instructions?

"You a virgin?"

Had the woman just asked her if she was a virgin?

"Never played before?"

Was she that obvious?

"Just put in your money." The woman leaned over to point to the lever.

Grayce could see the woman's pink scalp through her silver blue hair.

"Pull the lever when it feels right. Listen to your inner voice."

"Thank you." She hoped this would finish the gambling tutorial. She looked up to check on James. He was in the VIP room and moving toward Maclean's table.

Grayce shook her head. "No, James. No." She waved, trying to get James' attention.

James turned toward her and nodded.

The older woman asked, “You say somethin’, Darlin’?”

“Just talking to my machine.” Grayce patted the metal contraption and smiled.

She focused on James’ pursuit of Maclean. He was about to sit next to Maclean. She kept shaking her head. How did she get into this absurd situation?

James took the only seat available. She nodded her head in approval. “Okay, James.”

“What Darlin’? My name ain’t Jane.”

“What?”

“You just called me Jane.”

Grayce suppressed a giggle. She put a token in the machine, turned and looked behind her. No one was there. She couldn’t rid herself of the nagging feeling someone was watching.

James, with a cigarette in his hand, leaned toward an expensively dressed woman. He smiled, his striking angles softened with laughter. Grayce watched the older woman with heavy diamond earrings, taken in by his charm. “Oh, James.”

“Darlin’, my name’s Betty, not Jane.”

Had she spoken aloud again? Maybe the noise in here was making her lose her mind.

James was talking to Maclean. When she got her hands on James, she would slowly strangle him. James laughed and slapped Maclean on the back. Maclean gave James a disgusted look.

She leaned forward, breathless. “James.”

The older woman muttered, “So young to be hard of hearing.”

“I’m just praying to St. James.”

Grayce then pointed to the exit. James gave her a slight nod and continued to play. His face was wreathed in a gigantic grin when he pulled the chips toward him. He had won. Her incorrigible friend gave her a thumbs up. She dropped another coin in her machine.

A rough-looking man in a black suit and black shirt leaned over James. Her heart thudded to a stop. The gigantic neck and grim countenance didn’t belong to a waiter. He took James’ elbow and pulled him up. James resisted.

"Please, James."

"You praying again?" Betty smiled at Grayce and then said aloud, "St. James give me a winner." Betty then pulled the lever on her machine. Coins poured out of the machine while bright lights flashed and loud, brash music played. "Thank you, St. James." Betty gathered her coins into her cup; her face flushed with excitement.

Grayce, distracted by Betty's win turned back to see James brush the burly man's hands off. James didn't appear to be the least bit intimidated. He took a drag on his cigarette, stubbed it out in the ash tray, turned and smiled at the older woman. Maclean, with a dark sneer, watched James.

The man whispered to the disgruntled James who had an insolent smirk. The man took James's elbow. James shrugged it off and walked out of the lounge. The bouncer grabbed James' elbow and led him toward the exit past Grayce.

"Sir, I don't want to hurt you. You need to leave, no trouble. Don't come back. We don't tolerate cheating in this casino."

"Cheating?" James yelled. A few people turned. Most watched the machines, oblivious to anything but their hopes spinning against the odds.

"Sir, you were counting cards. We watched you and your partner at the slot machines."

Her heart did a tailspin. She battled against her need to hide and her need to dash, to run to the nearest exit. Inching her way behind one of the machines, she searched for other exits. She wasn't going to wait to be escorted out.

"Get your hands off me, you big brute. You're wrinkling my Burberry." James' theatrical voice was heard over the din. He was enjoying the drama.

Unlike James, she didn't want any drama and she didn't want Maclean to see her being escorted out. She walked to the side exit, her body tense, her muscles clenched, ready for flight. The blue domed ceiling, painted in a *tromp l'oeil* underwater fresco with cavorting salmon at the exit didn't provide the intended relaxation. She felt like the salmon, soon to be caught and eaten by a grizzly bear.

She anticipated footsteps behind her, a hand on her shoulder. But no one stopped her. Walking into the night air, a young man in a red jacket approached.

"Ma'am, may I get your car?"

"No, no, thank you."

Where was James? Had they arrested him?

In the dim light of the parking lot, shadows danced around her. She crisscrossed the lot, as if searching for a lost car, in case anyone was watching her. The silence felt menacing after the metallic bings, boings and blips of the casino. She wound her way around the lot to the entrance of the casino. People stood in a line under the canopied entrance, waiting for the valet to return their cars, water fountains cascaded in front of giant cedar doors.

Her cell phone rang. Startled, she had to squelch a scream.

James's voice was harsh, "Where are you?"

"Are you okay?"

"I'm at the car."

She didn't need her intuition. James was upset. "I'm coming. I came back to the entrance to look for you."

She took a different route through the parking lot back to the car. She climbed into the Beamer. "I thought they were going to arrest us."

"Arrest us?" James sniggered coldly. "For what?"

"I don't know. They thought we were counting cards. Isn't that considered cheating?"

"Let's get the hell out of here." James swerved between cars in the parking lot.

She leaned back in the leather seat and tried to calm her friend. "Your nonchalance was priceless. And your line about your Burberry was great."

James stared straight ahead. She waited for James' theatrical replay. He turned up the music. Lady Gaga blasted in the car.

"Honey, tell me," Grayce pleaded.

"Let's get to Meow. I need to be with my people."

James sped south to Capitol Hill.

Tonight was another failure to gain evidence. All she had accomplished was to upset her friend. Twenty minutes later, they pulled up in front of James' favorite bar.

She placed her hand on his arm. “Once we go in there, you’ll be surrounded by your friends. Are you sure you don’t want to talk about it? It’s my fault you were there.”

“It isn’t your fault that some big geek tried to manhandle me.”

“But you looked so calm and cool.”

“I had years to perfect that calm façade. It was the way I pissed my father off. He wanted to see me get manly and fight back.”

“We shouldn’t have gone.”

“Having a goon grab me brought back a few bad memories. It’s no big deal.”

James had always hidden his childhood experience with snide, self-deprecating comments. This was the first time he had ever acknowledged how difficult it had been.

“James. I’m sorry.”

“There’s nothing to be sorry about. My father was a bastard, but I walked away from all of his bullshit years ago.”

“Oh, honey. He never deserved you as a son.” Grayce squeezed James’ arm. Shewanted to put her arms around him and hug him but James wouldn’t welcome such an open display of affection.

“Well, the good news is that he feels guilty now. He tries to buy me off.” James gave another hollow laugh. “It’s definitely a Grey Goose night and it’s your tab. What else could I ask for?”

CHAPTER FORTY

An unnatural cry jolted Grayce awake. Standing next to the bed, Mitzi howled an ungodly sound, the poodle pulled hard on Grayce's wrist with her open mouth. Grayce sat up in bed. Dense smoke obscured her vision; hot air burned her throat and her nostrils. Fire!

Mitzi gave another yank and then dropped to the floor and began to crawl on her stomach, directing Grayce to crawl, guiding her to safety.

She had to call 911. Her phone was in the kitchen.

Grayce reached in the drawer of her bedside stand for her most prized possession. Her fingers clasped Cassie's necklace. Quickly putting the heart shaped pendant around her neck, she dropped to her knees. The closest exit was the back door. The windows in the bedroom and bathroom were too small for an escape.

Mitzi gave another ghastly howl, impatient that Grayce wasn't moving.

The smoke was thinner on the ground. And the floor was cooler. She crept toward the door as she called for Napoleon. His loud meow came from the kitchen. So much for her instincts, she was the last one to recognize the fire.

Holding her breath, Grayce followed Mitzi, trusting the poodle. After a few seconds, she was forced to breathe in the acrid air; a violent cough rattled her body.

Grayce crawled into the kitchen behind Mitzi. She had planned to wet a towel at the sink to wrap around her face. But the temperature in the kitchen was unbearable, as if she had descended into the scorching gates of Hell.

Searing heat blasted across her face; she put her head down and followed Mitzi. It was a short distance to the back door. Napoleon, her loyal companion, pressed his body against her side. Grayce inched blindly toward the back door. She couldn't see Mitzi through the gray haze but heard her nails clicking on the wood floor.

Grayce took short panting breaths through her nose. Air-hungry and dizzy, she had to fight the need to lie down. She had to get them out of the house fast or they'd all die.

Mitzi barked a dozen times from the direction of the front door. Red flames shot out of the back door. Grayce changed direction and began the slow crawl to the front door. Napoleon was next to Grayce's head, shepherding his mistress out of danger.

The smoke grew thicker, weighing Grayce down, slowing her movements. Heat pounded on her back, on her bare feet as if she was walking on searing rocks. She stopped. It was a small house. How much farther to the front door?

Napoleon nudged against her head, getting her to move.

When Grayce and Napoleon got to the front door, Mitzi's barks turned frenzied. Grayce tried to marshal her strength to stand, to open the door. She was dizzy. The sound of shattering glass vibrated in the airless space and then a rush of cool fresh air.

Mitzi had jumped through the glass window next to the door. Grayce pushed Napoleon toward the jagged hole. The giant cat jumped outside. Mitzi and Napoleon were safe.

Mitzi barked insistently, giving Grayce instructions from the front porch. Didn't Mitzi understand she couldn't fit through the hole? She gulped the fresh air, pulling the cool air into her scorched lungs. It hurt too much to breath. Everything hurt. She needed to lie down and rest. Once she rested she would be able to stand, go through the door.

A man's authoritative voice came through the broken window. "Ma'am, stay down. We're coming in."

CHAPTER FORTY-ONE

Davis stretched on the cot at headquarters. He and Grayce had hardly slept last night. This was turning into the most insomniac shift of his career. He was going on close to twenty-four hours without sleep. He half-listened to the portable radio next to his bed. The radio was on the dispatch channel, the usual late night urban grumblings—suicide, chest pain, OD's.

Unable to sleep, he replayed his list of possible suspects in the department. He couldn't bring himself to accept that one of the FI's might be the perpetrator. His colleagues had the skill to burn the shed and had the clearance to access his office. But if the bastard wasn't an FI, it must be one of the brass. Once he went down that path, there was no turning back. Ferette should've gotten back to him. The delay was making Davis paranoid.

He yawned and closed his eyes. He started to drift. The chatter on the radio continued in the background. "House Fire."

The fire was in Fremont. Grayce lived in Fremont. The fine hairs on his neck lifted. He listened for the address.

Grayce's house was burning. His throat tightened and his chest constricted, the air squeezed out of him. A rush of adrenaline pumped through him, his heart sped, his senses heightened. He bounded out of bed.

They had spoken a few hours ago. Grayce would be asleep with Mitzi and Napoleon. He switched channels on the portable radio to hear the exchanges on site. He listened to the assessment of the first engine. The second engine was on its way. Pulling on his boots, he held his breath, afraid to miss a word.

"A large poodle and cat on the front porch, the dog is bleeding, looks like he jumped through a window. Owner must still be in the house, someone, restrain the dog, looks like it might try to go back in."

Davis swallowed hard against the bile rising in his throat. He was going to toss his guts.

"Okay, got a location... woman down... blocking the door...too hot... Need to vent before going in. Use the picture window. Get the pole."

He prayed for the first time since his dad died.

He couldn't stop panting. He took a deep breath. He took another breath. He knew the exponential growth of an unchecked fire. He knew the risk of inhaling hot fumes. He knew too much.

He ran to his car with his radio blaring about the arrival of the two ladders and the medic rig. In the background, orders were shouted. The different crews readied to fight the blaze.

Acute anxiety fired every cell, his entire being focused on the radio. He waited for word from the first team about Grayce's condition. He gripped the steering wheel, his body drumming for action.

He listened to the team decide whether the fire had reached a temperature too hot to allow safe entry before dousing. He knew that every second's delay diminished Grayce's chances of survival. His mind closed to that possibility.

He pressed his foot on the gas. At least at four am, there was no traffic back-up. He sped along the empty streets.

"I need the medic." The harsh voice echoed in the interior of the Suburban.

They had gone in and gotten Grayce. She was alive. They had removed Grayce from the burning house. *"Put her here. Let's move. She needs oxygen."*

"House's empty."

He clenched the steering wheel. He felt lightheaded with relief. He listened for more details of Grayce's condition. Nothing more was said. The medics with the oxygen tanks would've moved away from the fire. The focus of the firefighters was putting out the fire. He heard a voice in the background. *"Someone get the cat off the stretcher."*

His stomach had a rolling sensation as if he might lose his greasy dinner. Grayce was on a stretcher. Was she conscious?

He crossed the bridge, spotting the plume of smoke. He was primed, primed for battle.

His mind was in a storm of pure emotion. Rage and the desire for revenge surged—worthless emotions, but they fueled his body and mind. He wanted to kill whoever had torched her house. He'd bet every arson case he had solved that Grayce's house fire was no accident.

Davis veered off the street and pulled to a stop on the sidewalk. He jumped out and ran toward the ambulance. Great clouds of gray blended with the haze, turning early morning into dusk.

He ran between the rigs and around the ambulance.

Grayce sat upright on the stretcher next to the ambulance. Over her blackened face, an oxygen mask covered her mouth and nose. She was swathed in blankets, her hair hanging over the mask.

His heart slammed against his chest. He had never seen a more beautiful sight. Napoleon sat at the foot of the stretcher. The medics hovered nearby. Mitzi spotted him and ran out from under the stretcher. "Good work, girl."

He never slowed his pace toward Grayce. Her eyes opened wide when she saw him. She tried to smile, pulling her lips upward under her mask. He knew it took a lot of effort.

Henderson, one of the medics, greeted him, "Man, are we glad to see you."

He nodded to Henderson, but couldn't speak. He walked to the stretcher and touched Grayce's face. He brushed her hair away from her eyes. "Are you okay?"

She nodded and started to remove her mask.

"No, leave it on. You'll feel better."

Davis turned to Henderson. "Does she need to go to the hospital?"

"She refused to go. Her vitals are stable. She wasn't unconscious for more than a few seconds. She's keeping up her sat's, even off the oxygen. She has abrasions, but I didn't find anything else."

Davis never took his eyes off of Grayce while listening to Henderson's report. "Thanks, Henderson."

"Your dog needs to have her cuts cleaned, but she won't let me touch her. She wouldn't leave Dr. Walters or her cat. I've never seen such a connection."

Grayce, surrounded by her menagerie, was struggling with her mask. He bent over and helped her remove it. Her emerald eyes glistened with tears.

"Oh, Davis. Mitzi, If Mitzi and Napoleon... " She swallowed hard. Tears streaked down her soot-stained face.

He unbuckled her belt from the stretcher and lifted her into his arms. He wrapped the blanket around her and carried her to the Suburban. He had never seen her cry. He felt like he'd been hit with a wrecking ball. He almost doubled over at the pain of seeing Grayce's tears.

"I might've died if it weren't for Mitzi and Napoleon."

He tightened his hold, pressing her against his body. He wasn't ready to hear the truth.

"If it weren't for…"

He cupped her head against his shoulder. "It's finished. You're safe." He couldn't listen; cold rage coursed through him.

"No, he isn't done."

Davis stroked her hair. "It's okay. No one is going to harm you."

"I've got to treat Mitzi, she's got cuts. Put me down. I can walk."

"I'll take care of Mitzi. Let me take care of all of you."

Davis realized his focus had been only on Grayce. He turned his attention back to Mitzi and Napoleon. The poodle and gigantic cat had followed him, walking side by side. "Good work, Mitzi and Napoleon. I'm going to buy you steaks and fish. You're both going to have a feast."

Grayce's laugh was forced, brittle, as if she might start crying again.

"Everyone in the Suburban."

He loaded Grayce and the animals into the rig. A car pulled up next to the Suburban. Davis turned to see the chaplain jump out of his car. "Niles?"

"I heard it on the radio, and came over to see if I could help."

Niles didn't usually get called in the middle of the night.

"Is she okay?" Niles stepped toward the car window.

Instinctively Davis stepped in front of the door. "She's fine. Some bastard torched her house." His suppressed rage resurfaced. He needed to stay in control. Later, he'd take care of the bastard who had tried to kill her.

CHAPTER FORTY-TWO

Grayce started to roll out of Davis' bed but was stalled when Napoleon jumped on her chest. She ran her hand along his head. "Are you okay, big guy?" She stroked along his spine. "What an adventure we had. Did I tell you how brave you were?"

"No, you fell asleep before you got to tell me." Davis appeared with Mitzi close behind.

Last night, Davis had scooped her off the stretcher and brought her to his condo. She remembered his gentle touch while he bathed and fed her soup, and then held her in his arms until she fell asleep.

Mitzi put her paws on the bed and licked Grayce's face. "How are you, Mitzi? How are your cuts?"

Grayce sat up, then realized she was naked. Her breasts jutted above the black duvet. She reached to pull the gray sheet but couldn't budge Napoleon and Mitzi.

"I've brought you breakfast in bed, sleepy head," Davis' voice was husky.

"What time is it?" She pulled on the covers, dislodging the animals a few inches, and managed to sit with some modesty.

"11:30." Davis placed a tray on her lap. "How do you feel?"

"I've got to get to work." She tried to move. She was trapped by the animals and the tray.

"Today's a recovery day for you. I called Hollie. She's rescheduled all your patients, but she wants to talk to you about a cat."

Grayce leaned back against the soft gray pillows. Everything in Davis' condo was color coordinated in gray and black, definitely a designer's work. "Thank you." She was unaccustomed to having anyone take care of her. It felt both embarrassing and intimate.

"I don't have any clothes." She paused and took a deep breath. "Do I still have a house?" She must've been in shock; she hadn't even given a thought to her house. All she could think about was that someone wanted to kill her.

"Your house is standing. I just got back from assessing the damage."

"Is it bad?"

"Not bad, mostly water and smoke damage. The fire was started on your back porch. You're going to need a new back door and deck."

Her stomach lurched at the smell of the omelet and potatoes that Davis had prepared. "Hard to imagine that someone deliberately damaged my little house."

Davis sat next to her. "It's okay. We'll get through it." He pushed her tangled hair away from her face. "Today is an "R-and-R" day. Tomorrow, when you're rested, you can face that unpleasant job."

She could only nod. This couldn't be her life. She kept waiting to wake and find out it was another of her nightmares.

"I got you breakfast. I hope you're hungry." His tone was excited, enthusiastic for the breakfast he made. How could she disappoint him? She pretended a hunger she didn't feel.

Davis' upbeat mood, the comfort of Napoleon and Mitzi, and the strong Earl Grey helped lighten the gloom sitting in her stomach beside the omelet and fried potatoes. "The food was great. Thank you."

She sipped her tea, watching Davis wander around the bedroom. The art on the walls was bold geometric shapes in gray and black and color coordinated with the bedding. An early picture of his family on the bedside stand was the only personal piece. Davis' chubby five-year-old hand was intertwined with his mother's.

"What is it, Davis?"

He hovered closer. His gaze clouded, impenetrable. "Seeing your house this morning…" He patted the poodle who lounged next to Grayce. "I'm glad Mitzi…"

Napoleon stood and rubbed his head against Davis' thigh. "…And Napoleon… were there to protect you."

Davis blamed himself for the fire. He saw it as a failure on his part. He should have told her about his suspicions; he should have watched out for her. He had confessed all of this last night. She ran her hand along the side of his face and leaned forward to kiss him. "You'll get him."

He returned her kiss, gently running his tongue along her lips, tasting her. "Him?"

She didn't want to have this discussion not after last night. Didn't he need her as much as she needed him? She wanted comfort and to give comfort. "The man on the wharf, he started the fire at my house, too." She leaned forward to kiss him again.

Davis pulled away. "How do you know it was the same man?"

"He threatened me."

"What?" Davis' bellow reverberated in her ears. The animals scattered.

"What in the hell are you talking about, Grayce? I know who burned your house."

Davis towered over her. She rearranged the pillow behind her back, trying to ignore his outburst. "You know who he is?"

"I found out this morning. He broke into my office. He used to be a firefighter."

He crossed his arms across his chest. "Damn it, Grayce. Tell me about the threat."

"He knocked me down my office steps. He said if I told you, he would kill you."

Davis' eyes were locked on her, his chest moving in and out at irregular bursts. "What? The suspect threatened you, and you didn't tell me. I'm the investigator and your…" He rubbed his hand along his tightened jaw.

Every contorted, harsh line on his face warned her he was barely in control. "When exactly did my suspect assault you?"

"The night before the party."

His eyes narrowed on her, examining, exploring her face as if he didn't recognize her. The muscles in his jaw tightened and he spoke in a low, intense voice, a voice she had never heard before. "Start from the beginning and tell me every detail."

She adjusted the sheet, trying to cover herself. Mitzi pushed her cold nose under her hand.

"I was working late. He somehow got into my office building. When I came out, he grabbed me and held me near the steps."

She decided to spare Davis the details of the preceding chase. He was upset enough. She tried to sound nonchalant as if the retelling didn't affect her. But her mouth was dry and her heart thudded against her chest.

Davis stood with his legs braced apart, arms crossed on his chest.

"He told me to stop my snooping and said if I told you anything you would pay. I kicked him and then he dropped me down the steps."

The silence was excruciating. She played with the spoon on the tray. Davis' rage was palpable. She imagined his nostrils were flaring, like a stampeding bull.

"Why?"

"At first, I didn't know what to do. I didn't want him to harm you. I planned to tell you tonight when you came over for dinner."

Davis paced. His restlessness permeated the room.

"Why didn't you tell me sooner?"

"I wanted to, but I was afraid he would hurt you if I did."

"You didn't believe I could defend myself?"

His voice was caustic, but she heard the pain.

"He's violent. Look what he did to my house."

Davis exploded. "There wouldn't have been a house fire if you'd told me." He bent over her as if he was about to shake her. She leaned back into the pillows.

"If I'd known, I could've protected you."

She wanted to escape. With no clothes, she wrapped herself in the duvet and stood. "I tried to do what I thought was best." Her feelings had progressed from guilt to irritation. She was the one who had gotten knocked down the stairs and escaped a burning house. "Why can't you understand?"

Davis gave her a cold, piercing gaze.

"I wanted to tell you but didn't know how without putting you in danger."

"I need time, Grayce. With no sleep in two days, I don't have any perspective." Davis walked toward the door. Was he leaving?

"What are you saying?"

"I've jeopardized your safety by becoming involved with you. I'm a fire investigator and you're a witness who has been threatened and almost killed."

She squeezed the duvet between her fingers.

"If we weren't together, you wouldn't have tried to protect me. You would've called me about the threats."

"Davis, please stop."

"Obviously, you didn't trust me."

Grayce had no answer. She hadn't expected him to blame himself for all that had happened. Davis was right. She hadn't trusted him but it wasn't about the danger, it was about trusting him with the truth about herself.

"It's complicated."

"Not to me." He continued to stand at the doorway. "Are there any more revelations you'd like to share about my investigation?" He hit his chest with his fist when he said the word "my."

His brows were forced together and his lips hardened. He had himself in control, in icy cold control. "Grayce, is there more? Anything else you've decided I couldn't handle?"

What did she have to lose?

"Maclean isn't to be trusted."

"What?"

"I got a bad feeling when I met him. I've tried to warn you."

He strode back into the room.

"I've tried to explain to you that I sense things others don't."

Mitzi stood and came to her side.

"Right, you met the guy once. He's been with the force twenty three-years, and I'm supposed to suspect him?"

As she had always known, he wanted facts not intuition. She lifted her chin. "He's got gambling problems; he isn't the good guy you think he is."

Davis moved quickly toward her. "How in hell do you know that he gambles?"

His aggressive posture made her step back. "James and I followed him to a casino. He's a regular and plays for big money."

"You and James followed Maclean?" The room echoed with his shouting. Davis stood still, too still after his outburst.

It did sound preposterous. "We decided to follow him, to test whether my instincts were correct." She was glad she hadn't revealed the vision of the scar. Davis would've gone ballistic. "I'm not sure if he's mixed up with the fire, but he isn't what he seems."

Davis picked up a pillow from the floor and threw it on the bed. "The whole time we've been together you've been playing investigator, following some crazy intuition. You wanted the excitement of being with an FI."

She started to answer but something about the way Davis looked at her stopped her.

His face flushed and his voice was hard, rough. "What a joke. I thought you were different, we were different."

His shoulders were hunched; his hands opened and closed in a fist at his side, his voice barely above a whisper. "Let me see if I can I get this straight. You went to Belltown to look for a dangerous assailant, you were assaulted by a suspect, and you followed my boss. You did all of this without saying a word to me."

"I told you about Belltown and I was planning on telling you about the assault."

Davis didn't appear to hear what she had said. He moved toward the door then turned and faced her. "What kind of woman needs to interfere in a criminal investigation?"

She didn't have a quick answer, how to explain a lifetime of hiding her gifts.

"I can't do this, right now. I'm afraid I'm going to say something I'll regret." He reached for the doorknob.

"It sounds bad the way you put it but I want you to know—I did it because I care for you," Her voice quivered, "It might not be the way you would've handled it, but it doesn't mean it was wrong."

He turned toward her, shaking his head. "You should've told me the truth. I can't stand women playing games. Daphne lied for weeks about sleeping with my best friend."

She swallowed any apologies. He was comparing her to Daphne. If he couldn't see the difference, there was no hope for them. "Where are my clothes?"

"I'll get them. Where are you going?"

"Does it matter?"

"I need to know. You're a witness. Your safety is at risk."

"Bollocks. It was only when I was trying to protect you I got hurt." She could feel her face getting hot from the anger simmering under her skin.

"You got hurt because you thought you could solve the crime. How can someone so smart be so stupid?"

The heat blazed in her chest as if she were breathing the hot smoke from the fire, burning her insides.

"I'm sorry—I didn't mean that the way it came out." He moved toward her as if he was going to touch her.

She backed away. "Everyone says that after making a nasty remark."

Davis' jaw clenched and his words were tight, enunciated, "I want Mitzi to stay with you to protect you."

She bent and petted the poodle. "Sorry, girl, but I don't need you to stay with me."

Wrapped in the duvet, she walked toward the door, not looking at Davis. "The man accomplished what he set out to do. I'm intimidated and done investigating."

Pulling the cover tightly, she walked into the bathroom. She needed to get out of Davis' condo.

Davis followed behind her. "I want Mitzi to stay with you."

She turned back with her chin raised. She used the same carefully enunciated tone he had used. "Thank you but it just complicates matters. Contact me if there's anything about the fire."

She slammed the bathroom door.

CHAPTER FORTY-THREE

Davis bench-pressed the 245 pound bar, feeling the slow burn in his arms and heaviness in his chest—guilt and remorse over his total loss of control with Grayce.

Niles' suggestion this morning that he remove himself from the investigation "because his personal feelings were involved" didn't help his frame of mind.

He and Mitzi had run miles this morning, but he remained agitated, unable to sleep or stay in his condo. So, he tried to blot out his feelings by working out.

Maybe Niles was right and in this situation, he couldn't maintain the detached perspective required of an investigator.

He paused between reps, lying back on the bench, trying to regroup. His sweaty T-shirt stuck to his back and the bench. He couldn't shake the image of Grayce, getting into the cab with Napoleon in her arms, refusing to look at him.

He had been much too harsh. He had actually told her he was glad she was frightened. He still couldn't believe he had behaved like such a jerk.

His arms strained with each rep, his neck tensing. He relaxed into the blaze in his arms, the familiar pain was comforting—this was something he could control.

Did Grayce have any idea how close she had come to being killed? He would never forget finding her on the stretcher, gasping into an oxygen mask.

He rested. Only one set of reps left.

He thrived on order. Nothing in his life had been orderly since meeting Grayce Walters. He had never been so regularly agitated and over reactive.

He added a new rule to his list of rules of investigation—*Never fall in love with a witness.*

Grayce had proceeded blithely along, believing she was capable of stopping criminals. She had ventured into the heart of danger, looking for a violent misfit. The city was filled with drug dealers and addicts.

He lifted the bar over his head, allowing the slow simmer of his anger to burn away. At least James knew karate. The idea of Mr. Fashion confronting some thug might be entertaining if he didn't know the threat involved.

"You bulking up to stop the next bastard who tries to stab you?" Chris Crosby, a climbing buddy and firefighter, stood over Davis, grinning. "Or you gonna let Mitzi take him down?"

He and Chris shared some sticky climbing experiences together.

"I'm trying to work out my theories on the investigation."

Chris sat on the bench next to Davis. "You want another perspective?"

Chris had always been willing to listen to Davis process his investigations during their long slogs up the mountain.

Chris lay on the bench and lifted the weight above his chest. "Can we talk while working out? I've got to get back to work."

Davis scanned the room to make sure no one could hear the discussion. He started his last rep, not looking at Chris. "I think the Russian mob hired Benson to burn the fire I'm investigating."

Chris suspended the weight over his head, his face turned purple. "Shit, Davis. Are you trying to kill me? You can't just drop A-bombs."

Chris put the weight on the ground and sat facing Davis. "Rob Benson is a torch for hire? You gotta be kidding me. And for the Russians? You're acting as if you're oxygen deprived."

Davis finished his last rep and sat up. "The guy who tried to stab me was possibly hired by the Russians."

"I thought he was a drug addict."

Davis had had no suspicions about the guy who tried to stab him until Grayce had maintained the street thug was a Russian hired gun. And Benson wouldn't have threatened her unless she had ventured too close to the truth.

"I don't have any proof but it's one theory. You remember Zach?"

"The FBI agent you brought to the Mt. Adams climb?"

"Zach told me that Russian organized crime moves heroin from Afghanistan through Russia to all different ports. It's a hundred billion dollar business for them. What if the Russian mob is bringing heroin through Fisherman Terminal?"

Chris was shaking his head. "You're crazy, man. This is Seattle."

"The mob went to a lot of trouble to get me off the case of a small wharf fire, trying to stab me, poison my dog. Only adds up if heroin is coming through in crab cases."

"But why start a fire on the wharf if they've got an operation there?" Chris asked.

"One of the many missing pieces in my theory. I don't have a reason for the fire. All I know is that the fire was done by an experienced torch."

"And you suspect Benson?"

"I went through our regular fire starters and no one is that good, then I looked at fired firefighters. And Rob was at the top of the list for talent."

"Rob was a good firefighter, but I can't see him reliable enough to get the job done without complete supervision."

"I agree. Someone else has to handle Rob. Someone Rob trusts, who can keep him in line."

Chris leaned forward on his knees, closing the distance between them. "Who?"

Grayce's house had been burned after she followed Maclean.

"I don't know. Did Benson have anyone he was close to in the department?"

"Benson was a belligerent asshole. Everyone tolerated him because he was a damn good firefighter."

"You're right. Niles was his only ally."

"What about the fire at your girlfriend's house? Did Rob torch it, too?"

"Shit, I didn't want everyone to know about Grayce. It puts her in danger if she's connected to me and the wharf fire."

Chris stood and hit Davis on the back. "Everyone knows the story of how you picked her up from the stretcher and carried her into the night."

Davis wasn't in the mood for jokes. He stood and walked to the small weights.

Chris followed Davis to the weight table. "Hey, I was just giving you crap. Do you think Rob lit her house?"

Davis didn't have a motive for Benson burning Grayce's house. She couldn't identify Benson as the torch on the wharf; it had been too dark. But Benson wouldn't know that.

Davis started his biceps curls. "The Russians might want to intimidate the witness. Except she didn't see anything." He didn't tell Chris that Grayce's investigating adventures might have gotten the mob's attention.

Chris stood next to Davis with a hand weight and started to do curls. "You've got to bring in the feds."

There was no way he was stepping aside in this investigation, not after an ex- firefighter had gone after his girlfriend. Davis uncurled his arm. From his assessment of her house fire, Benson hadn't planned to kill Grayce, just scare her. But fire wasn't something you could carefully manage. He curled his arm tightly. He was going to get the bastard, and, when he did, Benson would suffer.

"You're getting the same look as on the mountain when you're about to do something dangerous," Chris said.

Davis switched arms. "I'm going to involve Dan at ATF. Dan will give me some moving room to go after Benson and his possible connections to the department."

He wasn't going to mention his suspicions to Chris or Dan about Maclean. He needed more proof than Grayce's allegation. He just couldn't see Maclean involved with the mob, but Grayce said he had gambling problems.

"This is some heavy shit. You better let the feds go after the Russians. You don't want 'em coming after your girlfriend."

Davis wasn't going to leave Grayce unprotected. He would alert the police and Dan. Mitzi would be her guard dog. Hollie would help him get Mitzi in her office. He probably should talk with James about no more adventures. Grayce wouldn't like it, but he wasn't going to take any chances. Until this was over, he would be the only one investigating.

They needed to come after him.

Grayce slept most of the day on James's couch. Exhausted and needing solitude, she spent the day wrapped in James's silk bathrobe napping on his plush leather couch. Napoleon slept in a cocoon of the shiny red fabric at Grayce's feet.

"Have some more *Swimming Rama*. Carbs are best for a broken heart; they release some sort of hormone that's supposed to make you feel good." James reclined on the matching leather couch. Beer bottles and paper cartons were piled high on the Noguchi glass coffee table.

"I don't have a broken heart. Someone tried to kill me and burn my house down and Davis…"

"Whatever you say, Darlin'. Your house is going to be fine. I'll take you over tomorrow when you've rested. Honestly, there isn't that much damage. I'll get someone out there to rebuild your door and deck."

"Davis planned to take me over to my house." Her voice quivered.

"This is a little reminiscent of high school." James reached for the carry-out. "Remember when Tom Manyak broke your heart. We had a sad-in and lit candles."

"Hearts mended quicker back then."

"Yeah, it must've taken a whole week before you recovered."

She really must be in bad shape, since James wasn't offering love advice. He usually relished such moments.

"Where am I going to live?"

"With your parents?"

They both laughed, her first true laugh of the evening. Maybe it was the Thai beer she guzzled with her Swimming Rama and Tom Kha Gai.

"My mom wants me to move back into my old bedroom, can you imagine?"

"And of course, you couldn't say no?"

"My mom's been really helpful, handling the whole insurance thing and organizing the cleaning."

James raised his eyebrows. He understood her guilt about frightening her parents.

"Something in my mom's voice… she was happy that I had asked her to do something. She wants to be needed."

"I know, honey. You've spent a lot of time making up for Cassie dying."

Grayce sighed. She was doing a lot of sighing today.

"You are going to stay here and his majesty is invited as well."

Napoleon flicked his gigantic tail.

"Thanks, Jamesie. I can't stay here, but if you could keep Nap."

The marmalade cat stood, stretched, and folded himself back into the same curl.

"We boys can manage."

James and Napoleon both pretended indifference to each other when Grayce was around. James gave Napoleon run of the designer condo. When James' architecture company had developed the building, James had picked the top floor condo.

"Promise me you won't move home."

"I'm going to sleep on the futon in my office."

"That's dreadful."

James loved his creature comforts, as evidenced by his extravagant penthouse.

"I've slept there before. It's not bad."

The feeling of gloom descended around her like the fog settling over Puget Sound. She wanted to go home to her own little nest.

"My entire set of Louis Vuitton luggage is filled with your stuff. You should stay here."

"I can't." Grayce shook her head.

Her whole life had abruptly changed. Everything she took pride in—her house, her independence, gone. She was the one who took care of people—she disliked feeling dependent on her parents, on James. "I won't be good company."

"So? I'm not good company either." He threw back the beer.

"I can't. I need some time alone."

"Honey, this isn't the time to be alone. You need..."

"I don't know what I need. That's part of the problem."

"I know what you need or should I say who ..."

Grayce shook her head. "It's over. Davis went ballistic about my interference in his investigation; I thought he might strangle me."

"All that male animal stuff, I love it. Think about the make-up sex."

The usual James banter fell flat.

"James, it was more than an argument."

She stirred, causing Napoleon to jump down from the couch. Davis' anger made her restless. "Davis couldn't understand my not confiding in him. He saw it as total dishonesty."

James nodded again. "Daphne?"

Her stomach ached. Eating Thai food and drinking beer might not have been the best choice.

"Baggage," James said.

"What?"

"He doesn't trust you because of Daphne and you're afraid to trust anyone because you might lose them like Cassie. Mutual distrust, a recipe for failure."

She gulped the cold beer.

"Why can't you call him and explain? Tell him the truth about your abilities."

"You don't understand. Davis is roaring mad at me. I'm not sure I want someone who can't listen."

"Give the guy a break. He rescued you. The next morning he finds out you, his witness, has been threatened—kind of hard for an in-charge, macho guy to hear. You know you blind-sided him." James took a long chug on the beer. "I feel like such a man when I drink out of the bottle."

"Davis thundered around, acting like something out of an old Tarzan movie."

They both laughed. Maybe the beer was having an effect.

"From his viewpoint, you tried to cut his balls off."

"It's just like you to bring male anatomy into the discussion."

"He gets paid to protect people. And you told him you could do his job better."

"I was trying to protect him." She couldn't put a lot of feeling into her basic defense, and James' attitude was getting on her nerves.

"You know that isn't the reason. You're afraid to let anyone know."

A hollow pit formed in Grayce's stomach and moved upward into her heart.

"Honey, you really like the guy. You've got to take the leap."

"He was very clear; he thought it was insane that we followed his boss."

"He doesn't know you have special gifts. From his perspective, you're invading his domain. Men don't like that—it threatens their maleness."

She forgot that James had a male's viewpoint.

"It's not a great example, but what if Mitzi were really sick, and Davis didn't tell you, and he went off and treated her himself?"

"It isn't the same."

"What's the difference?" James reached for more of the lemon grass soup.

"I can't tell him about my vision and premonitions, not after last night. I just can't. He'll never believe it. I was ready to tell him but I knew, deep down, he'd never accept it."

She reached for the Kleenex. A barrier broke, the floodgates opened and she couldn't stop. Tears poured down her face. She tried to speak but couldn't. A great well of sadness had been tapped. She cried for her house, for Davis, and she cried for her sister. She cried for all of life's moments that she could never share with Cassie. The Christmas mornings, the Friday nights of potato chips and Diet Coke, her future without Cassie.

She feared her sadness and her tears would never end.

CHAPTER FORTY-FOUR

The sermon ripped right into his soul. Guilt and despair weighed on him. He bowed his head, praying for forgiveness, needing salvation. He had made his choices for the best possible reasons, but a man had died.

If only Benson had just done what he had been told. He should've known that the cocky bastard couldn't follow orders. Benson had no impulse control. Now Benson was dead and he was responsible.

Following the funeral service, he walked down the aisle. He greeted the crew with his usual composed smile. After speaking to the minister and the distraught widow, he walked to his car.

He couldn't go on with this charade much longer. Benson had tried to circumvent him and make his own deal with the Russians. The idiot broke into Davis' office to steal his files and then lit Grayce Walter's house, all to prove he had the "shit" to work for the mob without a handler.

He didn't want to think about what Zavragin had done when he found out about Benson's activities.

He blamed himself. He should've known Benson would have grandiose visions, see himself as a player. True to his criminal nature, Benson believed he was above the rules. He should've seen it coming; Benson's obsession with the color red had been a warning signal.

Then Davis' investigation had uncovered Benson's involvement with the Fisherman's Terminal fire and Zavragin had eliminated him. The Russians had staged the murder in Benson's storage unit to look like a suicide. They never left loose ends; loose ends led right back to the source. After a few laced drinks, Benson had passed out in the driver's seat of his Corvette with the engine running. Then they clipped a note to his sun visor, taking full responsibility for the fire, as well as several other fire fatalities the department had never solved.

Davis would follow the threads and uncover the proof that Benson was the torch. But Zavragin had that much right: dead men could give evidence, but they can't turn state's evidence.

He pulled his car out of the church parking lot and headed home. The freeway was open, no twisting lines of cars. He drove in silence. Benson's suicide and the confession note that admitted to lighting both fires would close the case for the department and delay Davis contacting the FBI to investigate the Russian's drug smuggling. Benson was their patsy.

Three more days and then his work was finished. He had cashed out his retirement.

He didn't expect that anyone in the department would understand. He hoped Davis might. But in the end, they would hold him responsible for Benson's death. And they would be right.

CHAPTER FORTY-FIVE

Grayce stood at Mrs. Leary's front door. Mitzi watched her from the car, barking frantically when Mrs. Leary opened the door. Grayce turned to find Mitzi jumping at the car window.

"Is that your dog, Dr. Walters?"

"She's a friend's dog, spending the day with me."

She had been out-maneuvered by Davis, who had dropped Mitzi off when she went to her parent's house to shower. Either she had to call him or accept Mitzi as her companion for the next few days. It was an easy choice.

At the sound of their voices, Mitzi began another frenzied round of barking.

"She's upset."

"She'll settle down in a minute. She misses her owner." Great, now she appeared cruel by leaving the dog in the car.

"Oh, I don't want her to suffer. Have her come in."

"Beowulf will be distressed by having a dog in his house," Grayce said.

Mrs. Leary took Grayce's hand. "Beowulf's not skittish. He loves dogs."

"I'm not sure Beowulf considers loving dogs as a compliment."

The older woman tittered, her warm eyes sparkling. Mitzi gave a pitiful cry.

The dog could have a career in Hollywood. "Are you sure Mrs. Leary? Really, Mitzi will settle down once we've gone in."

"I think Beowulf would like the company."

On cue, Mitzi gave her high-pitched yelp.

"I'll bring her in, but you must tell me if you feel it's too much for Beowulf."

The delicate woman patted her on the arm. "It's going to be fine. Don't worry."

She walked to her car and unlocked the door. "Nice job, you're invited in." The dog's entire demeanor went through a radical change. A relaxed Mitzi walked next to Grayce to greet Mrs. Leary.

"What a beautiful dog."

Mitzi sat on the porch and placed her head under the old woman's hand.

"You didn't want to be by yourself. I understand." The stooped woman leaned down and rubbed the dog's head. "Beowulf is sleeping in the living room. Please, both of you come in."

Mitzi, followed Mrs. Leary into the small living room, filled with an oversized chair and couch. Pictures of smiling children lined the side tables.

Beowulf slept on the couch. He opened his eyes, briefly acknowledging Grayce and Mitzi, but remained motionless. His respirations were shallow, but he didn't appear to be in pain.

Mitzi, venturing from Mrs. Leary side, walked slowly toward the cat. She paused, doing her own assessment, then gently licked the giant cat's head. Beowulf closed his eyes and purred softly.

Mitzi repeated the gentle gesture. Beowulf remained still. After a few more licks, Mitzi laid down in front of the cat.

"Isn't that amazing? Mitzi is offering comfort to Beowulf, as if he were visiting a dear friend in the hospital," Mrs. Leary said.

"You're right."

Grayce felt the familiar ache, the hole that opened up inside her, the gaping wound of grief. There were no further treatments, no magic healing that she could perform against death. There was nothing in her large fund of knowledge to stop the process of dying. When she had trained to heal, she never fully anticipated how often she would need to help animals die and then care for the people who loved them. And how often she would have to revisit her own loss.

It was Beowulf's time. Mitzi, without years of training, knew what needed to be done—gentle comfort.

"Come sit down, Dr. Walters. I appreciate that you and Mitzi have come. Beowulf knows you cared and did all you could."

She had come to help Mrs. Leary; instead, the woman was soothing her. Tears pooled in her eyes. She seldom cried, but, in the last few days, she had turned into a geyser.

"Come, sit down by Beowulf. I'll get the tea."

"You mustn't bother."

"It's no bother. It's ready."

"Thank you, that's very kind."

Mrs. Leary limped toward the kitchen.

"Can I carry the tray for you?"

"Not necessary my dear. I have a push cart. You sit with Beowulf."

Grayce sat next to the giant cat and put her hand on his head, barely touching him.

"Beowulf, it's almost time, my sweet friend. You've done your job."

Mitzi sat up. Like a lioness with her cub, she tenderly licked the cat.

"You've been a great cat. Mrs. Leary wants you to go. Your time to rest. Don't worry about Mrs. Leary. Mitzi and I will visit her."

Beowulf didn't open his eyes. He continued his shallow breathing. He waited for his mistress.

She looked into Mitzi's eyes. They both understood the moment. Mitzi put her head in Grayce's lap.

The three sat together, sharing a bittersweet peace.

Grayce drove away in silence. She wasn't in the mood for music. An erect Mitzi sat next to her in the passenger seat.

"Thank you for your help."

Mitzi leaned over and put her head on Grayce's arm.

"I'm sad too."

An inadequate word to describe grief, the primitive physical pain of loss, your body aching with misery, making it hurt to breathe, making it hurt to remember.

Grayce grieved. She grieved for Beowulf, for the light in Mrs. Leary's life now gone. She grieved for a relationship with Davis that might have worked if only she could've shared her real self.

Grayce was glad to have Mitzi going back to the office with her. Davis told Hollie he would come for Mitzi when the case was resolved. She refused to start reanalyzing their relationship and whether Davis could accept that she communicated with her dead sister, had visions from his dog, or that when she healed, she channeled her energy into a different plane of consciousness. Not easy things for a logical, left-brained man to accept, or a woman of science to explain.

CHAPTER FORTY-SIX

Davis steered his car around the speed bump in the trailer park. He pulled into Benson's driveway. The dilapidated trailer stood as testimony to Benson's alcoholic decline.

Davis had been desperate to find Benson, once Ferette had identified him from his keycard as the intruder who had broken into his office. His assignment on the West Seattle fire delayed the trip to Kent. And now he was too late. Benson was dead.

"Come on in." Betty, Benson's widow dabbed at her nose with a knotted Kleenex, a cigarette in her other hand.

Davis sat, avoiding the darkened spots on the threadbare couch. The haze of heavy smoke didn't lessen the reek of stale beer and garbage.

"I can't believe he killed himself." Betty gulped, trying to suppress a sob when she inhaled from her cigarette.

He couldn't understand why the woman grieved for the bastard who had treated her so badly. A memory of one of Benson's abusive, drunken scenes with his wife at a department holiday party flitted across his brain. Life with an alcoholic was never predictable or pretty.

"I know this is really hard for you."

The haggard woman couldn't be older than thirty-five. Her mouth was lined from years of dragging on too many cigarettes. Betty had probably been pretty in high school, with her blond hair and blue eyes.

"When was the last time you saw Rob?"

"We weren't together." She twisted the Kleenex. "But we were thinking of getting back together."

He could imagine the dysfunction. He really didn't want to hear the details of the abusive relationship.

"You saw him recently?"

"Last week."

"Did Rob find work after he got laid off?"

"Must've, he had money."

"What was he doing?"

"He said he was finally getting to be his own boss." She reached for another cigarette. "He bought that red Corvette. He kept it in storage so the paint would stay nice and shiny, but mostly so no one would steal it. He was going to take me to Las Vegas, just like the old days." She started to cry again. "He called me baby." Her face twisted. Black ran down her cheeks from the heavy mascara.

He shifted his weight on the musty couch. He hesitated. "Did Rob ever talk about killing himself?"

"He said he was like his dad, too mean of an S.O.B. to die." Her laughing bark was followed with a dry hacking cough. "It just don't make sense. He was so excited about the car, his new job, me..."

His gut was right. Benson wasn't a candidate for suicide. He would never take the blame for any of his mistakes.

"Was he still mad about being retired from the department?"

"He stayed pissed. You couldn't talk to him about it. After they let him go, he got real mean and his drinking got real bad. He would go on about how the department went down the toilet. He couldn't believe that they hired women and blacks but let him go over a little booze."

"Did he stay in touch with any of the guys from the department?"

Betty smashed her cigarette in the loaded ashtray. He was probably getting lung cancer, just sitting in the smoke infested room.

"I don't know."

"Did he ever mention anyone?"

"Only the nice chaplain."

"He never told you what his new job was?"

"Nah, but he liked it. That's why it doesn't make sense. Why would he kill himself, now?"

He waited through another ten minutes of a winding monologue. Betty wasn't going to reveal anything significant. Unsure of Betty's financial situation, he took a $100.00 bill out. "I don't think Benson would've liked flowers. You decide what to do for him."

"Thank you. I'm sorry you couldn't make the funeral. He looked real nice. I put him in his uniform. He would've wanted it. I had 'em dye his hair back to brown."

He tried to sound nonchalant, but his pulse raced. "Rob changed his hair color?"

Betty examined the $100.00 bill. "He got real mad when I told him I didn't like it. It was weird for a man his age to have red hair."

His gut did a little turn over before settling. "Did he say why he chose red?"

"Nah, just if I didn't like it, to cram it."

He walked outside, taking his first real breath since he'd arrived in Kent. His mind was buzzing. Benson had combined the brake fluid with chlorine to get the big bang. And with his 20,000 bucks, he'd bought himself a red corvette. Only one problem—red hair wasn't enough evidence to prove that Benson lit the fire.

Benson must've been the bastard who knocked Grayce down the stairs and lit her house. He didn't want to think about what he would've done if the asshole wasn't dead.

Davis got into his car, his brain trying to make all the connections. Assuming Benson was the torch, why had he burned Grayce's house after he threatened her? Grayce and James followed Maclean after the party so there wasn't any need to threaten her unless she was correct about Maclean's huge gambling debts and criminal connections.

But had Maclean killed Benson? It seemed too much of a fantasy. He couldn't see Benson organizing large scale crimes, negotiating with the mob. But Davis could imagine Maclean being incredibly competent at managing every critical detail of mob crimes.

CHAPTER FORTY-SEVEN

Grayce woke herself out of the nightmare. Her heart pounded against her chest, making it hard for her to breathe. She had been too late, too late to save Davis from falling from a great "height" but she couldn't remember whether it was a cliff on Mount Rainier, or the window in his condo, or a burning high rise, but Davis was falling, and neither she nor Mitzi could do anything to prevent his plummet.

A sense of helplessness and horror had colored the nightmare as she raced with Mitzi into a white space, weak-kneed, struggling to breathe through the thick air, struggling to reach Davis.

The dream shifted and slowed. Grayce watched, powerless, unable to move, as a man pushed Davis over the ledge of an empty void.

A cold tongue brushed her cheek. Struggling to wake, she opened one eye. Mitzi leaned over her. "I'm getting up."

Grayce rubbed the dog's head, scratched behind her ears. "How did you sleep?"

Grayce and Mitzi had spent the night on the futon in her office. Mitzi jumped off the futon and sat alert, close to Grayce's face. The poodle stared unwaveringly at Grayce. Her black eyes focused as if looking through Grayce's eyes, and seeing something beyond them.

"I had the strangest dream," Grayce said.

Mitzi listened with her head to one side, her ears up, her body tense.

"You and I were trying to save Davis from falling."

Mitzi thumped her tail, a slow steady beat.

"You know?" Grayce asked.

A thump and then another thump. Mitzi dropped to her stomach and pressed her nose under Grayce's hand and whacked her tail faster.

"The dream was an anxiety dream. We're both worried about Davis. I doubt we'll ever have to save him from falling. He's a mountain climber." Feeling a chill in the room, Grayce snuggled under the down comforter. Funny thing was, it hadn't felt like an anxiety dream at all. It felt like impending disaster, like it was going to happen—a premonition.

The ring of the office phone jarred her back to the present. She would let the message go to voicemail for Hollie. She had an early appointment with Dr. Z.

"I'm seeing Dr. Z today. Do you want to stay in the office with Hollie or come with me? You won't get away with your dramatics with Dr. Z. like you did with Mrs. Leary."

Mitzi stretched out her front paws and rolled onto her side.

"Okay. I'm sure Hollie will be happy to have your company."

Mitzi and she communicated in dreams? One more little piece of information to keep to herself.

Grayce sat across from Dr. Z, with his shiny bald head and keen eyes.

He poured tea from a 19th century teapot. His usually radiant face was solemn. "I've waited for you to come."

The fear and pain she had buried for so long poured out like the scalding tea. She couldn't understand what was happening. The peace and contentment she usually felt in Dr. Z's presence was gone.

"The man with the scar?" He asked.

She raised the cup to her lips. Her hand trembled. "I don't know. I tried to help Davis, but I made a mess of it."

"I'm sure you did your best."

"Davis is angry and hurt. He doesn't trust me. " She swallowed the hot tea in a big gulp. "He and his investigation have destroyed the equilibrium I've worked so hard to maintain."

"Your work has provided a safe haven to hide your gifts."

"I couldn't tell him about my abilities." Dr. Z knew how she had guarded her secrets, avoiding relationships, burying herself in her academics, then in her acupuncture practice.

"You would like to be someone different, someone you believe this man would love?"

Few words. They resonated deeply.

She sat back in her chair. "I don't know what I want."

"I think you know."

She sipped her tea, avoided looking at Dr. Z.

"You're done?"

"He doesn't want me interfering."

Dr. Z widened his eyes. "I can feel your loneliness."

A dull ache started in her chest. "I want what others have. I want something more."

Dr. Z shook his head. "More is being who you are, being truthful, truthful about your feelings for this man, truthful about your gifts."

She wanted to scream, shout. She had never gotten angry at Dr. Z before. She closed her eyes. She wouldn't, couldn't go down the path he was trying to lead her on, a path she had resisted all her life. "I can't… it's too hard."

"You're afraid of revealing yourself, your gifts. You want to be like others, even when it is evident, even to your logical mind, that you're different."

Dr. Z gently stripped away all of her self-deceptions. He wouldn't allow her to hide.

"My gifts didn't help me. I almost got killed. And Davis doesn't want my help."

"I don't think your gifts are the problem." Dr. Z smiled his first smile of the visit. "You're still learning how to use your gifts, is it not true?"

She nodded, remembering her dream about Davis falling into the void and her sense of impending disaster. Was it prescient or the result of anxiety?

"Fear still rules your actions, your thoughts."

"I'm not afraid. I searched for the man who tried to stab Davis. I followed Davis' boss, fought the man who attacked me, and escaped my burning house."

"I'm not speaking about your courage in the face of danger." He placed his smooth brown hand over his heart. "The fear here. You're afraid to love since it protects your heart from ever losing someone." He smiled. "Your light is very strong. Once you embrace it, the fear will diminish. You'll not be like others who spend many lifetimes resisting the light." His face radiated as if a light shone on him from another source. "What are your plans?"

"My plans?" She stared at the little man.

He stared back. Dr. Z was a gently fierce warrior.

"I can't help Davis. I promised him I was done investigating."

Dr. Z waited.

"I had a dream in which I tried to save Davis from falling into a void but I failed."

"Being deeply loved by someone gives you strength, while loving someone deeply gives you courage." He leaned forward and patted her hand. "You remember how much I like the poet, Lao Tzu, yes?"

His eyes were deep pools of light. "I'm sure you'll find your courage."

His words were like a child's lullaby. Grayce felt herself floating, floating in space, their boundaries morphing, coalescing. Dr. Z was transferring his strength, his courage to Grayce.

"Acupuncture will help, yes?"

His tender smile lifted her spirits.

Grayce glided to the nearby coffee shop. After the intense acupuncture treatment, she needed time to reenter the physical world. She hovered between unconsciousness and reality. She sat at a table away from the bustle and stared out the window. Bridging the world of unconscious knowing to outer reality took quiet and patience. Matters of the heart couldn't be forced.

Deep in her acupuncture treatment, deep in the quiet space of healing, Cassie's presence had enveloped her, bringing profound peace. The dark hidden caverns of her heart were filled with light by her sister's presence.

What had felt so difficult was easy now. None of the usual fear arose with the thought of revealing her gifts to Davis. Something inside had shifted, never to be hidden again. She was purging her fears of trusting, because of her love for Davis.

Dr. Z trusted her to do the right thing. Cassie was with her. Grayce would reveal her intuition to Davis, her vision of the scar, and now her dream about him falling. Davis could decide what to believe. She walked to her car, ready to face her office and the upcoming confession.

Her need for secrecy about her gifts wasn't the most important thing. Davis' safety had to take priority. Tomorrow, she would return Mitzi to his office. He needed Mitzi's protection more than she did.

She climbed the stairs to her office, two at a time, energized by her newfound determination. She wanted to talk with Davis but with clinic tonight, she'd have to wait to call and arrange to meet.

She wasn't sure if Davis could take a leap of faith and accept that there were illogical possibilities in the world. She felt the dull creep of pain. This was the problem with opening your heart. It hurt.

CHAPTER FORTY-EIGHT

Oblivious to the blustery weather, Davis left his office and marched the three blocks to headquarters. The chance that Maclean had been caught on the security tapes at Benson's storage unit was the hard evidence he needed to connect his boss to Benson. He had devised a logical plan; to pretend he had access to the tapes to entrap his superior. But he hadn't anticipated the illogical emotions twisting in his gut. He was about to precipitate a major scandal and ruin an officer's career.

He had disclosed his suspicions to no one. He wasn't ready to admit that one of their own was dirty. It violated every unwritten code of the department, every one of his values.

Proceeding through the hallways, he acknowledged his colleagues with a brief nod. Headquarters was home—filled with loyal, dedicated people who risked their lives every day for the citizens of Seattle. And one of his colleagues was a traitor.

He knocked on Maclean's open door. "Got a minute?"

In every direction of Maclean's office, Davis was confronted with the fruits of Maclean's twenty-three years of service. The walls were covered with awards, commendations, and pictures. Davis focused on the large black and white photo of Maclean with the chief. The two men had been friends for all those years.

Temperament aside, this man was brass. Doubt ran through Davis like a chugged pint of beer.

"What do you need? Have I missed a new fire?"

Maclean knew there was no fire.

"Still on the wharf fire," Davis said.

"Benson lit the damn thing."

"But why? What was in it for Benson?"

Maclean laughed harshly. "You aren't busy enough. Benson was pissed. He never got over being fired. He blamed the department. Who knows what else was going through his pickled brain?"

"I think he was hired."

"Someone paid for one shed to be burned?" The assistant chief walked around his desk, moving closer. Davis didn't budge. They were already facing off.

Davis watched Maclean's habitual scowl for a reaction. "But why a single shed on Fisherman's Terminal? Benson always struck me as a three-engine kind of guy."

Maclean showed nothing except a deepening of the pitiless crevices surrounding his mouth.

"This fire may lead to something big," Davis said.

"What in the hell are you talking about? The investigation is finished."

"Have you ever known me to chase half-cracked ideas?"

Maclean leaned back against his desk and crossed his ankles. "What's your theory?

Davis withheld the mention of drug trafficking and the Russian connection. He wasn't about to reveal his theory that Maclean was working with the Russians because of his gambling debts.

"Get on with it, Davis."

"Don't you find it strange that right when I'm thinking Benson could've done this job, Benson shows up dead?"

"That's your theory?" Maclean walked back to his desk. "Do you need to take time off? You're losing it. Maclean spoke slowly, implying with each punctuated word the irrefutable truth. "Benson committed suicide, get over it."

"Did he?" Davis asked.

Maclean sat down.

"Maybe it was a set-up? Made to look like a suicide?"

Maclean inspected the papers on his desk, never looking up. He opened his top drawer and shuffled through the contents. Maclean wasn't reaching for a gun, was he? It was an absurd thought, but Davis' body didn't distinguish the difference. His heart raced, the adrenaline pumped into his blood.

The assistant chief leaned across his desk and waved a stapler at him. "You're always bloody sure of yourself. You didn't get it right this time. Benson's death has nothing to do with your fire. The drunk went over the edge. Did you know he dyed his hair red to look like some god dammed comic book super villain?" Maclean stapled papers together. "Bought himself a red Corvette. I can see him thinking it was a fitting way to go out, in his brand new car. He was nuts; end of story."

"But that's my point. Where did Benson get the money to buy an expensive car? His wife said he had a new job."

"You interviewed his widow?" Maclean slammed the stapler down on the desk. "Benson's death is official police business."

Davis couldn't look at Maclean when he delivered the *coup d'état*. His heart thumped in his chest. It was easy to intimidate punks, but trying to trap his boss wasn't as easy. "I spoke with the owner at the storage unit where Benson kept his car. I'm going to review the DVR tapes. He's willing to have me look at the security tapes."

"Bullshit. The tapes are evidence." Maclean stood up. "Benson's death is under police jurisdiction. The dicks hate our investigators involved in their crimes. You piss them off and the chief will get a call."

Davis slowly inhaled and then exhaled, trying to keep to his planned script. "The cameras are at the entrance of the storage units. I want to make sure Benson was alone when he went into the unit."

Maclean's face didn't move—the same pig-headed stare. "The police have the tapes. If there was anything on them, we would've heard."

Davis felt like a rookie in his first interrogation. Was Maclean bluffing? Had Maclean wiped the tapes clean? With all of his investigative skills, Davis couldn't tell if his boss was lying. The man was a gambler. He knew how to hide his emotions.

"Drop it, Davis. That's an order."

Davis stepped closer to the desk. "Why? I've got the time."

"Just leave Benson's death the fuck alone." Maclean shoved his chair back and stood up. "And since you've got time, I've got a job for you. Show up for Ladder Seven's technical rescue tomorrow on the Space Needle. Bill Summerton's wife went into labor."

Maclean leaned over his desk. "Whit recommended you. Heard you're quite the mountain man. This will give you a chance to prove it."

The tiny hairs lifted on Davis' neck. "What time?"

"The schedule is posted. You'll be in the second group. I'll need you to dangle from the Space Needle."

Maclean's smirk was in his voice. The bastard was hoping to scare him.

"I'll be there."

"And Davis, drop the wharf fire. Let the insurance company waste their money trying to figure it out."

Davis turned and walked out. Frustration surged through him. His bluff to identify Maclean on the DVR tapes had failed. He didn't have access to the security tapes or the police reports. Maclean did.

He doubted the boys downtown would share their investigation. Damn turf wars between the FI's and the police.

Maclean wouldn't try to harm him on the Space Needle in front of the entire crew of Ladder Seven. Or would he?

Davis needed to put some distance between himself and headquarters. He raced down the steps, wanting to move, to shake the bad feeling about the department's traitor.

Grayce had accused him of delusions of invincibility. If only she could see him now, in deep shit and nowhere to turn. The department had no guidelines for accusing a superior of heinous crimes.

He would need to confide in the chief that his close friend and colleague had ties to the mob and might be a murderer. But he had no smoking gun to link Maclean to Benson. And no proof that Maclean had ties with the Russians.

If he spoke with the chief, he would precipitate an investigation by the feds with no loyalty to the department. He could see the media circus if there was a federal investigation of the fire department.

The rain had intensified since he left his office. Head down, he walked straight into someone. He felt the give of a plump body and heard a whoosh of exhaled breath.

"Davis, what the hell? Are you still in a bad mood about the Huskies' loss? Or should I say slaughter?"

Niles hovered over Davis. The tall Dane made Davis' six foot two inches feel short. As the biggest man in the department, Niles was also the softest. His round face, although lined, glowed with the exuberance of a puppy.

Davis' feelings of paranoia grew when he looked up at headquarters. "Don't remind me of the Huskies." He shook his head. "It's worse than the damn football game. There's someone dirty in the department."

Nothing registered on Niles' face when Davis blurted the shocking allegation. As the chaplain, Niles must be immune to bad news.

"Let's get out of the rain." Niles pointed to their coffee shop across Jackson. "You look like you could do with some java. If you're going to accuse someone in the department, you're going to need an ally."

Niles folded his oversized body into a beat up chair. He put half of a glazed doughnut into his mouth. He spoke while chewing, "Best doughnut in town."

"You eat too many of those and you might have to start working out." Davis tried to lighten the serious mood. He regretted his outburst and wished he could escape Niles' grave looks.

"What's this about someone being dirty?" Niles wiped his hands on the napkin.

Davis damned his impulse to confide in the chaplain. Now, he was trapped.

Niles' round face was filled with concern, his familiar calm voice reassuring. "You can trust me."

"I'm not one for conspiracy theories but a higher-up may be involved in arson for hire. There may be a connection between the wharf fire and the Russian mob's drug trafficking. Once I bring in the feds about the drugs, I lose all control of the investigation. I'm trying to find evidence to take to the chief before the feds take over and it becomes a bloody mess."

Niles kept his eyes trained on him. "What made you suspect someone in the department?"

"A friend was suspicious and alerted me to the possible connections with the brass."

"A friend in the department?" Niles asked.

"No. Someone outside."

Niles shook his head. "I can't imagine anyone outside understands how we work."

Davis felt defensive when Niles put it that way. Davis gripped his thighs. He sat forward. "She's very insightful."

"She? Meaning Grayce Walters?"

He hadn't planned to mention Grayce, but if he couldn't trust the chaplain, who could he trust? He couldn't grasp why he was hesitant to talk with Niles. He needed to bounce his ideas off of someone in the department, someone who understood the taboo about raising the possibility of a traitor.

"She doesn't know anyone in the department, does she?" Niles asked.

"She met him at the party. I don't know what alerted her, but she followed him to a casino."

"A witness followed one of our officers?"

He had the same shocked reaction as Niles when Grayce described following Maclean. He still didn't understand why she had followed him.

"Our man has a gambling problem, might be bartering his skills for his debts."

"Does Grayce work as an investigator? I thought she was a vet."

"She went off and followed…" Davis almost slipped and said Maclean's name.

Davis told Niles about the threats against Grayce and his suspicions about Benson's death. He hadn't planned to replay Grayce's close brush with death or his failure to protect her. He felt better recounting the entire case. Niles was a good listener with his quiet acceptance.

"You're sure you haven't been watching too many crime shows?"

"If you're giving me shit, just think what the chief's reaction will be?"

"What are you planning, Davis?"

"I need evidence to link the brass to the wharf fire and Benson's death."

Niles lowered his voice, "This is serious business."

Davis took a gulp of his coffee.

"What about Grayce?" Niles asked.

"What about her?"

"Is she still investigating?"

"Grayce better not be involved." Davis couldn't control the surge of anger slipping into his voice, his body. He didn't want Grayce near the Russian mob. They were ruthless. "Today, I confronted the brass. I tried to refocus the heat on me."

"You're playing a treacherous game." Niles' eyes darted back and forth, searching each person who walked into the coffee shop.

Niles' sudden apprehension made Davis tense. His gut clenched around the doughnut he had eaten. Niles didn't offer his usual encouragement for Davis' plan. Everyone seemed different today, or were his suspicions making him doubt everyone? "If anything happens to me…"

"Davis, nothing is going to happen to you. You need to rethink this before you make any accusations."

Davis had made a mistake, confiding in his friend. This wasn't the time for re-thinking. It was the time for action. He needed to get the evidence. "I'm not planning to accuse anyone until I have real evidence."

"Is there anything I can do?"

"Stay out of it, Niles."

"But…"

Davis shook his head. “If I’m wrong, what then? If I’m right, I think my man will show himself tomorrow. I’m assigned to assist in a technical practice, he’ll be there.”

Niles let out a slow whistle and shook his head.

Davis stood to leave. “Whit, on Ladder Seven, is a mountain-climbing friend. He’ll watch my back.”

CHAPTER FORTY-NINE

The cars in front of Grayce snaked slowly down Mercer Street. Like in her nightmare, she couldn't reach Davis, couldn't warn him. She swallowed hard against the panic gripping her throat and stomach, twisting them into tangled knots.

She had gone to Davis' office to return Mitzi as they had agreed, but hoped for the chance to talk with him. He wasn't in his office but had gone to the Space Needle to practice a technical rescue. Why would a fire investigator be part of a rescue exercise on the Space Needle?

He wasn't answering his cell phone and, according to the office assistant, he had left for the Space Needle an hour ago and Assistant Chief Maclean was in charge of the drill. She was living her nightmare.

Mitzi, on alert, her head and eyes pointed straight ahead, sat next to Grayce in the passenger seat.

Waiting in line to cross the bridge under repair, Grayce dialed her cell phone. "James… pick up…"

The phone continued to ring.

"Darlin', I'm in the middle of waxing my legs, I'll call you later."

"James, meet me at the Space Needle."

No response. Had she lost service? Then she heard James' throaty chuckle. "Is this a surprise party? It's not my birthday…"

"James, this isn't a joke."

"I can't meet you. I need all day to get ready for Gay Bingo."

"Maclean has lured Davis to the Needle. He's in danger."

"But, Darlin', Tony is here and we're testing my make-up with my new fabulous wig. We're on the final touches."

"Forget Gay Bingo." She didn't mean to shout, but she was wound tight.

"But…"

"You have to help me. Davis could die."

"All right, all right. La Bete is on her way."

"Call me when you get there."

Grayce drove faster than she should've down Westlake. The fear that she might be too late pressed against her diaphragm, making it hard to catch her breath. As if sensing her panic, Mitzi licked Grayce's face, trying to soothe her.

"We'll save him, Mitzi."

Grayce and Mitzi ran between the long lines of tour busses to the Space Needle's visitor's entrance. Chinese tourists filled the entire waiting area. Rapid-fire Mandarin echoed throughout the cavernous space as if she were in Beijing.

She couldn't see where the line to the elevator began. Squaring her shoulders, she started toward the elevator. No one responded to her gentle nudges. She pushed Beijing style, using elbows, shoulders, hands. Smiling and nodding, she made her way to the front of the line-queue Kung Fu.

Sweat beaded on her neck under her ponytail. She had worn her business suit and Jimmy Choos as a gentle reminder to Davis that she was a highly-regarded scientist. It was part of her plan for when she revealed her non-scientific abilities to Davis. This was her strategy before she discovered that Davis was on the Space Needle. Her professional image would work to her advantage. The burly security guard, earpiece in place, towered over everyone.

"Excuse me. I'm Dr. Grayce Walters. I'm part of the Fire Department's Rescue Team. Can you direct me to the area where I'm to join the fire department?"

The hefty man inspected her and Mitzi. "Assistant Chief Maclean didn't say anything about a dog."

"Mitzi works with Ladder Seven. She's a rescue dog. He may not have thought to mention her."

The guard scanned the crowd like a Doberman; his eyes darted back and forth.

"I need to get up there. Assistant Chief Maclean isn't going to be happy that we're late," she said in her most authoritative voice.

A rush of tourists pressed from behind when the elevator door opened. The security guard stepped between her and the tourists. He walked the few steps to the elevator and spoke with the operator. "Take Dr. Walters to the mezzanine level. She's joining the fire department."

She and Mitzi walked to the back of the elevator. She had no interest in the view from the glass doors. The tourists filled the elevator, taking pictures of Seattle Center and Queen Anne Hill from their cell phones. She caught a glimpse of the security guard on a walkie-talkie.

The elevator lurched and so did her stomach. She hated heights and had no need to watch their ascent. She closed her eyes. "Mezzanine level, ma'am." A path opened between the sea of tourists. Assistant Chief Maclean stood waiting.

"Dr. Walters and Mitzi, what a pleasant surprise."

Maclean stepped forward and grasped her by the elbow. His face was expressionless, but his fingers dug into her elbow.

Mitzi's low growl was in rhythm with the low rumble of the elevator.

"You're part of the Department's Rescue Team? How convenient." He dragged Grayce along the corridor.

Mitzi continued her low grumble and pulled on her lead toward Maclean.

"Keep that mongrel away from me or you'll regret it."

Grayce pulled Mitzi closer.

"Why in the hell are you here?"

"Where's Davis?" She asked.

"A little desperate, following your boyfriend to his job?"

Panic rippled through her body, making her shaky. "I need to see him."

Maclean's laugh echoed down the narrow hallway. "This is a rescue. No one is allowed to waltz up here. Either you can take the elevator down or wait for him in the mechanical room. What will it be, Dr. Walters?"

"I'll wait."

"It'll be a long wait. He's on top with Toni." He lowered his voice and leered at Grayce.

Grayce ignored Maclean's coarse remark. "Please tell him I've an urgent message."

She searched Maclean's face. Nothing showed in the harsh angles, but the muscles in his jaw were clenched, deepening the jagged lines along his mouth.

"This way, Doctor," He pointed to a metal door with a "No Entry" sign.

Mitzi brushed against her when they moved into the room. The dog's presence steadied her. Equipment and clothes were strewn throughout the room, serving as the staging area for the firefighters. Maclean's fury permeated the small space, making it hard for her to breathe. She tried to put some distance between them, backing further into the room.

"I don't know when Davis will be finished." Maclean emphasized "finished" with a fiendish laugh.

A bone cold chill ran up and down her spine, sending icy panic to every vertebra, every nerve pathway. How could she stop Maclean? If she tried anything, he would call security. She needed to find Davis. Where was James?

"As always, it was a pleasure, Dr. Walters." Maclean closed the door. She heard the lock turn.

Adrenaline raced through her body, making her as queasy as if she were tilting with the rotating Space Needle.

One part of her mind screamed silently, the other was grimly aware that she was reliving her nightmare. She was too late to save Davis.

CHAPTER FIFTY

James, in his favorite black skirt, silk blouse, red pumps and matching crimson Chanel lipstick, stood at the bottom of the stairwell leading to the top of the Space Needle. The flash of his volunteer I.D. for *The Outsider* had worked. He was about to interview Assistant Chief Maclean for Seattle's gay newspaper. The security guard didn't recognize the name of the newspaper and granted him admittance. The guard looked like more of a Sports Illustrated fan, probably the swimsuit edition.

"I'll get Assistant Chief Maclean."

"Oh, don't bother Stewart. He'll just get irritated with you. Give me a moment to get my camera," James said.

He was lucky that he had packed his camera in his Prada bag, ready for the evening. He and his friends loved to be catty and dissect every ensemble.

James batted his two pairs of false eyelashes. "I'm ready to go up. Thank you for your patience. You're such a thoughtful gentleman."

The blonde's sweet face colored with a charming pink. "Why don't I go first… high heels on stairs can be tricky?"

James' little black skirt was tight and short to emphasize his best attribute, his finely shaped legs highlighted by his red Alexander McQueen platforms. "Oh, how considerate of you to think of my modesty, but I'm really not shy." James squeezed the guard's arm.

The guard sounded breathless. "Hold on to the handrails. I wouldn't want you to fall."

From the bottom step, James watched the guard's tight bum. He needed to stay focused on his mission. He was here to protect Grayce and possibly Davis. He found it hard to believe that Davis needed his help but if Grayce had gotten herself into a dangerous situation, then he needed to be there for her.

He and the guard climbed two stairwells, each requiring an access code card. The fire department's presence on the Needle had lessened the tight security practices or he never would've been able to finagle this easy *entrée*.

He was in drag at a fire department practice to rescue super hero Davis, and had no plan for what he was going to do once he got to the top. He might let Grayce explain, if she were up there. But she hadn't answered her cell phone; and who knew where she could've gotten off to.

The guard lifted the heavy hatch, opening onto the dome.

"I can't believe you were able to open that heavy door. You don't look like you're that strong. James ran his finger down the man's arm. "Must be all lean muscle under that white shirt."

The guard reached down and assisted James to the tower. "First I need you to rope up and you'll need to stand right here. The firefighters will come to you." The guard placed the rope over his head.

James gave his high pitched giggle. "How sweet of you to be concerned I might fall off. What a spectacular day."

With the clear sky, James turned to take in both mountain ranges. Mount Rainier shined in all her glory as did Mount Baker. The sun dazzled the usual gray waters of Puget Sound.

"It's stunning. I'm breathless." He fluttered his hand on his well-padded chest.

Below them, two hunky firefighters and one tall blond woman stood chatting, unfazed by their precarious positions. The men were in T-shirts. And what specimens they were. This adventure surpassed Gay Bingo.

With the guard's signal, the firefighters, well roped-in, scrambled up the angle of the dome with ease. Everyone here was real. And for a moment, James wanted to throw all pretense and glamour away and become something unvarnished and true. He quickly came to his senses as he watched the men's thighs work. Yes, much better than Gay Bingo.

"James Dewitt, reporter for *The Outsider*."

The tall blond woman eyed him. "We already did a photo shoot this morning. We're wrapping up." Her stare was disconcerting. It took all his self-control not to check whether his boobs were still in place. Grateful for the rope snuggly wrapped around his waist since he was having trouble balancing in his McQueen platforms on the uneven surface.

The hunky firefighter, with dark sultry eyes, asked, "*The Outsider*?"

"It's really a personal piece: Why would you want to risk your gorgeous selves?"

He needed to tone it down. But this was way too much fun. "I'm really here to interview Assistant Chief Maclean. Where is the chief and has my photographer arrived?"

"Maclean is giving an interview for the gay newspaper? I don't believe it." The hunky stud laughed.

"I'm supposed to meet the assistant chief here. We tried to call him on the walkie-talkie. He hasn't responded," James said.

"Maclean's probably down directing Davis."

The blond bombshell chimed in. "Davis will love that."

"Where is Davis?"

"You know Davis?" The gargantuan woman scrutinized him from his Alexander pumps to his fabulous blond wig. He couldn't be sure if she saw him as competition or knew he was in drag.

"I've a mild acquaintance with him." He rolled his eyes, implying the opposite. "Do you know where my photographer or Davis might be?"

The security guard stood close to James. "There was no photographer. Assistant Chief Maclean allowed a woman access. She said she and the poodle were part of the rescue team."

He and the blond both turned at the same time to look at the security guard.

"She must still be at the mezzanine area," The guard said.

James didn't like the sound of Grayce meeting Maclean. "I need to find my photographer. Will you excuse me?" The situation grew more ridiculous. But what did you say in such circumstances. As Miss Manners would say, good manners never fail. "Thank you. Will Davis be down there too?"

"Davis is on the halo, about to fall off. I'm waiting to rappel down and rescue him." The blond stuck out her generous chest when she announced her forthcoming rescue. Definitely marking her territory.

For the first time since reaching the top, James felt a tingling weakness behind his knees. "How does Davis fall off?"

The dark-eyed, handsome dude spoke, "He's roped, as a Space Needle engineer would be who's working on the halo. And like a worker who might slip or get injured, Davis will fall and dangle. Toni will rappel down with that basket and rescue the victim, taking him to the ground." He pointed to a steel cage placed next to a neatly coiled rope.

He didn't like the sound of Davis dangling. There were too many possibilities for mistakes.

He had no doubt that Toni could save Davis, but only if she had a chance. He needed to get down. "I'm so impressed." He meant it.

"I've got to get my photographer and get down to the halo. I want to get shots of you coming over the edge. The angle will be fabulous." He had no damn idea what the halo was but he needed to find Grayce and get to Davis. "See you down at the halo."

James took the two steps to the hatch. The security guard took his arm. "I'll go first."

He didn't have time for flirty games. "Thank you."

CHAPTER FIFTY-ONE

Harnessed, roped, and tethered to a steel wire, Davis was perched on the edge of the flying saucer disc that surrounded the Space Needle. The crowd, five hundred and twenty feet below, looked more like scurrying beetles than people.

He waited for the signal to drop.

He wasn't nervous about the dangle. The operation was an efficient, well-run drill. From years of climbing, he knew every detail of every sequence. His body was primed. His senses heightened. His heart pumped against his chest, his muscles were tensed, as if ready to climb Mount Rainier.

Hyper-vigilant, he decided to walk the halo one last time. He had already inspected the entire surface of the three-foot wide, angled platform. He paid particular attention to the tensile steel cable encircling the halo. The thin wire must support his body weight when he hung suspended. He had found no hint of tampering.

He had also checked his own equipment. Harness, rope, and the carabineer connecting his nylon rope to the safety wire were in perfect working condition. All appeared secure. He trusted Toni's ability, assigned to rappel down for his rescue.

Tourists waved through the wire mesh and glass to Davis from the observation deck. Not feeling particularly social, he forced a smile and a nod.

What could Maclean possibly try with hordes of witnesses watching within a hand's reach?

He stood at the outer perimeter of the halo, gusts of wind whipped through his hair. Nothing stood between him and the one hundred and forty yards of hard ground below.

He wanted this whole damn business to be finished, so he could get on with his life. When this case was over, he was ready to grovel, beg, do anything to have Grayce back. He was glad she'd remained out of the investigation and safely at home with Mitzi. Wait a second, Grayce was supposed to bring Mitzi to his office today. And he'd forgotten, what with his entire focus on this Space Needle practice rescue. He felt a sinking sense of helplessness at the thought of Grayce believing he had forgotten her. How was he ever going to be able to explain to her? He shook his head and forced all thoughts of Grayce from his mind. He couldn't afford any distractions during this critical event.

Restless, he walked around the corner to find Whit, Lieutenant of Ladder Seven, and Maclean in discussion. Whit nodded and climbed through the exit. What the hell? He had counted on having Whit watching his back while he dangled.

He couldn't see Maclean's face but somehow he knew the man would be flashing his condescending smirk. He moved toward Maclean, ready for the confrontation.

Maclean stood in full uniform, his posture erect in his harness. He exuded his usual arrogance and confidence. Davis' blood ran hard and fast through him. The bastard was up to something.

"This is it, Davis."

Davis, set his feet apart, readying himself for the battle. He tried to hide his antagonism, his need to bloody Maclean's face. "Are they ready for me to go over?"

"Not yet. We're evacuating the observation deck. We don't want the tourists upset by your fall."

The hair on his neck and arms bristled in warning. "I was surprised you wanted me to participate in this drill."

Maclean peered over the edge. "Quite a drop. 520 feet."

Cold drips of sweat gathered under his arm pits. "Where's Whit?"

"He's coordinating the evacuation with the Needle's security team."

"Isn't that your job?"

Maclean's polished veneer of superiority disappeared. He squared his shoulders, and jutted his pointed chin. His voice was rougher. "Very good, Davis. Two years with the department and you're ready to run it."

"Whit's my climbing partner."

"After 23 years with the department, I decide who's here and who's not. Face it Davis, it's finished." Maclean's face was harsh. "You're in it up to your eyeballs for the shed fire and Benson's death." Maclean inched towards him, his dark eyes filled with contempt. "I wasn't supposed to say anything but the chief told me this morning that you're dirty. You son of a bitch."

"What the hell are you talking about?"

"The chief received a note from Benson, written before he died, pinning both fires on you. You hired him to burn the shed for the Russian's drug dealing operation."

Maclean's accusation hit him like a kick to the groin. His stomach contracted and his lungs stopped moving. He was air-hungry, breathless although wind blew across his face.

"The only reason you're part of this practice is because the chief didn't want to cancel...too costly. You're not to leave my sight and I'm to escort you back to the department once we're finished here."

A cold draft blew down his neck, chilling him. The wind was picking up. "And where's this note?"

He had been set up, but not by the assistant chief. Maclean's rage was real. Maclean wanted to beat the shit out of him, as would the whole department once they heard he was a traitor.

"I'm sure the chief won't mind sharing it with you. He knows it all, your association with Benson, your Russian connections and why the whole investigation came to a dead end. You didn't follow protocol and report the drug trafficking to the feds because the Russians were paying you. The chief wants to talk with you before he turns you over to the police. Lucky for you, he's more open-minded than I am."

Davis had been prepared for a physical attack, not for this revelation. Maclean was innocent.

"What about the witness's house?" Davis inched backward, positioning himself away from the edge. "Why would I burn my girlfriend's house?"

"Maybe your girlfriend is in it with you."

Pressure built in his chest. Grayce implicated in criminal activities caused a hot fury to consume his body. "Grayce mixed up with drug dealers? Have you gone crazy?"

Maclean showed no fear, stepping closer to the edge. "Then why is the little doctor here? She's even brought your dog. She's in it up to her bloody neck. I've got her locked up."

"What? Grayce is here?" He took the two steps toward Maclean. His hands tightened. He had never before wanted to choke the life out of anyone.

"She had the nerve to say she and the dog were part of the Rescue Team. She has an urgent message for you." Maclean smirked. "Can you imagine that?"

He stood closer to Maclean. "Where is she, you bastard?"

"She has it in her head that you're in danger. Where would she ever have gotten such a bullshit idea?"

He grabbed Maclean by the arms. "Tell me where she is or I swear I'll…"

"How dare you touch me?" Maclean threw his weight forward against him. The sudden movement caught Davis off guard. He stumbled backwards.

Maclean, his face mottled with fury, shouted. "Who in the fuck do you think you are?" He suddenly moved to grab Davis. "Do you know what we do with dirty bastards in our department?"

Grayce threw her full 90 pounds against the heavy steel door one last time. Breathless, she paced the small room, struggling to contain the terror that she was too late, too late to save Davis.

She had tried to pry the lock open with the various tools that hung on the back wall. In desperation, she had even tried her credit card. She was trapped.

Mitzi waited, poised at the door. Her low whining was a constant reminder of the mounting pressure to find Davis. Grayce tried to control her breathing. She whispered, more for herself than Mitzi, "Don't worry girl, we're going to find him."

Still "searching for service" flashed across her phone. Where was James?

She readied to shriek. Her cry might manage to draw Maclean away from Davis. The twist of the door knob stifled her shout.

An enormous firefighter opened the door. He stopped mid-stride and stared. "I wasn't expecting anyone. I'm Lieutenant Whit Henley with Ladder Seven."

Every instinct screamed for her to rush the door.

"Isn't this Davis' dog?" He bent down to pet Mitzi who was trying to find an opening around the firefighter's legs.

"Yes, it's Mitzi. Stay, girl."

Mitzi dropped to her stomach and gave a low whimper. She felt the same frustration as Mitzi. The lieutenant, oblivious to her distress, continued to pet Mitzi.

"I'm Grayce Walters, Davis' fiancée," she fibbed. "He wanted me to watch the technical rescue."

"Davis, the sly devil. He never said a word. I'm his climbing buddy, Whit."

Her face heated with the blatant lie. "Do you know where Davis is?"

"You're just in time. Davis is about to dangle off the halo."

Her heart hammered against her chest as if she had run straight up the stairs of the Space Needle. "He's going to do what?"

"He's our volunteer. He just dangles, harnessed, of course. Didn't he tell you? This is our favorite drill. Then one of my crew rappels down and rescues him."

"What's the halo? And how do I get there?"

"It's the flying saucer part just above us, but it's off limits—only the roped crew has access now."

"Is Officer Maclean with Davis?"

"I just left them. Came to get my jacket, the wind's picking up."

She felt light-headed as if she might pass out. Davis was on the Space Needle with Maclean and she couldn't get to him. Whit wouldn't break protocol, wouldn't be swayed by her explanation of Davis' danger. He would never let her up on the halo, no matter what story she manufactured.

"You can watch Davis dangle from the Observation Deck. I'm going there now to clear it of all the tourists. For some reason, the assistant chief doesn't want anyone watching this rescue." The firefighter rolled his eyes. "Who knows what the brass is thinking?"

She knew why. Maclean was going to push Davis off and he didn't want any witnesses. "Thank you for the offer. It might be more than I can handle to watch my husband-to-be dangle." Her heart felt like it was going into V-Fib, a rhythm that caused hearts to stop. She tried to shut out the vision of Davis hanging from the Space Needle.

"Don't worry about Davis. He and I have done a lot more dangerous ascents."

She didn't want to hear about Davis' climbing exploits. "Mitzi and I will wait for Davis here. He'll come here before he leaves?" Her mind searched for a possible escape. "Do you know if there's a lady's room on this level?"

"There's one on the left just before the stairwell."

"Thank you."

She tried not to break into a run when she left the mechanical room. She had to get up the steps before the lieutenant came out of the room. Mitzi raced ahead of her. She saw the long narrow steps leading to an open hatch. "Mitzi, wait, you can't go up there."

She kicked off her Jimmy Choos and commanded Mitzi one more time to stay. Grayce had no idea how she was going to stop Maclean. Where was James when she needed him? Nothing mattered, not her acrophobia, nothing but saving Davis.

She climbed the metal steps in her bare feet. Cool air blasted down the stairwell from the opened hatch.

She was gasping when she got to the top, not from the exertion but from terror. With only the blue sky above, she climbed onto the glaring white platform. She didn't need to look down to know she was high above the ground. Whit had said she had to be roped. She didn't see any ropes.

The wind whipped at her ponytail. She stepped back toward the stairs. The uneven surface caused a new wave of unsteadiness. Her heart surged in a jagged pulse.

She managed a small step forward. Sudden shakiness began in her knees and proceeded to a trembling that shook her entire body. Waves of panic surged through her. Fear kept her glued in place, paralyzed.

She had blocked out everything but the battle she was fighting to overcome her fear of heights. Her fright made her body stiffen. She saw a flash out of the corner of her eye. She gingerly turned her neck, terrified by the slight movement.

Ahead on the edge, just like her nightmare, Maclean grabbed Davis. Her heart clenched.

Davis broke free of Maclean's grasp. They fought on a tiny slope seeming oblivious to their danger.

She pleaded with Cassie for help then dropped to her knees and crawled. With each forward motion her hands trembled and the weak sensation hammered behind her knees. Neither man had seen her. Her body and mind were consumed by the need to reach Davis.

She kept her head down. It was at least another twenty feet to reach Davis. She was going to be too late. She focused on placing each hand forward. The wind blasted, the Needle swayed. Her heart thundered louder in her ears.

Mitzi rushed past her. The poodle jumped over Grayce and skirted the edge of the halo moving fast toward Davis and Maclean. Mitzi lips were pulled back, showing sharp gleaming canines.

Davis dropped his hands from Maclean. "Grayce? Mitzi get back." With her teeth bared, Mitzi growled.

Surprised by the commotion behind him, Maclean turned quickly. His sudden response pitched him backward toward the edge. He flung himself forward trying to regain his balance.

Like a sport spectator, Grayce watched him try to regain his balance, swinging back and then forward. Time slowed. The momentum of Maclean's waving arms had pitched him too far. He fell backward over the edge.

Davis jumped forward into the air and grabbed the falling assistant chief by his legs.

Maclean dangled upside down. His bellow shattered the silence.

Grayce leaned over to watch both men swing like a pendulum. Terror pulsed through her.

Whit and Toni, the rescue team rappelled down the halo. They landed in one powerful heave. Whit grabbed Davis' rope and pulled Davis toward him. Toni jumped into the air wrapping herself around Maclean from behind. An upside down Maclean swung with Toni. The team worked in synchrony. Davis and Whit slowly pulled Toni back above the Halo. Whit grabbed Maclean and lowered him onto his side on the narrow ledge. Maclean didn't remain lying down for more than a few seconds. He pushed himself upright.

Whit's face was contorted with fury. He shouted at Davis. "What the fuck happened?" Davis shrugged his shoulders.

The wind prevented Grayce from hearing any more of the conversation between the team. Toni stood nonchalantly, as if she rescued dangling upside down men every day. She probably did. Maclean had his back to Grayce, so she couldn't see his reaction.

In the next minute Maclean strode away from Grayce as if nothing unusual had occurred. She was able to hear him shout at Davis, something about headquarters. His last words she heard clearly, since he looked directly at her when he shouted. "Get your damn girlfriend and dog out of here."

Mitzi barked at Davis. Davis shouted, "Stay there, Grayce, don't move; I'm coming to get you." The absurdity of the situation hit her. Didn't he know she was too scared to move?

Whit and Davis moved toward her. Whit was in charge and wasn't going to be directed by Davis. "Don't move, Ma'am. I'll have you off quickly."

"Whit, I'll get her off."

"Why in the fuck are your fiancée and dog out here without being roped?"

Davis pulled Whit back. "It's okay. I'll get them down."

Both men glared at each other.

"I'll explain it all to you," Davis said.

Whit nodded and then went over the edge. It seemed no one in the Fire Department ever took elevators.

CHAPTER FIFTY-TWO

Davis walked swiftly toward Grayce with Mitzi following behind. Grayce hadn't budged.

"Grayce, I'm going to pick you up. Remember I'm secured to the safety line. Nothing can happen."

She managed a nod. She was petrified. He felt a rush of protective feelings. "Keep your eyes closed. I'll have you on solid ground before you know it." Davis lifted her trembling body. She was freezing, shaking with fear. He pulled her close to his heat.

Tender feelings, newly discovered, pulled at him. He pressed her against his chest. "It's okay. We're almost there."

A blond woman in a bright red blouse stood at the top of the stairs, fluttering hands adorned with sparkling rings. "Oh...Thank God, Davis. I thought you went over."

The voice sounded familiar, but the woman wasn't recognizable. She had layers of makeup, bright red lips and batted her eyelashes outlandishly.

"My God, Grayce, you went out there? And Mitzi?"

Grayce shook her head.

"Honey, are you all right? Grayce is terrified of heights. I can't believe you did it."

Why was Grayce, Mitzi and a girlfriend at the Space Needle? Davis wondered.

Grayce's voice shook from the shivering he could feel against his chest, "Please James, can we have this discussion on the ground."

"James?" Davis kept looking at the woman, trying to recognize James underneath the feminine clothes.

James put his hand on his hip in a seductive pose and batted his eyelashes. "Darlin', I saw the way you were checking me out."

"James!"

Davis had never heard Grayce so irate.

"No need to get testy, Grayce. I know you've been through a lot, but let's get things in perspective. Davis didn't fall off."

He watched James climb back down the stairs in his tight skirt. Davis held Grayce close. He unhooked himself and carried her down the stairs. He hadn't carried anyone for quite a while. Grayce made the task easy. She weighed less than Mitzi. "You thought I was going to fall?"

She murmured against his shirt. All he could discern was "Maclean."

James was putting his shoes on when Davis got to the bottom. Red high heels, no less.

Grayce pushed against him. "You can put me down now. I'm fine. It's just heights that scare me."

James handed Grayce's shoes to Davis. "Let the big strong firefighter carry you. You look terrible."

Davis didn't want to let her go. Mitzi jumped from the last steps and stood next to him. "You're still shaking. Let's see if we can find you a blanket or coat." He felt James' close inspection.

"It looks like you're in good hands, Darlin'." James pecked Grayce on the cheek. "I'm going to sneak out of here. I don't want to run into Dave, the security guard. It will be a great story with Grey Goose."

"Thanks, James."

James pursed his lips and threw a kiss toward Davis. "Honey, I'm available anytime to save Davis' ass. I can still make it to Gay Bingo."

"The police might need to talk with you," Davis said.

"Men in uniforms? Send them over."

"Don't go out of town."

James tittered. "And I thought you didn't have a sense of humor. Ta-ta." He waved his hands covered with chunky rings and red painted nails like a parade queen. He stepped into the elevator, pulling down his tight skirt.

Grayce pushed against his chest again. "Davis, I'm okay now. You can put me down."

He ignored Grayce's command and carried her into the mechanical room. Mitzi trailed close behind.

"I didn't recognize James. What a guy. Or should I say gal?"

She pushed again. "Davis, put me down."

He didn't feel like releasing her yet. He knew he was holding her as much for his own needs as hers. The whole scene with Maclean had been hellish and there would be a lot more to come. He kissed her head, inhaling her scent. He had missed her. He put her down slowly, feeling her small, lithe body move down his length. "I'm going to find something to warm you. He searched through the gear scattered throughout the small room.

She stood in the middle of the room, not moving or speaking. Davis wrapped the heavy regulation coat around her shoulders. He smiled down at her. "I think you should remain my fiancée."

That shook her out of her despondency. "I had to give Whit some reason. Or he wasn't going to let me stay."

"And rightly so."

She blinked, her large green eyes rounded. "You're upset that I came?"

He pulled her into his arms. "Not at all. I'm trying to understand what you thought was going to happen today."

"I was afraid that Maclean would push you off."

"So you and Mitzi came to save me." He wanted to laugh but knew by the way she chewed on her lower lip that she wasn't in the mood for humor. "I appreciate what you did, more than you'll ever know."

The elevator doors opened, to the sound of male voices.

"Let me do the talking. This is a bit complicated."

He kissed her quickly. Her lips were still cold. He wanted to warm his valiant rescuer, who had risked herself to save him. The voices came closer. With her pale color and the violet smudges under her eyes, she didn't look like the warrior woman who had climbed out on the halo to save him. Post-battle fatigue had struck.

"I'm not sure what's going to happen. It might be too late to call," Davis said. He didn't mention that he might be in police custody or possibly jail. He held Grayce close to his side while they waited for the valet to bring her car.

Grayce put her hand on his arm. "I don't think I'm going to be able to sleep. I don't care what time it is. You'll come over?"

Her long blond hair hung down, framing her face, making her look younger. He wanted to take away the air of vulnerability that clung to her now. He pulled her close. "I don't think I'm ever going to forget you crawling across the halo."

"I wasn't sure if you would understand my need to come here, to protect you."

He rubbed his lips against her cold lips. "I didn't think you came for the view, since it's pretty hard to see much from your knees." He could feel her smile against his lips. He wanted to make her laugh, to forget what had happened and what he faced next. Maclean thought he was dirty. Talk about irony.

"Excuse me, your car is here." The valet said.

He whispered into her ear, inhaling her sweet scent, the scent of innocence and goodness. "Honey, your car is here."

"My car?"

He couldn't resist her bewildered look. He kissed her again. "The young man brought your car."

Her face turned bright red. He reluctantly let her go. She began to dig in her gigantic purse.

He opened the back door. "Mitzi, come on girl. Get in the car." Mitzi barked and climbed over the seat into the passenger's side.

"Do you let her ride in the front seat?"

"I know it's not the safest place in the car, but she won't stay in the back. She wants to be near me."

"Smart dog. I feel the same way."

She ran her hand up and down his arms, touching, soothing him. "I'm sure the chief won't believe for a second that you're a criminal."

"Thanks, honey, for your faith. I'll call you when I'm done and you can decide whether it's too late for me to come over. You've been through a lot and once the adrenaline is gone, you'll see how tired you are."

"I'll be waiting for you, Davis." And with that, she got into her car. He watched her drive down the circular drive. He turned and walked back to his car. He didn't have Grayce's faith that the chief would believe him. The chief would want evidence. Evidence he didn't have.

CHAPTER FIFTY-THREE

Grayce held the hot teacup to her cheek and inhaled the fragrant jasmine vapors. Wrapped in a down comforter, she still couldn't get warm. Mitzi lay at her feet. Napoleon was curled in a tight ball, tucked into one of the soft folds in the comforter. Both animals were subdued, mirroring Grayce's mood.

She had been wrong. Maclean wasn't a criminal. Her cheeks heated with the memory of lying to Whit about being Davis' fiancée. Although mortified, she would do it again to protect Davis.

Her gifts weren't linear or a hundred percent accurate, but that didn't mean she should discount her instincts. Deep knowing resonated—Davis remained in danger. Someone in the department had accused him of working for the Russians.

She had been wrong because of Maclean's hostility toward Davis.

Dr. Z had reassured her that she was learning to tame her powers and should continue to bring them under control. She slowed her breathing, focusing on someone hostile to Davis, someone with a scar and a motive. She took another deep breath and closed her eyes to meditate.

Mitzi nudged Grayce's hand with her head.

"I know…he's still out there."

With her eyes closed, her eyelids flickered, deepening into relaxation. She slowly stroked Mitzi's head.

Instead of visualizing her white light, she visualized the scar. The same ominous dread surrounded her, the image of the puckered scar slithering up the man's arm.

Mitzi started a low growl.

Grayce closed her eyes tighter, willing herself into a deeper meditation, trying to see the details of the scar.

Mitzi jumped on the couch next to Grayce and howled in distress.

"I don't know, Mitzi. All I can see is a big arm."

The man's arm was huge. She wanted to laugh at the absurdity of her newest clue, a man in the fire department with a huge arm. She had narrowed the suspects down to at least half of the department.

Grayce went to her bedroom and opened her childhood pink jewelry box with the dancing ballerina. She fingered her sister's pendant, a golden heart with a ruby in the center.

Cassie would be laughing right now, entertained by Grayce's escapade on the Space Needle. No matter how embarrassing, Cassie would've remained firm in her acceptance of Grayce's gifts. Her hand tightened around the necklace. *"Cassie, I need your help. Davis is in danger."*

She didn't have any sudden insight except that Davis needed her help. She reverently placed Cassie's necklace around her neck, then dialed Davis' cell. He didn't pick up.

Waiting for him to call her back, Grayce, with Mitzi following, paced back and forth in the small living room

She sent a text. "Be careful. You're still in danger."

Mitzi gave another hair-raising howl.

"You feel it too. Something's about to happen."

Mitzi ran to the back door and jumped up, yipping loudly.

"I'm getting dressed."

Mitzi jumped at the door in response.

It was time to rescue Davis. Again.

Grayce and Mitzi scurried across the slippery cobblestones of Pioneer Square, determined to speak to Davis. The mist created an eerie twilight on the historic buildings. She could smell the salt water of Puget Sound in the thick air.

When she entered the silent department headquarters, apprehension grabbed at her, causing her breath to quicken and her pulse to race. The vast space was usually filled with bustling humanity. She walked toward the front desk in the strangely quiet building. Niles, the chaplain came down the hallway with a broad smile. Maybe this trip wasn't a mistake.

"What a surprise, Dr. Walters. I thought you would need to recover after this morning."

"You've already heard about the Space Needle?" If her cheeks got any hotter, she would catch fire.

"Davis told me about this morning's mishap before his meeting with the chief. I was worried and thought I should check on you."

Niles' concern for her caused a ripple of suspicion to wind its way through her.

The huge man bent down to pet Mitzi's head. The dog pulled back, retreating behind Grayce. Her anxiety was contagious.

"I had hoped to talk to Davis."

Niles' eyes examined her face. His close scrutiny felt intrusive, disturbing. "Are you okay?"

Instead of feeling reassured by the man of the cloth, she felt agitated, her senses overwhelmed. She had experienced this paradox before when the outer-world clashed with her inner-world and people weren't what they seemed to be, like friendly people who abused their pets.

"I got worried when Davis didn't answer his phone. I thought his meeting would be over by now. Is there any way I could see him?"

"Why don't you come into my office and I'll go check whether the chief's door is still closed. Come this way."

Niles pointed at the empty hallway. Grayce looked down the long white distance to Niles' office. Mitzi pushed against Grayce's leg. Her heart thudded loudly in the silent space.

"My office will be a calm place to wait."

His soothing voice grated on her frayed nervous system. She shook her head avoiding eye contact. "I'm more exhausted than I thought. I think I'll go home."

"My office is a refuge, a great place for Davis to meet you after his difficult meeting."

She scanned Niles' face. His skin was gray and there were dark circles below each eye. He looked exhausted, like he hadn't been sleeping. His eyes flickered with an emotion she couldn't decipher.

"Thanks for the offer, but I'll just wait at home. Come on Mitzi." Her nerves were jittery as if she had overdosed on caffeine.

Grayce started to turn when Mitzi lunged for Niles's arm. The poodle locked her teeth on Nile's shirt sleeve.

"Mitzi!"

"What in the hell?" Niles shook his arm, trying to dislodge the 100 pound poodle. Mitzi held tight to Nile's shirt and continued a menacing, low-pitched growl.

"Call her off, damn it."

Niles jerked his arm violently. The force ripped his shirt and sent Mitzi flying.

The poodle had bits of white fabric clenched between her teeth when she hit the wood floor.

A long jagged scar ran the entire length of Niles' forearm. All of Grayce's senses exploded—the sound of Niles' harsh breathing, the light bulb flickering above them, the threatening silence in the hallway and the revelation that Niles was the one, the connection to the mob.

Her heart ran marathons, racing against her chest. Mitzi stood and shook herself.

Niles inspected his arm for damage. "What is wrong with that dog?"

"Did she break the skin?" Grayce asked, trying to disguise the quiver in her voice, in her body.

"No. I'm okay," Niles grumbled.

"I don't know why she would act this way." Grayce bent and petted Mitzi, avoiding looking at Niles.

Mitzi acted on instinct. Grayce would do well to pay more attention to her own instincts. Grayce kept her back to Niles, afraid she would reveal her panic. "I know Davis will pay for the damage."

Grayce flashed through her options in escaping. She could scream for Davis but how would she convince anyone that

Niles' scar proved him as the conspirator. The man was the chaplain.

Niles weighed close to 300 pounds. To use aikido, she would need to provoke him, using his weight and momentum against him. She wasn't confident she could take him down.

Deciding to run from Niles was her best option with the possibility of using her aikido, Grayce gathered Mitzi's leash. "I'm taking Mitzi home. She's still upset about going up on the Space Needle."

Niles' voice darkened, "I'm sorry, Dr. Walters. I can't let that happen."

"Can't let Mitzi go home?"

"You know… don't you?" Niles edged closer. "I need one more day and this will be over. Trust me."

Mitzi growled.

Niles squinted, watching her closely, as if he knew her plan to run. He was right. She was going to make a dash.

"I never wanted to involve Davis. You're the one who got him to scrutinize the department."

Her stomach did flutters and flips, shooting straight to her knees making them rubbery, making it hard to stand.

"You know you should've stayed home. This wouldn't have been necessary if you had stayed out of it."

Grayce stepped back. Mitzi jerked on her leash, trying to get closer to Niles, to wedge herself between Grayce and the villain.

"If you hadn't put Davis on to the Russians." The desperation in Niles' voice made Grayce want to race right out the door.

"If Davis isn't taken into police custody, you're staying until my son gets on his plane."

"Davis didn't do anything." Grayce pulled Mitzi closer to her.

Backed against the wall, Grayce couldn't move away from Niles' menacing posture. Mitzi strained toward Niles.

"My son and his family leave Russia tomorrow morning. If they don't take Davis into custody, then you'll be my bargaining chip to convince Davis not to go to the feds until Nicholas escapes. "

"I don't understand."

"The Russian's expect Davis to be taken into custody. If the Russians find out that Davis is free to bring in the Feds, they'll never allow Nicholas to leave."

"I won't tell anyone until your son is free."

"The Russians miss nothing. They'll know. They have spies all over. I'm sure you were followed here."

Niles stepped toward her, his hand outstretched. "Don't make this hard on yourself."

She inched away from his hand.

"We'll wait for the outcome of the meeting in the annex. Davis has been with the chief for hours and should be finished soon."

"The annex?" She needed to get outside and run.

"It's where the firefighters used to sleep while the station was being remodeled." Niles guided her, placing his hand on her back.

Grayce recoiled from his touch on her back. Walking next to her out to the street, Mitzi kept up her insistent rumble.

"Right there is the annex." He pointed to a squat cinder-block structure, tucked between the red brick buildings of Seattle's oldest neighborhood. The annex was dark and looked like a WWII bunker.

At the sight of the bleak building, her nervous system heightened to a fine pitch. She hoped the high-octane tremors going through her body would subside once she started to run.

"What's the building used for now?"

"Administration and support staff."

Hyper-vigilant, she became aware of the rain dripping down her neck, the sound of the trolley scraping the tracks, the horn blast of the Bainbridge Island Ferry. Her muscles clenched, ready for the run.

"Please. Don't try to run. You won't get far."

As if Mitzi understood Niles' threat, the poodle jumped and attacked Niles.

Dropping Mitzi's leash, Grayce ran. She ran toward the trolley stop but no one was there waiting. She changed direction, moving toward Occidental Square. Her flats couldn't get traction on the uneven bricks. She slipped sideways. She cried out when the pain shot from her twisted ankle.

Grayce didn't look back. With her leash dragging, Mitzi caught up to Grayce.

Niles was gasping for air behind her. She entered the square, usually crowded at this hour. The incessant rain had cleared the area. A homeless man, cocooned in a plastic tarp, slept on a park bench. No one else was out in the rain.

Niles was shouting, "Grayce… wait." His voice was strained from his effort.

She had put a fair distance between them. Mitzi remained next to Grayce.

Grayce had to double back to get out of the isolated industrial waterfront. In her panic, she had over run. She had to get back to Jackson Street, where coffee shops abound. He couldn't abduct her out of a Starbucks.

She turned to make for the alley that ran behind the Department to Jackson Street. Niles was slow enough that he wouldn't be able to cut her off at the far end of the alley. Revitalized, she sprinted toward the alley.

Suddenly, her foot caught between two bricks. She crashed to her hands and knees on the pavement.

Ignoring the flash of agony, she pulled herself up, wiped her hands on her coat and grabbed Mitzi's leash. Niles was shouting something about Davis. Mitzi barked ferociously. She turned the corner into the alley. A lone dumpster sat in the long dark passage.

The smell of rotting garbage hit her in the face. Grayce hugged the wall, trying to put some space between herself and the putrid-smelling dumpster. The sounds of her footsteps and Mitzi's clicking toenails reflected off the brick buildings.

Two Norway rats climbed among the bags of garbage. An involuntary shudder shook her body with the nearness of the giant rodents.

The alley was black with no street light. Niles' footsteps echoed in the alley. His bulk didn't slow him down. Davis had told her that Niles had been an amazing athlete, but his prospects as a football star had ended with an injury.

At the sound of Niles' footsteps, she tried to increase her speed. Her lungs burned and the pain in her side throbbed relentlessly.

She could burst into the station and scream that Niles was chasing her. Would anyone believe her after her blunder on the Space Needle? She put her hand over Cassie's necklace. A deep sense of awareness of her sister gave her an energy burst. She sprinted.

She crossed Washington Street. A black SUV careened down the street. Two men in the massive vehicle headed the wrong way down the one-way street. The driver accelerated when Grayce dashed toward the next alley. Niles shouted something.

A short block and she would be free.

Niles followed close behind, gaining. No rat infested dumpsters in this alley. Mitzi ran next to Grayce.

Niles' footsteps got louder. A woman with a red umbrella passed in front of the alley. Safety was close. The coffee shop filled with people was in her sight.

She heard an engine revving when she and Mitzi crossed Jackson Street. The black SUV accelerated, ran the red light, aimed to hit them.

Grayce and Mitzi sprinted the last fifty yards to the coffee shop.

Niles bolted across the street, maneuvering to avoid being hit by a taxi. The driver of the SUV gunned the engine, bearing down on Niles. Niles didn't stand a chance against the 5,000 pound force. Niles flew into the air like a small bird in flight.

The chatter in the coffee shop stopped with the sickening sounds of Niles being struck, and the shattering of the windshield when he bounced on the hood. Motionless, Niles rolled off and crashed to the sidewalk.

An unnatural silence followed.

The SUV sped away.

Grayce ran out of the coffee shop to Niles. He lay face up with his eyes open. Blood poured from a deep laceration in his forehead. A pedestrian had bent over Niles, taking his pulse. He was barely conscious, his eyes were unfocused, his respirations shallow. The sirens started to howl. The fire station was next door to headquarters. Blood dribbled out of Niles' mouth.

Grayce knelt by Niles' head. Mitzi lay down next to Grayce. "I'm so sorry, Niles." Grayce took his cold hand in hers. She prayed silently for him, not understanding how this moment had come to pass. His face had lost all color.

Niles tried to speak, "Tell Davis…"

Grayce bent her head closer to Niles' white lips.

Niles closed his eyes. He gasped, "My son… I did it for my son."

She squeezed his icy cold hand tight.

Niles rasped, "In my prayer book."

Someone lifted her by the elbow. "Ma'am, I'll need you to stand back. Let me attend to him."

The medics bent down to attend to the chaplain. "Good Lord! It's Niles Olsen."

CHAPTER FIFTY-FOUR

Davis sprinted toward Jackson Street. Niles was down.

He saw the ambulance—a good sign that they hadn't taken Niles to the hospital yet. Davis pushed through the bystanders, reverting to his professional role, in control.

A crowd of blue uniforms huddled around Niles. At any minute, Davis expected to hear Niles' reassuring voice, making light of the situation.

Davis heard a familiar bark. Mitzi and Grayce stood with a policeman away from the medic crew. He couldn't take in all that was happening. Grayce was wrapped in a blanket, protecting her from the rain. Even at ten feet away, he could see her pallor. Mitzi yipped but didn't move from Grayce's side.

Davis could see above the heads to where Niles lay on the wet pavement. A full code was underway. Sean gave chest compressions, Lisa pumped the ambu-bag, and Ron stood back, paddles in hand, after defibrillation.

Sean slowly shook his head.

His giant friend lay still, his face ashen.

Davis' vision narrowed. He fought to stay upright. He couldn't breathe. He bent over, trying to suck air into his lungs. Niles was dead. He needed to stay in control. Take charge or he would shatter.

Silence filled the space around him, broken by Mitzi's yipping. Davis began to move, his feet unsteady on the uneven bricks. He walked toward Grayce, who stared into space, oblivious to his presence.

"Grayce?" His voice sounded flat and hollow.

Grayce walked into his arms.

He could barely hear her whisper, "He's dead."

He tightened his hold on her. Mitzi whined, a pitiful sound.

The policeman waited.

"Do you have what you need, officer?" Davis asked.

"I've got it for now."

Davis dug in his pants for his card. He handed the card to the policeman, appreciating the irony of the situation. If he and the brass had finished their meeting, he might not have retained his rank, and been able to pass out his FI card.

"I'm taking you back to the station." He put his arm around her and steered her around the crowd. He avoided the medics and his fallen friend. He pulled Grayce closer, trying to warm her.

"Honey, I'm taking you to the annex where we can get you blankets and something hot to drink." He didn't want Maclean or the chief to know she had been present when Niles was hit. Neither had been pleased by her involvement on the Space Needle

"Niles tried to take me there." Her face was colorless, making her green eyes enormous.

"What?"

"He had the scar… If it weren't for Mitzi…." She clenched her teeth in an attempt to stop the chattering. Her complexion was colorless; her lips were blue and pressed together as if in pain. "He was the one in the garden and my nightmare."

"Grayce, I can carry you."

She shook her head. "No, Davis, I can walk, I'm wet and cold."

He quickened their pace, guiding her to the annex, to an on-call room. She must be in shock since she didn't laugh when he handed her sweats, size XXL.

Sipping hot tea, her color gradually returned, first her face, then finally her hands and feet. Mitzi lay on top of Grayce's feet as a foot warmer. Smart dog.

Grayce lifted the Styrofoam cup to her lips. "Why didn't I suspect him? I'm thinking my intuition must not have worked since Niles wasn't trying to hurt you. He was trying to protect his son. "

Davis bent down to be face-to-face with Grayce. "Honey, take a deep breath."

"We've got to find his son."

He took her hands in his and rubbed them together to warm them. "It's okay. You don't need to worry about that now."

Grayce had implied that Niles was the dirty connection. She had to be wrong.

She closed her eyes. "I could've prevented his death… I should've known sooner, but I got distracted by Maclean's scar and his gambling."

"Grayce, breathe. It will help."

She wiped her nose with the oversized sleeve. "If I had known sooner, I might have stopped his murder."

"It was an accident. Niles was hit by a car."

Her long hair, wrapped in a turban, gave her the look of an Egyptian goddess. She shook her head, the towel swayed back and forth.

"Mitzi and I made it into the coffee shop but Niles was too slow." A shudder racked her body. "They're going to go after his son."

"You almost got hit?" He asked.

"The men in the black SUV. They ran the red light and aimed for Niles." Her voice shook. "He flew in the air…" She gulped for a breath.

"Men in a black SUV were chasing you and Niles?"

"I didn't know if they were after me or Niles since Niles was chasing me."

He pulled over a chair and sat in front of Grayce, knee to knee. He couldn't let his surge of fury that Niles had been pursuing her distract him.

"Tell me what happened."

"I should've trusted you. I'm so sorry. Niles was the traitor."

"Niles was dirty?"

She reached over and grabbed his hand. "I'm sorry. I know he was a friend."

"I don't believe it."

Agony turned and twisted in his gut.

"He's the one, the connection in the department."

"Niles set me up? He gave the chief the note that linked me with Benson and the Russian mob?" None of them had considered the possibility that Niles had authored the note. "Did Niles say why he accused me?" He coughed trying to hide the cracking emotion in his voice.

"Niles needed to delay the feds coming into your investigation to give his son time to leave Russia."

Davis couldn't remain still. He leaped up from his chair and began to pace. "Niles must have been in pretty deep." He stood over her. "Why did you come to the station? And what's this about your abilities could've prevented Niles' death?"

Grayce, still wrapped in her blankets, pulled away from him.

"I'm sorry Grayce. I shouldn't be dragging you through all of this... "

She tried to straighten her turban. His bedraggled combatant, with her hair tumbling out of the towel, looked like she had survived a major battle. He wanted to laugh at the absurdity of the situation. Maybe he was the one in shock.

He took her hands and squeezed them. "I'm glad you're okay."

Mitzi, who remained sitting on Grayce's feet, added a few tail thumps in agreement.

Grayce leaned forward and cupped his face, empathy reflected in her eyes. "I know this is hard for you."

He couldn't allow himself to feel anything. He needed to stay in control, to keep all of his buried feelings from spilling out. He stood up. "Did Niles say anything else?"

Grayce's bright eyes dimmed, she chewed on her lower lip.

"Was there anything else Niles told you?"

"He said, 'In his prayer book.'"

"Prayer book? I've never seen Niles with a prayer book."

A familiar voice interrupted. "Davis, you sure know how to ruin a girl's good time. I was on a major hot streak at Bingo."

James, dressed as La Bete, promenaded into the room. He stopped midway. "My God, Grayce, not again."

Davis stood to greet James. "I appreciate you coming. I need you to take Grayce home."

"You didn't need to call James. I'm capable of driving myself home," Grayce said.

Mitzi jumped on James, trying to plant a wet kiss on his face.

James had trouble bending in his red heels. "Honey, you're a beauty and you like other women." He petted the dog's head. "We've got to find you a tough bitch with a studded collar."

"Mitzi definitely likes this female." Davis looked back at Grayce, who was trying to pull up the sweats that were sagging at her feet. "Don't get up. You need to get some rest."

Grayce walked toward the men. "I'm better now. I just got chilled from the rain."

"Why are you wearing sweats that look like they'd fit Attila the Hun?"

"We don't have any firefighters under five feet," Davis said.

"Did you hear me, Grayce? You look like hell," James said.

"I was…" Her voice wobbled.

"Grayce needs to go home. She may have gotten hypothermic. She was outside in the rain." Davis gave James a very brief summary of the last hour's events.

"I'll get her tucked in."

"Do I have a say?"

Davis leveled his commander look. "You need to go home and take a hot bath."

"And where will you be while I'm following orders, sir?" Her towel had fallen from her head and her hair fell in disarray around her shoulders.

"I have to stay here and sort through this mess," Davis said.

"I don't want to leave you, not now, when…" She edged closer to him. Her voice had gotten soft, quiet.

"Mitzi and I'll wait outside. We are a bit *de trollop*," James said.

Grayce wrapped her arms around Davis. Her eyes searched his face. "I don't want you to be alone. I want to take that look off your face." Before he could reply she clutched his neck and pulled him down for a kiss.

Her lips covered his in a gentle but fervent kiss. So fervent, he forgot about her being cold, about sending her home, so fervent he forgot to breathe.

She kissed him again, whisper-soft kisses this time, whispers against his lips, cheeks, and eyelids, whispers that lingered and promised.

"I mean it this time, Grayce. I'm coming to your house tonight, no matter what time."

"I'll be waiting for you, Davis."

She smiled like Mona Lisa, a woman who knew her worth.

He smiled. Mona Lisa had gone home barefoot.

CHAPTER FIFTY-FIVE

Grayce was exhausted but couldn't sleep. She was cold, but couldn't get warm. She was tense but couldn't relax.

It was midnight and she waited for Davis to arrive. They would comfort each other, lessen the emptiness, this feeling of detachment, a feeling that Diet Coke and potato chips couldn't ease.

She reached for the remote and surfed the TV channels, looking for news about the accident. How would the fire department portray Niles' death? She prayed for Niles and his son, offering a silent plea for both of them.

The local station announced the breaking news at Pioneer Square. The channel hawked the disaster, panning a shot of Pioneer Square and then moving to the spot where Niles had been hit. An icy chill settled deep down into her soul.

She was about to turn off the TV when the final pre-commercial lead announced that a spokesperson from the fire department would be interviewed. Another commercial flicked onto the screen.

The fire department spokesperson's name *Helen Fitzsimmons, Public Information Officer* flashed across the bottom of the screen. The slender woman stood in front of fire headquarters. A picture of Niles, in full uniform, remained on screen during Helen Fitzsimmons' prepared statement.

Chaplain Niles Olsen was accidentally hit while crossing the street. There will be an investigation by the Seattle Police Department. The Chaplain will be mourned by the entire community. He has served the fire department with honor for 18 years.

Fitzsimmons concluded with a pledge that the fire chief planned a speedy investigation and promised answers surrounding the chaplain's death. The chief and the department offered their condolences to their colleague's family and friends.

Davis would need sympathy. He was hurting and would blame himself, thinking that somehow he could've prevented the tragedy.

Grayce flicked on her Enya CD.

She headed to the bathroom to take a hot bath, to heat herself, to soothe her frozen bones and soul.

Davis gripped the steering wheel, impatient to get away from the station. He shifted back into first and waited in the long line of cars merging to exit the Century Link Field—a fitting end to a nightmarish day, to be stuck in football traffic. The fans streamed down First Avenue. His timing had been off all day.

The traffic started to inch forward. A trip that should've taken twenty minutes was turning into an hour. He could still picture Niles bleeding on the cement, which was how the mob honored their promises. He ignored the hurt in his chest close to his heart.

Neither the chief nor Davis could imagine Niles immersed in a criminal life. Niles' disgrace and death had made Davis feel sullied. Grayce's deep integrity was the antidote he needed.

Grayce wasn't answering her phone. She must have fallen asleep. Not exactly how he envisioned their reunion. The aftermath of trauma was rough. The nights were hard after a shock. He wanted to be there, next to her, helping her with the stress.

The traffic started to move. Once away from the snarl around Century Link Field, he made the trip quickly to Fremont.

All the lights were on at Grayce's house. She must have fallen asleep on the couch. He wouldn't wake her; just reassure himself she wasn't upset. Davis climbed the three steps to her front door and peered through the windows trying to catch a glimpse of Grayce. He didn't see anyone.

He still had a key from his inspection after the fire. He stepped into the house. A singer's soothing voice crooned through unseen speakers.

If Grayce was asleep in her bedroom, he didn't want to wake her.

He walked the three steps to Grayce's bedroom. Napoleon jumped up on the bed, startling Davis into a whole body flinch. He stared at the cat. Napoleon stared back, then jumped down and rubbed against his leg. "Big guy, where is she? Walking Mitzi?"

A voice floated down the hallway, Grayce singing with the sound of water running.

He peered down the hallway. The bathroom door was ajar. Mitzi, back legs extended, lay in the bathroom watching Grayce take her bath. Lucky dog. Mitzi jumped up, her tail wagging. He bent and petted her, giving her a nice scratch under her chin. Grayce continued to sing along with the music, a haunting melody.

Mitzi sauntered to the bedroom as if she knew what Davis intended.

He didn't want to frighten Grayce. He should wait for her in the living room but her wafting flowery scent and her lyrical voice beckoned.

Just a peek.

He slowly pushed the door further open, leaning against the door jam. Immersed beneath the bubbles, Grayce rested her head against the edge of the claw-footed tub. Her hair was twisted on top of her head with a few curls clinging to her neck. She lifted her dainty foot to turn the water tap. Unaware, she kept her eyes closed.

He should feel guilty for being a voyeur but after the harrowing day, he deserved this indulgent interlude. She was tiny enough that the water covered her body, but his male brain had no trouble envisioning the sweet presence just below the surface. The idea of Grayce, hot and wet, was affecting his body, pooling heat in uncomfortable places. If he wasn't careful, he would soon be panting.

He should retreat to the living room, but his feet remained planted. Grayce was the perfect tonic after today's shock. She stretched her neck back. The movement lifted her breasts out of the water. His breathing got jagged, coming in bursts.

As if aware of his hungry stare, she opened her eyes and sat up, oblivious of her naked body.

"Davis you scared me."

His blood flow had left his brain and had headed to his nether regions. "I just got finished."

"Davis, are you okay?"

"I called your cell phone, but you didn't answer so…" He gulped. "I came to check on you."

"I didn't think you would be done so soon."

"I thought you might be sleeping. I didn't want to wake you."

His heart hammered against his chest, his breath uneven. He stayed leaning against the door. "You looked so relaxed, I hated to disturb you."

"I can't seem to get warm."

She wanted to get hot? His body core temperature couldn't get any higher. He struggled for words, trying to act nonchalant, "What's the smell?

"It's lavender. It's supposed to help you relax."

"I don't feel relaxed."

"What happened? Did Niles leave a letter, a message?"

"He hid a memory stick in his prayer book. The pictures and the spreadsheets exonerated me from any connection to the Russians and gave enough proof to nail them for drug smuggling. He did it all to get his son and his family out of Russia."

"Sounds like the man you knew."

Davis didn't want to think about Niles' decision.

"You look tense."

She had no idea the effect that her slick glistening body was having on him. He had a lot of pent up emotions that he knew exactly how and with whom he wanted to relieve them. She shifted in the tub, giving him a better view. His control slipped another notch.

"I'll wait for you in the living room." He turned back at the door. "Unless you need help getting out?"

A slow knowing smile crossed her lips, "You'll get all wet."

"I don't mind."

In two steps, he was across the bathroom, swooping down to pull her out of the water. She giggled. Heat radiated from her wet body.

"Grayce, you're killing me. You're so hot and slippery… and I've needed you ever since you left the station. It's been a nightmare. When I thought you might have gotten killed by those sleaze …but we're going to nail those bastards."

"I'm sure you will."

Inhaling the sweet scent of lavender, the sweet smell of Grayce, he pressed her wet body against him. "Let me love you."

CHAPTER FIFTY-SIX

Grayce stirred from her sleep. Davis stood at the window. With his back to her, he stared into the dark. His shoulders sagged as if the weight of the last day was too much to carry.

She scooched up and leaned against the headboard. Her shift in weight jostled Napoleon from the foot of the bed. The cat landed on all fours and headed for a more peaceful spot.

Davis turned. His large physique was silhouetted by the dim light from the hallway.

"You're not able to sleep?"

"I can't stop thinking about Niles."

Grayce patted the space next to her. "I'm happy to listen, whatever will help. I'm here."

He sat at the end of the bed, distancing himself from her. He was hurting and wouldn't want or accept an easy absolution.

"I've tried to put myself in his place. If only he had told me..." Davis said.

"If Niles confided in you that he was hiring ex-firefighters to do the Russian's criminal work, what could you have done?"

"I meant before those bastards had him trapped. I've got friends in the FBI. I could've helped to shield him and gotten protection for his son. I just can't understand why Niles would go out of the system."

"Maybe his son had warned him off or he didn't feel he could risk his son's life."

Davis clenched his hands on his thighs.

She scooted down the bed and placed her hand on top of his fist. "Honey, I don't think Niles wanted to involve you."

"He was willing to let me be a suspect in a murder investigation." He pulled his hand away.

"He was trying to buy one day until his son left Russia."

Davis shrugged. "I know, I know, but it was so senseless. And I'll never forgive him for threatening you."

"I think Niles panicked when I came to the station." She remembered her distress when Niles chased her. "I felt how desperate he was. I ran... I don't think he would've hurt me."

Davis jumped up and started to pace. "How in the hell do you know that? As you said, he was desperate. The Russians were moving in. He was a marked man. He cashed in his retirement and took out a big life insurance policy naming his son as beneficiary."

"I guess I'll never know what Niles planned but I want to believe he wasn't a violent man."

"I don't know. You think you know someone and then the whole thing blows up in your face." Davis dropped down on the bed.

Her hands lifted, molding his face. "Niles knew others would condemn him but trusted you to forgive him for choosing his son over honor. And you know why I know this, because you're a good man, Ewan Davis, and Niles knew it."

"You know a lot, don't you?" Davis smiled. It was his first of the night.

"And I know you're going to find his son and help him get away." Grayce ran her hand along his back. "I wish I could take all your pain away."

Davis grinned. "You've already done a lot to help relieve my pain, but I might need more pain relief. Animal doctors seem to know a lot about handling animal instincts."

Grayce moved back against the headboard. She curled her finger. "I haven't begun to show you my techniques for taming large dangerous animals."

He pulled her by her feet along the bed, bringing her down to him. He bent over and kissed her mouth. "I can't imagine what this night would've been like without you. I don't want to think about going to the station tomorrow when everyone learns about Niles."

Her arms tightened around him, bringing him down on top of her. “We’ll just have to fill your mind with better things.”

CHAPTER FIFTY-SEVEN

Grayce leaned on her elbow, watching Davis sleep. His massive bicep was draped over his face. His chest, covered in dark hair, moved effortlessly. If she stayed in bed, they might not get around to talking. She slid out of bed.

He rolled to his side but didn't wake. She wanted to run her finger down his muscular back to the little notch at the base of his spine. Last night had been about raw feelings, a scintillating blend of trust, comfort, and lust.

She walked to her closet and slipped on her soft yoga clothes. This morning was about their future. Davis had trusted her with his feelings, not an easy thing for a man who prided himself on control. She needed to honor his trust and reveal herself.

Touching her sister's pendant, she was filled with anticipation. After yesterday's events, she never wanted to waste another minute failing to grasp love, despite its complexities and contradictions. She prayed for Niles, hoping he had found peace. She prayed for his son—that he would honor Niles' sacrifice by living a free life.

She reached into the cupboard for the oats for her oatmeal pancakes with blueberries. Davis liked steak, potatoes, and eggs, doused with plenty of ketchup, and a generous side of toast for breakfast. Not this morning. She wanted to share her world, her life.

She mixed the yogurt and oats together and then began to fry turkey bacon. Napoleon lay curled on the floor by the sink, next to Mitzi. They were such an odd couple, like herself and

Davis, sensitive animal healer and macho man. She added the blueberries to the batter.

"Do I smell bacon?"

Davis wore his navy blue work pants, sans shirt or shoes.

"I didn't know you cooked," Davis said.

She beat the pancake mix, matching the rhythm of her racing heart. "I wanted to make you my favorite breakfast."

He took the two steps toward her and pulled her into his arms. "You're my favorite breakfast."

He ran his hand down her spine, causing chills and heat to dart along her skin. This wasn't going as she had planned.

"Aren't you hungry?" The question came out as a whisper, since her breathing had picked up speed.

"Starving." He proceeded to mouth tiny bites along her neck.

It was becoming difficult to resist. She pulled out of his arms. "We need to talk and I thought we could do it over breakfast. You're going to like these pancakes."

Frustration flashed across his face. His voice was gravelly, "Can we talk later?"

"I need you to understand something about me, before…" She groped for the right word. Had he been serious last night when he told her he loved her or had it been his passion talking?

Her stomach churned with uncertainty.

"Grayce, the bacon is burning."

The kitchen filled with smoke. She flipped the bacon. The pieces were black.

He turned her away from the stove. "Breakfast can wait. Let's talk." He didn't let go of her hand. He removed the pan and turned off the stove. "No fires while I'm here." He tugged on her hand and led her to the living room. Mitzi and Napoleon trailed behind.

She sat on the couch. Davis bent and placed a gentle caress across her lips. The giant cat jumped on her lap while Mitzi lay at her feet. Davis stood across from her.

"I want to talk with you about the fight we had over my interference in your investigation," she said.

"I know what you're going to say. It isn't like me. I was worried for your safety." His voice got louder, fierce, "My God, Benson torched your house and the Russians tried to run you down."

"You had every right to be mad," Grayce said.

"I'm not usually like…what did you say?"

"You had every right to be mad. I should've confided in you."

He stared at her as if he had won the lottery. "You're not worried that I'm too controlling, have anger issues? Isn't that what you want to talk about?"

Her own anxiety made her laugh out loud. "No, but I'll have to give it more thought, now that you mentioned it."

Davis didn't laugh. His eyes were focused on her face.

"I want to apologize for not explaining."

"You do?" He asked.

Now came the hard part, the moment that could destroy the harmony, their chance of a future. She could hear Napoleon's soft snuffles. Mitzi, picking up on the tension, put her head under Grayce's hand. She patted Mitzi's head. "It's okay, Mitzi. She looked up at Davis. "I haven't been honest with you."

Davis stood still. His stance stiffened as if he grew taller.

"Could you sit down? It's hard to talk when you're standing over me."

He dropped to the chair across from her, distancing himself. The tender lover was gone. Whatever he expected to hear, he didn't believe it was going to be good. He had a deep crease marching across his forehead and his lips were pulled tight into a grim smirk.

"I have been hiding certain things about myself."

Davis sat straighter in his chair.

"I'm sorry I didn't tell you sooner, but I was afraid you wouldn't understand or believe me."

"About the investigation?"

"Sort of."

"Grayce, I have no idea what you're talking about. I'm sure there is nothing you could tell me that would change how I feel about you. Well, unless you're involved with someone else."

He bared his teeth, feigning a smile and detachment she knew wasn't true.

"How could you think that after our nights together?"

"I was joking. Grayce what is it?"

"I have been hiding…"

He leaned forward, bracing his hands on his knees.

"I have rather strange abilities."

He stood and moved to the couch. He took her hands in his. "You've said that before. Tell me about your abilities."

"I… communicate with my dead sister and animals."

Davis laughed. "This is what has you tied in knots?"

It was her turn to glare.

"Honey, I know you have unusual gifts. I've watched you."

She pulled her hand away from Davis and stood up. "I'm not talking about my acupuncture skills. I know what animals are feeling. My visions show me what animals are thinking."

"Visions?"

"When I treat animals, I go to a different place, kind of like dreaming. I can feel and see what animals are experiencing. It's hard to explain in words. It's like another world, another consciousness."

She wrapped her arms around herself. "My sister's communication is easier... well, easier to explain but I'm not sure it's easier to understand." She rubbed her arms. "I feel Cassie's presence. I don't understand the connection, except I know my sister still tries to protect me."

Grayce walked back and forth in her tiny living room. "I've tried to keep my gifts hidden, but when I met Mitzi, I knew you were in danger. I tried to warn you without revealing how I knew."

Mitzi followed Grayce to the center of the living room.

"The first time I met Mitzi in my office, I sensed her fear, but I realized it centered on you. When I treated Mitzi after her poisoning, I had a vision of a scar. I didn't know at the time what it signified, but I was overwhelmed with a need to protect you. I've always known that I was different, but I've kept it hidden until I met you and Mitzi."

"A scar?"

"It sounds as weird as it was. I don't usually see images during treatments but when I was treating Mitzi, I saw a scar on a man's arm."

"I'm amazed and a bit in awe."

"I wanted to tell you, but it's easier not to divulge my gifts." A pressure was building under her ribs, making it hard to breathe. "I want you to understand why I acted the way I did. I had a dream—you were falling into a dark void."

She stopped and bent to pet Mitzi, who now sat in the middle of the living room, watching her.

"I'm not explaining myself well. As a child, my sister always believed in my intuitive abilities, but when she died my whole world collapsed. I've found it hard to sort out what is real and who to trust. I'm sorry I couldn't trust you sooner."

"Grayce come here." He reached for her.

She and Mitzi walked together to the couch. Grayce sat down. Mitzi lay at Grayce's feet.

"Let me get this straight. Even though Benson terrified you, you kept it a secret?"

She nodded and shifted away from Davis.

"Next, because you were convinced Maclean planned to hurt me, you came out on the halo although you're terrified of heights?"

"I didn't have a choice. I had no way of knowing if you were in danger."

"And you came to the department to protect me and got chased by Niles and almost run down by the Russian mob?"

Her palms were sweating. She never sweated. She rubbed them on her yoga clothes.

"Grayce, don't you realize what you've said?"

"I know what I'm trying to tell you."

"Which is?" He raised his eyebrows.

She was in a muddle. "I was trying to tell you I'm not the woman you think I am. I'm different than most people."

"You sweet idiot. I've always known you were different. Why do you think I love you?"

"But Davis, I told you I have visions that come from the mind of a French poodle."

"I didn't know you had such astounding gifts, but since the moment I met you, I've known you're the woman for me. I should've known when Henny wouldn't leave your side. I tried very hard to deny the immediate attraction, but I thought it was your little skirt hitched up to your thighs. I still haven't forgotten how you looked that day."

He took her hand between his. "Attraction isn't the right word. It was an immediate belonging, as if I met someone I've known all my life."

"But you're an investigator. You believe in facts."

"Right. You and I are different in all the ways I like." He cupped her hand gently.

"What are you saying, Davis?"

"I don't care if you have dreams or visions. All I know is that you tried to save me, even though you were terrified. Since my Aunt Aideen, no one has ever cared for me, tried to protect me."

"You don't find it illogical that I can sense unseen things?"

"I love your sensitivity. You make me and everyone who knows you feel cared for, cherished. You have an incredible gift of loving." He pressed her palms to his lips. "Animals and people love you because you make them feel safe. They get how sincere and innocent you are." He licked her palm. "Not too innocent, I hope."

A surge of pleasure shot all the way down to her toes.

"What was I saying? I got a bit distracted." He pulled her onto his lap. "I feel very privileged that you decided to protect me, care for me. I promise to work hard to deserve you. You saved the department and the chief from an embarrassing and painful public disclosure of Niles' involvement."

She relaxed. Her gifts had contributed to an honorable purpose.

"Every federal agency is now involved. The feds will be waiting for the Jupiter to dock. With the information Niles left, the FBI will have a case against Ivan Zavragin. Niles' son, his wife and grandson are all safe in the Witness Protection Plan."

"It's rather bittersweet. Niles sacrifices his life for a son and grandson he'll never know," she said.

"He chose their lives over his own."

Grayce didn't say anything more about Niles' decision. Davis had a lot of pain that would take time to heal.

"Grayce Walters is now a heroine and friend to the fire department."

She pressed her lips against his smile. "Davis, don't forget Mitzi."

He bent around Grayce to stroke Mitzi. "Sorry girl. I didn't mean to exclude you. You both did an amazing job."

"But Davis, you won't mind when other people find out?"

"Find out what?"

"That I'm not a run-of-the-mill veterinarian."

"What other people?"

"Your family, friends…"

"Are you kidding? My aunt already loves you and so will my sisters. They're warm, loving women, like you. By the way…is this gift of yours…" He twisted her ponytail around his fist and showered light butterfly kisses down her neck. "Genetic?"

"I don't know… I don't think so. My sister didn't have it."

Was he already thinking of children, their children? "Why do you ask?"

"I thought it might be hard on a son of mine to be logical and sensitive at the same time."

She pushed on Davis' massive chest. "Davis, what an outrageously sexist comment. One doesn't preclude the other. I want you to know that I'm a respected scientist."

"Honey, I know you're brilliant."

"You do?"

Davis fingered the one button on her shirt. "What part are you objecting to? The idea that our son might be logical and sensitive or that a male might be both logical and sensitive?"

She couldn't tear her gaze away from him. He was serious about the question. "I guess I'm not objecting to either. Any son of yours will be like his dad, logical and sensitive."

"Sensitive?"

"Yes, you, Mr. Macho. You have to be sensitive or insane to be accepting of me. And I happen to know you're not insane."

"I will be insane if you don't take off that soft shirt that is clinging to you so seductively."

Who would think yoga clothes were seductive? He pushed her back on the couch. Napoleon did a graceful leap to the floor and sauntered to Mitzi, who lay down with her paws on her head. Both animals seemed resigned to wait for breakfast.

EPILOGUE

Emily Chow, reporter for television station KZOQ, frantically ran her fingers through her straight hair, trying to restore the edgy look. Her $180 haircut wouldn't hold up in the torrential rain and wind of the winter storm.

She hated this whole depressing project of exploring homelessness in Seattle. Her editor wanted to showcase the new face of homelessness—returning military veterans. Emily disagreed. The ratings for the evening show proved Emily was correct.

Viewers needed uplifting stories like the story about Dr. Grayce Walters, a veterinarian who communicated with animals. Seattleites loved animals and other-worldliness. Dr. Walters was Emily's ticket to the anchor spot.

Emily resigned herself to another day of dispiriting stories. She hadn't gotten this far at KZOQ by going against the flow.

She shook her head, still trying to undo the wind damage. Futile. The VA medical complex, renowned for its treatment of war-scarred vets, served as the backdrop for the interview.

Emily forced a smile and walked over to greet today's family. Angie Hines, just returned from her latest deployment in Afghanistan, had disappeared after treatment for PTSD at the VA facility on Beacon Hill.

Angie's mother, dressed in her Post Office uniform, looked brittle, ready to shatter. The brother stood erect, definitely ex-military. His angular face registered no emotion, only steely control.

The mother might not be able to keep it together in front of the camera. Her editor wanted the woman's angle, working mom with a missing daughter—a little emotion was great, but too much meant they would have to reshoot.

She shook Mrs. Hine's hands. "I am sorry to bring you out in this rain." Emily ground her teeth together in another smile. "There is nothing to be nervous about. I'll ask you the questions we've already reviewed."

Mrs. Hines, a twisted Kleenex clutched in her hand, managed a half-hearted nod. The brother had the chiseled good looks to make it on TV.

"Just to make sure I'm clear on my facts, Angie graduated from Cleveland High School and then enlisted in the army. Is that correct?"

"There was no way of stopping Angie once she got an idea in her head." Mrs. Hines shook her head.

Angie's brother, Hunter Hines, showed no reaction.

"Something bad has happened to my daughter. She would never leave Ossie."

Emily hadn't heard about Ossie in the preliminary interview. "Who's Ossie?"

Hunter spoke, his voice a deep baritone, "Ossie is Angie's cat."

The mother swallowed a sob. "If that cat could talk, we would know what really happened."

Emily never believed in the idea of serendipity. "I know of a veterinarian in Seattle who is able to communicate with animals. Dr. Walters might be able to help you."

Emily ignored the force of the brother's cold inspection. She took Mrs. Hines's hand. "I'd be happy to set it up for you."

Mrs. Hines had just provided the missing part of the equation for Emily's nightly spot with the veterinarian. She and Dr. Walters would help animals reunite with their missing owners.

In the newspaper article about her helping the fire department, Dr. Grayce Walters came across as a very attractive and highly intelligent woman.

How could the doctor turn down Angie Hines' family? How could the doctor not want to be a celebrity? Dr. Grayce Walters would have fame and fortune. What else could a woman want?

AUTHOR BIO

Descended from a long line of storytellers, Jacki spins adventures filled with mystery, healing and romance.

Jacki's love affair with the arts began at a young age and inspired her to train as a jazz singer and dancer. She has performed many acting roles with Seattle Opera Company and Pacific Northwest Ballet.

Jacki has set *An Inner Fire* in Seattle, her long-time home. The city's unique and colorful locations are a backdrop for her romantic mystery.

Although writing now fills much of her day, she continues to volunteer for Seattle's Ballet and Opera Companies and leads children's tours of Pike Street Market. Her volunteer work with Seattle's homeless shelters influenced one of her main characters in *An Inner Fire.*

Jacki's two Golden Labs, Gus and Talley, are her constant companions. Their years of devotion and intuition inspired her to write dogs as main characters alongside her strong heroines.

A geek at heart, Jacki loves superhero movies-- a hero's battle against insurmountable odds. But her heroines don't have to wear a unitard to fight injustice and battle for the underdog.

To learn more about Jacki and her books and to be the first to hear about contests and giveaways join her newsletter found on her website: www.jackidelecki.com. Follow her on FB—Jacki Delecki; Twitter @jackidelecki.

Photograph by Michael Cole